THE DEATH SHIP;

OR,

THE PIRATE'S BRIDE AND THE MANIAC OF THE DEEP.

A Nautical Romance.

BY THE AUTHOR OF "GALLANT TOM," "THE SMUGGLER KING," ETC.

> The sea! the sea! the open sea,
> The blue, the fresh, the ever free.
> Without a mark, without a bound,
> It runneth the earth's wide regions round;
> It plays with the clouds, it mocks the skies,
> Or like a cradled creature lies.
>
> BARRY CORNWALL.

LONDON:

PUBLISHED BY E. LLOYD, 12, SALISBURY-SQUARE, FLEET-STREET.

———

1846.

THE DEATH SHIP;

OR,

THE PIRATE'S BRIDE AND THE MANIAC OF THE DEEP.

𝔄 𝔑𝔞𝔲𝔱𝔦𝔠𝔞𝔩 𝔕𝔬𝔪𝔞𝔫𝔠𝔢.

BY THE AUTHOR OF "GALLANT TOM," "THE SMUGGLER KING," ETC.

See p. 26.

CHAPTER I.

THE LEGEND OF THE DEATH SHIP.—THE WARNING CRY.

ON the summit of a lofty hill on the western coast of England, backed by scenery of the most diversified and romantic description, and immediately proximate to the vast waters of the ocean, a large, black, and ancient stone building reared its head, and there had stood from time immemorial, bidding defiance to the ravages of age or tempest.

For what purpose it had originally been built, there were no records extant to show, but it was now, and had been for many years, the residence of a stout, staunch, and benevolent yeoman ; who, after having passed his youthful days in the service of his king and country on the perilous deep, had retired with his family to this strange edifice, on the proceeds of his hard-earned savings, and the bequest of a deceased relation, which enabled him to live in comfortable independence, if not in affluence.

Michael Belford (for such was the veteran's name) would not have exchanged his unsightly dwelling for a palace, and rude though and cheerless as was its outward appearance, the comforts within far more than compensated for it.

There, then, stood the old stone house, braving both time and weather ; the boiling sea, when it howled in its tempest wrath ; the furious hurricane that carried devastation around, alarmed not its peaceful and contented inmates ; and often was that lonely dwelling frequented by many humble inhabitants of an adjacent village, who always found a hearty welcome and assistance from honest Michael, as far as his means permitted, in the time of need.

Gloomy winter had now spread his hoary mantle over the face of nature ; bleak winds swept the bare summits of the hills and precipices ; fearful storms frequently howled and foamed in the neighbouring offing ; every vestige of foliage was torn from nature's tall, variegated, and luxuriant bosom, and the deep valley presented to the eye a desolated blank of universal whiteness. No more did the shallow rivulet meander over its pebbly channel ; its water was now bound in icy fetters ; arrested were its wanderings, and its lucid current was congealed in the dismal silence and chill of death itself. All nature's beauties slept, but to awaken again to increased glory, like the careworn spirit escapes from its earthly tenement to the realms of immortal bliss.

No longer the feathered choir attuned their downy throats to dulcet strains of harmony, but on the leafless branches sat moping, or pecking the wild berries left by the ravages of unpropitious skies ; it was the scanty pittance allowed to nature's little commoners. Here and there, upon the snow-encrusted earth, a plumy victim found a spotless grave. The winter squirrel, now crouched, almost famished, in the hollow of an aged tree, upon whose plenteous boughs he had lately fed, till the appetite was sated with the luxuriant banquet. All, all was rapacious, and nothing satisfied.

The day had been bitter cold ; the frost was nipping, but no snow had fallen, and scarcely was there a breath of wind stirring. The forenoon passed away, and the darkness gradually increased ; the sky was black as marble, or a funereal pall, and everything gave token of a coming storm. The day, which had been scarcely distinguishable from night, closed, and an universal and impenetrable darkness prevailed. By slow degrees the winds arise, louder and louder, until they howl together in fierce contention and strife, like demons exulting over their destined prey, and savagely anticipating the total wreck of human nature. Heaven protect those unfortunate beings who are exposed to the fury of the elemental strife in this terrible hour !

Around the old stone house the tempest howled with terrific violence ; the windows rattled in their frames ; and even that firm building, which had bravely stood the test of ages, was shaken to its very foundation. But from its lower windows gleamed the red reflection of a cheerful fire, and between the pauses of the blast, the hearty laugh that rose upon the air, showed that all were happy within.

Cheerful indeed was the party assembled around that happy hearth, apart from the sympathy they felt for their less fortunate fellow-creatures who were exposed to the horrors of the storm. It consisted of Michael and his wife, Kit Hayward (an old friend of the family, who often called in to see them, and enjoy the pleasure of their company), and Frank Trevors, a handsome youth, whose fine bright eyes were rivetted upon an object, who seemed to engross the whole of his attention, notwithstanding he at times took part in the conversation, and was always foremost in the merry laugh which followed any joke uttered by the senior members of the company.

And who was the fair being who brought the glow of rapture in the face of Frank Trevors, and kindled the fire of admiration in his eyes? It was she who had been the companion of his earlier days, the being who constantly occupied his thoughts, whose smiles it was his greatest triumph to obtain—the one fair being whom he would have braved death in its most terrible shape to serve,—the young, and lovely daughter of Michael Belford.

And, surely, Rosetta Belford was a being formed in nature's most perfect mould for universal love—to raise the soul to rapture and a sublimity of admiration of the most lovely portion of God's creations! To say that the poet's muse, or the painter's pencil, could do anything like adequate justice to her transcendent charms, would be presumption.

For fifteen years had Rosetta bloomed to shed a bright lustre upon her sex, and to impart happiness to her fond parents and all who knew her. Her form was the animated portrait of her mind : truth, benignity, pure and unstudied delicacy, the meekness of sensibility and the dignity of innate virtue, claimed the esteem, whilst the bewitching countenance captivated the heart of every beholder. She was tall, and finely proportioned ; her complexion, though not insipidly fair, nor partaking of the masculine shade of the brunette, was all that the most ardent admirer of female delicacy could imagine or desire ; the freshness of health glowed upon her cheek, while the lustre of her dark blue eyes borrowed its splendour from the unsullied flame that gave her mind the perfection of intellect.

Milder even than the cooings of the ring-dove was her voice, and her smile was the gentle harbinger of tenderness and complacency. The poet's lines convey but a faint portraiture of her :—

> " Light, lovely limbs, to which the spirits play,
> Gave motion, airy as the dancing spray,
> When from its stem the small bird wings away.
> Lips, in whose rosy labyrinth, when she smil'd,
> The soul was lost, and blushes swift and wild
> As are the momentary meteors sent
> Across the uncalm, but beauteous firmament.
> And then her look !—Oh ! where's the heart so wise
> Could, unbewilder'd, meet those matchless eyes ?"

In short, she was everything that fancy could picture or conviction adore ! Perfection could go no further.

Such, then, was the party assembled in the stone-house on the awful and momentous evening on which our narrative commences. But ever and anon Rosetta would raise her eyes towards the window as the roaring blast swept by, and while compassion filled her gentle bosom, she uttered a brief but fervent prayer to Heaven for the protection of the houseless wanderer, or those poor creatures who had to brave the fury of the tempest on the wide waste of troubled waters.

" Ay, my love," observed Michael, " and may Heaven preserve us from a visitation of the Death Ship, for wherever and whenever it appears some awful event is sure to follow."

The females shuddered, and Michael, after a pause, continued,—

" Ah! it is just five years this very night since she was seen buffeting about off this coast, with her white sails reflected upon by the ghastly blue lights she had hoisted, and looking like so many giant spectres of the deep, and the frightful emblems upon her black flag as visible as at noonday. Chase was given to her, but she dashed before the wind like a spirit of the ocean, over which she had supreme control, and vanished as if by magic. Great were the calamities which followed this visit : a storm arose that lasted for four days, and raged with greater violence than ever I, all the years I was at sea, remembered before."

" Gracious Heaven !" cried the terrified Mrs. Belford : " well do I remember it, and reason enough have I to do so ; for, alas, Michael, you know, that very night we lost our poor boy, and ——"

" True—true," interrupted Michael, with much emotion ; " but it is no use to think of the sorrows of the past ; poor boy, he is a saint in heaven now, and at this moment is very likely supplicating the protection of the Great Commander for us all."

Tears started to the eyes of Rosetta at this melancholy reminiscence, and she hid her face in her mother's bosom, while she listened appalled to the conversation that followed.

"And then the dreadful cry that proceeded from the strange form which flew past our house and down the hill with the speed of lightning," said Mrs. Belford; "it still seems to ring in my ears. Oh, truly, it was a most awful event. No one could discover the features of that mysterious being, but you know there were many who, at the time, did not hesitate to assert that it was seen to enter the Manor House."

"Psha, dame!" returned Michael, "that must have been all imagination, for, although there are strange things rumoured of Sir Horace Middleton, and he is certainly a man of very eccentric habits, we must not believe all we hear."

"He is a miserable old dotard," said Kit Hayward, "and it's little enough the poor in the neighbourhood have to thank him for; and then, there is that harum-scarum nephew of his, Raymond Middleton, who only appears at the Manor House now and then; and the less he does so the better; he—but this is nothing to do with the subject we were talking about. Michael, from what you have said, one might be inclined to think that this vessel was the very devil's ship, and was manned by beings of another world."

"Why, you see, Kit, I am an old sailor," answered Michael, "and, although they spin remarkable yarns, and some of them entertain strange superstitions, such as the Flying Dutchman, and all that sort of thing, I flatter myself that I am not so foolish. Certainly, the extraordinary events connected with the Death Ship, and the manner in which she has for so many years been able to escape from pursuit, are enough to create fearful ideas; but she is known to be a notorious pirate, though some go so far as to assert that she is commanded by Lucifer himself."

"Has she ever been engaged with any vessel?" asked Frank.

"Engaged, ah! times and oft," answered Michael, "and in all parts of the world; and bloody engagements they have been, for but few ever lived to tell the dreadful tale, and they have been saved by a miracle."

"Was she ever seen near this coast before the times you mention?" asked Kit, eagerly.

"Ay," replied Michael; "every five years for the last twenty years, and always on the same day of the month. But have you never heard the story of Hugh Clifton, who is supposed to have been the captain of the Death Ship, and may be so still for what I know?"

"I have heard something about that guilty man," said Kit, "but could never gather all the particulars."

"Then I will tell you all about it," returned Michael; "but first throw another log on the fire, dame, and replenish the glasses, for it is a fearful tale, and we shall need something to refresh us while I relate it."

"Oh, Heaven! what was that?" exclaimed Rosetta, in a voice of terror, and starting from her chair, while she gazed towards the window.

"Nothing—nothing, child," replied her father. "What did you think it was?"

"I—I thought I heard a dismal cry, such as that my mother has described," faltered out Rosetta.

"God bless us!" cried the alarmed Mrs. Belford.

"Nay, Rosetta," observed Frank, "it was only your imagination; rest assured it was no more."

"It was only the howling of the tempest," remarked Michael; "but had not you and your mother better retire to another room, for you are in no condition to hear that I am about to relate?"

"No—no!" answered the maiden, endeavouring to recover herself, for she was anxious to hear the story. "It—it could only have been fancy, and certainly the horrors of this night are enough to create strange and fearful ideas in the breast."

"True," coincided Michael, "it is an awful night; but here we are safe from harm. So do as I desired you, dame, and then for the legend."

The dame obeyed, and then she and her daughter having drawn their chairs closer to Michael and his companions, he thus commenced :—

" It is now more than twenty years since Hugh Clifton resided in this part of the country, and in this very house !"

"In this house !" cried the listeners in a breath ; and Rosetta and her mother trembled violently.

" Yes," answered Michael ; " in this house ; it is useless to deny it, for you would probably hear it some time or other. But he was then good and esteemed, and few would have believed that he could become the wretch he afterwards did. He once lived in happiness, and endeavoured by his industry to gain an honest livelihood for himself and family. He was a fisherman, but fortune at length frowned upon him. He was capsised in a storm—his only son sank to rise no more, as it was then supposed, and Hugh with difficulty reached the shore. But from that moment all his hopes were wrecked ; he became reckless of his future destiny, and ruin came upon him. Principle at the same time fled, and with his wife he retired farther up the coast, where he became one of those wretches, who make the shattered bark, tossed on the foamy deep, their plunder."

" Miserable wretch !" ejaculated Kit.

" True, he was ; but no one was ever driven more rapidly down the stream of crime. The misfortunes he had met with seemed to steel his heart against every feeling of humanity, and he commenced a terrible war upon his fellow creatures. I need not describe to you what miscreants those wreckers are ; but Hugh Clifton appeared to take a delight in endeavouring to surpass them all in atrocity. Blood, human blood, he shed with indifference, so great was his thirst for gold ! Gold—gold ! that was his only thought by night and day, and he cared not whom he might sacrifice to obtain it."

" Oh, God ! and he was the inhabitant of this house !" ejaculated Rosetta, with a shudder of horror, and once more glancing towards the window, as if she expected the grim visage of Hugh Clifton, or his ghastly phantom, to be glaring upon her.

The tempest continued to increase rather than to abate in violence : and the lightning blazed in at the window, adding to the terrors which had taken possession of the damsel's feelings. Frank whispered to her some words of confidence, but her cheeks remained blanched, notwithstanding she was so eager to hear the remainder of the tale, that she resisted all the endeavours of her father to persuade her to retire.

" But his wife, Michael," said Kit Hayward ; "did she become as bad as himself ?"

" In some respects she did," answered Michael, " of course she was aware of his unlawful proceedings, but it is said she knew not that he had ever shed the blood of his fellow creatures. How true that may be, I cannot say. Well, some time passed on in this way, and the more success that Hugh met with, the more it lured him on to crime, the more he trampled with impunity upon the laws of nature. Well, so goes the story, as I had it from the lips of an aged man when first I came to this place. One fine summer's evening, Hugh Clifton walked forth from his lonely hut, and made his way to the sandy beach. He had been for the last few weeks unfortunate in his guilty course, and his mind was more than unusually stern and determined. It was a dead calm, and the ocean was spread before him, glittering beneath the sun's departing rays, scarcely ruffled by a single billow. His eyes rolled wildly to the west, and the calm scene that met his gaze added to the discontent of his guilty mind. Then he muttered a bitter curse, for when Nature wore her gayest smiles, fortune frowned upon him. The setting sun damped all his guilty hopes. He paced the beach, and more disordered became his brain, and more bitter were the curses he growled in the rage and disappointment of his soul. Oh, it must have been terrible to have seen that unhappy wretch at that moment. But the crisis of his evil destiny was approaching.

" One little cloud now appeared, and the villain's hopes revived. That cloud might turn the balance yet. He laughed wildly as this thought darted across his brain, and with a savage smile, he directed his eyes towards the south, in which that one little cloud, black and portentous, had met his eager gaze. Gradually the wind arose, and rippled the bright blue waters, while the departing sun was hid behind

a misty veil. The wrecker's steps became firmer every moment, and his countenance more calm, as his eyes wandered over the ocean. The winds still more
powerfully arose, and the billows gently heaved. Fast the varying clouds gathered
upon the horizon; but ere the last rays of the sun sank in the bosom of the ocean, a
distant speck appeared on the horizon, which the wrecker's eye quickly marked, and
he laughed aloud in fiendish exultation. He knew it to be a ship, and soon her
scudding sails were distinctly revealed to him. But now dense clouds overhung
the ocean; but the wind had increased, the waves foamed and bubbled, and rolled
beneath the stormy influence; the thunder in heavy peals shook the air, the lightning's flash ever and anon illumined the foaming deep, and revealed to Hugh Clifton
his hoped-for prey, rolling and struggling with the mighty waves, hastening fast to
a watery grave. Mingled hopes and fears filled the villain's breast, lest the shattered bark should perish ere she could approach near enough to afford him his
wished-for booty. But on she came, rushing and plunging, anon her signals vying
with the roaring thunder. Hugh Clifton prepared his lantern, and displayed it before a rock, which was now obscured by the bounding surf, and the crew of the
hapless vessel beholding the beacon, were lured to their destruction. Nearer and
nearer she came, and in a loud, hoarse voice, the wretch shouted to them to steer
that way. A few minutes more, and one loud, one hideous shriek was heard, which
rose even above the voice of the thunder, or the howling wind. It is the piercing
shriek of death. The vessel had struck upon the fatal rock, and the next instant
the ill-fated crew were engulphed in death."

"Oh, horrible!" exclaimed Rosetta, shuddering at the dreadful recital.

"Ay, my lass, it was," said Michael; "but still the most fearful part of the story
is to come. Hugh Clifton viewed the awful work of his hands with mingled feelings
of exultation and fear. But not all of the crew had perished; one still survived,
and struggled with the waves to reach the shore. Clifton watched him with eager
eyes, and when he saw the bounding billows heave him to the beach, he hastened
towards him. 'Save me! oh, save me!' the unhappy man gasped forth in a faint
voice. 'Yes, thus! thus!' shouted the ruffian, and at the same instant plunged his
knife in his victim's heart. Then he stooped over the bloody corpse, and commenced
searching his pockets, with the hope of finding money or jewels, for what apparel
the unfortunate man had on, denoted him to be something more than a common seaman. He searched in vain, for nothing but an old coin, suspended from his neck,
could he discover; and muttering fearful curses, he raised the still warm body from
the earth, and was about to plunge it in the deep, when a piercing shriek sounded in
his ears, and his arm was arrested by some one behind. He dropped the corpse
upon the blood-stained beach, and terrified, turned round to see who the person
was that had stayed him in his purpose, and the blue lightning's vivid glare revealed
to him the ghastly countenance of his wife! She had beheld him plunge his knife
in the defenceless man's breast, and then, for the first time, knew that her husband
was a murderer! We must imagine the scene that followed; but at length the
eyes of the wretched woman were attracted to the coin which her husband still held
in his hand, and snatching it from him by the lightning's flash, eagerly examined it.
A frightful scream escaped her lips, and she directed the murderer's attention towards it. 'Look! look!' she cried, 'it is the very coin we placed around the neck
of our child in his infancy!'

"The guilty man did look, and his blood froze with horror as he recognised the
well-known bauble. Then with delirious haste they both stooped and examined the features of the murdered sailor. Every lineament of that countenance,
though changed by manhood and by death, was the same, and a particular mark on
his right breast, and some papers, which they found in one of his pockets, and had
escaped the observation of Clifton, confirmed them in the horrible truth. Hugh
Clifton had murdered his own son!"

Michael paused, for the feelings of his auditors were worked up to the highest
pitch of horror, and it was some minutes before they recovered themselves.

"And did it ever transpire how the unfortunate son of Hugh Clifton was rescued from a watery grave in the first instance?" interrogated Hayward.

"No," answered Michael; "but it is supposed that he had been picked up by some vessel, and on his recovery had been induced to enter the service."

"But the sequel of this fearful tale, Mr. Belford?" asked Frank, eagerly.

"When the wife of Clifton had made this dreadful discovery," continued Michael, "she uttered one piercing shriek, and immediately sank insensible upon the corpse of her murdered son. The murderer, for a few moments, stood appalled, and gazed vacantly around him; his eyes seemed to burn in their sockets,—his broad chest heaved with a convulsive feeling, and the large drops of agony rolled down his cheeks; then, with a loud and hysterical laugh, he dashed wildly from the spot. But he returned no more to his hut. His wife was shortly afterwards found, but she lived no longer than to relate those dreadful particulars. Hugh Clifton was seen no more in the neighbourhood of his horrible crimes."

"Then what is there to connect him with the Death Ship?" asked Kit.

"Why, it is said that one of the crew of a vessel which had been attacked by the pirate, and who alone had escaped from the awful massacre that took place, knew Hugh Clifton well, and had declared positively that the wretch who was acting as captain of the Death Ship at that time, was the same. The legend goes so far as to state, that Clifton, after the murder of his son, had sold himself to Satan, and became the master of a vessel, the crew of which certainly appear to act more under supernatural agency than anything else. Others assert that Hugh destroyed himself, and that it is his troubled spirit that haunts the spot of his hideous crime, and this spot, whenever that awful cry is heard, which I have described. Certain it is, that whenever the Death Ship has appeared off this coast, it has been in the same month, and on the same date, as when the horrible event took place. Such is the legend of the Death Ship, and may Heaven preserve us from another visit, I pray."

"Amen!" ejaculated Mrs. Belford; "and may we also soon leave this house altogether, for I shall never be able to sleep quietly in it again."

"Psha! dame," interposed Michael; "I thought you possessed more good sense than to talk thus; what have we to fear who never did anybody harm, if even this old building, for which I have so great a regard from particular circumstances, was once the residence of the villain Clifton?"

"Oh, mention not his name," said the old woman; "for it freezes my very blood with horror."

"I am sorry that I related the story to you," said Michael, "since it has taken such an effect upon you. But replenish the fire and the grog, for it is impossible that our guests can leave the house while the tempest continues to rage so violently. We will talk about something else."

The storm did, indeed, rage more terrifically than ever; the roaring wind and heavy peals of thunder were deafening, and the vivid flashes of lightning rendered the horrors of the hour complete. In vain Michael endeavoured to engage his companions in cheerful conversation; their thoughts were totally engrossed by the fearful legend he had related, and the terrors of the night served to increase the oppressive weight of their feelings.

Suddenly, however, the storm appeared to have ceased, and a deathlike silence still more awful succeeded. Not a breath of wind seemed to stir, not a sound could be heard, and they looked at each other with amazement, as if something of a dreadful and mysterious nature was about to happen. Neither of them could speak, and it was quite evident that the same strange and indefinable feelings presided in every breast.

But it was only for a short time that this solemn silence lasted, and then it was broken in a manner which served to appal them all. A low moaning sound was at first heard, like the distant sighing of the wind; louder and louder it became, until it swelled itself into one piercing shriek, of such magnitude that human imagination could form but a faint idea of its horror. Rosetta uttered a cry of terror, and clung to her father, while they all stared at each other aghast, and for some time neither of them could utter a syllable.

The fearful sound died away in lengthened echoes upon the air, and then again the storm arose with renewed violence; peal after peal of thunder following each other in rapid succession, and shaking the very hill upon which the building stood to its centre.

"Merciful Father protect us!" at length she gasped forth; "this cannot be treated with indifference; we all heard that fearful cry, that cry to which no human voice could give utterance."

"It is certainly very strange, and very alarming," observed Kit Hayward. "I am not much given to fear, but never, in the whole course of my life, did I before hear a cry like that."

"After all," said Michael, "I am inclined to think that we suffered our fears to deceive us, or that it was only the scream of the sea-gull."

"No, Michael," returned Kit, shaking his head, "a thousand sea-gulls combined could not have produced such a cry as that."

"It was just such a cry as we heard on that fatal night five years ago," remarked Mrs. Belford, violently agitated, and looking in the pale face of her trembling daughter, who was still clinging to the arms of her father.

"It might only have been the distant roaring of the troubled sea," remarked Frank Trevors; "we must endeavour to combat those fears."

They again seated themselves, and by degrees became more calm, but still Rosetta in vain tried to banish from her mind the horrible impression that the extraordinary event, coupled with the awful recital of her father, had made upon it.

It was not long, however, before they were again startled, for between the pauses of the thunder, the loud report of a gun reverberated upon the air.

"It is the signal from a ship in distress," said Michael. "May Providence save the poor fellows in their dreadful emergency."

Boom! boom! again and again came the report, and Michael's excitement increased.

"I can no longer hear these awful appeals without responding to them," he said; "let us hasten to the beach, and see what assistance can be rendered to the unfortunate beings who may yet be snatched from a watery grave."

"Oh, for Heaven's sake, forbear, my dear father," ejaculated the terrified Rosetta, "remember the danger, remember the night, the fatal night when ——"

"Rosetta, love," interrupted her father; "and think you that any fear of danger can restrain me in this hour, when my poor fellow-creatures are struggling on the verge of eternity? No, no; I am an old sailor, and should despise myself did I suffer for a moment a feeling of fear to overcome my sense of duty. Hark! again! Come, come, Hayward, you, I know, will accompany me; Frank had better remain here to take care of the females."

"Husband, dear husband, do not venture," supplicated Mrs. Belford; "what assistance can you render to the unfortunate creatures in such a storm as this, and should any harm befal you ——"

"Oh, I fear it not," said Michael, putting on his hat, and placing a bottle of rum in his pocket; "look for my speedy return. Come, Kit, there is not a moment to be lost."

"I am ready," said Hayward, "and may God prosper us in our efforts."

Michael hastily embraced and kissed his wife and beauteous child, and he and Kit then darted from the house, and made their way down the hill as fast as they could. They watched them with anxious eyes till they were out of sight, fervently offering up prayers for their safety. Then they turned their eyes in the direction of the ocean, which the lightning revealed to them rolling, and foaming, and tossing its spray to the clouds; a frightful sight, at which the heart sickened; and the soul quailed beneath the mighty wrath of God!

"Come away, Rosetta, come away," said Frank, gently urging the lovely damsel from the door, "this is no sight for you. Come, come, and let us pray to Heaven for mercy to those who are exposed to all its horrors."

Rosetta suffered herself to be led away, and sinking on a chair, exclaimed,—

"Oh, God! who can brave the horrors of this night? My poor father, what will become of him?"

See page 12.

H it was truly madness for him to enter upon this adventure," said Mrs. Belford, " and after what has already occurred, I fear that something dreadful will this night take place."

"Nay, Mrs. Belford," observed Frank, " we must not encourage those apprehensions; an All-merciful Providence will always watch over and shield from danger those who act from the same benevolent and humane feelings as your husband."

"Oh, may your words prove prophetic," ejaculated Rosetta ; " but my heart misgives me. That awful, foreboding cry ; never shall I be able to get it out of my ears again."

"Endeavour to forget it, Rosetta," urged Frank.

"Oh, never, never ! it is impossible ! Hark ! did you not hear a sound ?"

"Nothing but the voice of the tempest," answered Frank ; " you have suffered the wild tale your father related this evening to make too powerful an impression on you, Rosetta."

"It was a dreadful story," remarked Mrs. Belford, looking fearfully around her. " In this very house, too, the miscreant, Hugh Clifton resided. Oh, what could induce my husband, if he was aware of that fact at the time, to take this place ?"

"And what harm can befall you by dwelling ere ?" demanded Frank.

"I shall never more be able to move through any of its chambers without fear," answered the old woman; "I shall fancy I see his grim and savage countenance at every turn, and think ——"

"Oh, mother! dear mother!" interrupted Rosetta, trembling with terror at the thoughts these observations conjured up.

Mrs. Belford ceased, seeing the pale looks of her daughter, and Frank persuaded them to retire to an inner apartment, where the horrors of the storm might not be so apparent.

They complied; but, scarcely had they entered the room, when a crash of thunder more terrific than any that had been heard during the tempest, shook the whole building, and transfixed them all to the spot with the violence of the shock. It had not subsided an instant, when all again became as still as if the world no longer existed, and then low moaning sounds were heard, which became louder and louder, and again was heard that awful, that indescribable shriek, which had before appalled their senses, almost congealing their blood in their veins with horror.

Rosetta uttered a piercing scream, and immediately sank insensible in the arms of Frank Trevors. Mrs. Belford was scarcely in a better condition, and it was some time before she was sufficiently recovered to render any assistance to her daughter.

"My God! my God!" she cried, "this can be no deception; it is a warning of some dreadful approaching calamity. My poor husband will never return; I knew he would not; oh, why was he so rash as to venture forth on such a hopeless errand such a night as this?"

"Pray calm your fears, madam," expostulated Frank, "and see to the recovery of Rosetta. I cannot account for this strange sound, but still I would believe that it proceeds from nothing but natural causes—the wind whistling among the rocks, probably."

Mrs. Belford shook her head incredulously, and then went to get some restoratives for Rosetta.

CHAPTER II.

THE BURNING SHIP.—THE AWFUL MOMENT.—THE RESCUE.—THE MANIAC OF THE DEEP.

MICHAEL and his companion, in spite of the fury of the tempest, made their way to the scene of horror; but, the farther they proceeded, the more hopeless they became that they should be able to render any assistance, for what boats could venture forth to the rescue of the unfortunate creatures in such a storm? However, Michael resolved, that if there was the least chance, he would not hesitate to make the attempt.

As they approached the rocks, they heard the loud shouts of the people who were there assembled, and saw the lights that blazed from the numerous torches they carried. On arriving at the spot, what was the scene which presented itself? At some distance from the shore two vessels were battling with the furious waves; one entirely dismasted, and the other black and indistinct, at some short distance from her. On they came, pitching and heaving; the foaming ocean roared, heaving them upon each billow, sometimes mountains high, at others burying them deep in despair. But still the numerous persons congregated together could only gaze appalled without being able to render them any assistance, and the nearer they approached the various reefs of rocks that there stretched themselves into the sea, the nearer were they to inevitable destruction. The thunder roared, the lightning flashed, the winds howled, the sea gulls screamed, making up a combination of horrors which language must fail to pourtray. Still nearer and nearer they came, but yet they were far from the shore; but Michael was now glad to see that they were steering towards the less dangerous part, and his hopes slightly revived.

"They may yet be saved!" cried Michael, as he rushed towards a small creek. "Man the boats; let us not stand here gazing when the lives of our fellow creatures are in such dreadful peril ; even should we perish, we cannot do so in a better cause. Come, Hayward."

" Are you mad, Michael?" said a voice near him, and grasping his arm ; " what boat, think you, could live an instant in such a sea as this?"

Michael turned round to gaze at the speaker, and immediately ejaculated,—

" Ah ! Martin Trevors !"

It was the father of Frank who had spoken. He was a tall man of robust and muscular appearance, but there was something particularly stern and repulsive in the expression of his features.

" Trevors," continued Michael, " I have braved many as heavy a sea as this in a frail and shattered vessel, and cannot remain passive on such an awful occasion as this."

" Psha !" returned Trevors, " is your life of so little value that you would risk it thus ? Recollect, you have a wife, a daughter ; we have all of us wives and children, and who could repay them for our loss ? They must take their chance."

" Take their chance, Trevors ? Can you talk thus ?"

" Ay ! what help can we render them ? One, I know, will weather the storm, or the devil is out of luck altogether."

" What mean you?" demanded Michael, fixing upon him a look of astonishment.

" Perhaps a few minutes will explain my meaning," answered Trevors. " The shattered hull may struggle against the waves, but let the black looking craft get nearer to her, and her destruction is certain."

Michael fixed upon him another look of amazement, and then turned his gaze once more towards the two struggling vessels.

More than half an hour elapsed, when suddenly the tempest abated in violence, and then gradually entirely subsided. The winds became lulled, and the waves no longer rolled in gigantic wrath.

" Thanks to Heaven," exclaimed Michael, " they will yet be saved. To the boats, lads, to the boats !"

Scarce had he given utterance to the words, when a terrible report was heard, that rattled across the deep like a field of artillery, and was succeeded by mingled shouts of apparent exultation and piercing cries of horror and despair.

" Did I not tell you so ?" said Trevors ; " see, the black craft is alongside the hull, but she will not be there long."

" By Heaven ! she has poured a broadside into her."

" Even so."

" And see, flames are issuing from the shattered vessel."

" The black craft has fired her, no doubt," said Trevors, complacently.

" A pirate ! a pirate !" shouted Michael ; " to the boats ! to the boats ! we may yet save some of the poor fellows."

" You had better remain where you are, if you are wise," said Trevors, " or you will never return to reveal the secret you may discover. Behold, the flames now shoot on high, casting a broad reflection around ; the black craft boldly wings her flight over the unruffled waters ; you may hear the shouts of her daring crew ; by the light from the burning hull you may see her flag ; say, what do the emblems upon that flag denote her to be ?"

" The Death Ship ! the Death Ship ! the Death Ship !" burst simultaneously from every voice, and even the countenance of the stoutest there was blanched with terror.

On, on flew the bark of death, away and away, nor could the shouts of exultation from its fiendish crew be drowned by the frantic shrieks of despair from the unfortunate wretches on the burning vessel,—on, on, on and away, until she could scarcely be distinguished from the black clouds which hung like a curtain over the ocean. Not a soul offered to move ; they were all paralyzed to the spot ; but the piercing shrieks of those who were on board the burning vessel. They could see them distinctly rushing madly through the devouring element, others plunging into the deep to meet a death as certain though less horrible. A few moments more and she was burnt to the water's edge, and only a few floating timbers remained to show that she had ever existed! Michael was the first that was aroused into action—

" Lose not a moment!" he cried; " we may yet not be too late to save some of the poor fellows."

He rushed to the boats, and was followed by Kit Hayward, and several of the others; but Trevors remained behind, and seemed to take little or no interest in the scene. Quickly Michael and Hayward, and one or two more, jumped into a boat, and made off towards the spot where the scene of destruction had taken place, one of them carrying a lighted torch, but although they saw portions of the unfortunate vessel, they beheld nothing of the crew, and began to suppose they had all perished, when a wild and frantic laugh met their ears, and by the light of the torch they beheld at some short distance the form of a human being standing upright in a small boat, and with arms extended above his head, as if he was about to plunge into the deep. They shouted aloud to him, but whether he heard them or not, they could not tell, for he sunk back in the boat, probably from exhaustion, or the emotion consequent upon the prospect of deliverance.

They were not long in coming up to him, and, dragging him into the boat, prepared to return to the shore. It was a boy, apparently about sixteen years of age. His features, although pale, were handsomely formed, and his hair hung in a profusion of natural ringlets over his neck and shoulders. He had nothing on but his trousers and shirt, but they were not of that description which sailors usually wear. He was quite insensible.

They quickly gained the shore, where Michael placed the poor boy on his knee, and moistened his lips with some of the spirits he had brought with him, with the hope to revive him, but it had no effect. He then, with the assistance of Hayward, lifted him up, and made his way towards his dwelling, happy to think that he had been the means of saving even one human being from so terrible a death.

They had not proceeded far when a dark form flew past them with the rapidity of lightning, at the same time uttering a cry that made the air resound again, and smote the heart with horror. He was out of sight in an instant.

" It is the same mysterious form I beheld on the former occasion of the appearance of the Death Ship," said Michael; " what can unravel this strange and awful mystery?"

" It is, indeed, strange and awful," said Kit; " but let us make all the haste we can to your dwelling, and see what can be done towards the restoration of this poor boy."

" Ah," observed Michael, " Rosetta and my wife will be dreadfully alarmed for our safety. Heaven send that nothing may have happened to them."

Hayward returned no answer, and increasing their speed, they soon began to ascend the hill, on the summit of which Michael's house stood. Rosetta had recovered, and, with her mother and Frank, was standing at the door of the house eagerly looking out for them. When she beheld her father and Hayward, she ran joyfully towards them, but when she beheld the burthen they carried she started in amazement.

" He is not dead, is he?" she interrogated, eagerly.

" No, no, poor boy, he still breathes," replied her father, " and Heaven send that we may be able to restore him."

They now entered the house, and placed the insensible form of the youth on a couch, and Rosetta and her mother gazed at his interesting countenance with the deepest sympathy and admiration.

" Poor child, poor child," cried the compassionate dame; " how did you save him? But his clothes are not wet; he does not appear to have been immersed in the water."

" Now, my good dame," remonstrated Michael, " pray do not ask any questions; the story is too long to tell you now; with all speed see what you can do to restore the lad to sensibility."

" Oh, it has been an awful night," said Mrs. Belford ; " we saw the reflection of a fire from the ocean, and ——"

" Now, now, enough," interrupted her husband, impatiently ; " you shall know everything by-and-bye."

Mrs. Belford needed no more, but speedily procured some vinegar and other restoratives, with which she bathed the youthful stranger's temples, whilst Rosetta looked on with feelings of the deepest interest and anxiety. But for a long time the humane efforts of the dame were ineffectual, and the unfortunate boy showed not the least signs of returning life.

" Alas !" said Rosetta, in a voice which showed her feelings, " he is dead. See how ghastly pale he looks."

" No, no, my love," returned her mother; " he still breathes, and I do not despair of yet being able to restore him."

" Some hot water, wife," suggested Michael ; " some hot water to place his feet in ; that may have the desired effect."

Rosetta flew to get it, and returned in an instant. The youth's feet were then placed in it, and after a few minutes he evinced signs of returning animation, and heaved a deep sigh.

" Thank God !" cried the old woman, " he will recover. I'm sure he will. What a handsome little fellow. Poor boy! poor boy !"

Rosetta could not remove her eyes from him, but watched his recovery with the greatest anxiety. He sighed again, and then he gently opened his eyes, but gazed on vacancy, and seemed entirely unconscious of surrounding objects. But oh, what eyes were those whose lustre now met the gaze of those by whom he was surrounded ! Beaming with a strange expression, 'tis true, but yet so eloquent in their wildness ; so soft, yet so sparkling; so wandering, yet so intelligent. No one could contemplate them without admiration, and pity, and love. And then the beauty of his countenance; it combined all the delicate graces of the girl, with the more masculine nobleness of the youth. His features were formed in the most perfect mould, and vainly might the sculptor exhaust his skill in endeavouring to do justice to them. His complexion was fair almost to maiden whiteness, and his beautiful auburn hair hung in graceful curls around his high pale forehead, and down his neck, nor had the recent adventure he had met with been suffered to disarrange them. He was, indeed, altogether an object which the eye could not dwell upon without the deepest interest and sympathy.

Rosetta's eyes wandered from him to Frank, and although she had hitherto thought the latter very handsome, she could not but acknowledge to herself how much he suffered by comparison with the fair and youthful stranger.

" Thank God !" exclaimed Mrs. Belford, " our efforts have not been in vain. My poor boy," she continued, kindly approaching him, and taking his hand, " look up, and fear not, you are with friends."

With a strength and activity they thought him incapable of, after his late exertions, the poor boy bounded from the couch on which he had been placed, and, standing erect, fought and struggled as though with an enemy, and then in tones which made the place re-echo again, although his voice even in his frenzy was wildly melodious, he exclaimed,—

" Unhand me ! off ! off ! off ! See you not the flames ? Hark how they hiss, and roar, and crackle ! See, see, they gather around me ! The planks on which I stand are burning—my feet are scorched—my eyes are blinded with the smoke. I will remain here no longer ! Although a boy, I feel the strength of a lion in my despair—let go your hold ! Ha ! ha ! ha ! Did I not tell ye that it was madness to attempt to arrest me in my purpose ? Through flame, through smoke I go; away—away !—now—now to the deep, to the deep. One plunge and all is over."

And stretching his arms above his head as if to make the plunge, he threw himself prostrate on the floor before any one could prevent him. Michael immediately raised him, but he had again became insensible, although he breathed freely. Once more he was placed upon the couch, and Mrs. Belford moistened his lips with a cordial, and continued to bathe his temples.

"Poor lad," said Frank Trevors, compassionately; "his mind wanders."

"Ay, no wonder that it should," observed Michael, "considering the horrible situation from which I rescued him. But, perhaps, a night's rest, if he can obtain it, will restore him; such a trial has been too much for his youthful strength to bear."

"Has then a vessel been destroyed by fire?" asked Frank.

"Yes, yes," answered Michael; "and this poor boy was probably aboard of her."

"She was struck by the lightning, I suppose, sir?" said Frank, who could not restrain his curiosity.

"Struck by the lightning!" repeated Mr. Belford; "no—no, but basely fired by—but not to-night. Again I request you all to restrain your curiosity till to-morrow. Heaven be thanked that I have been made the humble instrument of saving one individual from a dreadful fate, though, alas! many poor souls I fear have perished. Your father, Frank, however, will tell you all about it to-night, I dare say."

"My father!" ejaculated Frank; "was he then present at the dreadful scene?"

"He was."

"And took he no part in endeavouring to rescue the lives of the unfortunate creatures?" asked Frank.

"He did not," replied Michael.

"Strange, most strange," exclaimed the youth, and a feeling of shame and astonishment agitated his breast; "and yet my father is no coward."

"I do not believe that he is; but—but he is a man whose real character and motives it may perhaps be difficult to understand. However, I do not wish to talk about that which does not concern me."

"My father's habits I own are uncouth and mysterious," observed Frank; "and it is a source of much regret to me; but that he should not have exerted himself in the cause of humanity does, indeed, surprise me. The hour is getting late, and the storm has now entirely subsided. I will return home."

"And as I am going your way, Frank," said Kit Hayward, "and can do no good by remaining here, I will accompany you. Good bye, my friends. I will call to-morrow, and hope by that time to find that this poor lad has recovered. Alack! alack! perhaps it would be better that Heaven would take him, for he may have lost relations, friends, all, in that dreadful calamity."

"I trust to God that he has not," returned Michael; "but if he should, Providence has placed him under my care, and in me he shall ever find a friend and protector."

"Well spoken, Michael," said Kit, "and I know you will be as good as your word."

"Ay, that I will; Michael Belford never yet forfeited his word, and he is not going to do so now, especially on such an occasion as this."

The eyes of Rosetta sparkled, and she pressed her father's hand with a feeling of gratitude and love which she could not restrain.

"Ah!" exclaimed Mrs. Belford, "who could refuse protection to one so young, so handsome, and so unfortunate?"

Mr. Hayward and Frank then took their leave, and Mrs. Belford renewed her kind attentions to the insensible young stranger.

"He seems to sleep calmly," said the dame.

"Yes," answered Michael; "and may it be the means of restoring him to reason. Unfortunate boy, he has, indeed, had a narrow escape from a horrible death. Oh, dame, this has been a dreadful night. Heaven preserve us from such another."

"It is no more than I expected, Michael," replied the old woman; "it is, indeed, the fatal night, and the Death Ship——"

" Mention not the name of that fearful, that mysterious vessel," interrupted Michael ; " dame, this very night I again beheld it."

" Gracious Heaven !" ejaculated Mrs. Belford and her daughter in a breath, and shuddering with horror.

" Oh," continued Mrs. Belford ; " how grateful then ought we to be that you have returned in safety. But do not keep me in suspense, Michael ; let me know everything."

" I would fain not relate the facts at present," replied Michael, " for you have already had enough to shock your feelings. Rosetta, child, you had better retire to rest, for it is now late. Your mother and myself must remain here to watch this poor boy."

" I am not tired, my dear father," said Rosetta ; " and—and pardon me if I say that my curiosity is excited to know all the particulars you have to relate."

" Nay, child," returned her father ; " you have already heard and seen enough this night to terrify you ; and were you to hear what I have to detail, you would not be able to sleep to-night, or frightful dreams might disturb your rest."

" Indeed, my father, I am not such a coward as you take me to be," observed Rosetta, coaxingly. " Suspense would make me more uneasy than anything you can have to relate."

" Well, well, e'en then remain ; and now listen to me, both of you."

Rosetta and her mother were all breathless attention, while Michael detailed, as briefly as possible, the awful and extraordinary circumstances with which the reader has already been made acquainted. Their horror and surprise may readily be imagined. Notwithstanding all their promises, they trembled violently, and looked around them with fear, as though they expected to encounter the terrible and unknown captain of the Death Ship, at every glance.

" Gracious Heaven !" exclaimed Mrs. Belford, when he had concluded, " how strange, how awful and mysterious are these events. Surely it is enough to make one believe that this terrible vessel must carry on its operations under the influence of supernatural agency."

" Why you see, dame," returned Michael, " I am not a man to believe in such things ; but, as you say, it is very remarkable and alarming."

" And why do not the government take some steps to capture her ?" asked Mrs. Belford.

" Why, you know very well that they have done so," replied Michael ; " but it is all to no purpose. She always contrives to elude them, in spite of all their vigilance, and so many years have now elapsed since she was first heard of, that I suppose they despair of ever being able to do so."

" But the conduct of Martin Trevors," said Mrs. Belford, " how strange."

" True, but you know it is all of a piece with him. His conduct is altogether ambiguous."

" And he appeared, you say, to be aware of the presence of the Death Ship ?" said the dame.

" He did," answered Michael ; " and also of her intentions. I know not what to make of it."

" Nor I," observed Mrs. Belford ; " and you could not learn the name of the unfortunate ship that was destroyed ?"

" Certainly I could not."

" And think you that this poor boy was on board of her ?"

" I have very little doubt of it," replied Michael ; " and should he recover his senses, he probably can give us every information."

" Hapless lad," said the dame, " his troubles have indeed commenced early ; I wonder who he is."

" That we shall, doubtless, soon know," remarked Michael ; " he is a noble, looking youth."

" Yes," coincided Mrs. Belford ; " and yet so fair and gentle withal in appearance. Never did I before gaze upon so beautiful a countenance. Hark ! he sighs in his sleep, and now he awakens. Caution, Michael ; we must be careful, or he is so far exhausted by the sufferings and excitement he has under-gone, that he may never recover."

The youth, before the old woman could come to the conclusion of this speech, had started from the couch, and sinking on his knees in the middle of the room, clasped his hands vehemently, and while his countenance evinced the greatest agony, he thus exclaimed, in piteous accents, addressing himself to some imaginary individuals,—

"Mercy! mercy! mercy! Shed not her blood;—she is my mother, my own, my good, kind mother! Oh, she was ever most kind to her poor Julio; she soothed me to rest when the tempest raged, and the angry waves roared with dreadful fury. Send away those frightful men! What has she done that you should seek her life? And what would become of Julio, should you take her from me? Ah! you mock my supplications. You laugh my prayers to scorn! Monsters! monsters! monsters! Oh, my poor brain!"

He covered his face with his hands, and sobbed convulsively.

"Say nothing to him," said Michael in a whisper to his wife; "this burst of natural grief may relieve him."

A pause ensued, during which the unfortunate youth continued to sob and weep bitterly. Rosetta and her parents watched him with the deepest pity and interest, but at length he again started to his feet, and staring wildly about him, cried,—

"See! see! they grasp her arms, those arms that have so often enclosed my neck, and strained me to her heart with maternal fondness! They point their glittering weapons at her breast! God! God! will nobody rush forward to save her? Mother! mother! They bear her from me, and now—that piercing shriek! Despair! despair! the bloody deed is done, and Julio is parentless! A plash! a plash! Ah, they have thrown her mangled body in the deep—but she is not dead! No, no. See, her body rises on the waves! She clasps her fair hands!—fair—no, no, they are no longer fair! they are crimsoned with her own blood! She sinks—and now—again she rises! I yet catch the loved glance of her eye! I hear her voice, as she is carried by the cruel waves far away from me—'Julio! Julio!'—again! again! And shall I not obey her summons? Monsters, release me; you have doomed her to death, and we will perish together! Let go your hold—ah! she sinks from my sight!—the waves are stained with blood! Fiends are hissing in my ears! My brain is on fire! Mother, mother, mother! Ha! ha! ha!"

He could no more, but staggering forward, sank exhausted in the arms of Mrs. Belford.

"Wretched, wretched boy! your troubles must surely have been great to have worked this destructive effect upon your intellect," said Mrs. Belford.

"They must, indeed," coincided Michael; "from all that we can judge, his mother has been savagely murdered."

"Alas!" sighed Rosetta, the tears starting to her eyes, "I fear that his reason has fled for ever."

Again Julio (for such appeared to be his name) revived, and looking with a vacant expression of amazement and doubt upon Mrs. Belford and her daughter, he said,—

"Who is it that holds me? I am not mad, though they said I was! No—no—let me go—I will not harm you! Poor Julio cannot harm any one. He is only a weak, friendless boy!"

"You are not friendless, unfortunate boy," said Mrs. Belford, in her kindest accents; "you are with those who will protect you, cherish you—love you."

"Love! what, love Julio?" repeated the maniac, with a vacant stare; "but no, you are not she that I used to love! You are not she who used to kiss and weep upon my cheek, and call me her only comfort, her darling boy. Ah! me! there is no one to love Julio now. Oh, she was so beautiful! Did you ever see her? No, no, no; and you will never see her now; the angry waves have swallowed her up! I shall never again hear the song she used to sing to me in

childhood. Oh, it was such a sweet—sweet song. Shall I sing it you? Yes, I will, for you look so kind and gentle, and I know you will not mock me Hush! hush!"

And then in a voice of such plaintive sweetness, that it brought tears into the eyes of those who heard it, the hapless youth sang the following words:—

"My cherub boy, my cherub boy,
   Lie still upon my breast;
It is unto a mother's heart
   Thy little head is pressed.
Nay, start not at the moaning wind
   That fitfully sweeps by;
A mother's soothing voice shall be
   Thy gentle lullaby!
               Lullaby! lullaby!

"Soft be thy sleep, my cherub boy,
   And ——

"Oh, my poor head! I cannot remember the rest. But I shall never hear it again! Never again! Ah, me!"

He drooped his head upon Mrs. Belford's shoulder, and became lost in his own wild wanderings. Again he raised himself from the arms of Mrs. Belford, and passing his hands across his forehead, appeared to be endeavouring to recollect himself.

"Where am I?" he cried; "have I been dreaming? Yes, yes, poor Julio's is now a life of dreams—of fearful visions! I do not hear the roaring of the tempest! I do not see the devouring flames that enclosed me on every side, nor hear the screams of the poor creatures for help when there was no help nigh. Where am I? Where am I?"

"Fair youth, you are safe," said Michael, "you are where no harm can reach you."

"Safe! safe!" repeated Julio, in bewildered accents; "where are those frightful men, and what strange faces meet my gaze? I know you not. And who are you?" he continued, fixing his bright but bewildered eyes upon the lovely countenance of Rosetta, "you are very pretty, but you are not my sister—oh, no, and yet I once had a sister, who was as fair as you, but she died, died when I was very young, and I have no sister now. Will you not be my sister?"

Rosetta was overcome with emotion, and knew not how to reply.

"Ah, me!" sighed the maniac, "you refuse! Julio has no one to love him now." Then suddenly starting with an extraordinary wildness of gesture, he cried, "hark! hear you not that piercing shriek? It is borne by the night wind across the wide waste of waters! It is the shriek of despair—of death! Will no one fly to the sufferer's aid? It is a mother's voice that calls upon her child! They have mangled her body with their dreadful weapons, and thrown her into the deep! Haste, haste, or she will sink—she will perish! No, you stir not—there is no pity in your breasts! Wretches, her blood will be upon your heads! Again that shriek! Can you hear it unmoved? Let me then go—you shall not hold me. Mother! mother! I come; your boy—your Julio will die with you!"

Again he sunk exhausted in the arms of Mrs. Belford, and was borne unresistingly to the couch. For awhile he remained silent, and then without moving or opening his eyes he once more sung in a voice of the most touching and melancholy sweetness the words of the simple ballad:

"My cherub boy, my cherub boy,
    Lie still upon my breast;
It is unto a mother's heart
    Thy little head is pressed.
Nay, start not at the moaning wind
    That fitfully sweeps by;
A mother's soothing voice shall be
    Thy gentle lullaby!

                        Lullaby! lullaby!"

The last words were scarcely audible, and as they died away upon his lips, he sunk into a state of unconsciousness.

"The dreadful events he has hinted at have certainly deranged his intellect," said Michael; "it is terrible to see one so young cast upon the ocean of misfortune. I fear his history is a terrible one, but here I swear to become his future protector, and to guard him to the best of my power from the cruel enemies he has doubtless in existence."

"Heaven bless you for that vow, Michael," said his wife; "and rest assured that the Almighty will assist you in your Christian designs."

"I do not fear that he will not, my good dame," replied the benevolent Mr. Belford, "and I only hope that the time will arrive when this dark mystery will be unveiled, and the wretches who have been guilty of such cruel deeds be brought to punishment. Poor fellow, he seems to sleep calmly now; oh, may it remain undisturbed, and that the morning's sun may restore to him the light of reason."

Rosetta and her mother fervently responded to this humane wish, and Michael then urged his daughter again to retire to her chamber, as he was fearful that the unusual excitement of the eventful evening might otherwise make her ill.

"It would not be safe to leave the youth," he continued, "so your mother and me will watch by him till the morning. Go to your chamber, Rosetta, and fear not ; all good angels will watch around your pillow and guard your innocence from every harm."

Rosetta embraced her parents affectionately, bade them good night, and casting one eager glance upon the pale but handsome countenance of the unfortunate Julio, retired from the room.

When Rosetta had reached her chamber, she placed her lamp upon the table, and sitting down, gave herself up to the variety of thoughts which the strange and impressive events of the night naturally gave rise to in her mind. But all the horrors of the evening were superseded entirely by the last adventure, and her deepest sympathies were excited for the unfortunate and interesting Julio, and when she reflected upon the piteous observations he had made use of in his wild ravings, her heart was moved to compassion, and she wept tears of the gentlest pity.

It has been before stated that Rosetta possessed a soul of the most delicate sensibility, and it must, therefore, be expected that the misfortunes and the affliction which had befallen one so young, would make the most powerful impression upon her ; but there was something so peculiar in the circumstances connected with Julio, his bereaved reason, which might never be restored to him, and his friendless state, that more than usually affected her. And then his handsome features, his graceful form—never had she before seen anything to approach their excellence, and she could never cease to admire them. She blushed not to do so, for she did it in the genuine innocence and purity of her soul.

The terrors of the evening were forgotten, and after some time passed in reflection, she offered up her prayers to the Supreme, in which she did not forget the name of Julio, and, retiring to her couch, sweet and balmy sleep soon descended upon her eyelids.

CHAPTER III.

THE RED MANOR HOUSE.—THE MISER BARONET.—THE HORRORS OF CONSCIENCE.—THE INTERVIEW.

THE residence of Sir Horace Middleton, or, as he was commonly called, "the Miser Baronet," was situate about half a mile from the dwelling of Michael Belford, and was known by the name of the Red Manor House. It was a spacious building, probably more than two centuries old, and had evidently been erected for some person of consequence; and, indeed, the gentleman who had possessed it previous to Sir Horace, kept up the establishment with true old English magnificence and hospitality, and was a blessing to his tenants and dependents, contributing to their necessities with a liberal hand, and studiously consulting their welfare and prosperity.

Our narrative commences about the year 1780, and some twenty years prior to that period, the Red Manor House, having been for some time unoccupied, was purchased by Sir Horace Middleton. He was then a man about forty years of age, said to be a widower, and having no family but a boy whom he called his nephew, and who, at that time, was not more than three years of age.

The personal appearance of Sir Horace, even at that period, was anything but prepossessing. He was a tall, spare man, always habited in clothes of the oldest fashion and meanest texture. His features were sharp, his cheek bones very high, and his complexion sallow. His eyes were small, and always cast down beneath a pair of very bushy brows, and, when speaking, he never by any chance ventured to raise them towards the countenance of the person whom he was addressing. A smile was never seen upon his features, and, in fact, anything in the shape of cheerfulness or complacency appeared to shun him as an alien.

Two servants, an old woman who acted as housekeeper, and an aged porter, the very counterpart of his master in attenuated appearance, formed the whole of his establishment; but he brought with him a steward, who soon proved that he was very well qualified to transact the business of his worthy employer. It must have been a terrible thing to Sir Horace when he was under the necessity of employing a tutor for his nephew; and it was a matter of general marvel how he could ever have found it in his heart to burthen himself with this little relative at all.

By many it was believed that his real name was not Sir Horace Middleton at all, and that he had very good reasons for concealing it; but whether that surmise was correct or not, we must leave it to time to develope. Albeit he was believed to be very wealthy, but the way in which he had gained his riches was a subject that was frequently mooted; and various conjectures, all, perhaps, equally vague and unjust, were as frequently hazarded upon it.

His tenantry were not long in discovering the actual cruelty and oppressiveness of his disposition. He raised the rents, and if quarter-day brought not the money to the very hour, ejectment was the certain consequence. Remonstrance was useless: it was a word that was expunged from his vocabulary, if, indeed, it had ever been there, which was rather doubtful; and his certain reply was, "I am poor—very poor, and I must have my rents, I must have my rents." The consequence of this was, that tenants sought other landlords, and his estate, which had once been one of the richest in the country, became little better than a complete waste. Thus does avarice generally defeat its own purpose.

Thus sordid, oppressive, cruel, and inhospitable, it must be expected that Sir Horace Middleton was universally despised and hated; the wealthy would not associate with him, and, indeed, he sought not their society. Scandal attached more evils to his character than perhaps it merited; he never walked forth from his now gloomy residence, which was but seldom, and that in the darkness of night, but he was followed by the secret curses of those who had felt his tyranny; in fact, he was universally shunned, despised, and suspected.

His nephew, as he grew up, although he evinced none of the darker features of his uncle's character, but on the contrary, a levity and recklessness of disposition directly opposed to it, was treated with very little more respect. He quickly showed that the seeds of vice were strongly ingrafted in his nature: how should it have been otherwise, brought up as he was under such unfavourable auspices? Principle appeared to be a stranger to his breast, and all his actions augured a future career of profligacy and crime.

He was a handsome youth, spirited and active, and probably, under proper tuition, might have made an ornament to society; but his predilection for extravagance seemed to increase with his uncle's parsimony. It was probably this that induced his uncle to yield to his inclinations for a sea-faring life, and, at the age of fifteen, young Middleton commenced his nautical career as a middy on board the Antagonist; and such was the perseverance with which he pursued his maritime studies, and the spirit and bravery he displayed upon many occasions, that he quickly arose to promotion, and had he not been naturally vicious, might have shone with honour and distinction, both in public and private life.

No doubt Sir Horace was glad to get rid of his nephew, and whenever he returned to England his reception was none of the most agreeable description; but his nephew bore it all with becoming patience and prudence, for he knew sufficient of his relation's character to be aware that to incur his severe displeasure would be to deprive himself of the hoard of wealth he one day anticipated possessing.

Thus years rolled on, and with advancing years so did the avarice of Sir Horace and his mysterious habits increase. He had no one now to watch his secret actions; he was left to the uninterrupted enjoyment of his propensities and the furtherance of his dark plans; but was he a happy man? Ah! no; the withering blight of conscience was continually upon him; it haunted him day and night, presenting to his tortured imagination the frightful forms which the deeds of past years conjured up; the canker-worm of conscious guilt gnawed at his heart; and the miser, as all misers are, was a trembling, restless, quivering wretch in the midst of all his riches. He shunned the light of day as though he dreaded that it would reveal his secret thoughts and actions to the world, and bring down upon him that just retribution which his crimes merited. But there were other fears which constantly haunted him, fears of such a terrible nature that he was often almost overwhelmed by them, and at times he was worked up to a pitch of frenzy. There was *one*—one dread being living that haunted him as severely as his conscience; *one* who held his destiny in his hands; upon whose word hung his very life, and that *one* was placed in such a position that he dared not murmur, while he was forced to become the slave of his power.

And there were other forms that would constantly presented themselves to the miser baronet's fancy—forms that made the very life blood freeze within his veins as they rushed upon his imagination, and his soul shrink appalled, and quail beneath the weight of its own guilt.

Often had Sir Horace been observed, when the darkness of night enshrouded the earth, standing with folded arms upon one of the loftiest rocks, and gazing with a wild, yet eager glance across the broad waters of the deep, as if watching for something. Ever and anon he would pace with disordered steps backwards and forwards, but never were his eyes for an instant removed from the ocean, and as the beams of the moon reflected on his cadaverous countenance, he looked like some ghostly and troubled spirit that was doomed to wander over the scenes of its former crimes. Then again he would pause and listen as if he expected, yet feared the approach of something, but when nothing but the rippling of the waves met his ears, he would give utterance to an indistint exclamation of disappointment, and clasp his hands together with an air of agony that was truly pitiable to behold. Sometimes he has been known to remain there till the hour of midnight was past, when he would retrace his steps to his dismal dwelling, to darkness and thought.

It was on the evening of the tempest described in the first chapter of our tale, that there were seated in the kitchen of the Red Manor-house the two amiable and worthy domestics of Sir Horace Middleton, Grisselda Skinflint and the venerable phantom of mortality, Simon Snipe. A small lamp on the table sent forth a feeble and flickering ray, just sufficient to render their cadaverous and lank countenances visible to each other.

"Ah, Simon," said the old woman, with a long drawn sigh, " you sport with my passion; you treat me cruelly; but it's like the whole of your faithless, cruel, deceitful sex. Would that I had never set eyes upon you; would that I had been born where man was unknown; then I should not have experienced this sorrow. Have you not promised thousands of times to make me bone of your bone, and flesh of your flesh? and now it seems that I shall neither become one nor the other. It is very cruel of you, Simon, it is barbarous thus to sport with my virgin love."

And here the old woman applied one corner of her apron to each of her eyes, under the delusion that she had something there to wipe away.

" Gracious Heaven !" cried Simon Snipe, " these are shocking times, indeed, when youth, unwary youth, must be constantly pursued by the wiles of woman. Oh, Grissy,—oh, Grissy !"

" Why do you not keep your promise, then ?"

" Think of the expense, Grissy," said Snipe; " think of the money it would cost to get married—a perfect fortune. Monstrous !—Besides, our dear master would never give his consent to our union."

" It is a poor excuse, Simon," said Grisselda, " and you know it is. Our master is an angel, a perfect angel, and I know he would never, he could never be so cruel as to blight the hopes of two fond hearts."

" Grissy !" said Simon, with a look of horror, " would you bring ruin upon the baronet ? Think of the expense of a family. We might have children, dear Grissy."

" So you have said for the last forty-five years that we have been courting, Simon ; but, should it so happen, you know we are both good economists, and could make the burthen light to us."

" Well, there is something in that to be sure," returned Snipe.

" Besides," continued the old woman, " how happy we should be in a sweet communion of souls, Simon."

" True, true, Grissy."

" Never did nature so truly form two beings to meet together."

" You are a coaxer, Grissy," simpered the skeleton porter.

" Ah, Simon, I knew you would relent ; I knew your faithful, generous nature too well to think otherwise."

" Oh, Grissy, Grissy, you are a sad tempter. A man must be marble whom your charms, your fascinations, could not allure."

" You promise, then ?" eagerly demanded the old woman.

" I do, on my knees, dear Grisselda ; I vow that in three months from the present date, should our master give his consent, that the holy bands of matrimony shall unite our fates."

" Oh, joy, joy !" exclaimed Grisselda, " rise, sweet youth, and ——"

" Let this fond kiss seal at once my sacred vow !"

And the venerable lovers tottered to each other's arms, and sealed the bargain in the aforesaid manner upon their skinny lips.

" Dear Simon," said Grisselda, after a pause, " temperance and frugality, you know, is always our motto, those blessed principles that have been instilled into our breasts by our honoured master ; but I think upon this auspicious occasion we may indulge in a jug of ale."

" A small jug, Grissy," returned Snipe, " a half pint will be sufficient for us both, and we can dispense with our allowance to-morrow at dinner time."

" Very true, Simon," answered his aged companion, and she left the kitchen, and in a few minutes returned with a half pint measure full of a certain liquid which, while labouring under some extraordinary monomania, they had baptized table ale.

" May we not as well have our supper, Grissy ?" asked Snipe, " and then we can enjoy this excellent beverage with it."

The old woman assented, and went to the larder, but quickly returned with a countenance more elongated than before.

" There is nothing in the larder, Simon."

" Nothing ?"

" Not a morsel !"

" Where's the corned beef?" inquired Simon.

" Gone !"

" And the soup ?"

" All gone !" replied Grisselda.

" What every drop ?"

" Every drop, Simon, as I'm a living sinner."

" Powers of gluttony !" cried Snipe, with a groan of horror ; " what, three good pounds of corned beef, with soup, gone, all gone, in a little more than a week ? Oh, monstrous extravagance ! We shall ruin Sir Horace, we shall completely ruin him, Grisselda, if our appetites increase at this enormous rate. We cannot afford to drink his ale ; put it back, Grissy, put it back."

Grisselda obeyed : and it was some time before the worthy pair recovered from the shock their nerves had sustained by the discovery of their " monstrous extravagance," as Simon Snipe called it.

" It is a very awful night, Grissy," at length said Snipe.

" It is indeed, Simon," coincided his companion. " Dear me, how it thunders, and how fearfully the lightning flashes."

" Just such a night as it was five years ago, you remember, when the Death Ship made its appearance."

" Ah, so it is ; and I'll warrant it will visit this coast to-night," observed the old woman.

" You may be sure of that," said Simon, " or Sir Horace would not have been absent from home. Every five years, Grisselda ; every five years, you know."

" True, true ; but what connection can our master have with that dreadful vessel ?"

" Hush! hush! Grissy ; we must not be curious; we have an excellent master, and it behoves us not to pry into his secrets."

" Right, Simon, you say very right ; and I would not for the world endeavour to do so. But Heaven forbid that Sir Horace should return home in the same dreadful state of agitation that he did this time five years ago."

" I hope not," observed Snipe ; " but we must be prepared for it."

" I have often thought, dear Simon," said the old woman, after a pause, " I have often thought ——."

" Well, what have you thought, Grisselda ?" demanded her ancient lover.

" But you will be offended, Simon ; you will be angry."

" No, no. Tell me what you have thought?"

" Well, then, dear Simon, it has often occurred to me that you were not unacquainted with the secrets of Sir Horace."

" Powers of curiosity !" cried Simon, with a look of indignation which made his aged companion start and tremble ; " what I—I, Grissy ? Let me hear another hint of such a thing, and I will retract the vow I have made, to make you my wife, for ever !"

" Oh, gracious ! Simon, dear Simon," ejaculated Grisselda, greatly alarmed, " forgive me ; it was very wrong of me to say such a thing, and never, never will I do it again."

" Think of the consequences," said Simon, with awful emphasis.

" I do—I do—oh, foolish woman, that I should be so rash."

" Remember the oath we took to Sir Horace, never to reveal what we saw or heard."

" Oh, yes, yes."

" Never to dare to pry into his conduct," continued Snipe, with the same solemnity and energy of manner.

" I remember it all ; I remember it all."

" Then tremble ere you again attempt to disobey the solemn injunctions of Sir Horace."

" I do tremble, Simon ; I do tremble."

" And so you should."

" Indeed I ought. But let the matter drop, Simon, and say that for this once you will forgive me."

" For this once, then," said Simon with dignity, " I will condescend to pardon you ; but offend so again, and we are for ever made enemies."

" Never, never, will I offend so more, dear Simon."

" Then—you are pardoned," said the skeleton porter ; and he reseated himself with all the dignity natural to a functionary of his particular importance.

A pause of two or three minutes ensued, when Grisselda, having recovered from the trepidation into which the anger of Simon had thrown her, ventured to observe,—

" In two or three days young master is expected to arrive at the manor, I understand."

" Yes, plague on him," growled Simon, " and it would be quite as well if he were at the bottom of the sea, for what good he is."

" Lor bless me, Simon, you don't say so."

" But I do. He sets everything at sixes and sevens when he comes, with his noise and his racket, disturbing our beloved master from his studies, and turning the very house upside down. Besides, look at the extra expense, Grissy; it is horrible."

"So it is, Simon," coincided the old woman.

"For my part, I think Sir Horace has done quite enough for him," continued Snipe, " and now that he is made a captain of, he ought to be contented to keep himself."

"So I think, Simon."

"I am afraid that he will bring some trouble upon Sir Horace before he has done with him."

"Heaven forbid."

"He is so wild and extravagant, you know."

"Very true. But Sir Horace must not yield to all his extravagances," said Grisselda.

"Ah, Grissy," remarked Snipe, "how you talk; you know what a good, kind, generous, easy gentleman our master is, and that is the reason that young Middleton takes the advantage of him."

"Exactly so; I know it well, dear Simon. Every person but ourselves I believe seek to take an advantage of him."

"They do, Grissy, they do," sighed Simon; "and it is well for him that he has two such trustworthy servants as we are, or God knows what would become of him. Bless my soul, what a terrible peal of thunder that was!"

"Awful!" replied Grisselda; "I hope my master will not be long before he returns."

"I think we might extinguish the lamp," said Snipe, "for we have plenty of lightning, without wasting the oil."

"Very true; but Sir Horace will require a lamp when he comes back, and, therefore, we had better be in readiness for him."

"Very true; I did not think that, Grissy. But, hark! was not that the bell at the gate?"

"It was," answered the old woman; "it is Sir Horace, no doubt. Haste, Simon."

Simon took up the lamp, and hurried as fast as his feeble limbs would permit him to the door, but before he could reach it the bell was pulled with greater violence than before.

He opened it, and Sir Horace, pale as a corpse, rushed into the hall, and snatching the lamp from the old man's hand, darted up the staircase which led to his own private apartments. Having entered the gloomy wainscoted room, in which he usually indulged in his secret meditations over the midnight oil, he sunk on a seat, and panted for breath. More fearfully pale than usual was his repulsive countenance; his eyes rolled wildly in their sockets, his lips were livid, and large drops of perspiration bedewed his temples. A more fearful spectacle of horror could not be imagined.

It was some moments before he could give utterance to a sound; his lips moved, but the words he wished to articulate died away upon them. At length he clasped his forehead vehemently, and groaned aloud.

"Another night—another night," he at last gasped forth; "another night of unspeakable horror! Oh, Heaven! when will this cease? When—but fool! wretch! why do I murmur? it is but the reward I have brought upon myself; it is but the penalty of my crimes! And this is the happiness my darling gold has brought me! Such is the misery with which gold obtained by the shedding of human blood supplies its votaries! Miserable infatuation! Why do I not shake it off? Why not—but no, no, I cannot—I must still cling to it—it purchases me life, and I dare not die! But what a life! Oh, horror! horror! The curse of avarice has brought me to this, and now I am so entangled in the meshes of those who hold me in their power, that I cannot escape!"

He paused, and reflected deeply, and then a ghastly smile suddenly overspread his features, as he started from his seat, and exclaimed,—

"But I have the gold! ha! ha! yes, I have the gold! The object of my ambition is mine, though I have had to wade through blood to obtain it! No matter, no matter, 'tis mine! 'tis mine! And hourly can I feast my sight over

the glittering hoard. Who dare accuse me of crime, while I have gold—gold? Ha! ha! ha! I will laugh them to scorn, I—ah! whence comes that dismal cry? What awful groans from restless spirits are those that vibrate in my ears? And see, they rise before me! Another! another! and another! all ghastly, mangled, and bloody! They hover round me in a circle, grinning upon me, and pointing their fleshless fingers towards me! Away! away! I will not gaze upon ye! Rest, rest in your unhallowed graves, your murderer's time is not yet come! No, no, they mock me! And now they gather closer round me—I feel their icy touch! Help! help!"

Again the wretched man sunk exhausted on his seat, and burying his face in his hands, was for some time unable to utter another word, and afraid to look up.

At length the violence of his agony became somewhat abated, and he once more raised his head.

"It was but a delusion, a sickly delusion of my brain," he said ; "I must banish this weakness, and reflect calmly. I have had years enough experience, of bitter experience, not to act in this childish manner. I have the means of purchasing security; and, therefore, should deport myself with a bold carriage, and not as —— Who's there? Who knocks?"

"'Tis I," answered a voice outside ; "I would speak a few words with you."

"I—I cannot see you," answered Sir Horace ; "I am in no mood for converse ; seek me to-morrow."

"Psha!" returned the man outside; "what nonsense is this; I have left my home on purpose ; I will not detain you many minutes ;—unlock the door."

Sir Horace muttered some words of dissatisfaction between his teeth, and slowly arising from his chair, unlocked the door, and gave admittance to Martin Trevors.

It has before been shewn that Martin Trevors was a man of mysterious character, but nothing had yet transpired in the neighbourhood where he resided, to create any suspicion that he was an improper one. True, he was very reserved in his habits, and did not associate much with his neighbours, Michael Belford being the only one with whom he was on intimate terms, and his visits to him were not frequent.

He had several fishing-boats of his own, and was supposed to be in very comfortable circumstances. He had brought Frank up with care and attention, and the youth looked upon him with the greatest reverence, notwithstanding his manners towards him were never characterised by any particular kindness.

"You look pale, Middleton," he said, after he had gazed at him for a moment or two ; "you tremble. Will you never conquer this cowardice?"

"Cowardice!" repeated Sir Horace ; "oh, Trevors, after the night of horror I have passed, after what I have heard, after the terrible threats that have been held against me, can you wonder at my present emotion? Can you call it by the name of cowardice?"

"I do," answered Trevors ; "I always like to call things by their proper names, and I repeat that this is cowardice. Have you not gold? Cannot you purchase silence? Then what have you to fear?"

"Gold! gold! Trevors!" returned Middleton ; "ah! you are like the rest ; you will ring that word gold in my ears, and proclaim me rich, when I am poor, very poor indeed."

"Bah! are you mad to talk such stuff as this to me?" said Trevors ; "do I not know all your secrets?"

"Alas! alas!" sighed the miserable man.

"Hark ye, Horace Middleton," continued Trevors ; "it is not conscience that makes you wretched; you never possessed a very keen one; I know you well, it is the dread, the horror of parting with your money that tortures you."

"And should it not? Has it not been dearly purchased? Alas! how dearly purchased. The past ——"

"We will not talk of the past," said Trevors ; "but the present. You have seen him?"

"Seen him!" groaned Sir Horace ; "oh, yes—or why this agitation? I have seen him, and in five years more ——"

"Your bones will be whitening on a gibbet, very likely," added Trevors.

"Trevors! Trevors! say not so," cried the wretched man, every limb trembling with terror, and his countenance becoming more ghastly than before. "Come you here to torture me? They—they will not hang me! I have gold!"

"Ha! ha! ha!" laughed Martin Trevors, scornfully. "How soon the thoughts of the gallows will alter your tones ; just now you said you were poor, very poor. Ha! ha! ha!"

" Oh, Trevors, spare me ; I am an old man, spare me."

" Well, well," returned Trevors, " I wish not to torture you, and make you more wretched than you already are. I have a secret for you."

" A secret ?"

" Aye, and one that no doubt will afford you much gratification."

" Name it, name it, quick," said Sir Horace, impatiently.

Trevors approached him nearer, and whispered some words in his ear, which at present the reader must be content to remain in ignorance of, but whatever they were, no sooner did Sir Horace hear them than the expression of his countenance changed, mingled satisfaction and horror were stamped upon them, and starting back a few paces, he stammered out,—

" Trevors, you are not attempting to deceive me ? Is this true ?"

" I tell you again, it is," answered Trevors ; " you have nothing more to fear from them."

" This—this is good news, indeed," ejaculated Sir Horace.

" Good news," repeated Martin Trevors, with a look of scorn ; " good news Horace Middleton ; what has become of your conscience, now, eh ?"

" Do not, do not, Trevors ;—you rack me."

" Well, I came not here to do that," said Trevors ; " I have brought you good news, as you call it, which has cost me some trouble to obtain, and now I claim my reward."

" Reward ?"

" Aye ; I stand in need of twen y guineas, I will borrow it of you.'

" Borrow it of me ?" repeated the old man, with a shudder ; " borrow twenty guineas of me ?"

" Yes, to be sure," answered Trevors ; " and I know you will not refuse me."

" Twenty guineas—twenty guineas," muttered Sir Horace, and each time he repeated the words they were like so many daggers to his heart ; " it is a large sum of money, Martin, a very large sum ; will not less do ?"

" No, not a guinea less," answered Trevors.

" Well, well—I—I suppose I must let you have it."

" Of course, you must."

" But not to-night, Martin," said the old man, looking fearfully towards the secret trap which led to the precious hoard ; " to-morrow, Martin, to-morrow."

" Very well, to-morrow then be it," replied Trevors ; " but, remember, I shall expect it then without any more hesitation. You know me, Middleton ?"

" Alas ! too well," groaned Sir Horace.

" Or, perhaps," rejoined Trevors, with a significant look, " you might have said more properly, that I knew you too well."

" But—but—can I trust you, Trevors ; you will not betray me ?"

" Not while you keep faith with me," replied Martin.

" I will—I will !" gasped forth the wretched old man, with a look of terror.

" Then good night, to-morrow I shall call for the twenty guineas."

With these words Martin Trevors stalked from the room, and the old man once more locked and bolted the door. He looked around him with a fearful expression of countenance. Conscience was at work within his breast, terrible, busy conscience, and he started at his own shadow upon the wainscot, conjuring it up into some frightful apparition. He sank again in his arm-chair, and his attenuated frame was shaken by some powerful emotion. A more wretched picture of abject guilt, yet clinging to the wealth he had sinned so deeply to obtain, could not be imagined.

" He wished me good night," he said, in hollow, trembling accents, " good night—when will there be a good night for me ? I might hope for one, were they all gone, and no evidences of my guilt remained. Twenty guineas—twenty guineas ! It is a large sum, an enormous sum. But he must have it, I dare not refuse him. They are all robbing me—they all seek my gold—that gold I have purchased so dearly—yes, every coin is steeped in blood, the blood of those—oh, God ! let me not think! God! how dare I call upon his name?   What have I to do with God?"

And the sacred name died away in a choking tone in the guilty man's throat, and he covered his face with his emaciated hands, groaning with mental agony, and swayed his body to and fro, unable to support the weight of dreadful thoughts which crowded upon his perturbed brain.

A pause of some minutes ensued, and all was dismal silence in that lonely chamber. The storm had entirely ceased, but the dead stillness that had succeeded it was almost equally awful. Sir Horace again raised his head; during that brief interval his mind had wandered back to other scenes and early days, presenting a terrible contrast to the present.

"And yet I was once innocent, guiltless, honourable; then I could bask in the sun's rays, and everything upon which my eye gazed, appeared a joyous sylvan scene," he soliloquized; "I could laugh with the gayest, and mingle with the fair and lively, the good and virtuous, conscious that I was worthy of their society. Oh! would that I could recall those days; that I could again become the happy, cheerful being I was then. But a dreadful change came over me; the spirit of cursed avarice entered my breast, and I was hurled down the stream with impetuous fury, the demon urged me on; gold, gold was the beacon that lured me, and I would not suffer anything to impede my progress to the wished-for goal. I learned to laugh when men said that an unspotted conscience was man's richest treasure. Gold! gold! the fiend whispered in my ears, will purchase everything; he who has it not, must be the slave of those who possess that mighty talisman! Gold! gold! get gold, rang in my ears incessantly; it banished every other thought from my breast; virtue, honour, conscience, humanity, all yielded to its influence. One passion alone possessed my breast; 'twas the love of gold! and I obtained it, but how? Oh, that the dreadful past could be banished from my memory! But no! it will arise! it will stalk before my distracted imagination! Oceans of blood seem to flow before my eyes! Grim phantoms arise upon the surface! They laugh at me; they mock at me with their ghastly looks, and pointing to the purple stream, shout in my ears gold! gold! gold!"

Hoarse and fearful were the tones in which Sir Horace uttered these words, and he again buried his face in his hands, and became lost in the horror of his reflections. Suddenly, however, he again started to his feet, and changed was his tone and aspect.

"But I have it!" he ejaculated; "yes, yes, I have not struggled in vain; I am rich—rich, and who dare accuse me of crime? Ha! ha! ha! who dare say that Sir Horace Middleton is a murderer?"

He looked around him as though he expected some one to reply to his question. Then he tried the room door, to be certain that he had secured it properly, and advancing to the further end of the apartment, he applied all his strength to an old chest that stood there, and removed it from its situation. This done he returned to the table, and, taking the lamp in his hand, he stooped down and searched for something in the flooring. He found it; it was a secret spring, but so ingeniously contrived, that it would have puzzled the minutest search to discover it, unless it was by those who were aware of its exact situation. Again Sir Horace looked around him suspiciously, to be sure that no prying eye was watching his actions, and listened attentively to catch the slightest sound ere he would venture upon his examination. He pressed hard upon the spring, and a small trap flew open, beneath which was an iron depository of considerable depth. This was the miser's secret hoard; here was deposited the glittering treasure, to obtain which he had sacrificed his soul.

Bag after bag, most carefully tied round, Sir Horace brought forth, and placed upon the floor, counting them as he did so, and repeating it when they were all arranged before him. Then he laughed—a strange unearthly laugh, in the unnatural delight of his soul.

"They are all here!" he cried; "all filled with the bright, the yellow ore, and, why, then, should I be wretched? Am I not rich? Ha! ha! ha! very, very rich.

These are the golden fruits of my labours. But I have them now; I have them now, and the tempter has kept his word."

Again and again did the guilty wretch count over the bags which contained his ill-gotten wealth, and, every time he did so, he laughed the more.

"But Martin Trevors," he at length observed, "he will not fail to come tomorrow, and he truly said that I dare not refuse his demand. No, no, he does indeed know me too well."

He untied one of the canvas bags, and turned a portion of its contents out upon the floor. He gloated over the glittering pile, and then he rubbed his long, bony hands together, with the most unbounded satisfaction. He counted out the money he had promsed Trevors, and with every coin he uttered a deep sigh. Then he carefully tied the bag again, and depositing it with its companions in the secret place of concealment, he closed the trap, and once more drew the old chest over it.

"Twenty guineas," he repeated, when he had re-seated himself in his old armchair, and counting the money over in his hand, "it is a large, a very large sum, and to be sacrificed in such a manner. It is as much, or more, than it costs me to keep my whole establishment for a whole year, although my servants have most voracious appetites. But he suddenly added, after a pause, "I wonder if what he told me was true, and that they are ——"

He would not finish the sentence, for the words seemed to choke him in trying to give utterance to them, and he trembled excessively, and feared to look around him.

Whatever was the secret information that Martin Trevors had imparted to him, we cannot at the present stage of our narrative pretend to say, but various and remarkable were the effects the recollection of it had upon the baronet. Sometimes he would shudder and tremble with convulsed horror, then he would burst out into wild laughter, and pace the apartment with all the gestures and airs of a maniac, muttering at the same time strange unintelligible words to himself; again he would sink in his chair, and become buried in deep and gloomy meditation.

At length the old clock in the hall of the manor-house struck the hour of two; Sir Horace started up at the sound, and, taking his lamp, he slowly quitted the apartment. Most carefully he locked the iron door that opened into it, and then traced his way along the gloomy gallery, towards his chamber. To rest? ah, no; could such a miserable wretch as Sir Horace Middleton ever rest?

CHAPTER IV.

THE COVERED PORTRAIT.——THE TERROR OF JULIO.——THE MEETING.

SEVERAL days elapsed after the events recorded in the foregoing chapters without anything worthy of particular notice taking place. Michael had endeavoured all he could to ascertain the name of the vessel that had been destroyed by fire on the awful night selected for the commencement of our narrative, in the hope that it might afford some clue to lead to the discovery as to who the interesting boy Julio was; but his efforts were all in vain, every vestige of the ill-fated ship had been destroyed, every soul on board of her, with the exception of the young stranger, had perished, and thus the only chance of obtaining the desired information rested on the restoration of the hapless youth to his senses. Several bodies had been washed on shore, but nothing was found upon them to unravel the painful mystery, and Michael at length gave up the task in despair, and left the solution of the remarkable circumstances to the wisdom and will of Providence.

The wild delirium of Julio had ceased; he seemed to be conscious of the kindness bestowed upon him by the benevolent persons under whose care he had been so miraeulously placed; but still his senses wandered, reason, in fact, seemed to have quitted her seat entirely, and they could elicit no more from him than that his name was Julio, and to the more awful facts which seemed to be connected with his history, they feared to allude, lest it should throw him into those dreadful paroxysms which had so exhausted him on the night when he was rescued from his perilous situation by Michael Belford. One thing, however, appeared certain, namely, that his mother had met with an awful and untimely fate, and that in his presence, and no wonder that so bloody and inhuman a scene as he had described in his madness should have turned his brain. But who that mother was, or who is her savage assassin were, of course, is involved for the present in the deepest mystery.

Michael had procured him a suit of clothes, in which he had been induced to dress himself, and nothing could surpass the childish delight with which the poor boy viewed himself. He laughed in all the exuberance of jocund mirth and pleasure, and his fine eyes sparkled with a brilliancy and an expression of so peculiar and touching a nature that it brought tears into the eyes of the lovely Rosetta and her parents.

"Why do you cry?" said the maniac boy, turning suddenly towards them, and fixing an earnest look upon them. "Why do you cry? Is it because you see Julio so fine? Oh, it is a long time since he wore such fine things before, and looked so smart. How pretty, how very, very pretty. And you have given me all those beautiful things? Oh, how kind—and, indeed, I will love you dearly for it."

"Will you, my poor child?" said Mrs. Belford, kissing him with as much fondness as if he had been her own offspring; "then shall we be more than repaid."

"But you must not cry," said Julio, "for it will make me unhappy to see you weep, who have been so good to me. And yet dear mother would have wept for joy, could she have seen her Julio so fine. You never saw her, did you? No: and you will not see her now, for she is dead—dead, and left poor Julio alone. But, come, come—I will take you to her grave; you will find the sweetest flowers blooming over it, and ——. No! no! no!" he suddenly added, with renewed frenzy: "the cruel ocean is her grave! The wild waves rush and roar over her mangled form! They pierced her bosom—that bosom in which I have so often nestled—with their deadly weapons, and then cast her in the yawning deep. Hark! do you not hear that piercing shriek? It comes from the wide waste of waters! —it is the cry of a mother for her child! 'Julio!—Julio!'—there again! Does it not ring in your ears, and freeze your blood with horror? Fly!—fly to her rescue, or she will sink for ever! Mother! mother!—I at least will hasten to save you or perish with you."

He rushed towards the door, but was arrested in his progress by Michael, who by the most kind and soothing means restored him to calmness, and reseating himself by the side of Rosetta, who had listened to him with the deepest emotion, he relapsed into silence, sometimes passing his fair hands across his forehead, and seeming to be endeavouring to recall his scattered thoughts.

The graces of Julio's form were now displayed to the best advantage; and never did a figure more finely modelled meet the sight. Strength and activity were united to youthful delicacy and elasticity, and true nobility and dignity were predominant in every action. It was melancholy to behold so much perfection laid waste, wrecked by the desolating hand of sorrow. How terrible was it to reflect upon the misfortunes of that fair, young boy! What a bright intellect was, perhaps, destroyed for ever, ere yet its powers had been permitted to blossom to maturity! Rosetta gazed at him, and her heart warmed with a sister's affection, a sister's sympathy towards him. Brief as was the time since she had first beheld him, to her glowing imagination it seemed as if they had been acquainted from childhood; and she pictured to herself all the sorrows he had experienced as vividly as if she had been intimately acquainted with them. And the poor bereaved boy would sometimes cast towards her such looks—so wild, so strange, yet so full of feeling, so expressive of that which his wonderment would not permit him to give utterance to, that the damsel felt her emotions increase at every glance, and her innocent affections strengthen towards him.

"You weep, too," he said, after a pause, and gently approaching her; "why do cry? Is it for poor Julio?—do you, then, pity me?"

"I do—I do, indeed," answered Rosetta, with an energy she could not restrain.

"Oh, this is kind!" said the youth; "very, very kind; and you are so beautiful!

Oh, that Julio had such a sister !—how, how he would love her! And will you not let me call you sister ?"

" Yes—yes, poor youth !" replied the blushing and agitated damsel.

" Oh, joy ! joy !" exclaimed the maniac, his fine eyes sparkling with redoubled brilliancy. " Speak on, speak on — I do love to hear you talk : your voice is so sweet, so heavenly ; it reminds me of my poor mother—she whom the savage monsters murdered. Oh, God !"

" Dear Julio," said Mrs. Belford, in her tenderest and most compassionate accents, anxious to divert his mind from that dark and fearful theme.

" But no, I will not weep," he resumed, " for she is a saint in Heaven. But you will call me brother, and I will be happy. Happy !—ah, me ! No more !—no more !"

He uttered the last words in a tone of melancholy plaintiveness that must have touched the most insensible heart, and again, for a few moments, he relapsed into silence and thought. Once more he raised his head and looked anxiously towards Rosetta ; then he timidly approached her, and in a voice of the utmost simplicity and sweetness, said,—

" But I do not know your name : will you not tell it me ?"

" Rosetta."

" Rosetta !—Rosetta !—oh, what a pretty name ! I shall not forget it ; no, no ; though my mind wanders, and there are many things I wish, but cannot now recollect. And you shall be my companion, and we will sit together and talk of my mother. I will sing to you the sweet songs she used so often to sing to me ; and then we will wander together to the sea-side, and I will point out to you the spot where the cruel monsters consigned her body to the deep, and ——"

He seemed suddenly to lose all recollection of what he was talking about, abruptly broke off, passed his hand two or three times across his forehead, sighed heavily, and resigning the hand of Rosetta, which he had taken, walked silently to his seat, and seemed unconscious of all around him.

Towards night Julio always became less tranquil : he would walk often to the window, and look out upon the gloom beyond ; then his distracted imagination would recall all the horrors of that dreadful night described in our first chapter, and the exclamations he made use of were truly piteous to hear. But at length the violence of his delirium would exhaust itself, and he would become comparatively calm.

Sometimes reason appeared to be struggling hard to regain its ascendancy in the unfortunate youth's mind : its light, for a short time, faintly beamed in his eyes, and he would fix the most eloquent looks upon Rosetta and her parents, seeming to be at a loss to find words to give expression to what he wished. But it was only transitory ; he would suddenly press his hands on his temples, as if to collect his bewildered thoughts ; a vacant look, an idiotic laugh would follow, and all again was darkness and gloom.

" There is no hope : alas ! I fear not the least hope !" Mrs. Belford would observe, when the maniac boy was not present ; " his reason has fled for ever."

" No, dame," returned her husband, " I will not despair ; with care and attention he may yet be restored to his senses. We must endeavour to amuse and divert his mind in every way, and above all, we must be careful never to allude to the dreadful circumstances under which he was saved from death."

" True," coincided Mrs. Belford. " Ah ! poor youth, his is indeed a most cruel fate ; to be deprived of his parent in the horrible manner I have no doubt he has been ; and so young to be cast upon the wide world without a friend or protector."

" Say not so," said Michael, " for are we not his friends ? Are we not his protectors ? I feel as much interest in him as if he were my own relative, and when I desert one so young and so unfortunate, may Heaven desert me."

" Nobly spoken, dear Michael," ejaculated his wife, " and I know that you will not fail to keep your promise."

" No, by Heaven, I will not ; I will cherish him the same as if he were my son, and no exertions shall be wanting on my part to penetrate the strange and fearful mystery connected with him."

" Should both his parents be no more, I fear there will be but little chance of that," said Mrs. Belford.

" But we have no reason to suppose that such is the case," returned Michael ; " he has never made any particular allusion to his father, and he, at any rate, may yet be living."

" He may. But, after all, may not poor Julio have been an idiot from his birth, and the terrible tale to which he has just given utterance, in his wild delirous ravings, be nothing more than the offspring of his disordered imagination ?"

" No," answered Michael ; " that I consider to be impossible, or, at any rate, very improbable. Madness could never invent so terrible a tale. Besides, the circumstances under which I saved him, the appearance of the Death Ship, the burning of the vessel, all seems to confirm it. I fear it is, alas, too true ! that his mother has been most foully and barbarously murdered, and that Julio witnessed the dreadful deed ; and may the vengeance of Heaven overtake the monsters who could perpetrate so hideous a crime ; and it will, too, depend upon it it will, dame, for the all just God never yet suffered such wretches to escape unpunished, however great their triumph for a time may appear to be."

" True," coincided Mrs. Belford ; " but what could have induced the miscreants to take the poor woman's life ?"

" As for the reasons," replied Michael, " it is, of course, impossible for us to form a probable conjecture."

" Could Julio and his mother have been on board the Death Ship ?"

" It is not improbable," answered Michael.

" Oh, dreadful !" ejaculated Mrs. Belford ; " I shudder when I think of it. But is it not remarkable that they did not sacrifice the poor boy as well ?"

" It is," said Michael ; " but altogether this awful business is so much enveloped in mystery, that the deeper we reflect upon it, the more we must become bewildered. We must, however, guard Julio with a watchful eye, for his life may yet be sought by his secret and terrible enemies."

" Alas ! it may," answered Mrs. Belford ; " and even with all our care and precaution we may be unable to shield him from their power. God send that we may, for should anything now happen to the unfortunate child, I should feel it as severely as if he were my own son."

" Fear not, dame, Providence will aid us in our benevolent efforts."

Thus ended the conversation, and Michael and his wife retired to rest.

Julio slept in a room adjoining the chamber of Mr. and Mrs. Belford, so that they might be ready to hasten to him immediately, should he require their assistance in the night. They would frequently hear him, for hours after they had retired to repose, pacing the room, and talking wildly and incoherently to himself. Sometimes he would laugh aloud in frantic wildness, and at others convulsive sobs would escape his bosom, and the melancholy but rumbling lamentations he gave utterance to were truly pitiable to hear. Then he would commence singing in such plaintive tones that the heart must be insensible indeed that could not be melted to pity and compassion.

This room had never been used by Michael and his family, and, in fact, he had usually kept it locked up, and seemed to have some particular reasons for wishing no person to enter it. It was in consequence of its contiguity to their other chamber that he had probably placed Julio in it.

It was a small, but rather handsome apartment, but still it gave evident tokens of the neglect of many years, notwithstanding Michael had done all he could to render it comfortable before placing Julio in it. The wainscot and flooring were of polished oak ; the former displaying some very rich and curious carved work, which showed the taste of the original proprietor of the old stone house.

In one corner of this room was a recess, before which a dark curtain was drawn ; but what it concealed Mrs. Belford had never been able to learn, although her curiosity had often tempted her to press her husband upon the subject, and he had cautioned her never, if she had the opportunity of so doing, to attempt to discover. Still she had frequently, with that curiosity which is inherent in womankind, been tempted to disobey those injunctions, especially since Julio, being placed in that apartment, offered her every means of doing so.

It was on the third night that the maniac boy had been placed in this chamber, that Mr. and Mrs. Belford, as they were about to prepare to retire to bed, were alarmed by hearing his loud and frantic screams, and rushing into the room, they beheld him on his knees before the recess, with clasped hands, and trembling with emotion and

horror.   He had withdrawn the curtain, and his eyes were fixed with terrified earnestness on the object it revealed, and to which the eye of Mrs. Belford now wandered with eager curiosity. It was but a portrait which Michael had so long kept concealed with such peculiar care, but it was such a one as the eye could not rest upon without the deepest interest.

It represented a man of about thirty, attired as a fisherman, standing on the sea-beach, and resting on a boat-hook. But the countenance was one upon which it was impossible to gaze without strange feelings, far from pleasant, entering the breast, so strongly was it marked, and such was the singular expression of it. The complexion was pale, almost to cadaverousness; the lips seemed ready to part to address you, and whichever way you turned, still the large black eyes appeared fixed upon you. A profusion of long black hair hung in ringlets over the neck and shoulders. To say that the features were not well formed, nay, that they were not very handsome, would be untrue; but still there was something so stern and repulsive about them, that they inspired awe rather than admiration.

Michael and his wife approached Julio and raised him from his knees, but he started at their presence, and, pointing at the portrait with the greatest wildness of gesture and demeanour, he exclaimed,—

"Look! look! he is there! he is there! He glares upon me just the same as I have seen him do upon my poor mother and myself, when she sought to soothe him to calmness and to abate the fury of his rage. So he looked when he struck her to the earth, although I clung to his knees, and with tears implored his mercy. Hark! hear you not his terrible curses? see you not the ferocity of his looks? He threatens me,—he frowns upon me,—he calls me wretch, imp, all those dreadful names he has so often called me; and yet I know not why, for sure I ever sought his love, but he spurned me. See! again he frowns upon me;—oh, that dreadful frown! He will kill me, as he did—no—no, it was not he that did it;—but save me; oh, shield me from him!"

"From whom, my poor child?" said Mr. Belford, with compassion.

"From—from my father," answered Julio, with peculiar and awful emphasis on the word. "But no, I must not utter the name; he told me so, and oh! too well I know the terrible consequences of disobedience to his commands. He comes, he comes!—oh God! Mother, mother! I call upon your spirit to protect me;—help, help!"

Cold drops of perspiration chased each other down the maniac boy's face, and every limb trembled with the most convulsive emotion; but still he kept his beautiful eyes steadily fixed upon the portrait.

"Julio," said Michael, "quiet your fears; no one here can harm you; you are with your friends, after God, your best friends."

"Friends!" repeated the wretched youth, "I have no friends; they have all deserted me. Julio is alone; he has lost his mother, his dear mother; she was murdered; he has no one now—he has no one now,—and what friends are powerful enough to protect me against that—my father? See, see, he is approaching. He will strike me to the heart.—Well, well, welcome death! it will restore poor Julio to his mother in heaven."

Michael cautiously approached the recess and drew the curtain over the portrait.

"See, Julio," he said, kindly and persuasively, "he is gone now."

"Gone, gone!" repeated Julio, glancing eagerly towards the recess; "ah! has he then, indeed, been so merciful? But you have not killed him? you have not harmed him, although he is so terrible? You must not injure him, because he is my father, and my poor mother used to teach me to pray for him, and to love him. And so I did, but he loved not me; oh, no, and yet I know not why. Yes, yes, he is gone—gone—and perhaps it was, after all, only a dream. Oh, I often dream such strange, such terrible dreams now."

"It was but a dream, Julio," said Michael; "do you not know where you are?"

"Yes, yes," answered the maniac, "I do know where I am. Julio is not mad, though you may think him so. I am on board ship; I am tossed on the raging waves; hark how the thunder roars! see how the lightning flashes! And now behold! she lies gasping and bleeding upon the deck. She calls me wildly to her, but they snatch me from her dying embrace. Monsters! they will not allow the murdered mother to clasp her child in death. Leave go your hold; you shall not keep me from her. Oh, that I had strength! And see, they raise her mangled body in their rude arms;—they plunge her in the deep. The waters are crimsoned with her blood. She sinks—she rises again; she clasps her hands; 'Julio! Julio!' she shrieks, but the fierce tempest mocks her cries; they hold me from her, and—and, horror! horror! she sinks for ever. The air is scorching hot; the flames gather round me; I cannot breathe; I—I——"

The poor youth could say no more; his strength was completely exhausted, and he sank insensible in the arms of Mr. Belford. They removed him to their own chamber, and placed him upon the bed, keeping watch by him during the remainder of the night; but he was not restored to consciousness till the morning, and then he seemed to have lost all remembrance of the event of the previous night. Michael Belford now made arrangements for Julio to sleep in another apartment, and again locked up the room containing the portrait that had so much alarmed him.

"And why have you kept that portrait so carefully concealed, Michael?" inquired his wife, when they were alone.

"Because it represents a man whose name is associated with every crime," answered Michael, "and I feared that to gaze upon it might excite your alarm. Besides, it was one of the conditions I entered into on taking this house of the former proprietors, never to suffer it to be made the subject of idle curiosity, or to remove it from its present situation."

"And why, if he set so much value on it, and was so fearful of its inspection, did he not take it away with him?" asked Mrs. Belford.

"That I know not."

"Whom does it represent?"

"Hugh Clifton," replied Michael.

"Oh, Heaven! and this was his house?"

"Even so. But I was wrong to make you acquainted with his history; then your fears would not have been excited in the manner I see they are now."

"Poor Julio!" observed Mrs. Belford; "there must be some reason in his fearful ravings, or he would never have been so struck and alarmed on beholding the portrait. He called him his father."

"That is very probable," observed Michael. "It is now, I believe, five-and-twenty years since Hugh Clifton quitted these parts, and, even if he lived, it is not likely that he would marry again."

"But Julio and his mother may be in some way connected with him."

"They may be; but still I do not see how it is possible," returned Michael. "The event is very extraordinary, but, notwithstanding, it throws little or no light upon the mystery."

"You have have said that it was reported Hugh Clifton became captain of the Death Ship."

"True; but still it is only rumour, and we should not pay any particular attention to that."

"It is evident that he was a terrible and desperate man."

"He was; but I am inclined to think that more was attributed to him than he merited."

"What mean you?"

"Why, it is my opinion that Hugh Clifton never became in any way connected with the Death Ship, but that he perished by his own hands, after the dreadful murder of his son," replied Michael.

"But you have said that a person who had escaped from the slaughter committed by the crew of that fearful and mysterious vessel, had seen him in that capacity."

"He might have been mistaken."

"But he knew him well, you have stated," said Mrs Belford.

"He asserted so," answered her husband; "but still he might have been deceived. However, one thing appears certain, namely, that the unfortunate mother of Julio was barbarously murdered, and that either by her own husband or his orders."

"Oh, it is horrible to think of it," ejaculated Mrs. Belford; "what could she ever have done to merit such a dreadful end? Poor Julio, yours is indeed a dark, a terrible, and mysterious destiny."

"It is," coincided Michael; "and let us pray to Heaven to restore him to his senses, so that he may be able to reveal to us the particulars of his melancholy history. It may not yet be too late to procure him justice."

"Alas! I fear that it is. Has not his ill-fated mother perished?"

"I fear that is too certain," returned Michael; "but if she has indeed met with a dreadful and untimely end, her blood cries aloud for vengeance on the heads of her cowardly and inhuman assassins."

"Which may the most just and Almighty God visit them with," fervently ejaculated Mrs. Belford.

"He will, he will, depend upon it," replied Michael; "the shedders of human and innocent blood may escape for a time, but retribution, terrible retribution, is sure in time to overtake them."

The following day Julio never alluded to the portrait, and it was quite evident that he had forgotten all about it. He remained quiet and tractable, but he seemed unhappy whenever Rosetta was out of his sight. He would fix upon the beauteous damsel looks of the most fervent but innocent admiration, then he would laugh with the most extatic delight, call her his "pretty sister," and press her hand to his lips.

"Oh, we will be so happy, so very, very happy," he cried; "and when the bright summer comes we will ramble among the green fields and meadows, and gather the wild flowers that bloom in our path, and I will form a beautiful garland of them for your hair, Rosetta. You will not chide poor Julio, and refuse his gift, will you? Oh, no, I'm sure you will not, for you are so gentle and so good, and besides you are my sister. You told me I might call you so, and I will, and love you too, for, ah me! I have no one but you to love now."

"Nay, Julio," said Mrs. Belford, "you forget; you promised that you would love me and Mr. Belford."

"Oh, yes, yes," eagerly cried the hapless boy, "I must, I do love you, too, for you are so good to me; you give me such nice things, and have dressed me so smart, so very smart; ha! ha! ha! Don't I look fine? Julio is quite a young gentleman now. Ha! ha! ha!"

And then he laughed with all the hilarity and freshness of childhood, and surveyed his person with the utmost admiration. But suddenly his countenance and his manners changed, and with a heavy sigh, he said,—

"But no, these are not the clothes that Julio should wear; they should be dark, black, black as the clouds of night, for she is gone! she is dead! Oh! mother, mother!"

He paused awhile, and drooping his head, sighed as if his heart would break. Again, however, he recovered himself, and once more taking the hand of Rosetta, he observed,—

"Yes, yes, we will wander in the fields together, sister Rosetta, when the sun shines bright above our heads, and the little birds welcome us with their song. No angry storms shall howl to alarm us, no foaming billows roll beneath our feet; I like them not, for they swallow up all that is dear to us. No, no, all sunshine, all sunshine!"

Poor youth! brief had been the sunshine you had ever experienced, and dark and terrible were the clouds which were still impending o'er your head. Mr. and Mrs. Belford sighed as these thoughts occurred to them, and Rosetta could only express her feelings by her looks. Thus would Julio continue to talk at intervals throughout the day, and Michael and his wife sought every opportunity which seemed to present itself, to elicit from him more particulars of his history, and to ascertain the name of his parents, but without success, and they abandoned the attempt in despair, leaving it alone to time and chance to unravel the mystery.

In the course of the day we are now describing, they were somewhat surprised by the sudden and unexpected appearance of Martin Trevors. It was the first time Michael had seen him since the night of the tempest, and his conduct on that occasion had left no very favourable impression upon his mind; however, he greeted him with his usual cordiality and friendship, and Trevors walked into the parlour, but no sooner had his eyes rested on Julio, who was seated by the side of Rosetta, than he started, and altogether evinced much amazement and emotion. Julio stared vacantly upon him, but seemed not the least moved at his appearance. Michael beckoned his daughter to lead him from the room, and she obeyed.

"Why did you send him hence, Michael?" demanded Trevors, taking a seat.

"Why, the poor boy is a maniac," answered Michael; "and I thought his wild ravings might interrupt our conversation."

"A maniac!" repeated Trevors; "are you sure that his madness is not assumed?"

"Assumed!" answered Michael; "oh, no, one so young could never act with so much deception; besides, what motive could he have for doing so?"

"That may be seen hereafter," returned Trevors.

"Martin Trevors," said Michael, warmly, "your observations astonish me; I should have thought that the misfortunes of this poor boy would have excited your pity rather than your suspicions."

"Well, well," said Martin, "we will not quarrel upon the difference of opinion. And so this is the lad you rescued from the waves the other night?"

"It is," answered Michael; "and I thank Providence that enabled me to do so, and trust that the time will yet come when I shall be able to penetrate the mystery that is connected with him, and to bring the guilty to justice."

"I would have you beware what you do, Michael," observed Trevors; "recollect it was the Death Ship that fired the vessel, on board of which this youth, in all probability, was, and should you incur the vengeance of that fearful crew, I need not tell you that the consequences would be dreadful to yourself and all connected with you."

"I will dare anything to protect the innocent," said Michael, firmly. "I am an old seaman, Martin Trevors, and am not to be frightened at trifles. There has been some foul work here, and I feel that it is my duty, to the best of my ability, to endeavour to discover the truth, and see the injured righted."

"Well, you know best," said Trevors; "but what do you intend to do with the boy?"

"Keep him—protect him, as if he were my own, until I can find out those who have a claim on him, and will render him justice," answered Michael.

"Psha! why burden yourself with a stranger?"

"And what would you advise me to do with him?" demanded Mr. Belford.

"Send him to a workhouse, and that would take all the weight and responsibility off your hands," replied Trevors.

"And this is what you would do with him, had he fallen into your hands?"

"It is."

"Mr. Trevors," said Michael, unable to restrain his warmth, "I am surprised at your observations, and am sorry to find that humanity forms so small a portion of the ingredients of your nature. This poor boy's mother I believe to have been cruelly murdered, and he is thrown upon the wide world;—it has pleased the Almighty to deprive him of his reason, and shall I abandon him to the tender mercies of those whose characters at the best of times do not stand very high for kindness or sympathy in the misfortunes of their fellow-creatures? No, if I do may all the troubles which can befal me descend upon my head; if I do, may—may—may I be d—d! and that's swearing to it!"

"Come, come," said Trevors, who began to think that he had proceeded almost too far; "I did not intend to put you out of temper; I merely threw out a suggestion, which you are at liberty to avail yourself of or not."

"I am much obliged to you all the same, Mr. Trevors, but I certainly shall not avail myself of it," returned Michael, sharply; "and there is one thing I must say, since you urge me to it by your observations, had I been as indifferent as yourself on the terrible night of the tempest, this poor boy would have met with a watery grave."

"Well, well," replied Martin, coolly, "it was a mere matter of taste; you had your whim, and I suited mine; so there ends the business."

"And may I ask," said Michael, "how it was that you knew of the presence of the Death Ship before any one else recognised her ; and how it was that you seemed to be so well acquainted with her intentions ?"

Martin Trevors looked somewhat surprised at these questions, and he hesitated for a moment or two before he returned any answer.

" Why, the whole of it is," at length he replied, " I was nearly the first upon the beach, and immediately recognised her by the glare of the lightning. As for her intentions, I knew nothing of them, but merely guessed them from the manner in which she seemed to bear down upon the other vessel."

This explanation was anything but satisfactory, but Michael took no further notice of it, and after some other conversation Martin Trevors arose, and took his leave.

" By all the infernal host," muttered Trevors to himself, as he bent his steps towards his home, " I am almost certain it is the boy.   His features are so like, and the circumstances of his mother's death correspond exactly.   I must keep a watchful eye upon him, and consider what is best to be done, for I may turn this adventure to good account ;—but not too hastily."

Busied in these thoughts he hurried on his way, and soon reached his dwelling.

" The conduct of Martin Trevors more and more surprises me," said Michael, when he was gone; " there is a mystery about him which I cannot solve."

" At any rate," remarked Mrs. Belford, " he cannot boast of very humane or Christian feelings."

" He cannot, I am afraid."

" How unlike him is Frank, his son, in disposition," observed Mrs. Belford.

" Yes," answered her husband ; " Frank is a worthy lad, and deserves to do well in the world."

" Which I have no doubt he will," remarked the old woman ; " and you know he loves our daughter, Michael."

" As for that, dame," returned Michael, " they are both too young to think about love yet.   They are mere girl and boy, and although they have been companions from childhood, their affections cannot be supposed to be fixed yet, and they may see others who may create more powerful sentiments in their breasts. Frank has never said a word about his love yet."

" True," said Mrs. Belford, " but his looks have spoken quite as forcibly as words could have done."

" Tut, tut, tut, dame," said Michael, impatiently ; " we must not talk in this manner; it is time enough for such children to think about love; why they hardly understand the word yet."

" If they are so ignorant, it is not all young people who are," returned the old woman, archly ; " at any rate, we can answer for it that we were not, Michael, eh ?"

" Ha ! ha ! ha !" laughed Michael ; " right, right, my old lass ; we began betimes, and as we agreed that it was never too soon to begin to love sincerely, I suppose we must allow Frank and Rosetta the same privilege, and leave them to take their chance."

" And I am certain that neither of them will ever do anything that will bring disgrace upon our names," said Mrs. Belford.

" True, dame, true," coincided Michael, " of that I am confident.   But there is time enough for them to think about marriage yet.   Besides, they have never acknowledged that they love each other, that I am aware of."

" No," returned the dame, " but there can be very little doubt of it; and if their sentiments are reciprocal, I do not know any lad more worthy of our daughter's hand than Frank Trevors."

" As I have said before," remarked Michael, " I am perfectly of your opinion ; but still the conduct of his father far from pleases me."

" He cannot help the faults of his father, Michael."

" He cannot; but we must have a proper understanding with Martin Trevors before we can venture to proceed any further in the matter."

But when Michael Belford was left to himself and reflected upon the singular conduct of Trevors, he felt far from satisfied with it, and considered it was very strange, to say the least of it. The unfeeling observations he had made respecting Julio were the more remarkable, as he could have no particular interest in wishing to see him abandoned, neither could he have any just cause for making use of the unfeeling remarks he had, or of suspecting that the unfortunate boy was an impostor. The surprise and agitation which he had also evinced on beholding Julio, had not been unnoticed by Michael, and altogether he was greatly perplexed to find a reason for it. Austere and reserved as he knew Martin Trevors to be, still he had expected that at least the dreadful circumstances under which the youth had been saved, and his melancholy situation, would have excited his sympathy and compassion, and the more he reflected on it, the more he became shocked at the utter heartlessness he had displayed. Had he really known the character of Trevors, and the manner in which he for years had been connected, his astonishment would not only have been at an end, but he would also have shunned his society with disgust and horror.

Michael had hitherto kept Julio strictly confined to the house, but at length, fearful that his health might be impaired by it, and hoping that change of scene might tend to restore his wandering reason, he determined to take him out for a walk. The poor boy was delighted when he was made to understand this, but he implored most fervently that Rosetta should accompany them, and Michael, seeing no reason to object, complied with his request.

It was a fine winter's morning when they walked forth from the house, and descended the hill. The air was keen and bracing, and the sky was clear and bright, unspotted by a single cloud. It would be impossible to describe the delight of Julio as they proceeded; he bounded over the earth playful as a young fawn, laughing and shouting in all the wild exuberance of his glee, and turning every now and then to be sure that Rosetta had not left them.

No one, to have seen the maniac boy at that moment, with his laughing, joyous, rosy face, and his lustrous eyes, could ever have imagined that he had so deeply drank from the poisoned cup of sorrow. And anon he would draw back to point out to Rosetta some fresh beauty that occurred to his delighted imagination, and express his admiration in language of such simplicity that it made an immediate impression upon the heart, and left behind it a melancholy feeling of regret that so bright a mind, so keenly susceptible of all that is lovely and fair in creation, should be laid waste, and should have to relapse into the gloom and horror of its own sad retrospections.

Michael and his daughter watched him with redoubled interest, solicitude, and sympathy. And he was happy in that brief respite from dark and horrible remembrances; his heart was allowed to bound with all the buoyancy of his nature; he seemed as if he had entered upon another world; as though he had escaped from the fœtid vapours of a noisome dungeon to breathe the pure and exhilarating atmosphere of fresh life. The darkness of his sorrow had dispersed before the light, the air, the sweets of liberty! Fondly Rosetta and her father hoped that it would work a happy change upon his reason, and that it would be productive of the most favourable results; but, alas! these sanguine and fervent hopes were not fated to be realised. Transient was the period of joy that hapless youth was doomed to experience—like the feeble ray emitted by the lamp carried by the gaoler to light his wretched prisoner to misery, darkness, and despair.

" Come, come," he said once more, taking the hand of Rosetta and her father, and urging them forward; " this way, this way ;—I hear the rippling of the waters! We will wander to the sea-shore, and I will show you Julio's native home!—Oh, it is so beautiful to look upon the scene when the billows dance beneath the golden sunbeams, and the dolphins skip and play, and the sea-birds skim over its bright surface. Come, come, we must not miss the glorious sight! Hark; again the rippling waves invite us! Fear not—the sky is clear and bright, no angry storms will arise to terrify us. Oh! it is dreadful to view the tempest's wrath—to hear the wind howl in concert with the foaming billows, and——but come—come—this way, this way!"

And again the poor boy darted of with speed, and in all the hilarity of his spirits, and Michael and his daughter followed him, still encouraging hope, and watching with admiration, mingled with melancholy feelings of pity at the unbounded gaiety of his actions.

They reached the rocks on which Michael and his companions had stood on the night of the tempest, and watched the destruction of the ill-fated vessel, whose name they had not been able to ascertain. The heart of Michael sickened when he recollected the appalling horrors of the eventful night, and still did the frantic shrieks of the wretched sufferers seem to ring in his ears. Again in imagination he saw the fierce flames soaring to the sky, and throwing their horrid reflection upon the ocean and all around. But how different was the scene upon which his eyes now rested! Calm and beautiful, it appeared impossible that such a scene could ever have been distorted in so hideous a manner—that upon that broad expanse of bright blue waters, reflecting the fair canopy of heaven, such a scene of awful destruction could have taken place.

We have said before that the day was beautifully clear, and the air, although keen, was sweet and invigorating, giving lightness and buoyancy to the spirits; and the gentle breeze that came from the waters imparted a healthy glow to the blood, bracing the nerves and banishing every feeling of languor. Here and there the hardy fisherman pursued his avocation, and in the distance might be seen the white sails of many a gallant vessel, stretching and swelling themselves to the favouring breeze.

For awhile Julio darted from rock to rock, pointing with expressive gestures across the sea, and again laughing in the joyousness of his heart. Michael and Rosetta kept close to him, fearing that he might once more be seized with one of his wild deliriums and commit some rash act.

"See, see," he said, at length running towards them, and pointing to the calm scene before them; "is it not beautiful? How vast the expanse of water—how blue, how clear, how bright! But why do I stand here?—why do I not seek my native element?—Yes, Julio's home is there!—Upon those clear waters he was born, and the murmuring waves were his gentle lullaby. But they were not always calm and gentle as you see them now. Ah me! that ever poor Julio was born. No, no—they were not always calm, they were not always calm. Black clouds darkened the sky; thunder shook the vault of Heaven! The penguin quitted its rocky dwelling—the seamen screeched; the furious blast arose, swelling the waves into raging mountains; volcanoes of foam, spreading destruction around. Yes—yes; the sun of Julio's happiness had set; they sought *her* life—she who had nursed me with such unbounded affection, and whose only source of joy was in my infant smiles. The butchers, yes!—they pierced her bosom with their glittering blades; in vain she supplicated for mercy,—mercy! it was a stranger to their remorseless breasts. Hark! that cry! it is my mother's dying shriek, as they precipitate her mangled body into the yawning deep. Mother! mother! oh, God! and is there no one at hand to save you from the blood-thirsty wretches? No, no! You implore in vain; you talk to hearts of marble! Oh! why do they not suffer me to share your fate?—Why is Julio permitted to live, since all that rendered life valuable to him is snatched from him? They hold me back! they mock my tears, my entreaties; they scoff at your cries, my mother! And now behold, the waves are crimsoned with your blood. Do you not see it?—all red, red, and hideous. Can you mark this sight unmoved? Do not hold me! Let me fly to save her, ere she sinks for ever in that purple flood! Mother! mother! I fly to save you, or to perish with you. Off! off! my mother's voice calls upon me, and I feel a geant's strength! Off! off! I say! you shall not prevent me from rushing to her rescue."

Thus saying, the maniac rushed forward, and would have plunged into the deep had not Michael and his daughter prevented him, and the latter, laying her hand upon his arm, in an impressive tone repeated his name. Her soft and gentle voice seemed to recall the poor youth to his senses; his looks became less wild and agitated, and sighing deeply, he ejaculated—

"Poor Julio is mad—yes, mad,—ah! he has had enough to make him so;

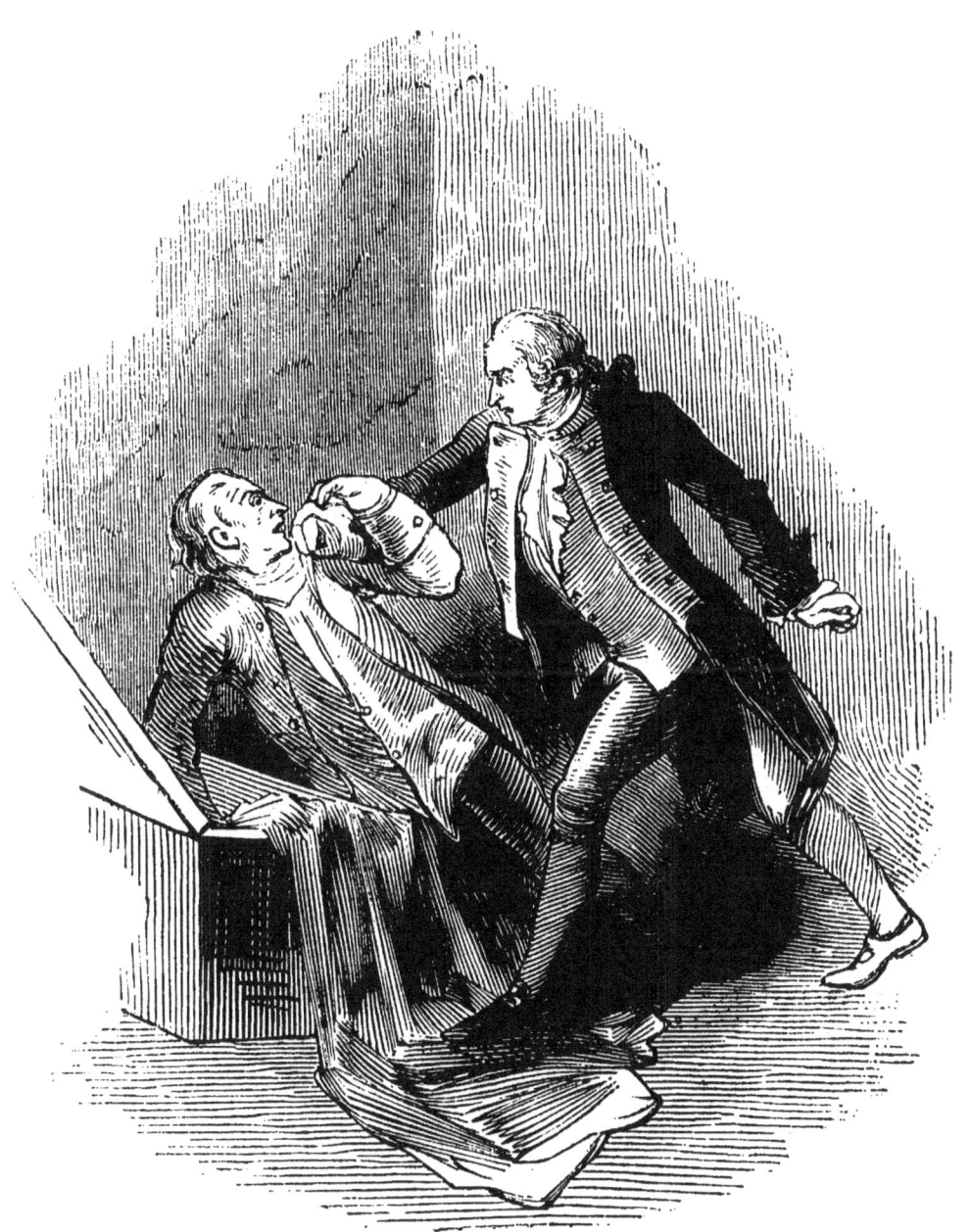

but I will not harm you; oh, no, I will not harm you, for you are so good and kind, and you have permitted me to call you sister!—Sister! oh, it is a pretty name, but Julio has no sister!—No, no, she died when very, very young! Was it not fortunate that she did not live to see her poor mother murdered as I beheld her?—Oh, it was a dreadful sight. Had you but heard how she prayed for mercy, for the sake of her poor child! but they heeded her not; they mocked her anguish, and—oh, my brain! how it aches and burns at that dreadful thought. Ah me! ah me!"

He could say no more; the power of his emotions overcame him, and drooping his head on the shoulder of Mr. Belford, he wept bitterly. Michael and Rosetta were glad to see this, for they were in hopes that it would abate the violence of his paroxysms, and afford his wandering, desolated mind some relief. They watched him with silent compassion, and then gently urged him to move from the spot.

Again Julio raised his head, and his countenance was now serene, and even cheerful. His elegant eyes wandered with an expression of delight over the wide expanse, and his cheeks once more glowed with pleasurable excitement. They continued to saunter along the beach, and every moment some fresh object attracted the attention of the youth, and called forth his simple but impressive expressions of admiration.

"Oh! it is beautiful!" he ejaculated; "so very, very beautiful. And yet the sea is not always so calm and lovely as it now appears. No, no—I have seen it when it was dreadful to look upon, and the dark spirits of the storm held their deadly court, mocking the efforts of the mariner to steer his gallant bark. And I have seen it—but no, I will not think of that,—it is beautiful now, and as such, my ocean home, I hail you! Come, come, this way. Oh, we will daily wander to these rocks, and gaze upon the wonders of all before us. And I will tell you the marvellous tales I have heard the sailors relate, and sing you the songs I have heard them sing. And tell you all the fearful particulars of the Death Ship!—No, no,—I must not tell that awful story; it would freeze the blood in your veins to hear it; and yet 'tis true, alas! too true; and yet she still ploughs the ocean, carrying horror and bloodshed wherever she appears, now here, now there, now everywhere! Woe! woe to the unfortunate beings who encounter that bark of death!—She comes in the storm; she comes in the darkness of the night, and destruction follows in her track. No, no; I will not shock your ears by that dreadful tale. Oh, horror, horror! What a poor lonely wretch has she made of Julio."

"And is it to this terrible vessel you owe all your misfortunes, my poor boy?" asked Michael, eagerly; and thinking this was a favourable opportunity of eliciting the mysterious particulars from Julio he was so anxious to know.

"Oh, yes," answered the maniac; "to the monsters belonging to that fearful ship, I owe everything!—They—but I must not repeat the dreadful tale; my brain burns when I think of it, and,—and I feel that I am mad! and you would be mad if you had suffered as I have done! Oh, that Julio could not think at all."

"Wretched boy," thought Michael, "most surely your sufferings have been great. Heaven help you."

"And you pity me," said Julio, looking earnestly at Mr. Belford; "I see you do, for your looks are kind and compassionate, and indeed I will love you for it, and never disobey you, for Julio can be grateful—yes, very, very grateful, though his mind is a wreck, and happiness can never more be his."

"Unfortunate youth," fervently ejaculated Michael, "I do indeed pity you, and I will be to you a protector, a father ——"

"Father!" repeated Julio, with a shudder of horror; "oh, do not mention that name, I tremble to hear it. Father! oh, God! what terrors arise to my imagination when I think of him! I see his fearful looks, those looks he always fixed upon me and my poor mother. I hear his fierce accents as he spurned my infant caresses. But you will protect me from him; you will not suffer me again to fall in his power; say that you will not, and I will try to be happy, and to think no more of the terrible past."

"Fear not, Julio," answered Michael; "all that I can do to protect you I will, and Heaven I trust will assist me and shield me from all harm."

"Thanks, thanks!" said the maniac, his bright eyes sparkling with gratitude, and again pressing the hand of Mr. Belford. "Julio then will not fear! He will laugh to scorn the frowns of fate, and smile, and sing in the gaiety of his spirit. Gaiety, ah! no! what have I to do with mirth? I should be sad, very, very sad; for is she not taken from me? Am I not left alone to think and weep? Weep, weep! yes, I should weep scalding tears, tears of blood—tears of blood!"

And he covered his face with his hands, and hysterical sobs choked his utterance. Michael placed his hand gently on his shoulder, and spoke to him in soothing accents. Julio raised his head, stared at him vacantly, and then bursting into a wild laugh, he once more bounded over the rocks, making the air resound with his frantic mirth.

"But we had better now return home again, Julio," said Michael, at length; "the air is keen, and we have already extended our walk much farther than I at first intended."

"Home! home!" repeated the youth, casting his eyes over the clear waters of the ocean; "yes, 'tis there! There is Julio's home, for is he not the ocean child?"

"We will come here again to-morrow," said Michael. "Every day we will walk here, and you shall gaze upon the scenes so pleasing to you, if you will promise me you will endeavour to become calm."

"Calm!" repeated Julio, passing his hands across his forehead,—"what is that? I never knew what calmness was. I—but I will tell you a secret why I love the boundless sea, and do so like to listen to the murmuring of the billows. My mother sleeps beneath them, and methinks I hear her spirit's gentle voice in every breath of air that is wafted from their swelling bosoms. She calls upon my name, just as she used to do when she hugged me to her heart, and covered my infant cheeks with her fond adoring kisses. Oh, it was cruel not to suffer Julio to rest with her who loved him so tenderly."

He sighed deeply, and, apparently unconscious of all around, and completely absorbed in his own dismal and fearful thoughts, he suffered Michael to take his hand, and lead him from the spot. They left the rocks, and had entered the path which led towards their home, when they were suddenly startled by hearing an exclamation of mingled astonishment and alarm, and looking up, they beheld Sir Horace Middleton standing before them, his countenance more than usually ghastly pale, his lips quivering, and his eyes glaring wildly upon Julio, as if he had encountered some frightful apparition. He was standing within a few paces of them, and seemed completely transfixed to the spot, with conflicting feelings of amazement and terror.

Michael bowed, but was too much taken by surprise at the singularity of the baronet's looks and demeanour to speak, and Sir Horace appeared not to notice him, but remained with his eyes still rivetted upon the maniac youth, who seemed to experience a feeling of terror, and clung still closer to Mr. Belford.

At length Sir Horace advanced nearer towards them, and fixing a glance upon the features of Julio, which seemed as if it would penetrate to his very soul, he ejaculated in a hoarse and trembling voice,—

"Powers of darkness, what fearful delusion is this? Who are you that appals my very soul to gaze upon you? Speak! speak!"

"Sir Horace," said the astonished Michael, "may I ask the reason of this extraordinary emotion? What do you see in this poor maniac boy, that should so violently alarm you?"

"Fiend! fiend!" shouted the guilty man, covering his face with his hands, and trembling in every limb, "why do you torture me thus? Those eyes, those features so like—oh, horror! horror!"

And without daring again to look upon Julio, but uttering a deep groan, Sir Horace darted precipitately from the spot, and was immediately out of sight, leaving Michael and his daughter completely overwhelmed with amazement and perplexity.

Michael had long been aware of the mysterious habits of Sir Horace Middleton, and had been inclined to believe that the strange reports which were raised against him, were not entirely without foundation, but his conduct on this occasion surprised him more than all, and he was quite at a loss to account for it. The great terror he had evinced on beholding Julio, and the remarkable words he had made use of, could not have been created without some powerful cause, and the more he reflected upon the circumstance, the more he was at a loss to form even the slightest reasonable conjecture upon it. The fearful observations he had made use of, and his ghastly looks, in which all the horrors of a guilty conscience were so strongly depicted, had greatly shocked Rosetta, and she felt a great relief when he was gone, notwithstanding her curiosity was much excited by his extraordinary manner.

Julio had met the keen and penetrating gaze of Sir Horace with a vacant look, and had listened to his words apparently quite incapable of understanding them; but when the baronet had hastily retreated from the spot, he followed with his eyes the direction he had taken, and clasping his hands together, he laughed aloud in his madness.

Michael took his hand, and looking kindly and persuasively in his face, moved towards his dwelling, his mind filled with a variety of conflicting thoughts, and the words of Sir Horace strongly impressed upon his recollection. He saw plainly that Julio was surrounded with many dangers, of the nature of which he could not form any adequate conception; he might involve himself in considerable trouble by the interest he took in his mysterious fate; but still he was determined, let the consequences be whatever they might, that nothing should daunt him in the prosecution of his praiseworthy designs, but that he would protect the poor bereaved boy to the utmost of his power with the same care and determination as if he had been his own son.

With every fresh incident that occurred, Rosetta also felt her interest and sympathy for Julio increase; the cruelty of his fate excited her tenderest feelings, and fervently she prayed to Heaven that the time would come when he might be restored to reason, and that happiness might again be his, although so dreadful must have been the events which had taken so powerful a hold upon his mind, that there were times when she feared that these humane wishes could never be realized. It was shocking to behold one so young, so handsome, so prepossessing, reduced to such a melancholy state, and Rosetta could hardly believe that there were such monsters in existence as could have been guilty of the atrocities that Julio described in his wide wanderings, or that those horrors had been perpetrated by the hands or the commands of his own father! What could the unfortunate mother of Julio have done to have merited such a horrible fate? And why had the life of the maniac boy been spared, since it seemed that he was equally an object of hatred? She was lost in a labyrinth of fruitless conjecture, and the more she ruminated upon it, he more did she become bewildered.

Mrs. Belford had been anxiously awaiting their return home, and no sooner had Julio entered the house, than he flew to the arms of the dame with the most unbounded joy sparkling in his eyes and glowing in his handsome countenance, and kissed her hands with all the same affection as if she had been his own mother.

"Poor boy," said Mrs. Belford, "who could behold you without sympathy and affection? Heaven look down with mercy on you, and release your mind from the darkness which at present obscures it. And so, Julio," she added, in her most tender accents, "you are pleased with your walk, my child?"

"Oh, yes, yes," answered the youth, "it was so beautiful; oh, it was most kind to take poor Julio to gaze once more upon those scenes he loves so well. The ocean was so calm and lovely, that it seemed to invite me to its tranquil bosom; but yet they would not let me go; why would they not permit me to return to my native home, when the spirit of my poor mother called upon me? She sleeps there, you know; far, far beneath those bright blue waters, and the spirits of the deep watch around her in their coral caves. Savage men cannot harm her now. No, no, poor soul—poor soul, she is at rest. Oh, why am I not suffered to join her? I have no business here!—no business here!"

"Nay, Julio," expostulated Mrs. Belford; "you must not talk thus. It is not the will of the Supreme that you should yet join the unfortunate parent whose loss you mourn; but you will be once more united in Heaven!"

"Ah!" exclaimed the youth, "it was so she used to talk to me, when the wicked men had threatened to snatch her from me. And, oh! what bitter tears she would weep as she said so, and pressed me to her bosom, covering my face with her fondest kisses! Ah! me! would that the time would come, for Julio is tired, tired of this gloomy, cruel world."

"Julio," observed Mrs. Belford, "you know it is wicked to talk in this manner, and——"

"Wicked!" interrupted Julio. "I must have been very wicked, or I should not have been punished as I am; I must have been wicked, or my poor mother would not have been taken from me. But she was so good, so kind; she taught me to pray, and I did; I prayed to Heaven for blessings on her head; oh! I must have been very wicked, very wicked, or Heaven would have listened to my prayers; alas! why was Julio ever born, to become so wicked? But I will wander again to the sea-beach, and Rosetta shall again attend me, for she is my sister, my pretty, kind sister. Yes, and you shall accompany us also, if you like, and I will point out to you all the beauties of the ocean, and show you the spot where my dear mother sleeps. The sun always shines on that beloved spot, and all is calm and tranquil, for Julio's mother rests there. I heard her voice to-day; the sea breeze wafted it to my ears, and oh! it was so heavenly, I could have listened to it for ever. Will you not come and listen to it with me? You will; it will bless you; yes, I know it will, for you are so kind to Julio."

"Julio," said Michael, "will you not accompany Rosetta to another room? she has something to tell you."

"To tell me?" said the youth, his eyes glistening. "Oh, yes, I will go any-where with dear sister Rosetta. Come, come."

Rosetta understood what her father meant, and smiling sweetly upon Julio, she suffered him to take her hand, at the same time that she felt a trembling and irre-sistible sensation at her heart, and they quitted the room together.

Mrs. Belford perceived, in a moment, that her husband had something to impart to her, and she eagerly inquired what it was. Michael made her acquainted, in a few words, with their meeting with Sir Horace Middleton, and his extraordinary behaviour, and the observations he had made use of on beholding Julio, to which the dame listened with the utmost attention and astonishment.

"What can be the meaning of this?" she said, when Michael had concluded.

"I am entirely at a loss to imagine," answered her husband; "but had Sir Horace beheld some frightful apparition, he could not have exhibited greater agitation."

"I fear that Sir Horace is a bad man," observed Mrs. Belford.

"Aye; I am inclined to believe that the reports which have been circulated about him are not all unfounded, and that his conscience is not entirely clear. But why he should evince so much terror when he saw the boy, is a mystery I cannot solve."

"And the words you have mentioned, are you certain he made use of them?"

"Certainly, dame," replied Michael. "I could not be mistaken, and never shall I forget the looks which he fixed upon the countenance of poor Julio. Dame, if it was not the consciousness of guilt that called up that powerful emotion, my name is not Michael Belford."

"Heaven send that he may not be in any way connected with Julio," said the dame, "or much do I fear what the consequences might be."

"It is strange," remarked Michael; "and yet I cannot believe that the features of any individual could make so terrible an impression, unless there was some greater reason than we can possibly, at the present, conjecture."

"Poor Julio!" observed Mrs. Belford, "yours is, indeed, a dark and mysterious fate; may Heaven shield you from your enemies, of which I fear you have too many."

"I will protect him, dame, with the same care as if he were my own offspring; and something tells me that, in spite of all the dangers with which he may be threatened, and the trouble that I, perhaps, shall be put to, which I care nothing about, I shall ultimately be able to do so effectually."

" Could we but be the means of restoring the poor child to reason, all might be accomplished, and the wretches who have been guilty of such atrocities be brought to justice. If the mother of Julio has met with the horrible fate he describes in his wild ramblings, is it not wonderful that he was suffered to escape?"

" It is," answered Michael; " and the more I reflect upon it, the deeper do I become involved in mystery. From what, however, the poor boy has this day stated, I am inclined to believe that it is to the crew of the Death Ship that all the atrocities are to be traced."

" Ah!" ejaculated Mrs. Belford, with a shudder of horror, " that dreadful vessel, which seems to defy every power. Alas! if it is indeed so, how can we hope to protect the unfortunate, persecuted boy?"

" There is a just God on high, dame," replied Michael, solemnly, " who will not fail to aid us. In Him we will trust, and fear not but all will yet be well."

" I have often been thinking, Michael," observed his wife, " of that fearful cry that has always been heard on the night of the appearance of the Death Ship, and the mysterious form which has been seen flying with the speed of the whirlwind. Report says that it has been seen to enter the Manor House, and, if such is the fact, it seems to me that there is good reason to believe that the dark suspicions attached to the character of Sir Horace Middleton are not without good reason."

" True, dame," returned Michael; " and we may think what we like, but we must be careful what we say."

" Yes," said Mrs. Belford; " but I will say this, and I do not think there are many who will not coincide with my opinion— it was a bad job for the poor people in this neighbourhood when Sir Horace put his foot in it. Is he not a sordid, miserly wretch, whose mercenary disposition has driven many an honest person from the beloved home of his forefathers, and brought distress and poverty upon him?"

" Alas! what you state is too correct, dame," answered her husband. " Heaven pardon him, for I fear he has much to answer for."

" He has; and many a heart has he broken to accumulate his ill-gotten wealth, which, if we may judge from his appearance and habits, proves to him rather a curse than a blessing. I like not his emotion on beholding Julio, and we must guard him from him with a watchful eye."

" Aye," replied Michael; " but still I know not why we should apprehend any danger from him; he cannot in any way be connected with the boy."

" You cannot undertake to say that, Michael," remarked his wife, " especially after the terror he betrayed on beholding him."

" True, true; but still I will be upon my guard," said Michael.

" It is absolutely necessary that you should be so, for should any harm befal the unfortunate boy, I should never forgive myself."

" It shall be no fault of mine, dame, if it does," returned her husband. " Ah! depend upon it, there is a dreadful tale to be revealed yet, and Providence, I trust, will in its own wise time bring everything to light."

" Most sincerely do I hope so, and that poor Julio's misfortunes may prove to be not so severe as his wandering imagination depictures them."

" Alas! I fear that there is too much truth in them. It must have been something horrible which could have made a maniac of one so young."

" It must, indeed," coincided Mrs. Belford; " but you know, I believe, more of the particulars of Sir Horace Middleton's history than you have thought proper to unfold, and his conduct to-day makes me curious about it."

" Dame," replied Michael, " I know nothing more of him than I have heard; how should I? and you know I never like to run down a man for what report says of him."

" Well, I believe you. But did you ever hear that Sir Horace was married?"

" I have heard that he was," said Michael; " but it is said that his wife died in a foreign land; at any rate, Sir Horace was reported to be a widower when he came to reside here. But we have nothing to do with his family affairs, you know; and how can his having been married or not affect us?"

"It may, for it might be the means of unravelling the mystery of his character, and ultimately show whether he is in any way connected with Julio."

"Psha, dame!" impatiently remarked Michael; "you are talking nonsense; how could it do that?"

"I know not," replied the dame; "but far more unlikely things than that have come to pass. Did you ever hear whether Sir Horace ever had any children?"

"I never did," replied Michael, "but if he did, I should imagine that they died, or from his parsimonious habits he would never have burthened himself with his nephew."

"Ay, and it is a matter of surprise that he did so whether or not. But after the occurrence of to-day, I shall always look upon the baronet with greater suspicion than ever. It is evident that his conscience severely smote him, and that he imagined he saw the resemblance of some person whom he had injured, or he would not have been so alarmed, or made use of the observations he did, when he beheld Julio."

"It is a subject on which it is impossible to form a reasonable conjecture," said Michael; "but see, Rosetta and Julio return to the room, and we must be careful what we say; all that I have told you must be kept a profound secret, or it might be the means of thwarting the plans we have in contemplation."

"You have no occasion to fear me, Michael; you know my prudence well."

"True, true, but silence."

Mrs. Belford obeyed, and Julio and Rosetta entered the room. During the whole of that day Julio never once alluded to the meeting with Sir Horace Middleton, and it seemed indeed as if he had entirely forgotten it, or, at any rate, that it had made little if any impression upon his mind; but Michael could not banish it from his thoughts, and he became still more perplexed and uneasy the longer he reflected upon it. Sir Horace could never have evinced so much terror if he had not some powerful reason for it, and the dark suspicions he had always entertained of his character were greatly strengthened by the circumstance. He, however, kept his thoughts to himself, and determined to watch the baronet with a cautious eye. The behaviour of Martin Trevors was also not forgotten by him, he knew that he frequently visited the Manor House, and when he remembered his indifference on the night of the tempest, and the strange and unfeeling remarks he had made respecting Julio, also the emotion he had displayed on beholding him, he considered that there was something about his character which needed explanation, and he resolved to be guarded in his future behaviour towards him, and to endeavour to ascertain, if possible, whether he was really the sincere friend he pretended to be.

Frank Trevors had not visited the dwelling of Mr. Belford as he had been accustomed to do, since Julio had been there, and when he did, his manners were far less cheerful than usual; he would gaze with the most intense earnestness upon Rosetta and Julio alternately, and when he observed the compassionate attention which Rosetta bestowed upon the unfortunate maniac, a heavy gloom would pass over his countenance, and not unfrequently a sigh would escape his bosom. Could it be that Frank was jealous of her kindness to the maniac? Rosetta noticed the change in his behaviour without being able to divine the cause, but an unaccountable and disagreeable sensation took possession of her bosom, and she felt a restraint in the presence of Frank which she had never experienced before, and as that sensation gained ascendency in her breast, so did her compassionate sympathy for Julio increase.

Frank Trevors, as has been shown, had never yet ventured to reveal the passion with which the numerous charms of Rosetta had inspired him; and although the damsel had always looked upon him with the utmost esteem, as the friend and companion of her youth, the least idea of a more tender sentiment had never yet entered her breast. She was yet too young to become acquainted with the passion, and had she but been aware of the real sentiments which Frank had ventured to encourage towards her, she would have trembled with maiden timidity, and probably have avoided his society altogether. But the time was coming when she would know all —and the real feelings of her own heart to be revealed to her in characters that were n ot o be mistaken. She was to be awakened to a full sense of misery and anguish and to find that she was destined to inflict sorrow and disappointment upon one whom she had ever esteemed as a brother.

CHAPTER V.

THE AGITATION OF SIR HORACE MIDDLETON.—THE ARRIVAL OF HIS NEPHEW AT
 THE MANOR HOUSE.—THE PROFLIGATE AND THE MISER.—THE SCENE IN THE
 OLD VAULT.—THE OATH.

WHATEVER it was that had so alarmed Sir Horace Middleton on beholding Julio, as described in the previous chapter, we are not prepared to say, but certain it is that he had not experienced such a shock since the memorable night of the tempest, and the mysterious appearance of the Death Ship. On leaving the spot he darted wildly towards the Manor House, every limb trembling with agony, his face covered with his hands, as though he would shut out some object too frightful to gaze at, and large drops of perspiration rolling down his cheeks with the power of his emotion. What pen shall describe the dreadful thoughts which were at that moment passing in his mind? Had all the spirits of the dead arose from their grave to confront him, he could not have betrayed greater horror than he did on that occasion. He feared to look around him lest his eyes should encoutner some ghastly object, but still the countenance of the maniac boy was as vividly present to his imagination as if he was then gazing upon it. Not all his efforts could shut it out, and on he rushed heedless whither he went, and giving utterance to strange and incoherent expressions as he proceeded.

At length he arrived at the Manor House, and hastily and violently pulling the bell, the door was opened by Simon Snipe, who stared at him with amazement.

" Gracious goodness, my honoured master," said the faithful domestic, " how very pale you look, and ——"

" Silence, fool, and begone!" interrupted Sir Horace, fiercely, and pushing him aside, said, " mind that no one interrupts me in my chamber, at the peril of my eternal displeasure—at the peril of your life, mind."

" Oh, ye—ye—yes, my dear master," stammered out Simon, as the baronet rushed past him ; and when he was certain that he was out of hearing, he added, " Mad !—mad as a March hare ! He called me, Simon Snipe, his faithful Simon Snipe, his factotum, his everything, a fool ! and that is an unquestionable proof of it. Oh, certainly the world will soon be at an end, since things have come to this pass. A fool ! Oh, gracious !"

And turning up his eyes with horror at the remembrance of the insulting epithet, the phantom of a porter slowly made his way to the kitchen to communicate his thoughts to his companion in starvation.

Sir Horace having gained his own apartment locked the door, and threw himself in a chair ; for a few minutes he was unable to utter a word, but stared vacantly around him, his disordered imagination still conjuring up the countenance he had so recently gazed upon, and which brought with it all the most terrible recollections of the past.

" Those features, each one expressing a ghastly volume ! Oh, methinks I see them now !" he at length exclaimed. " What demons are at work to torture me thus ! And it was reality ! Yes ; it was no phantom of the distempered imagination that I gazed upon. Oh, so like, that each lineament of that fair countenance came like a dagger to my heart ! And yet I was told that I should never gaze upon them again !—that death had swept away all those I dreaded, but those to whom I am the slave, away ! Who is this boy that has so suddenly crossed my path to kindle afresh the raging hell of conscience, and fill me with nameless apprehensions. What eyes were those which gazed so wildly yet earnestly upon me? —whose laughter that still rings in my ears, as if to mock my anguish? Comes he here to denounce me ? Oh, I have been deceived, and they do but mock me to make my sufferings and my disgrace the more severe. Martin Trevor, the tale you

told me, and by which you lured me out of my gold, was false.   But beware—beware!—you shall not triumph!   No, no; I have money—ay, and can purchase
your destruction.   You told me they were no more—but this boy, who is he?   His
countenance is an answer to my question : but what brings him here?   Why did
they suffer him to escape, to blast me with his presence?   Oh, those features!—
would that I had never beheld them!   For ever more will they be present to my
imagination.   But he must be removed ; yes, yes, he must, he shall be removed ;
such damning evidence of my guilt must not be supposed to exist.   And yet, I may
be mistaken ; he may not be the brat that I suspect; or, if he is, what has Horace
Middleton to fear from a friendless wretch like him?   He dare not accuse me ; for
have I not money and influence to crush him?   Ha, ha, ha!   I will be calm—I
will no longer be a coward!   Gold, gold, will purchase anything—anything, but —
peace of mind!   Ah, there is the sting—there is the bane of all my joys!   Conscience,
why cannot gold stifle your hideous voice?   But let me not give way to this weakness.   Have I not boldly dared for many, many years, and shall I now turn coward?
No, I will not ; and for this boy ——"

He was interrupted by a knock at the room door, and, starting hastily to his feet, he demanded, in a voice of anger—

"Who's there?   Who dare to interrupt me in my meditations?   Speak!"

"It is I, my honoured master," stammered out the voice of Simon.

"Wretch!" cried Sir Horace, "did I not command you not to approach me, or to suffer any one else to do so?"

"You did, my esteemed master," said the porter, in drivelling tones; "but pray pardon me, I merely came to inform you that young Captain Middleton has just arrived at the Manor-house."

"My nephew?" exclaimed the baronet.

"Yes, Sir Horace," replied Simon.

"Curses light on him!" growled Sir Horace, "I wish he had been at the bottom of the sea.   What brings him here at this time?"

"Shall I desire him to come to you?" demanded Simon.

"No—no, idiot!" returned the baronet furiously; "tell him—tell him I am engaged: I cannot see him at present—tell him to go to—to—to go to the d——l; I must not be disturbed."

With this very kind and polite message to a nephew whom the old baronet had not seen for more than two years, Simon Snipe departed, and the miser was once more left to his gloomy and guilty cogitations.

"Here is another source of torment and expense to me," he observed, "and all through my foolish good nature and benevolence.   What right have I to be burthened with my brother's child, especially after the enormous sum of money he has already cost me for his education?   Bah!   I am an old fool, and shall never rest until I have let this wild harum scarum spendthrift ruin me.   What business had my brother to marry a beggar, and throw his offspring upon my charity?   But he knew my weakness: he knew my kindness and generosity of heart, and took advantage of it.   Had I acted as I ought to have done, I should have placed this boy in the workhouse when a child, and then I should have had no farther trouble or anxiety about him; but now I have gone so far, I suppose I shall never be able to get rid of him.   No, no; I fear he knows me too well, and, perhaps, it might be dangerous if I were now to discard him.   I suppose he will have the impudence to make another demand upon my purse, to supply his extravagances, and the house will be turned upside down while he remains in it.   But he shall find me not so foolish as I have been.   No, no; I have been too liberal—far too liberal; and what thanks do I get for it?   I feel convinced that he laughs at me for an easy old idiot, behind my back, and no doubt would be happy to see me in my coffin, for he flatters himself that he would then come into possession of my gold.   But let him beware, or he may chance to find himself deceived.   More expense! more expense! everybody imposes upon the old man, and will not be satisfied until they have brought him to ruin.   Would that he had been a hundred miles off; how can I see him in my present state of mind?   Hark! that is his voice; he is singing—the profligate! he will drive me mad."

The voice of Captain Middleton now resounded through the house, singing the following words, in tones far more noisy than harmonious:—

> "Jolly, jolly, let us be jolly;
> Man was not made to indulge melancholy.
> Care to the devil, away with all sorrow,
> Enjoyment to-day, never think of to-morrow.
> The red wine we'll quaff from o'erflowing glasses,
> And sweeten its flavour by kissing the lasses!
>   Jolly, jolly, let us be jolly;
>   Man was not formed to indulge melancholy."

Sir Horace shrugged his shoulders as he listened to this boisterous ebullition of mirth, and then he muttered a curse between his teeth.

"What am I to do with this wild, dissipated boy?" he exclaimed; "I shall go mad if he remains in the house long   Well, it is a just punishment to me for my foolish generosity; but did he not know me so well, I would not long be pestered with him."

He tried to assume as much composure as he could, but still the image of Julio would present itself to his imagination, and then quitted the room, and descended to the hall in which his nephew was seated, still carelessly humming to himself the burden of the song we have above quoted.

Captain Middleton was really a fine, handsome young man, of tall and commanding figure, but still there was an expression in his countenance which showed the wild and reckless rake, and prevented that feeling of respect and admiration his appearance would otherwise have created.

When Sir Horace entered the hall, he immediately arose, and advanced cordially to receive him, but the baronet met him with a frown, and muttered an impatient "Bah!" between his teeth.

"My dear uncle," he said, "I am most glad to see you again, and looking so well. After ploughing the waves and helping to drub the enemies of our country, I have once more cast anchor in the old house, where I hope to pass a few weeks in the enjoyment and the pleasure of your society."

"Humph!" growled the old man, "and it would have been quite as well if you had cast your anchor anywhere else but here, for I am in no humour to encourage your foolery; and let me tell you at once, that the less I have of it the better."

"Nay," said the young man, "and is this the way you welcome me, uncle, after so long an absence? But I know you do not mean what you say; it is only your eccentric way. You're too kind, too generous-hearted, to entertain any such ideas."

"Ah! because I have been a good-natured old fool for so many years, you think I am always to remain so. But hark you, sir; if you think that I am going to encourage your extravagances you are much mistaken; I have already impoverished myself to bring you up like a gentleman, but I can do so no longer—it is not in my power. I—I am poor—quite poor, and see nothing but ultimate ruin before me."

"Poor!" repeated his nephew, and he secretly cursed and despised the miser in his heart.

"Yes, poor!" reiterated Sir Horace; "whoever thought that I was rich? They must be mad to do so; but—but I tell you again, that whatever may have been my former circumstances, they are now changed, miserably changed; I have experienced losses; banks have failed, and ——"

"And have your speculations on the sea also failed, dear uncle?" demanded young Middleton, with peculiar emphasis.

The baronet started, and his countenance underwent a most powerful change. He grasped the arm of his nephew, and glared fiercely in his countenance, as he exclaimed in a hoarse voice,—

"Boy, what mean you?—What dare you insinuate by those words? You must not, cannot suspect ——"

"I suspect nothing, uncle," answered Captain Middleton, who was fearful that he had proceeded too far; "I merely thought that, perhaps, ——"

"Boy," interrupted Sir Horace, with increasing agitation, "you must not venture even to think, as you would dread my curse, my everlasting anger. Speculate! what have I to speculate with? Any one to hear you talk would think that I was rich, and—and—but once more I warn you, never to dare to hint at such a thing again, or—or you little imagine what the consequences might be to yourself."

"Sordid old wretch!" thought young Middleton, as he viewed the agitation and alarm of the miser; "however, keep hoarding on, keep piling up your golden treasure in your coffers; it will purchase rich sport for me when your old bones shall be mouldering in the grave, or bleaching on a gibbet."

Sir Horace, after fixing his keen eyes sternly and earnestly upon his nephew's countenance, walked backwards and forwards across the room, muttering some incoherent words to himself; and it was quite evident that his mind was greatly disturbed by the hints which Captain Middleton had thrown out. At length his countenance changed, and forcing a conciliatory and truckling demeanour, he said,—

But come, come, Raymond, you do not mean what you say, I know you don't; but you know I am getting old, and perhaps I am testy. I have a deal of care on my mind, Raymond, a vast deal of care and anxiety, and cannot bear to be spoken to as you have done. Should you openly talk thus, what would the world think of me? They might entertain suspicions—they might call me miser and—but I do not wish to quarrel with you. You know how kind I have ever been to you, how I have indulged you even to foolish fondness, when, Heaven knows, I could but ill afford it. But we will say no more about it; and—and I am glad to see you, Raymond, very glad, and to prove my sincerity, we will take a glass of wine together; rare stuff, my boy, it has been many years in bottle, and I only indulge myself in a glass of it at times and seasons, for it is very expensive, you know—very expensive."

Sighing deeply, and shaking his head as he uttered these words, the old man rang the bell, and on Simon Snipe making his appearance, he perfectly astounded him by ordering him to bring a bottle of wine, and such other refreshments as the scanty larder afforded.

Raymond could not help viewing his uncle with feelings of disgust and hatred; but he knew it was to his interest to disguise his real sentiments, and he therefore observed,—

" Well, uncle, it is my place to ask your pardon for anything I may have said that is unpleasant to you, but you know I am only a rough unpolished seaman, and we are sometimes apt to let our tongues get the weather-gauge of our reason."

" Ah! ah! just so," said Sir Horace; " I can excuse you, Raymond, I can excuse you."

The wine was now brought, and the baronet looked at it with a melancholy eye as if it was so much of his heart's blood, while Raymond filled two glasses, and taking up one, observed,—

" Well, here's health, long life, and prosperty to you, uncle."

" Ah!" growled the old man, also taking up his glass, " I—I thank you for the toast, but it will be of very little use to me. Health I never had—I am always ill; care and anxiety have ruined my constitution. I have been dying for years, I feel it, although no one pities me;—long life! how can I, who have lived threescore and ten, expect it? and, as for prosperity, I have never prospered, boy, and I never shall,—always miserably poor—miserably poor. Heaven only knows how I have struggled with the difficulties I have to contend; only that I have a patient and energetic mind, or I must have sunk under them long ago."

And the wretched old man sipped with his wine, and sighed and sighed again. Raymond could scarcely help expressing his disgust, as the mercenary and sordid hypocrite gave utterance to the above words; but he knew what the consequences would be if he did so, and he therefore disguised his feelings.

" Come, come, uncle," he said, " you must not talk so; I shall have the happiness of seeing you yet live many years, and it will be my study to tend to your comfort. I shall be your companion for some time at the Manor-house, and intend to make a merry time of it; these old walls shall wear a smiling aspect they have not done for many a day, and ——"

" Boy! boy!" interrupted Sir Horace, with a look of the greatest alarm, " know you what you say? Would you bring ruin at once upon me? No, no, I must have none of these extravagances; it is only madmen that indulge in them. I cannot afford to pay for mirth."

" Women, wine, and mirth, are the only enjoyments of life."

" Horrible! horrible! Raymond,—you are a profligate; but—but you will not remain long in England, will you? It is only for your own good I speak. I —I am very glad to see you, but still your stay here will only be short, will it?"

" Nay, sir," returned young Middleton, " you cannot be in such a hurry to get rid of me; I know you are not, it is only your eccentric way."

" I wish the waves had swallowed you up ere you could again have set foot on these shores," thought the baronet.

" Yes," continued Raymond, " here for a few weeks I shall stay to keep you company, and to enjoy myself ; then once more to sea, and after another cruize I shall have sown my wild oats, and may probably settle myself down to sober matrimony."

" Matrimony !" repeated Sir Horace, in a shrill voice, and with a look of horror ; " do not dare to think of it ; there is misery and ruin in the very name. What business have you with a wife ? You cannot keep her ; and mark me, Raymond, I will not consent to your marrying—not a shilling shall you ever have from me. A wife, indeed !"

" A mistress, then !"

" More dreadful still !" cried Sir Horace. " Boy, are you mad ?"

" Ay, uncle," answered Raymond, " *in love !*"

" Love ! love !—impossible ! Why, you were but a boy when you left England, and what should you know about love ?"

" And she whom I admire is but a child, if you will have it so ; but yet has she continually occupied my thoughts since I have been away, and I shall not rest until I have beheld her again. Uncle, in spite of all you say, we cannot resist our passions, and I would encounter any risk, brave every danger, to obtain the gratification of them in this instance."

" Libertine ! profligate !" exclaimed the baronet, " you shock my ears."

" Say not so," returned Raymond.

" And what is the name of this girl who has thus made a slave of your reason ?" demanded Sir Horace, sternly.

" Rosetta Belford," answered his nephew.

" The daughter of a beggar," remarked the baronet, with a frown.

" But yet she has charms that have enslaved my imagination."

" Would you make her your wife ?"

" No, but I would triumph in my desires," said Raymond ; " Rosetta is a conquest worth struggling for."

" Forbear, forbear, young man," said the baronet. " Would you bring ruin and disgrace upon my unsullied name ?"

Raymond could scarcely repress a smile of contempt.

" I must again behold her," said the libertine ; " I cannot restrain my desires ; she—she must be very lovely by this time."

" Bah !" ejaculated Sir Horace, impatiently ; " I caution you once more to abandon your guilty thoughts ; to forget her as you value my future friendship and favour. If you persist in these dangerous propensities, nothing but destruction can follow. Reflect well upon my words, and see that you obey them, or take the consequences. I will now leave you to yourself for awhile, for I must be alone ; you have already interrupted me in my meditations."

With these observations, Sir Horace quitted the Hall, and once more betook himself to his own apartment, muttering curses as he went on the circumstance that had brought his nephew once more to the Manor-house, and his own folly and good nature, which had induced him ever to take him under his protection at all. And yet he looked upon him with dread ; he feared to offend him, for he imagined that he knew too much of his guilty transactions, and the hints he had thrown out respecting his secret speculations on the sea, confirmed him in that belief.

" Would that he had perished in his infancy," he ejaculated, " or that I had never been fool enough to burthen myself with him. He knows me, and like all those who do, he takes advantages of it, and in a moment might betray me to destruction. But he will not—dare not ; he will not venture to whisper a word that may work me harm ; he thinks to possess my gold, and that will purchase his silence ; in the meantime I may contrive some means to get rid of him. Oh, it is a fine thing to possess the yellow gold ! it quiets the tongues of babbling fools, and protects us in our secret transactions. But for the gold ; what would have become of me long since? Stern justice would have laid her unrelenting hand upon me, and the gibbet would have claimed me for its victim. And shall I always escape? Oh, let me not think, or my fears will overcome me. That boy, too, who like a hideous phantom crossed my path to-day; whenever I think of him my blood freezes with horror. But I must have been deceived; it could not be him my conscience imagined. I must see Martin Trevors upon the subject. But I will not alarm myself; if it should, indeed, be the youth I suspect, what have I to fear from him? He knows me not, and therefore cannot bring me into any danger. Let me be calm, or by own conduct I shall betray myself. Oh, guilt! guilt! thou art a coward after all."

With these words he walked into his apartment, and, locking the door, gave himself up to the gloomy reflections which tortured his guilty soul.

"And so," soliloquized Raymond, after he had quitted the Hall, "this is the cordial reception that I meet with from my worthy uncle, the sordid wretch whose whole soul is wrapped up in his coffers, and to fill which he has shrunk not from perpetrating the most hideous crimes. But 'tis well; there is no love lost between us, and I only watch my opportunity to appropriate to myself his ill-gotten wealth, and then the sooner the hangman claims him the better. He would make an admirable scarecrow! ha! ha! ha! And does the old idiot think that he will always be able to hold me in the trammels he now does? He will find himself most wofully mistaken. He little imagines that I already know so much of him as I do, or his craven soul would quake with fear. In a moment I could betray him to destruction; but all in good time;—I must have money to carry on the schemes I have in contemplation, and the old man's secret hoard must supply me with it. What would be his alarm, did he but know them? was he aware that I have, at this time, a tight little vessel of my own not far from here, supposed to be a fair trader, but which is manned and fitted in every way for the life of freedom in which I mean to embark? I feel that I was never intended to fight the battles of my country, and to wait patiently for honours and distinctions. No, I am for a life of liberty; I would become the rover of the seas, and held those in terror who now rule me as masters. Let those seek an honourable name who value it; I do not. Rosetta Belford, too, she is still living in this neighbourhood, and I must behold her, nay more, I will accomplish my designs against her, or perish in the attempt!"

He paused and reflected deeply, and all the bad passions of his nature rapidly strengthened and gained ascendancy over him, and he paced the room, filled with the most guilty determination.

Raymond Middleton, as has been shown, had frequently seen Rosetta before he quitted the Manor-house, and, even young as she then was, her extreme beauty had excited the most powerful passion in his breast, a passion base as it was powerful, and he secretly marked her for his future victim. Absence had not been able to conquer these guilty thoughts, and he looked forward to the time when he should return home, that he might have an opportunity of putting his villanous designs into effect, determined as he was, by some means, to get the damsel in his power. Now that Sir Horace had left him, and as it was not likely that he would see him again, probably for some hours, he resolved to walk forth towards the residence of Mr. Belford, with the hope of seeing Rosetta, but at a loss to know how he could introduce himself to Michael's dwelling, without exciting some suspicion in his breast; and he was well aware that the best opinion was not formed of him by the persons who resided in the neighbourhood. However, he quitted the Manor-house, and walked slowly on towards the place of his destination, weighing in his mind, as he proceeded, the dark projects which occupied it. The morning had been very fine, but the afternoon set in cloudy and threatening, and Raymond had not advanced far on his way, when some heavy drops began to fall, and the rain soon descended in a rapid shower. He wrapped his cloak closer around him, and increased his speed.

"This is fortunate," he said; "it will form an excellent excuse for my seeking a shelter in Belford's house, and obtaining the gratification of my anxious wishes. Rosetta, I cannot rest until I behold you again!"

He hurried on his way, and soon came in sight of Michael's dwelling, and, ascending the hill, knocked loudly at the door, which was speedily opened by Mr. Belford himself, who started back with some amazement and confusion, on beholding the nephew of Sir Horace Middleton.

" Do you not know me, Mr. Belford ?" said Raymond.

" Captain Middleton, I believe," answered Michael, but in tones which were sufficient to show he did not consider him a very welcome visitor.

" I have been overtaken by the storm on my way to the Manor-house," continued Raymond, " and must, therefore, request you to accommodate me with a shelter until it has abated."

" Certainly, sir," answered Michael, with his usual politeness, and immediately ushered Raymond into the parlour of his clean and comfortable dwelling.

Raymond looked anxiously around the apartment, but when he beheld no one but Mrs. Belford seated there, he felt greatly disappointed and vexed ; however, he took a seat by the fireside, with an air of as much composure as he could assume, and awaited to see whether Rosetta made her appearance or not.

" It was lucky that I was so near your house, Mr. Belford, when the storm came on," he observed ; " for it now comes down violently, and I should have been wet to the skin before I could have reached the Manor-house."

" No doubt of it, Mr. Middleton," answered Michael ; " but I dare say you have weathered many a worse storm than this at sea, or even the tempest that raged off this coast a few days since, when the Death Ship, that harbinger of woe, made its appearance."

" The Death Ship !" repeated Raymond, with some degree of interest and emotion ; " did she then again visit this coast ? Let me see, it must have been then just five years after her former appearance."

" It was," returned Michael.

" I well remember the time," observed Raymond, appearing for a time to forget himself. " It was then for the first time that I began to suspect that my uncle—" he bethought himself, and, seeing the look of eager curiosity which Michael had fixed upon him, he felt somewhat confused, and added, " Ay, ay ; the pirate is the devil's own craft, that's certain, Mr. Belford ; but did anything particular happen on the occasion of her last appearance ?"

" Happen !" repeated Michael ; " ah ! Captain Middleton, it was a dreadful night. A noble vessel was destroyed by the pirate, even whilst struggling against the fury of the battling elements ; burnt to the water's edge, and out of all her crew and passengers but one poor creature's life was spared, and that an idiot."

" Indeed !"

" It is true, sir," said Michael ; " and then there was a repetition of all the same horrors which occurred five years before. There was that strange, wild cry that rose even above the howling of the storm, the same mysterious form was seen to dart with the speed of the whirlwind from the rocky caverns, and take its course towards the old Manor-house, and——"

" Towards the Manor-house ?"

" Even so ; and it is said that it has been seen to enter there."

" Mr. Belford," observed Raymond, with looks of incredulous astonishment and emotion, " you—you must be mistaken."

" Such is the report, Captain Middleton," returned Michael ; " but I cannot undertake to answer for its truth."

" Well, well ; we will talk no more upon that subject," said Raymond. " I am glad to see you looking so well, and your worthy dame, too ; why, I declare she looks as young as ever."

" Yes, captain," replied Michael ; " thank God, with the blessing of a clear conscience, we are enabled to weather the storms of life pretty well."

" I am glad to hear it," remarked Raymond. " And your daughter, the fair Rosetta, I trust that she is also quite well."

" I am much obliged to you for your good wishes, sir," replied Mr. Belford ; " my dear child is well and happy."

"Ah!" ejaculated Raymond, led astray by the eagerness and impetuosity of his own base thoughts, "you should, indeed, be proud of such a daughter, Mr. Belford; she was, in truth, a beauteous creature, formed to captivate the eye and the heart of every beholder. Methinks I see her sylph-like form now, as it gambolled over the green fields, in the playfulness and vivacity of youth and innocence, her bright eyes sparkling like diamonds of light, and her silken tresses—"

"Sir," interrupted Michael, with a look of anger, "this fulsome flattery is far from agreeable to me. I know that my Rosetta is fair, I know that she is good, and I need not the tongue of praise to make me properly appreciate the treasure with which Heaven has blessed me."

Raymond bit his lips, and could not conceal the confusion and vexation which the warm reproof of Michael excited in his breast, but he quickly recovered himself, and said,—

"Pardon me, Mr. Belford, if my admiration of your lovely daughter has caused me to express myself with too much apparent warmth. You cannot, of course, imagine that I meant to offend you?"

"I know not why you should seek to do so; but excuse me, Captain Middleton, I am an old man, and am not altogether ignorant of the world. My experience has ever taught me to look with an eye of suspicion and mistrust upon the honied accents of extravagant adulation and flattery. Sincere and virtuous admiration never descend to them."

Raymond felt more confused than ever, and he secretly cursed the old man's keen penetration in his heart. He made some stammering answer to Michael's last observation, and then remained silent for a few minutes, and walking to the window, looked out, apparently watching the progress of the storm. He then resumed his seat, having regained his composure, and entered into a conversation with Michael upon other subjects. Suddenly he was startled by hearing a voice of such melancholy but bewitching sweetness, that it rivetted his whole attention, singing the following words:—

> "Hark! hear you not the howling winds,
>   That drown the sea-mew's cry?
> And see you not the lightning's flash
>   That glares across the sky?
> But hear you not that piercing shriek
>   Above the tempest wild?
> It is a mother's dying voice
>   That calls upon her child!
> And see! ah, see! that mangled form
>   Now rises on the wave!
> Help! help!—you mock!—she sinks!—she sinks!
>   The ocean is her grave!
> Mother! mother! mother!"

The last words of this wild melody were uttered in tones of such frantic despair, that they were truly appalling to listen to, and Raymond, filled with amazement, turned to Michael, and said,—

"What means this, Mr. Belford? From whom did these remarkable words proceed?"

"From the poor maniac boy, whom I told you I rescued from a dreadful fate on the night of the tempest," answered Michael; "but see—he comes."

Julio then entered the room, leaning on the arm of Rosetta, and with his eyes cast towards the ground, apparently unconscious of all around him.

Raymond gazed at him for an instant with a feeling of the deepest interest, but his eyes almost immediately wandered to his beauteous companion; and as he gazed upon those incomparable charms which time had ripened into perfection, his bosom throbbed with admiration, and the sinful passions he had so long encouraged gained an ascendancy over him which he found it impossible to conceal. All that his imagination had formed of the captivating beauty of his intended victim fell far short of the reality, and he could at that moment have fallen at her

feet and worshipped her with all the strength of his unholy sentiments.   But the
attention which she paid to the unfortunate Julio excited his jealousy, and he was
already prepared to hate him with all the fierce loathing of his nature.

Rosetta, when she beheld the unexpected guest, shrank back with maiden
timidity, and she felt a sensation of dread at her heart which she could not
conquer.   She slightly courtseyed to Raymond, and then leading Julio to her
parents, she took a seat by their sides, and hid her blushing face from the earnest
glances of the young captain.   Julio rushed to the arms of Mr. and Mrs. Belford,
and embraced them with all that ardour of affection, as if they had been his own
parents.

"Fair Rosetta," said Raymond, at length recovering himself, and disregarding
the suspicious and offended looks of Michael and his wife, "do you not know me?
I am your old friend, Raymond Middleton, who, thanks to the accident of the storm,
has been led to your dwelling, and who gladly avails himself of the opportunity to
express his pleasure at again beholding you, and to see you well."

He advanced towards the confused damsel as he spoke, and tendered his hand, but Julio suddenly starting from the embraces of Mr. and Mrs. Belford, and darting in between them, exclaimed,—

"No, no; you must not approach her, for she is Julio's pretty sister, his own Rosetta, whom he loves so fondly, and whom he would protect with his life. Ah! you smile; but those smiles cannot deceive Julio. You would offer fine, flattering words to allure and betray, but in vain. Go, go—I know you."

Raymond Middleton started back a few paces, and bit his lips, and staring at the maniac with amazement; but he saw the necessity of stifling his rage, and observed, in assumed accents of pity,—

"Poor boy! this is indeed madness. But ——"

"Mad!" interrupted Julio. "Who says I'm mad? No, no; I am not mad—my mind does but wander; and have I not had enough to make a wreck of my poor brain? Oh! yes. But you are a sailor; I know you. And just like you, just so handsomely dressed, did *he* appear—he who—no, I dare not, cannot mention his name. I am forbidden to speak it, and would that I could forget it; for, oh! how my blood freezes when I think of it. You are a sailor, and Julio will tell you a tale of horror, if you have a heart formed for pity. He will tell you how the tempest raged, and how the death's crew shouted in mockery of it, and in that fearful moment could perpetrate a deed of blood from which even fiends would shrink appalled. Yes, yes; he will tell you how they snatched him from his mother's arms, and laughed at her cries for mercy. Hark! do you not hear her voice? See you not their glittering blades, and ——

> " ' Hark; hear you not the howling winds
>   Which drown the sea-mew's cry?
> And see you not the lightning's flash
>   That glares across the sky?
> But hear you not the piercing shriek
>   Above the tempest wild?
> It is a mother's dying voice
>   That calls upon her child!
> And see! ah, see! that mangled form
>   Now rising on the wave!
> Help! help!—you mock!—she sinks!—she sinks!
>   The ocean is her grave!
> Mother! mother! mother!'

Ha! ha! ha! it is a goodly tale, is it not? A goodly tale—a goodly tale!" And the wretched maniac laughed again, then sank in his chair, and became lost in the gloom and horror of his own wild thoughts.

Raymond Middleton could not help viewing Julio with the deepest interest; but compassion was foreign to his nature, and he quickly again removed his eyes from him to Rosetta, who, however, concealed her countenance from his gaze, and felt ashamed and uneasy at his presence. There was a boldness in his demeanour which alarmed her, and in spite of all her efforts to the contrary, she could not but entertain a sentiment of repugnance towards him, and a dismal foreboding that he harboured thoughts which might be conducive to her future misery. She could see, from the looks of her parents, that they entertained no good opinion of him; and if all that she had herself heard was true, she was certain that it was not without just reason that they did so.

"And have you not been able to ascertain," said Raymond, at length, removing his eager glances from Rosetta, as he perceived that Michael and his wife watched him with suspicion and displeasure; "have you never been able to ascertain the name of this unfortunate youth's parents, or whether there is any truth in the fearful story which his madness describes?"

"I have not," answered Michael; "but I fear that it is too correct, and that there has been some monstrous work—some fiendish deed of blood. It must have been something indeed dreadful that could thus make a wreck of the reason of one so young."

"It is very strange," remarked Middleton; and the words of Julio still vividly impressed themselves upon his memory; "and know you not the name of the vessel which was destroyed by fire?"

"No."

"And what do you mean to do with the lad?"

"Do!" answered Michael, "why, that which it is the duty of every Christian to do towards his fellow creatures in distress, to be sure—protect and befriend him to the utmost of my power, till I may be enabled to learn the particulars of his melancholy history; and then if I find him to be parentless, and the victim of cruel persecution, which I firmly believe he is, I will adopt him, love him as my own son, with the certainty that Heaven, and the consciousness of doing that which is right, will amply reward me for any trouble or anxiety to which I may be put."

"Well, well," said Raymond, "I commend your feelings, and hope that they may never be abused or imposed upon."

"Abused! imposed upon!" repeated Michael, warmly, "oh, do not apprehend that. Think you that I have anything to fear from the ingratitude of this unfortunate lad? It would be a gross libel upon human nature to imagine such a thing."

Raymond returned no answer, for he knew not what to say, and again his eyes wandered to Rosetta; and as he gazed upon the fairy-like proportions of her form, the unlawful passions he had suffered to enter his breast increased in strength, and he secretly vowed that nothing should prevent the gratification of his wishes. He could have dwelt upon her image, but he saw plainly enough that he was far from being a welcome guest at Michael's dwelling, and, as the storm had now subsided, and there was no further excuse for his prolonging his stay, he arose from his seat, and thanking the old people for the accommodation they had afforded him, he turned to Rosetta, and said,—

"Farewell, Miss Belford, and rest assured that there is no one who more sincerely esteems your parents and yourself, than Raymond Middleton."

"We are obliged to you, Captain Middleton," said Michael, in reply, "for the friendly feeling you profess towards us, and trust that you will never find us to be unworthy of them, or the esteem of all the rest of our fellow creatures."

Raymond felt enraged and abashed at the frigid coldness of Michael's manner, and once more bowing to them all, he quitted the house.

"Well, I am glad that he is gone," remarked Mr. Belford. "I am sorry if I do him an injustice, but there is something in the appearance and manner of that young man, which give me a bad opinion of him, and the more seldom he honours us with his visits, the better I shall like it."

"Ay," said Mrs. Belford, "I am perfectly of your opinion, Michael, and sorry enough I am that he has returned to this neighbourhood. It is well known that he is a wild and unprincipled libertine, and that he caused much misery and uneasiness amongst our neighbours when he was here before."

"True, dame," coincided her husband, "but we know his character, and must therefore be guarded against him. By Heaven, if I knew him to harbour a thought against Michael Belford or those belonging to him, most dearly should he repent it, elevated though he may think his station to be."

"But he will not dare to attempt anything of the kind, Michael," said his wife.

"He had better not; but did you not notice the bold looks he directed towards your daughter?"

"Oh, my dear father," ejaculated the blushing Rosetta, "what do your words imply? I know not how it is, but I feel both terror and repugnance in the presence of Captain Middleton; but surely he cannot entertain a thought towards my wrong?"

"I know not, child," answered Michael, "but I repeat that I like him not, and I know that I need not caution my dearest Rosetta to beware of him."

"Rosetta!" ejaculated the maniac, suddenly starting up and gazing around him, "who would dare to harm my kind sister, Rosetta? But no, they must not, they shall not; Julio would fight for her, protect her, and in the cause of Rosetta, he would possess the strength of a tiger; for I have promised to love you, have I not, my dear sister?"

Rosetta pressed the unfortunate youth's hand in silence, for she was too much agitated to give utterance to a word, and a short time afterwards Frank Trevors arriving at the house, the conversation ended, and all parties resumed their wonted composure.

"They view me with suspicion—they penetrate my real character," soliloquised Raymond Middleton, as he retraced his steps towards the Manor-house ; " the coldness of Michael Belford and his wife convinces me of this, and assures me that I have nothing to expect from persuasion.   But it matters not ; my mind is made up, and nothing on earth shall alter it.   I have beheld the beauteous Rosetta again, and my determination is strengthened. She must, she shall be mine, and that before many days have passed o'er my head.   I have only to accomplish my designs against my sordid old uncle, and then to put my other plans into execution.   I must see my trusty comrades of the lugger, and obtain their assistance,—then to commence my daring career, in which I prognosticate the most glorious success.   That boy, that Julio, as he is called, I like not his appearance or his words, maniac as he pretends to be.   Then the looks of intense affection with which Rosetta eyed him,—they were poison to my soul.   But no matter, I will keep a watchful eye upon him, and if I see any further reasons to strengthen my suspicions, I shall no doubt find a ready way to dispose of him.   And now I remember that Frank Trevors was always her companion and favourite from childhood, and that his attentions spoke of something more powerful than mere friendship.   He must also be watched ; I must suffer no obstacles to remain in the way of the gratification of my desires."

Thus soliloquising, Raymond arrived at home, and entered the Manor-house.   He was soon afterwards rejoined by Sir Horace, who was more composed in his demeanour.   He had seen Martin Trevors — had related to him his meeting with Julio, and the emotion which his features had occasioned him, but, whatever was the answer and advice which Trevors had given him, we know not ; however, it seemed to have been of that nature to satisfy him, and to allay his secret terrors for the present, although dark thoughts still crowded upon his mind, and rendered him, as he must ever be, doubtful and wretched.

"So you have returned," he said, addressing himself to his nephew. "Ah ! I thought the old Manor-house would not suit your taste.   It is dull and melancholy, only a fit abode for an old man like me, and I wonder that you should ever have come back to it."

"It was only my anxiety to again behold you, my dear uncle, that caused me to do so," returned Raymond, with an hypocritical smile.   "Where should I go on returning from a long and perilous voyage, but to the house of my only relation, my friend, the protector of my childhood, my benefactor?"

"Bah !" growled the baronet.   "I dare say you entertain a very great affection for me—are very grateful to me, like all the rest of the world.   But you cannot deceive me ; no—no, I am not to be deceived.   But whither have you been ?"

"I took a stroll among the old scenes so familiar to me," answered Raymond, "and was overtaken by the storm, when I sought shelter in the house of Michael Belford."

"Michael Belford !" repeated Sir Horace, "then you saw Rosetta ?"

"I did.   Oh, she has grown more lovely than I could ever have anticipated."

"Psha ! I want to have none of your foolery.   But—but, tell me, Raymond, did you not behold some one else there besides Rosetta and her parents ?"

"Yes—a boy—who appears to be a maniac, and whom Michael Belford rescued from death."

"Curses light upon him for the same," said Sir Horace, bitterly.

"How ?" exclaimed Raymond, with some astonishment.   "What means this emotion, uncle ?"

"Emotion !" cried the baronet.   "Boy, you do not notice any emotion in me. No, no.   What have I to be alarmed at ?   But did you not observe the features of that youth ?   Did not the resemblance to ——— ?"

He paused and recollected himself.

"To whom, sir ?" interrogated Raymond, eagerly.

"No one, no one. I knew not what I said; but, oh, there is something in that countenance which I can never forget; I would have given worlds had I never seen it. It haunts me like a hideous phantom, and,—but what a very fool I am to talk thus. It cannot be he—Martin Trevors has convinced me of that. Raymond, did you hear the maniac speak?"

"I did," replied Raymond. "He talked wildly of storms at sea, of the crew of the Death Ship, and of the fearful murder of one he called his mother."

"His mother!" gasped forth Sir Horace, and his countenance became ghastly pale, and his lips quivered. "Of the crew of the Death Ship? Ah! what dreadful thoughts are these that again rush upon my brain? How terrible is the coincidence! By h—l! Martin Trevors must still be endeavouring to deceive me. But I will learn the truth of this. They told me they were no more, and ——"

"Who were no more?" demanded Raymond, with increased amazement and avidity; "to whom do you allude?"

"Ask me no questions, boy," returned Sir Horace, fiercely, "fool, fool that I am, to have no more guard on my tongue. But yet he is an idiot; he knows me not, and what have I to fear from him?—Raymond, heed not what I say; I—I am mad at times. Yes, I must be mad, or I should not give utterance to such vague and wild observations. Oh, torture! torture!"

Thus incoherently raving, the baronet covered his face with his hands, and sank on a chair; then he again started suddenly up, and without saying another word to his nephew, he rushed from the room.

"It is the demon of a guilty conscience that racks your brain," remarked Raymond, when he was left alone; "truly, you are a worthy being, and I ought to be proud of such an uncle. But what can he mean by the words he has just now uttered? What can the maniac boy have to do with him? Whose likeness does he trace in his features?—Oh! I would give something to be thoroughly acquainted with all your dark secrets; but I think I already know enough to make you yield to my demands, and to keep you in fear of me, and it shall not be my fault if I do not ascertain more."

Raymond did not behold his uncle again till supper time, and then he was reserved; but his countenance plainly showed that his mind was distracted with torturing thoughts, and Raymond frequently caught his eyes fixed upon his face with the most intense earnestness, as if he would penetrate his very soul.

The meal being over, Sir Horace arose, took up a lamp, and bidding his nephew good night, he abruptly quitted the apartment. Raymond did not remain long after him, but also taking a lamp, he made his way to the chamber in which he used to sleep when he was before at home, and which he found all ready prepared for him. But he was not inclined to retire to rest for the present, and sat reflecting upon the events of the day, and maturing his future deep laid and guilty designs. The recent observations of Sir Horace had made a deep impression upon him, and his interest was more than ever excited respecting the maniac boy, to whom he had alluded with such fearful emphasis.

"It is evident," he said, "that notwithstanding his efforts to disguise it, he suspects this Julio to be some one whom he has reason to dread, and I must endeavour to discover it, for it may tend to aid me in my plans, and place Sir Horace more securely in my power. It is only by intimidation that I can expect to gain my ends, and them I am resolved to accomplish at all hazards. Gold I must and will have, and where can I so properly apply as to the coffers of my uncle? Of what use is wealth to the sordid miserable wretch? only to torture his restless and covetous mind, or perhaps, to purchase him a respite from the gallows! It is enough that he has accumulated it; my business, as a dutiful nephew, is to take the anxiety off his mind, and to spend it for him. Ha! ha! ha!—that is a task which I think I can accomplish in a masterly manner, and I do not see why I should not have a share in his wealth as well as others."

Thus he continued to soliloquize for some time, and then his thoughts once more returned to Rosetta, and the coldness of the reception he had met with from her and her parents.

"It is evident that the damsel looks upon me with dread and repugnance," he said, "and therefore the only chance of success depends upon my own determination. Force must and shall make her mine, and when I have once got her in my power, I will convey her to a place where her friends can never discover her, and where any resistance on her part to my will, will be entirely useless. Yes, Rosetta, however safe you and your parents may think you are, you are mine as securely as if you were at the present moment in my power. But my plans must be executed promptly; yes, there must be no delay, lest something which I cannot at present foresee should arise to thwart them. I will see about making arrangements for putting them into effect by to-morrow at the latest."

The clock had long since struck the hour of eleven, but still Raymond was so busied in reflection that he did not think of retiring to bed, and the longer he ruminated, the more he became determined in the prosecution of his guilty plans.

"Disgrace, opprobrium will attach themselves to my name," he said, "but what care I for that? I have already learnt to treat the world's hatred with indifference, and I shall then be in a position to hold it at defiance. They may term me robber, pirate; I shall not be ashamed of the titles; even those who appear so good, so virtuous, and so honourable, would look but sorry wretches were they stripped of their hypocritical disguise. Men grow rich by preying upon their fellow creatures, and why should I not share in the spoil? Honour, honesty, I find are beggarly qualities, and therefore will I have nothing to do with them. Those fare the best who become the greatest villains, so give me your bold-faced scoundrel before the drivelling, honest fool. I'm for a life of liberty and enjoyment, and I care not by what means I obtain it. But I wonder if the old dotard has retired to rest? I should like to listen to his midnight soliloquies, for they might furnish me with some valuable information. All is still in the house, so I will even venture to his chamber-door, and perhaps my curiosity may not remain ungratified."

It was a strange thought, but still he could not resist the temptation, little anticipating the adventure that was in store for him. Taking his lamp in his hand, he silently opened his room door, and listening to ascertain whether anything was stirring, he cautiously began to ascend the stairs leading to the gallery on which the chamber in which Sir Horace Middleton slept, opened. On arriving at the door, he perceived that a light was still burning in the room, but all was still, and he began to think that his uncle had indeed sought his couch, when suddenly he heard him stirring in the chamber, and soon afterwards give utterance to some incoherent words. There was a recess in the wall in which he concealed himself and shaded his light, and so near to the door that he could have an opportunity of hearing all that passed.

The baronet seemed to be pacing the chamber with disordered steps, and talking wildly to himself, but it was some time before Raymond was enabled to distinguish a syllable. At length Sir Horace spoke in under tones, and then his nephew plainly heard the following words,—

"I dare not brave them; I dare not mock at the threats of those terrible men, for they would denounce me to the world; they would betray me to justice—to the gallows; and what would then Sir Horace Middleton appear? A monster of the blackest dye—a robber, a murderer! Ah! what sound was that? Methought that some hollow voice repeated the word, and called me murderer. But no, it was only my disordered imagination. Oh! that I could learn to brave the fearful upbraidings of conscience, to forget the past, and not to anticipate the future. No, it will not be—it will not be. I have hoards of glittering gold, but it cannot purchase that. The Death Ship, that vessel of blood and horror, to which I ——"

Raymond could not catch the conclusion of this sentence, important as it was, and for a few moments afterwards Sir Horace ceased to speak. At length he said,—

"It is the solemn hour of midnight, and all but one are at rest. It is the dismal stillness of death which prevails. Oh, how doubly awful to me! I must not yet retire to my bed. No, no; I have a fearful task to perform, and it must be at this hour, when there is no eye to watch me, or to pry into my awful secrets. I must forth, and gaze upon that which I have not looked upon for many a dreary year. I cannot endure this horrible suspense; but would that my dreadful task was over. Courage! courage!"

Bound up to a pitch of the most breathless curiosity, Raymond more securely shaded his lamp, and compressing himself into the smallest compass within the recess, he awaited the appearance of Sir Horace. He did not have to wait long; the room door was slowly and cautiously opened, and the wretched man emerged into the gallery with the lamp in his hand, and cast a fearful glance around him. There was an expression in his cadaverous countenance that was truly appalling to behold, and it was rendered, if possible, still more ghastly by the faint and sickly reflection which was cast upon it by the light from the lamp. He paused for an instant, and seemed to listen with the most profound attention; but the sighing of the wind was all he heard, and with silent footsteps he proceeded along the gallery.

He did not venture to look back, so that when he had proceeded some distance, Raymond ventured stealthily to follow him with noiseless steps, lest his slightest tread should catch his breathless attention, and prevent the gratification of that unconquerable curiosity which the conduct of his uncle had excited in his breast.

When Sir Horace arrived at the end of the gallery, however, he paused at the top of the staircase, and Raymond drew back into the shade. And now the miser ventured to raise the lamp above his head, and to look back with timid eye upon the little distance he had traversed; but although he could behold nothing but the rude figures on the carved oaken wainscot, he started and trembled, for no doubt the poor guilty wretch conjured up forms in unison with those frightful images presented to his conscience, and the murmuring, moaning midnight wind at that moment swept along the gallery, like the dismal lamentations of troubled spirits.

And it was awful to gaze upon the ghastly countenance of that guilt-tortured, shivering old man, and a feeling of pity might have entered the breast of humanity that so hoary-headed a man, whose age should command respect and reverence, had become so fallen, so abject, so despicable, in the midst of this bright and beautiful world, where God has supplied such abundant, such inexhaustible stores for the happiness of his creatures. But disgust dries up all the sources of pity, which would otherwise flow to the sordid miser.

Of what a strange and incomprehensible mixture of propensities is the mind of man composed. Perfection it can never conscientiously arrogate to itself, although virtue sometimes finds within it its natural tenement; but vainly may we look around for an instance wherein either vanity, avarice, ambition, inordinate passions, or frivolous pursuits, do not, in some degree, contaminate its purity, and tarnish its most brilliant attributes.

The warmth of a vigorous imagination in youth leads the giddy mortal through the flowery paths of prodigality, till dissipation plunges him in a gulf of hopeless misery. In vain does the sinking victim, struggling in the whirlpool of destruction, supplicate the commiserating hand of friendship to snatch him from the torrent that overwhelms him; he that falls by his own imprudence, falls unpitied, for age forgets the errors of its earlier years, and avarice deadens the soul to every exquisite sensation of philanthropy.

And the miser, what is the earthly hell in his fancied paradise that he creates for himself? How the poor worm drags on his weary way to the grave! Shrinking under the gripe of misery, craving for that which in fact he possesses in such abundance, without knowing how to enjoy; looking with fear and suspicion on his fellow creatures; shivering in voluntary anguish over masses of treasure, and, possessing the means of every gratification, pines out an irksome existence in poverty and sorrow, till he sinks into the grave abhorred and unlamented.

The latter were the thoughts which flashed upon the brain of Raymond Middleton in that brief space of time while he gazed upon the pale, livid, careworn countenance and attenuated form of his guilty uncle, and still more fearful ideas began to suggest themselves to him. What business had one so vile in this world? Stood he not there a foul curse, a blight upon it, fearing to use the means he had of enjoyment, and preventing others from the possession of it? Could it be a sin to rid the world of such a locust? What unbounded pleasure might his hoarded riches procure! They were alone; no mortal eye watched them! It needed but one determined blow, but one brief struggle to secure wealth and independence, and —— but he paused, and shuddered at his own thoughts; no, no, he was not yet so deeply plunged in crime to become a murderer, and the murderer of a poor, feeble, defenceless old man, his own relative, and who, at any rate, with all his faults, had brought him up from childhood, protected, educated, provided for him, when he had no other friend in the world. Guilty, cruel, heartless as he had undoubtedly been, he could not imbue his hands in the blood of his own kinsman.

And now the old man began to descend the stairs, his footsteps sounding hollowly in that still and dismal hour, and again Raymond stole cautiously after him. He suffered him to reach the bottom of the staircase, and crossing a small hall open a door at the extremity, then followed him. He was surprised that the old man did not close the door after him, but, of course, he suspected not that he was watched, and was, perhaps, fearful that the noise it would make might disturb the inmates of the house, and be the means of interrupting his secret and mysterious purpose; and Raymond, after a short pause, entered the apartment upon which it opened. All was involved in darkness, and Sir Horace was not there.

"Ah!" thought Raymond, "I am baffled in my design; the old man has escaped me by some secret means with which I am unacquainted. D——n! and shall not my curiosity after all be gratified?"

He groped around the stone walls with the hope of finding a door, but he was disappointed, and was unable to form any idea, for a moment or two, by what means the old man had escaped him. But at length, casting his eyes towards the floor, he beheld a faint streak of light, as if issuing from some narrow crevice, but the next instant it was gone. He knelt down and felt about the spot where he had seen it, and his hands came in contact with a trap door which was not quite closed. With much difficulty he raised it, and then descended a broken flight of steps which he found underneath it.

He groped about, and turning an abrupt angle of the narrow passage in which he now found himself, he once more beheld the faint glimmering of the lamp the miser carried, and caught an indistinct view of his form, as it slowly threaded that dreary subterranean avenue.

Damp and dull was the atmosphere of that passage, which appeared of great length, and Raymond felt it most oppressive, but his anxiety would not allow him to abandon his intention and return. The passage was narrow and winding, and in some parts so very low that he was obliged to stoop to prevent his head from coming in contact with the roof. The ground was on the descent, and Raymond as he proceeded was certain that it must be far beneath the surface of the earth, and stretched to a considerable distance from the old Manor-house. For what purpose it could have been originally designed, he could not imagine, and he was the more surprised that the conscience-stricken baronet should have the courage to venture to such a dismal and loathsome place at that solemn hour.

The passage seemed to be interminable, and at times Raymond almost lost sight of the light emitted by the lamp, and it was only the hollow reverberation of the miser's footfall that convinced him he was still upon his track. In a few moments the light again entirely disappeared, and he could no longer hear the sound of the old man's feet. But still Raymond groped on his way, and pursuing the winding of the place, he shortly again beheld the glimmering of the light, and perceived that it proceeded from beneath a low archway at the farther extremity, where it appeared to be stationary, and he therefore concluded that Sir Horace had reached the termination of his nocturnal ramble. He made towards it, and venturing to peep beneath the archway, he found that it led into a large vault or rocky cavern.

The miser had placed his lamp upon the earth, and was at that time employed

in exerting all his strength to remove some large pieces of rock, which, when, after much labour, he had succeeded in doing, Raymond was surprised to behold the bright beams of the moon, and the wide expanse of the ocean spread beneath its rays.

Sir Horace looked out from the aperture, and seemed to inhale with moment-ary pleasure the fresh breeze that was wafted from the deep. And now, again, did terrible thoughts and temptations force themselves upon the mind of Raymond.

" The waves dash against this rocky cavern," he reflected; " one moment and they might engulph the form of the miser for ever; it could never be discovered how he had met with his end, and his hoarded treasures would then be mine beyond dispute, and I should have ample means to carry all my designs and wishes into effect. But no—no, I cannot, will not shed his blood; let that be the task of the executioner."

He was interrupted in these reflections by the observations of the old man, who still continued looking out of the aperture.

"All is still," he soliloquized, "save the murmuring of the waves as they dash against these stubborn rocks. Welcome sounds—welcome sounds: ye speak to me of liberty when danger might threaten me from those I fear. Thus could I escape even when death were at my heels. Only one beside myself knew of this secret retreat, and he is now no more, therefore I am quite secure. Many a time have I watched the Ship of Death from this rocky cavern, when no human eye could behold me, or penetrate my dark and important secrets. With hope, with anxiety, but horror, have I watched that fearful vessel, when no one knew of its approach but myself. But enough; let me to my task."

Sir Horace now again proceeded to replace the pieces of rock in their former position, and Raymond then turned his attention to a closer inspection of the cavern. It was very spacious, and seemed to be rather the work of nature than of art. It contained several seamen's old chests, and rusty swords, and broken fire-arms were strewed about, so that Raymond was inclined to think that it had at some period or other been a retreat for smugglers, by its close proximity to the sea, it was so well calculated.

The miser, having closed up the aperture, moved a pace or two forward, with faltering steps, and took up the lamp. Raymond was secure from his observation, and he therefore watched him narrowly, and felt the greatest anxiety to know what would be the result of this midnight adventure. The countenance of his uncle still retained its ghastly hue, and his eyes glared fearfully around the place; he trembled violently and seemed to shrink appalled from the task he had undertaken. He then sunk on one of the chests, and covering his face with his hands, for a moment or two appeared afraid to look up.

"All is still in this retreat of gloom and horror," he at length said, slowly raising his head, and glancing around him. "I am alone, with my own dark thoughts and the fearful evidences of my guilt. But, oh! what a death chill comes over me, and strange hissing, moaning sounds seem to vibrate in my ears. Ah! what was that?"

He started as the wind whistled mournfully through the different fissures of the rocky cavern, and every limb shook with the power of his emotions.

"No, no," he resumed, after a pause, "what a coward fool I am; it was imagination, all imagination. It was but the murmuring of the waves, or the sighing of the wind; and yet can I wonder that such terrible fears should assail me in this place? The foul deeds of former days dart upon my recollection, and —but away with thought. I who have dared so much, should not shrink appalled from the recollection of what I have done. And here secure, concealed from every human eye but mine, are the witnesses of my guilt. Let me see—let me see, and make sure that they have not been discovered. Be calm, be firm, my heart—I—I—do not fear; no, no—what have I to fear?"

Still as he thus spoke the old man trembled in every limb, and the emotion visible in his countenance plainly showed the terrors of mind he was enduring, notwithstanding all his efforts to the contrary.

Raymond watched him with increased curiosity, and scarcely dared to breathe, lest he should discover him, and he knew not what the consequences might be if that should be the case.

Sir Horace walked towards a chest of cedar of peculiar make, in a remote corner of the cave, but from the position in which Raymond stood, the rays of the lamp plainly revealed to him every action. The miser stood before this old chest for a few seconds, and as he fixed his steadfast gaze upon it, his resolution again appeared to falter.

"Bah!" he ejaculated; "how strange, how very strange it is, that I cannot resist the cold shivering tremor which comes over me whenever I approach this secret depository. And why have I not consigned its contents long since to the deep, and thus at once and for ever have got rid of a portion of the cause of my horrors? But no, some secret, some irresistible power prevents me, and still I cling to them as I do to my gold. Hush! hush! I—I must not speak of my gold; even these very rocks may have ears, and should it be discovered that I am rich, men would seek my life that they might possess themselves of my treasures. But who can hear me in this place ? No, no—here, at any rate, I can in safety commune with myself. That likeness, I must once more gaze upon it, and satisfy myself that I have not suffered my imagination to mislead me in the resemblance which I fancied the features of that boy bear to it, for, after all that Martin Trevors has told me, I cannot yet persuade myself that he has not attempted to deceive me. Now then for the trial."

He took from his pocket a small bunch of keys as he spoke, and applied one of them to the lock of the chest, but his hand trembled as he did so, and it was not without the greatest difficulty that he opened it. When he had succeeded in doing so, he clasped his hands together, and appeared to gaze aghast at the contents that were revealed to his view.

"They are all here," he observed; "all here; sad, dreadful memorials of crime—of blood—murder! Ah! who spoke? Who accused me of murder? Who dared in this solitude to say that Sir Horace Middleton had shed the blood of innocence? Fool! fool!—weak idiot! It was but the echo of my own voice; what eye can watch me ? what ear can listen to me in this secret retreat? None, none. I will be firm."

He now stooped down, and took from the chest an elegant female dress of white satin, which he held up with shaking hands.

"Ah!" he cried, in a hoarse, husky voice; "it is her bridal dress—the dress she wore when she wedded herself to a fate of horror. When she gave her fair hand to a monster, in all the confidence of her heart. Oh, how young, how beautiful, how innocent was she then. And yet she, the wife of my bosom, the mother of my child—I could murder, barbarously murder—goaded on by infuriate jealousy, and the taunts and threats of that fiend in human shape, Hugh Clifton, who held me in his power as a slave. He, the pirate captain, the monster commander of the Death Ship, the—but away with such thoughts—why should I repent of a crime which justice demanded? Was she not guilty? yes, yes, could one so beautiful really love a man like me? No, she was a base deceiver, and—oh! agony! agony! conscience will torture me in spite of all my efforts to stifle its voice."

He let fall the dress, and clasping his burning temples, seemed for awhile completely absorbed in the frenzy of his dreadful thoughts. Suddenly he started, and gazed appalled into the chest.

"Blood! blood!" he cried; "the life-blood of a murdered wife is before my eyes. Why do I not rid myself of this awful relic? Why not consign it to the waves, that would wash it for ever from my sight? But could the waves as easily efface it from my memory? No, no; there it is imprinted in indelible characters—in characters of fire."

He groaned in the misery of his thoughts, and for a short time remained silent and inanimate as a statue. Raymond continued to gaze at him with eager eyes, and disgust, hatred, and other fearful passions occupied his mind. One moment he was half inclined to rush upon the old man, and accelerate the terrible retribution of Heaven, which must some day overtake him, but still he shuddered at the thought of shedding the blood of his own relation.

Sir Horace at length recovered himself, and again turning to the chest, took from it another dress, which, as he held it up in the light, Raymond perceived was stained in several places with blood. But a moment the guilty wretch held it, and then dropping it on the earth, covered his face with his hands as if he would shut it from his sight for ever. Again he started, and looked fearfully around him, as if his ears were once more assailed by the mournful lamentations of the troubled spirit of his murdered victim.

"Psha!" he ejaculated; "why will those terrible fancies still present themselves to my imagination? What have I to dread? Nothing—nothing; I am alone, far from the haunts of man, and cannot be discovered or overheard. But one task more, and then my business is done, and I will again to my chamber. Ah! 'tis here—'tis here."

He took from the chest a small portrait of what, as well as Raymond could perceive, appeared to be a young and beautiful female, which the old man gazed at with eager and frenzied eyes.

"Ah!" he exclaimed, "the countenance is the very same; every feature, every expression—the sight palsies my very soul, and I could almost imagine the boy stood before me. Fiends of hell!" he continued, letting fall the portrait; "I have been deceived! they are not dead, they still live as damning evidences of my guilt, to appal me with their sight. But I will not be foiled—I will not be betrayed; no, no—more blood, more blood must be shed to shield me from detection."

"Villain!" cried Raymond, unable any longer to contain himself, and at the same time rushing into the cavern. The old man turned round appalled at the voice, and when his eyes fell upon the person of his nephew, the horror and alarm that shook his frame may be imagined, but cannot be described. But with a wild and unnatural cry he rushed upon Raymond, and endeavoured to hold him in his feeble grasp, while his eyes glared fearfully in their sockets, and his bosom was convulsed with terrible emotion.

"Ah! wretch! prying, sneaking wretch!" he cried; "you have discovered my secret; you have heard all—you possess the damning knowledge that would consign me to the gallows, but you shall not betray me. No, no—I feel myself imbued with the strength of a giant, and never shall you quit this cavern alive."

"Hoary-headed monster!" exclaimed Raymond, as he pressed his fingers in the wretched old man's throat; "I have indeed discovered your secret. I know you now in your true character; your own words, when you thought that there was no one to listen to you, have condemned you, and here are the bloody evidences of your guilt. Oh, would it not be a just retribution were I now to take your life, and consign your miserable carcase to the deep?"

The wretched miser writhed in the grasp of his nephew, and his features were distorted with agony. He made several ineffectual efforts to speak, but at length faltered out,—

"Raymond—nephew, boy, for the love of Christ take your hand from my throat—I—I am choking. Raymond, oh, spare, spare!"

Raymond gradually relaxed his hold, and hurled his uncle from him, who sunk upon his knees, trembling convulsively, and with clasped hands, he fixed his ghastly eyes upon the countenance of the young man, as he exclaimed,—

"Mercy, mercy, Raymond, nephew, dear nephew—mercy for the poor old man. You will not murder me; remember I am your own flesh and blood; your father's brother, who has been so kind and good to you. Mercy, Raymond, mercy."

It was a pitiable, a melancholy sight to behold that miserable, aged wretch, crouching at the feet of his nephew, and begging for that mercy he had never awarded to others. Raymond viewed him with contempt, but no feeling of pity entered his breast. Neither was his indignation or horror sincerely aroused at the crimes which his uncle had committed; he rather exulted in the idea that he had now got him in his power, and could compel him to yield to his wishes, however extravagant they might be, and he was fully determined to take every advantage of it.

"Mercy," he repeated, frowning severely upon him; "what mercy ought an old villain like you expect, or dare to claim?"

"No, no, Raymond, dear Raymond; call me not a villain—I am your uncle; your kind uncle—your benefactor."

"You are a villain," replied Raymond; "a villain of the blackest dye."

"No, no; you mean not what you say."

"Shameless old hypocrite. Murderer!"

"Murderer!"

"Yes; dare you deny your guilt?"

"Yes, yes, no—dear Raymond, but ——"

"Have you not by your own words acknowledged your guilt?" demanded Raymond.

"No, no," faltered out the wretched old man; "you must have mistaken me, Raymond; I did but rave, I ——"

"Liar! Are not these blood-stained relics undeniable proofs of your crime? Gaze on them, old man, and proclaim your innocence if you dare."

Sir Horace did gaze towards them for an instant, and then, with a groan of horror, he hastily averted his looks, and covered his face with his hands.

"Spare me—spare me," he again cried; "I—I do acknowledge everything."

"Ay, you must, miscreant."

"Oh, forbear—forbear!"

"Are you not the murderer of your wife?"

"Hush!—hush! We might be overheard. Oh, Raymond, pity me."

"Pity you," replied Raymond, with a look of the most unbounded contempt; "what pity do you desire, who never showed any to others?"

"But I am an old man—a wretched old man."

"Ay, and you deserve to be so."

"Say not so, dear Raymond. You will pity me."

"Is not the blood of your wife upon your head?"

"Yes, yes, but I do repent."

"Repent, liar! are you not still carrying on your career of iniquity? Do you not even contemplate shedding more human blood?"

"No—no," said the alarmed baronet, still crouching at the feet of his nephew; "you did not hear me say so. It was madness—I knew not what I uttered—my mind was wandering."

"Bah! Sir Horace," returned Raymond, "this is idle mockery; you stand confessed a cold-blooded murderer—the gallows claims your forfeited life."

"No, no—I must not die—I dare not die; let me live for repentance; you will not hang me, Raymond—you will not betray me to a shameful death. Think of all the kindness with which I have ever behaved to you. I have gold, and you are my heir, dear Raymond—yes, yes, I have struggled and struggled; saved and saved, and all for you, dear Raymond, all for you."

"Liar!"

"For shame, Raymond; call me not such harsh names. Am I not your uncle?"

"Ay, and have I not reason to be proud of the connexion?"

"Truly so, dear Raymond, for you will be rich, very rich—when—when I am no more."

"Indeed?"

"Yes, all my gold will be yours; all my hard-earned savings will fall into your possession; but you will not betray me? Let us destroy these fearful things, and bury the past in oblivion."

"No, no," hastily ejaculated Raymond, "not one of them shall be destroyed. They shall remain securely locked in the chest in which you have so long deposited them, and of which I must possess the key."

"You possess the key?" cried the old man, with increasing alarm.

"Yes, I must in future take charge of such precious relics."

"What would you do, dear Raymond?"

"Avail myself of the advantage I have gained."

"Oh, no, you would not—could not be so cruel."

"Cruel! this comes well from your lips," returned Raymond.

"To you, at any rate, I have always been most kind and generous," said Sir Horace.

"Oh, most generous," answered Raymond, with a sneer; "however, I intend to put your generosity to the test."

"What mean you?"

"I promise to spare your life."

"Oh, thanks! thanks!"

" On certain conditions."

" Name them, dear Raymond, but be not too severe."

" You think, then, your life is not worth a very expensive purchase," said Raymond, ironically.

" Do not mock me, Raymond ; for mercy's sake do not mock me," gasped forth the old man.   " Name your terms, and let us leave this awful place.   Oh, would that I never entered it."

" You must swear to comply with them, whatever they may be."

" Swear, Raymond ?   No—no."

" It is the only way by which you can purchase my secrecy."

" But at least first let me know what it is you demand of me ?"

" No, it can matter little to you to know them beforehand," returned Raymond, " since you can only preserve your worthless life by complying with them."

" Alas ! alas !"

" Come, no delay ; no hesitation ; swear by all your hopes, on this blood-stained relic of your murdered victim, to yield implicit obedience to what I shall demand of you."

" Mercy, mercy, Raymond !"

" No equivocation, old man, I am determined," said Raymond, holding up the blood-stained garment before the eyes of the trembling Sir Horace ; " swear."

" I—I swear," groaned the baronet, averting his looks in horror.

" 'Tis well," exclaimed Raymond, with a look of exultation.   " You have sworn, and now remember that your very life depends entirely upon the manner in which you keep your oath."

" Oh, Raymond," groaned the old man ; " and what is it you demand of me ?"

" First, that you shall never attempt to remove the contents of this chest without my knowledge and consent," said Raymond.

" Alas ! alas ! what terrible reasons have you for exacting such a promise ?" tremblingly asked Sir Horace.

" It matters not, such is thy will ; do you promise ?"

" I—I do, but is that all you demand ?"

" Oh, no," said the libertine, with a bitter, exulting sneer.   " I have one demand to make, and then I may be satisfied."

" Name it—name it."

" You have acknowledged that you have gold—that you are very rich."

" No, no, Raymond—I could not say so ; I knew not what I said."

" Bah !" impatiently cried Raymond ; " this subterfuge will not avail you—you have boasted of your generosity."

" Oh, dear Raymond," returned Sir Horace, " you know I have been very generous to you, and that I have impoverished myself to———"

" I told you I would put your generosity to the test," interrupted Raymond.

" Well, well."

" I know my presence here is an annoyance to you."

" Oh, no, Raymond, you mistake me.   Have I not ever given you a hearty welcome on your return to Manor-house ?"

" No trifling.   However, I am willing to leave you immediately."

" Leave me, Raymond ?" said the old man, eagerly.

" Yes, and these are the terms.   You have gold in abundance ; more than you can require for your scanty wants.   I am poor, and must see life, indulge in all its gaieties, and seek those pleasures you have always denied yourself. One thousand guineas will satisfy my present demands, with a grant of five hundred annually, and the sole possession of your fortune at your death."

The old man turned more ghastly pale than before, and again sinking on his knees, gasped out,—

" Boy, nephew ! recall your words.   A thousand guineas ! five hundred annually !   God help me ; where is a poor old man like me to find the money ?

Oh, mercy, mercy! Dear Raymond, after all my kindness to you, would you bring me to ruin?"

"Remember your oath; I am not to be trifled with."

"Bethink yourself, Raymond; you cannot be so cruel."

"You have to choose between that and an ignominious death," returned Raymond.

"Oh, horror, horror!" groaned the miser. "But think of the exorbitant demand, Raymond; I will give you money, but do not extort from me so large a sum."

"Not one guinea less will I take."

"Ruin, ruin!" ejaculated the old miser, and he sobbed like a child; "my gold, my gold!"

"Do you comply?"

"I—I cannot."

"Then you must take the consequences."

"No, no—you will spare me."

"You know my determination."

"At least give me some time to consider."

"It requires no consideration. To-morrow the money and the deeds must be mine. Once more I ask you, do you consent?"

"Alas! alas!" returned the wretched miser, beating his breast in despair; "I must—I do."

"Enough, dear uncle, benevolent uncle, amiable uncle," said Raymond Middleton, in a voice of the most bitter sarcasm; "by so doing your secret is secure; dare to break your oath, and the world shall immediately know you in your real character; these damning evidences of your guilt be brought forward against you."

The old man still covered his face with his hands, and groaned in greater agony than ever. At length he suddenly started to his feet, and grasping his nephew by the arm, ejaculated, in a voice hoarse with emotion and terror,—

"Boy, you have got your wish; you have extorted the promise that dooms me to beggary. Let us begone; let us leave this dismal place, I am cold—cold, and ——"

"Stop," said Raymond, coolly; "it is first necessary that you should see I deposit all these important articles again in the chest, and secure the key."

"Oh! hide them from my sight," cried the distracted baronet, recoiling with horror; "let me not again behold them. Oh, fool! fool! Why did I not destroy them long ere this?"

Raymond returned no answer to this, but replaced the clothes in the chest, and took up the portrait, at which he gazed with the most intense curiosity. The extraordinary resemblance which the features bore to those of Julio, struck him with the utmost surprise, and when he recollected the observation of his uncle, his curiosity was more than ever excited.

The portrait was that of a young female apparently not more than seventeen years of age. The features were beautiful and regularly formed, and the mild blue eyes beamed with an expression which seemed imbued with life, and fascinated the heart of the beholder. Raymond for a few moments could not remove his eyes from it, and it created the deepest interest and admiration in his breast.

"And whom does this lovely portrait represent?" at length he demanded of his uncle.

"Spare me, spare me!" cried the conscience-stricken man; "conceal it from my gaze, I cannot bear to look upon it."

"Old man," said Raymond, with solemn emphasis, "and could you shed the blood of one so beauteous as this?"

"I did not shed *her* blood; I—torture me not, oh, torture me not."

"Is not this the portrait of your wife?"

"No, no—forbear."

"I must, I will, know whom this represents," said Raymond, in commanding tones.

"Do not urge me. What good can it do you to know ?—Let us begone."

"When you have satisfied my inquiries. Of whom is this the likeness ?"

"Of—of her I believed to be my daughter !" groaned Sir Horace, and his limbs shook fearfully as he uttered the name.

"Your daughter ?"

"Yes, yes; oh, agony !"

"And does she still live?" asked Raymond.

"I—I believe not ; no, no, she is dead, or ——"

"And was she murdered also ?"

"No," returned Sir Horace, shrinking within himself, and scarcely able to support his tottering form,—"who said that she was murdered? who,—boy, boy, you drive me to madness ; are you not satisfied with what you have already learnt? Let whatever may be the consequences, I will not answer any more questions."

"Beware, old man, beware !" said Raymond ; "however, I will not at present urge these questions, although your agitation convinces me of your guilt. Oh, you have been in truth a villain."

"Hold, hold ! no more ; let us begone."

"It is a pity that so fair a portrait should be locked up in this old chest," observed Raymond ; " I will keep it out of respect to my beauteous cousin."

"No, no," cried the terrified miser, and attempting to snatch it from the nephew's hand, "not for worlds should that portrait be seen by any other eyes than those which now gaze upon it. Destroy it, but do not, I beseech you, attempt to remove it from this place."

"Well," said Raymond, " to show you that I am not altogether unmerciful, I will again deposit it in the chest, until I may require it on some future occasion."

Sir Horace made no reply, but still averted his looks from the portrait, which Raymond having returned to the chest, locked it, and put the key in his pocket.

"Remember your promise," he said, turning to the old man, " and rest assured, that, as you keep it, so will I keep mine. Not an article must be removed from this cavern, without my knowledge and consent. Do you hear me, Sir Horace ?"

"Alas! I do," sighed the wretched man. "Come, come! let us away !"

"Take the light and lead the way," said Raymond, in accents of insolent command ; "you know it better than I do."

Sir Horace looked at him imploringly, and then with a trembling hand he took the lamp, and led the way from the cavern, followed by Raymond, but as they proceeded along the dismal subterranean passage, he frequently started, and exhibited the same terror as if his eyes had encountered some ghastly phantom.

At length they reached the Manor-house, and Raymond having procured another lamp, lighted it, and turning a peculiar look upon the old man he said,—

"Remember your oath ; to-morrow we meet again."

Sir Horace only answered by a groan, and hurried into his chamber, locking the door after him, and Raymond Middleton re-entered his apartment.

"I triumph! I triumph !" he exclaimed, in a tone of exultation, when he was alone. "Oh, I expected not to make so rare a night's work of it as this. The old miscreant! I have then discovered some of his secrets, and have him securely in my power. He dare not break his oath, for if he did he knows that I should not fail to denounce him to the world as a murderer. How dark is the catalogue of crimes he has perpetrated ; but there is much more that I have yet to learn. He mentioned the name of Hugh Clifton, and I have good reason to believe that he is connected in some way with the Death Ship ; well, well, be it so ; in a short time even that desperate vessel may find a successful rival on the ocean, and the name of Raymond Middleton shall strike an equal terror into the breasts of all who hear it. I have played my cards well, and secured fortune, to carry me on in my well-formed designs. Ha! ha! ha!—I will soon empty the old man's coffers, and then the sooner he falls into the hands of justice the better."

He paused and reflected.

"But the daughter of Sir Horace," he resumed, "can she be still living?— No, I do not think it is likely that she is, or she would ere this have sought her relation. No doubt she has perished by the villain's orders. The boy,

oo, whom Michael Belford saved from the burning ship; how striking the resemblance that his features bear to the portrait, and which seemed to excite strange thoughts and fears in the breast of Sir Horace when he contemplated it. There is some important mystery connected with this which I must endeavour to solve. But this must be subject to further consideration; at present I have quite enough to occupy my attention. Rosetta Belford must be mine; she has excited my most ardent passions, and they shall be gratified. I shall leave the Manor-house to-morrow, very likely, and then I can concoct and put my designs into execution without suspicion. Once let me get the beauteous damsel into my power and it will be useless for her to attempt to resist me."

Thus soliloquizing, Raymond Middleton remained for a short time, when he retired to rest and soon fell off into a sound sleep, from which he did not awake till daylight. No dreams disturbed his guilty mind, and even the good and innocent could not have enjoyed more tranquil repose. But the time was coming when rest would become a stranger to him, and the horrors of a loaded conscience would continually haunt his imagination.

CHAPTER VI.

THE TERRORS OF SIR HORACE MIDDLETON.—THE THOUGHTS OF MURDER.—THE DEMAND COMPLIED WITH.—THE DEPARTURE OF RAYMOND.

How terrible was the agony of the wretched miser when he entered his own chamber. He sunk in a chair, large drops of perspiration stood upon his aching temples, his lips quivered, and for a few minutes he could only give utterance to the most mournful groans, swaying his body to and fro, at the same time, in the greatest possible anguish.

" Lost ! lost !" he cried at last, " cursed, ruined for ever ! Oh, that I should have so long cherished a viper to work my destruction ! Why did I not abandon him to his fate in childhood ? Fool ! fool ! to abandon my own child, and take the beggar brat of my brother under my protection, and thus am I rewarded. My secret discovered, he holds me entirely in his power, and at his mercy. Mercy ! What mercy can I expect from a reckless spendthrift like him ? Has he not boldly told me that he intends to take advantage of his knowledge, and I must submit entirely to his extravagant demands, or he will denounce me to the world. One word of his, and an ignominious death is inevitable. Oh ! that the waves had swallowed him up ere he could again have returned to his native land. My gold, too, that I have purchased so dearly, that I have sinned so awfully to accumulate, he will have that from me. I must not, dare not refuse to comply with his extortions, for my life is in his hands. To-morrow; but a few short hours. Oh ! how I dread the time. What can I do ? How escape the horrors which surround me ? There is no way, no way but one. Ah ! by his death I should be released from these fears, these dangers. Had I anticipated this, he should have perished long since. But even now it may not be too late. All is still ; there is no one to observe me. Probably he sleeps ; could I but obtain access to his chamber, the deed might be accomplished before he could offer any resistance. I feel urged on by madness and desperation. It shall be done ; fortune favour me, and rid me of one whom I now so justly fear. I will wait a short time, however, so that he may be securely locked in the arms of sleep, and then to his chamber, even though fiends should rise to obstruct me. My gold, my treasured gold,—I will not be robbed of my gold."

As the guilty man thus spoke, he took up a knife which was lying on the table before him, and with an unearthly chuckle concealed it in his bosom. Then he relapsed into silence and thought, and with every passing moment his savage determination gained fresh strength, while the expression of his countenance became perfectly hideous.

In this manner nearly half-an-hour passed away, when Sir Horace started to his feet, and snatching up his lamp, exclaimed,—

" Now, now, the time has come ; I can wait no longer, the deed shall be done, and Raymond Middleton shall never wake again. Courage, courage, for on this hour depends fortune, life, everything.'"

The wretched old man cautiously opened his chamber door as he gave utterance to these fearful words, and listened to catch the slightest sound which might give him cause for alarm, and prevent the execution of his atrocious purpose.

But all was quiet; it was totally improbable that any one would be stirring in the house at that hour, and this thought emboldened him, and with increased determination he proceeded along the gallery towards the chamber in which Raymond slept, with noiseless steps, and his bosom swelling with impatience.

He arrived at the door of the chamber, and perceived a light burning within. He paused, scarcely dared to breathe, and listened attentively, but the only sounds which met his ears convinced him that his intended victim slept soundly, and he ventured to try the door. Raymond had neglected to lock it, and the next moment Sir Horace was standing by his bedside, and gazing upon his countenance with wild and eager eyes. Here, then, the man whom he now so feared and detested was completely at his mercy, and one determined blow would rid him of him. He grasped his knife, and approached nearer the sleeping man; but when he would have struck the fatal blow, a trembling came over him, and his arm fell useless by his side. The groans of his former murdered victims seemed to ring in his ears, and he could imagine the ghastly countenance of his deceased brother in the features of Raymond, reproaching him for the awful deed he contemplated. His resolution was gone, and covering his face with his hands, he groaned in agony, and retreated from the chamber.

When he had regained his own room, he sank exhausted with the power of his feelings in a chair, dashing the knife from him, and giving himself up to all the bitterness of his anguish.

"No, no," he groaned, "I cannot, dare not take his life. I cannot imbrue my hands in his blood; coward that I am, when I had such an opportunity of ridding myself of my fears, and saving my gold. Am I, then, to leave him to triumph? To laugh at me, mock me, and hold me in constant submission to his will? Yes, yes, my dastard fears will not permit me to do the deed, and ruin, shame, and misery is the only prospect before me. Oh, wretch! wretch! now am I, indeed, punished for my crimes. But I, who have dared so much, to tremble now! Curses light upon my weak hand, which could not strike the blow."

Again he arose from his seat, and traversed the apartment with hasty strides, and in a state of mental anguish which it would be impossible for any language, however powerful, to do adequate justice to.

"Would that I could see Martin Trevors," he said, "he might advise me how to act; and, perhaps, contrive some means to remove the object of my fears. Ah! even now it may not be too late to secure myself from Raymond's threats, and to adopt efficient means to prevent him from troubling me again. I will see Trevors in the morning, and then—but no, I have already trusted him too much, and cannot depend upon him. Despair meets me on every side, and the triumph of Raymond is complete. And is it to endure this life of ceaseless misery that I have plunged my soul to perdition? Oh, that I had never sinned, for what is gold ill-gotten? Can it purchase peace—happiness? No. It is a fearful curse that pursues its wretched votaries to destruction. Each glittering coin serves but to add a sting to his overloaded conscience, and to render life a burden to him, that life which, if properly occupied, might have been made a means of happiness to himself, and a blessing to his fellow-creatures." But yet, with all life's misery, the idea of death presented ten thousand more terrors to Sir Horace Middleton, for death was constantly depictured to his restless imagination in ever accumulated and various forms, each surpassing itself in horror. And such is the miser's enjoyment, such, at least, is the only enjoyment which ill-gotten gold can purchase. It becomes, when fettered through crime, perverted from a blessing into a curse.

How often wretched, misguided, avaricious man labours to create the fiends that worry him to madness. How deep does avarice plunge him into the vortex of crime, until life, amidst abundance of the glittering dross for which he has incessantly struggled, becomes a hell to him, and which he only clings to, dreading to meet the still more awful purgatory beyond the grave.

In the moments of his greatest delight, the miser, while gloating o'er his secret treasure, the pile that dazzles as if in mockery, the iron voice of conscience will obtrude and thunder in his ears the horrors of futurity, and his coward soul shrinks amidst even all its earthly wealth.

Such is the certain reward attendant on the miserable wretch's sordid labours, and yet the mad, infatuated fool proceeds until overwhelmed by despair, sinking in destruction, and securing for himself an immortality of execration.

The mind of the guilty is a phantasmagoria of the most hideous images; a frightful exaggeration of all that is horrible in conception, a gloom upon which no light ever breaks, unless it is to render despair still more visible. His whole career is a series of doubts, and suspicions, and apprehensions. The smile of seeming friendship may beam upon him, but it adds to his torture, for he knows himself unworthy of it, and he fears to encourage it, lest his own guilt should be made the more apparent, and detection, shame, and punishment, should follow.

Such was the state of the mind of Sir Horace Middleton on the eventful and awful night we have described. Such were the alternate feelings that harassed his burning brain, and rendered him doubly wretched to what he had been. On every side he found himself foiled, notwithstanding all the pecuniary successes that had attended his crimes. He sinned but for the profit of others who held his life in their keeping, at their mercy, as a security for the faithful fulfilment of his bond. And what was that bond?—the forfeiture of all that bright gold by extortion, which he had waded through blood to obtain possession of. He was their absolute slave. His dreadful secrets were known to them; and once if he dared to refuse their demands, his doom would be sealed—an ignominious death upon the scaffold, a shouting, exulting multitude; the gallows was the only perspective his terrified imagination could contemplate.

And now—oh, most torturing idea!—his nephew, the boy whom he had nurtured from childhood, held him in his power; he mocked at, he triumphed in his sufferings, and would doubtless take every advantage of the knowledge he had obtained. He had told him so—he was about to plunder him of his gold! Yes; but a few hours, and he must yield to his demands, extravagant as they were, or he knew well what the consequences would be. He must pander to his imprudences, or become the inmate of a prison, have all his vices unmasked to the world; stand forward a convicted murderer, clothed in all its most hideous and revolting deformity, and plunged at once into that awful eternity he so dreaded to meet. His life hung upon a thread, or the price which he paid for its preservation. That price might be ruin, and then he would be thrust forth upon the world a poor, helpless, outcast wretch, without the means to purchase security. While he possessed wealth, he felt as though fortified against detection, although it could not procure him peace of mind; and was he to be deprived of that protection by the boy who was already under so many obligations to him, whom he might have left to misery and starvation in his infancy? The thought was madness! What extraordinary weakness was it that had urged him to take under his protection the beggar brat of his brother, when he had discarded his own offspring?

"Oh, idiot, worse than idiot, that I have been!" he exclaimed, "why had I not rather pressed my fingers in his throat, and in infancy stifled the life which was to render me miserable? What saw I in his puling, senseless face to excite my pity or my love? Pity, love!—ha! ha! ha!—no, it must have been mad infatuation, for what have those sentiments to do with my nature? What is their value in the market? I feel shame—shame that I should ever have been so weak. But why should my hand have trembled but now when he slept and was within my power? But one blow, and my secret would have been secured and my gold saved; but now ——"

He started, and looked around him with a pale and ghastly expression of countenance; for again to his terrified imagination strange and fearful sounds were presented, and he could almost swear that solemn voices called him "Villain and murderer!" But it was conscience only that conjured up these ideas, and imparted nameless terrors to every breath of wind that sighed around the building. And now more terrible than ever did he feel it to be alone in that gloomy chamber;

and yet in his present state of mind he would have shrunk from human observation. His every glance, he was convinced, would reveal a dark and guilty history, and hasten the consummation of his fate. One moment he was half inclined to rush forth from the house, and give vent to his feelings in the dark and stilly air, where no one could hear him, where no eye could gaze upon the madness of his actions; but still an irresistible power rivetted him to his chamber, and still he gazed upon its gloomy walls, picturing all sorts of hideous phantoms, and laughing in the frenzy of his horror.

And now another thought equally agonizing rushed upon the brain of the wretched old man. Raymond knew that he possessed gold; he was determined to gratify his avarice, and what might he not dare to do, to rob him at once of his treasure? He might seek his life, and how could he defend himself against him? He shivered at the thought, and tottering to the door of his chamber, narrowly inspected it to see that it was secure from intrusion, but finding it locked and bolted, he became a little more composed, and again resumed his seat.

"No, no," he soliloquized; "he would not dare to make any such attempt, for fear of the punishment that would follow; and how could he save himself from detection? Besides, he would then be foiled in his designs, for he knows not where my money is concealed—no, no, he knows not that, he knows not that—ha! ha! ha! No one knows where my gold is secreted, and therefore am I safe. And yet I wonder that they have not long since forced the secret from me by threatening to denounce me unless I divulged it. Ha! that thought; I tremble to think that it may yet occur to them, and then, indeed, am I lost!"

He pressed his shrivelled hands to his burning temples as these ideas occurred to him, and continued for a few moments lost in maddening meditation.

"But why do I not fly from the dangers which surround me?" he said at length; "why do I not escape to some distant part with my treasure, where I may live unknown, unsuspected? Alas! whither can I fly where those I fear may not find me and wreak upon me their vengeance? So terrible is the power they hold over me, that I dare not brave it—I cannot escape from it. Here must I remain and chance my fate, whatever that fate may be."

Again he groaned as these thoughts crowded upon his bewildered and distressed brain, until at length shivering with cold, and worn out with excitement, he threw himself upon his bed, and pressing his hands upon his eyes, endeavoured to find forgetfulness in sleep. And the miser-murderer did sleep—but oh, what a sleep! Did it afford him any respite from the horrors of his conscience? Did he experience one moment of forgetfulness? Oh, no; forgetful, balmy sleep is only destined for the innocent and care-oppressed victim of unmerited misfortune; the murderer can never know rest. Sleep brought with it but accumulated horrors, and fostering imagination held its court over his heated brain with fiend-like malice.

The guilty wretch fancied himself alone in a spacious cavern lighted by innumerable lamps depending from the roof, and which cast a dazzing reflection upon the glittering treasures it contained. Around and at his feet heaps of gold were piled, as far as his gloating eyes could stretch; all the wealth of the world seemed to be there deposited, and all, all was his. Oh, how the miser clucked and rubbed his bony hands together, as he paced the cavern round and round, and tried in vain to count the innumerable piles; and then he raised it by handsfull, and let it fall again in a brilliant shower, laughing in perfect extacy at the music of its chinking sound.

"All, all is mine!" he shouted. "All, all is mine, and who shall rob me of a single coin? Ha! ha! ha! I am master of all the treasures of the earth, and all mankind must bend the abject slaves to my supreme power."

Suddenly terrific peals of thunder shook the cavern to its centre; the lamps shed forth a blue and ghastly hue, and wherever the glittering heaps of gold had stood but a minute before, the eyes of the appalled miser rested upon grim and ghastly phantoms of every shape, grinning hideously upon him, and pointing their skeleton arms towards him. The cavern resounded with their horrid sepulchral laughter, and the dreamer felt the air hot and scorching as a furnace. He tried to shriek in the horror of his feelings, but the sound was stifled in his throat; then he gazed around for some place of outlet by which he might make his escape; but whichever way his eyes turned, they encountered the same frightful spectres, who shouted in awful exultation at his despair and agony.

At length he gazed towards the end of the cavern, and there beheld an opening which admitted light and air. With a frantic cry he rushed towards it; liberty seemed before him, and oh! how much dearer did that now appear to him than the countless wealth of which he had but a few minutes before imagined himself the master. He had reached to within a few steps of it, when again the thunder rolled, the earth cracked beneath his feet, and there arose before his eyes, to impede his path, a female form in robes of blood-stained white, whose unearthly countenance and hollow eyes froze the very current in his veins, and transfixed him to the spot like a statue. Oh, well did he know those pale, pale features, nor could he remove his eyes from them, so fixed, and powerful, and soul-appalling was their gaze. Once more he tried to shriek, to sink on his knees before the ghastly vision, and implore for mercy, but in vain, and the hollow laughter of the phantoms around mocked his despair.

Suddenly the scene changed, the spectres faded from his sight, the earth appeared to shake under him, the cavern entirely disappeared, and he found himself on a small raft tossed about on the open sea. It was night. Dreadful was the tempest that raged, the mountainous waves roared and foamed, tossing him one moment to the clouds, and the next burying him in their bosoms; but still he remained firm on the raft, as if he was bound there by some inscrutable power, and doomed to endure all the horrors of the storm without the least hope of any termination to his misery. How gladly, the miser imagined in his dream, would he have averted the mercy of immediate death, by plunging at once into the deep; but not a limb could he move, and on he was dashed with the speed of the whirlwind over the terrific billows, amidst the roaring of thunder, and the lightning's frightful glare. Upon the raft was an open chest—its contents were gold, an inexhaustible treasure. Oh, bitter mockery to the wretched votary of avarice in his awful and hopeless situation. His soul shrunk with disgust at the sight, and in the madness of his despair, he shrieked aloud for help, and pressed his nails with agony into his hands until the palms streamed with blood. The howling wind, the roaring waves, and the deafening voice of the thunder, alone replied to his frenzied cries, and still on, on was he driven with the most frightful impetuosity. And what would then the miser have given but for a sight of land, or the prospect of assistance? Even all the riches of which he was now in his dreadful situation possessed, and that wealth which he lately considered himself master of.

And now as he proceeded, hurled along at the sport of the waves, the raging ocean seemed to change to blood, and hideous, shapeless spectres flitted about the raft, and rose upon the crest of every billow, grinning and mocking, and taunting him, with frightful gestures, adding their sepulchral laughter and wailings to the howling of the tempest, and pointing to the purple gulf upon which the wretched man was tossed.

Suddenly, as he imagined, an impenetrable darkness enveloped all around; he felt himself raised by some invisible power to his feet, and hurried along with the greatest rapidity. He was on land—he no longer heard the roaring of the ocean, but still the thunder reverberated in the heavens, and the lightning's broad flash at intervals darted across the earth; but still at present the dreamer was unable to distinguish anything closely; all before him was little better than chaos, and he might almost persuade himself that he was travelling over the regions of space, for his feet seemed scarcely to touch the ground, so quickly was he hurried along.

For a long time this strange journey was continued, but at length the darkness gradually dispersed, and the dreamer beheld himself proceeding along a wide road which seemed to lead to a town. Hundreds of persons were crowding along with the greatest precipitation, and their faces marked with the greatest excitement, as if they were in pursuit of some extraordinary sight, and the miser recognised in several of their countenances persons whom he had seen before. He addressed himself, as he thought, to two or three of them, and inquired where he was, and whither they were going ; but they returned no answer, and seemed not to notice him, but still they hastened on their way, and he was hurried along in the same course by some secret power, which he could not resist.

As he approached nearer the town, he could hear the loud shouts of a vast multitude, intermingled with the solemn tolling of a death-knell, and he imagined that in every tone his name was uttered, coupled with the word " murderer !" How the blood congealed in his veins, and fain would he have stopped in his course, but he could not. Louder and louder grew the shouts, and louder and louder became the tolling of the death bell, until at length he suddenly stopped, and found himself in the midst of an immense crowd of persons, and at that moment felt a hand cold, colder than ice, upon his arm. He looked up, and beheld by his side the grisly phantom of one of his murdered victims, whose hollow eyes were fixed with terrible earnestness upon his countenance.

" Look, look !" it cried, in awful accents ; " behold the reward of avarice, the fate of the miser-murderer !"

The eyes of the dreamer instinctively followed the direction to which the bony fingers of the spectre pointed, and rested on a gallows, beneath which was a cart containing the executioner and the wretched criminal about to suffer. God ! how he trembled ; and in that miserable culprit he saw an exact counterpart of himself, in dress, in form, in feature, everything. But, oh, how ghastly pale and livid was the countenance of that pinioned quivering wretch. And now the hangman proceeds to place the halter around his neck, to affix it to the fatal beam.

" Mercy ! mercy !" shrieked the dreamer, but to his imagination, although he gave utterance to the words, they seemed to proceed from the shadow of himself beneath the gallows. " Mercy ! mercy !" he again implored ; " spare me ! spare me ! do not hang the gray-headed old man ; take all my gold, leave me to beggary, to misery, but let me not die this horrible death !"

Terrific shouts of execration and derision from the assembled multitude followed this appeal, and the hangman proceeded to perform his bloody office. The cart was drawn from under the screaming wretch, and his body swung in convulsive writhings in the air. The dreamer beheld his frightful agonies, his awful death struggles ; he felt them all himself ! a weight of lead was upon his brain—a thousand daggers seemed to pierce his body—sounds more deafening than the loudest thunder vibrated in his ears—his chest was bursting—in vain he tried to breathe—flames of fire danced before his eyes—horror, agony, burst the bonds of sleep, and Sir Horace Middleton sprang from the bed, and sank upon his knees with clasped hands, and the cold drops pouring in torrents down his cheeks.

" Mercy ! mercy !" he shrieked, in tones that resounded through the building. " Save me, save me ! Oh, Christ ! save me ! I must not, will not die. I——"

He could utter no more ; but clasping his forehead with a groan of convulsive agony, he sank prostrate and insensible upon the floor.

Again he recovered his senses, and rising on his knees, looked with a shuddering feeling of horror around him. The grey dawn was just breaking through the window of his chamber ; but to the eyes of the wretched man every object appeared grim, and dismal, and indistinct.

" Where am I ?" he cried ; " do I still live and breathe ? Have, then, my appeals for mercy been heard, and am I saved from that dreadful fate ? In my own chamber ! How is this ? Where is the shouting, the exulting crowd, the fierce executioner, the gallows on which I lately writhed ? Ah ! can it have been only a dream ? Yes, yes ; but, oh ! what a dream ! My blood freezes with horror at the recollection. And is this to be my fate ? Am I not rich, and will not that save me from such a death ? Oh, my brain !"

Once more he covered his face with his hands, and groaned in the anguish of fearful reflection ; then he started suddenly to his feet, and staggered to the door. He tried the lock ; it was secure as he had left it when he had thrown himself on his couch.

" It was but a dream," he ejaculated, " it was but a dream ; but oh, the remembrance of it appals my very soul. And will not my wealth procure me one moment

of peace, of forgetfulness?   Oh, that I again possessed the innocence, the poverty
of youth.   Would that I had never, never sinned, how happy might I now have
been!   But reflection maddens me.   Away with thought! let me endeavour to fly
from myself.   The atmosphere of this room is hot; I cannot breathe; I will inhale
the morning breeze, and try to recover myself."

He slowly and cautiously unlocked the door of his apartment, and issued forth,
securing it after him.   Then he paused in the gallery, and listened, but no sound
met his ears; the inmates of the house were yet wrapped in the arms of sleep, and
he proceeded with silent steps along the gallery, and descended the stairs of the
hall.   He unbolted the door, and emerged into the open air; it came fresh and
reviving to his agitated spirits, strength seemed to be suddenly imparted to his
enfeebled limbs, and he hurried on laughing aloud in the very madness of his joy at
finding himself at liberty.   The poor wretch suddenly rescued from an ignominious
and horrible fate could not have felt greater delight than he did at that moment,
and he continued on his way exulting in the certainty that he was still free, that all
the horrors he had experienced were but the wild creations of his disordered imagination; but still that dream he could not efface from his recollection, and the
consciousness that it might be realised shook his soul with terror.

He was heedless of the way he took, his mind was so completely absorbed in his
own thoughts; but at length he paused to take breath, and found himself standing
upon the cliffs to which he had so often wandered, with the ocean stretched wide
before him.   Calm and unruffled were the waves, and the first golden streak of day
was just appearing in the eastern horizon, casting a chaste and mellow reflection
upon the clear blue waters.

But no charms had this lovely scene for the mind of the guilty miser, and with
his arms folded across his chest, he gazed for a time with a listless eye upon all
around him.   Then all the horrors of his dream rushed upon his memory, and to
his distracted imagination the ocean again appeared raging in all the fury of that
dreadful tempest to which in his vision he had been exposed.   He could fancy himself once more bound and rivetted to that fatal raft, tossed and dashed about at the
mercy of the contending elements, a thing of hatred and the vengeance of offended
Heaven.   Again he heard the voice of " the ethereal lion ;" the lightning blazed
around him, and he tried to shriek for mercy and for help in vain.   And now the
same ghastly phantom flitted about him, the same unearthly cries vibrated in his
ears, and he fell prostrate on the spot where he had been standing, overpowered by
the insupportable horrors of his distempered fancy.

He recovered, and once more rising to his feet, he wiped the perspiration from his
temples, and gazed around him.

"It was but imagination," he said; "but oh, how horrible!   Cannot I fly anywhere from thought?   Is my brain ever to be distracted by these fearful images?
Die on the gallows!   Never!   Have I not the means of rescuing myself from such
a fate, and ending at once this misery?   One plunge into these deep waters, and all
is over.   Over! oh, no!   In this world it would be, but how could I meet that
terrible eternity?   Ah, no! I dare not die; I must still live on, though my life be
worse than a state of living death."

He paused, and clasped his forehead in anguish; then he remembered the trial he
had to undergo that day, and his very soul trembled again.

" I must meet that hated, daring boy," he said; " I must yield to his demands;
he will extort from me my gold, and I can see no way to avoid him.   Oh, weak fool
that I am, how have I entangled myself by my own misguided conduct!   Had I
never burthened myself with him, even now I might have been safe, and have set
detection boldly at defiance.   How shall I act?—what can I do?   My brain is bewildered with my own thoughts.   Should I again appeal to his mercy and forbearance?   Pshaw! that would be useless; he would only again mock at my supplications,
insist upon my compliance with his demands, or threaten me with the gallows.
And am I to sue to this boy, my own nephew, the wretched dependant on my
charity and benevolence?   The idea is madness.   Oh! why did my hand tremble
when he lay helpless before me?   Why did I not strike the blow which would have

rid me of these fears? Despicable coward that I am, I richly merit all that may befall me. There is but one way in which I could rescue myself from his power, for I dare not trust the whole of my thoughts to Martin Trevors. Could I but see the dreaded being with whom I am connected, he might be safely removed on board the vessel, and would never trouble me again. But it is too late now, and it is useless for me to think of it. I have nothing to do but to yield, for Raymond's triumph is, alas! too secure. But the sun has arisen; my absence from the house may be discovered, and suspicions dangerous to my peace and security be excited. I must return, and endeavour to find courage to meet him."

He turned away from the spot as he spoke, and slowly retraced his steps to the Manor-house, vainly trying to gather resolution as he proceeded. He dreaded the interview with his nephew, but yet he well knew that there was no way of avoiding it; but the idea of parting with so large a sum of money as Raymond had demanded tortured him worse than all.

" Could I persuade him to postpone his resolutions, if only for a few days," he muttered to himself, " I might then find some means, devise some plan to defeat him altogether, and rid myself of him entirely. He must not be suffered thus to triumph over me, without at least another effort on my part. Thoughtless idiot that I was, not to discover that he was watching me last night, then this would not have happened. He would still have remained in ignorance of my secrets, and from him, at any rate, I should have been safe."

He now arrived at the manor-house, and entered by a private door, of which he possessed the key. He passed on quietly towards his chamber, and from the still-ness which reigned in the house, he was inclined to think that neither Raymond or his two domestics had yet arisen, so that he might still have some time left him to reflect, and prepare himself for the meeting.

When he had entered his room, and secured the door, he sat himself in a chair, and for a short time remained buried in profound and torturing thought.

" It is no use," he said at length ; " I see no means of escaping, no way to avoid the demands of this bold, extravagant, and ungrateful boy. Should I dare to refuse him, what can I expect but that he will immediately put his threats into execution, and then I am lost, ruined, destroyed. Oh, this is as bad as the torments of the damned ! But I must arouse myself ; it is needless to give vent to these vain re-grets ; I have brought myself into a snare from which I cannot escape, and must endeavour to make the best of a bad bargain. He must not know where my money is concealed, so I must be prepared to meet him. Now's the time, when I am alone, and no one can observe me."

He advanced to the chest, and removing it, opened the secret trap, and, with eager eyes, once more gazed upon his treasure. As he did so, his frightful dream flashed upon his memory, and he could almost fancy he again beheld the hideous forms that had so appalled his imagination, grinning upon him from the secret aper-ture, and he turned away with a sickening sensation of horror. But he quickly re-covered himself, and, with a trembling hand, took from the depository ten canvas bags, each containing one hundred guineas, which he placed before him, and gazed at them for some few minutes with a melancholy earnestness of expression, and sighing deeply. Then he counted them over,—

" One, two, three, four, five, six, seven."

And so on till he came to the last, when he sighed more deeply than before, and beat his breast in agony and regret.

" Ten !" he ejaculated ; " ten teeming bags of the bright yellow gold !—one thousand guineas !—one thousand ! each coin of which has been obtained by care, anxiety, crime ! And must these be given to an improvident boy, on whom I have, in my generous fondness, already expended so much ? My darling hoard, must I so recklessly and cruelly impoverish ye ? The curse of hell light upon the mischance which compels me to do it. And year after year, day after day, will ye be di-minished, hard-earned treasures of my soul, till I have not one to gladden my eyes, and the poor old man will be left a beggar. Oh, that thought !—it drives me to distraction. And must I, indeed, part with ye ? They might as well rob me of life as to plunder me of my gold ! Life !—no, no, no—not of life ; I dare not think of dying, for I feel that there is a terrible eternity beyond the grave, and that I am not prepared to enter into it. But it must be so ; Fate has conspired against me, and I have no other alternative but to yield to the fearful necessity."

With another sigh, Sir Horace placed the bags of gold in a small cabinet, and then closing the trap-door, replaced the chest over it, and, re-seating himself, be-came once more lost in meditation.

He was aroused from his lethargy by a knock at his chamber door, and, starting hastily up, he demanded who was there.

" It is only I, Sir Horace," answered the voice of old Grisselda. " Breakfast is ready, and young master awaits your appearance with much ——"

" D——n your young master !" passionately exclaimed the baronet ; but in a mo-ment recollecting himself, he added,—

" Well, well, begone ; I will attend directly."

The old woman departed, without venturing to make any farther observation, and Sir Horace paced the room for a few moments in a state of the greatest agitation.

"He awaits my appearance with much impatience," he said; "no doubt he does —curses light on him. Oh, had I not been a coward-fool, he would not have had an opportunity of beholding me again. Now then for the meeting, from which I shrink with dread. But away with this cowardice; I must try to be firm, and put on a bold front, or he will not fail to take advantage of it, and force me to compliance with his every will and demand."

He tried to assume an air of composure and determination as he spoke, but he succeeded very badly, and any one who had seen him at that moment must have noticed the agitation to which his mind was a prey.

He left his room, and made his way to the apartment in which the breakfast was prepared; but he paused at the door, and hesitated, as he heard his nephew carelessly singing the burthen of a song, and all his apprehensions were renewed with redoubled force. He entered; Raymond left off singing, and fixed his eyes with a peculiar expression upon the cadaverous countenance of his uncle, who shrunk from the glance, held down his head, and with difficulty took his place at the table, trembling at heart, as though he had been arraigned at the bar of justice to answer for all the crimes he had committed.

Raymond watched him for a few moments in silence, and while a feeling of disgust and contempt arose in his breast towards the miserable, guilty old man, he exulted in the triumph he had obtained, and the certainty of the success of the designs he had in contemplation.

"Well, Sir Horace," he said at length, in a sarcastic tone, "I hope you slept well after your exertions last night?"

The baronet started and looked at him aghast, and his lips quivered with extraordinary emotion as he faltered out,—

"Slept—slept; oh, it was a sleep; may I never experience such another. But torture me not, Raymond; you mock me, and —— but no more, no more. Talk of something else."

"Aye, uncle," returned Raymond, "we shall have something else to talk of presently."

"Not here," gasped forth the old man, looking round him timidly, as if he expected or feared that some one was listening to them.

"Well, well, I am not particular," said Raymond, with the utmost indifference, and exulting in the emotion and alarm which his wretched relative exhibited; "of course you do not forget your promise and your oath?"

"No, no—forbear, forbear!"

Raymond could scarcely repress a laugh of scorn, but he remained silent, and suffered his uncle to indulge undisturbed in the thoughts which tortured him. The repast was finished, Sir Horace having scarcely eaten a morsel, or once removed his eyes from the floor, when Raymond arose and said,—

"Now, uncle, to business."

The old man started, turned more ghastly pale than before, and in a trembling voice faltered out,—

"To business, Raymond! what—what mean you?"

"Psha! this is trifling; you understand me; just now you said you had not forgotten your oath."

"Alas, alas!"

"It is no use repenting now. Shall I attend you to your chamber? if not, we must discuss the business here."

"Oh, no, not for worlds," ejaculated the alarmed and trembling Sir Horace; "we might be overheard, and if we were ——"

"Why," added Raymond, with a sarcastic smile, "it might not be altogether so well for one of us. Lead the way, Sir Horace."

"Bethink yourself, Raymond, reflect; you are not cruel, I know, do not then be ungenerous."

"What folly is this? I thought I made you perfectly understand me last night.

"Give me but a few days to consider."

"Not a day; not another hour!"

"Oh, this is most unkind."

"I have no time to waste; I want to depart from the manor-house, I have better sport in view than I can meet with here."

"But you are not going to leave me so soon, are you, dear Raymond?" said the baronet, in whining, hypocritical accents.

"Aye, this very day," answered his nephew; "I dare say you will be very sorry to be rid of my presence."

"Yes, yes, Raymond, for it is a long time since we met before, and you know ——"

"Bah! to business, to business."

"Raymond," said the old man, mustering some semblance of courage, "you treat me with cruel ingratitude; I have protected you, provided for you from childhood, when you had no other friend in the world, and is this the way you would repay me?"

"Aye."

"By plundering me of my gold."

"Your gold!" repeated Raymond, with a bitter sneer.

"Yes, my gold, my precious, hard-earned gold," replied Sir Horace, with increased firmness; "but what if I now refuse to comply with your demands?"

"Why then you know the consequences," answered Raymond; "beware, old man, your gold would not save your neck from the halter should your guilty deeds be made known."

"Oh, Raymond, you surely would not, could not be so cruel as to denounce your own uncle, your kind benefactor."

"I will adhere to my promise; you know best whether it would be prudent or not to remain faithful to yours."

"I will make a fair, a handsome provision for you, Raymond, and when I am no more all that I possess you know will be yours."

"I have already made the bargain," answered Raymond, "and to no other will I agree. Come, I am tired of this delay."

Sir Horace groaned, and cast a piteous, imploring look at his nephew, but he saw that it was useless to appeal to him, that he was perfectly inexorable and determined, and he slowly moved from the room, and led the way to his chamber, followed by Raymond. When they had entered it he locked the door, and sinking into a chair he became lost in despair and agony.

"Come, Sir Horace," said Raymond, after a brief pause, "this is no time for the display of these emotions; I came here to act with promptitude and decision, and I expect you to do the same. I want money, and I must and will have it; give me my demand, and, so far as I am concerned, your guilt will remain a secret from mortal knowledge."

"Raymond, dear Raymond," cried the miserable old man, sinking on his knees, "I implore your mercy, I humbly supplicate you to relent, and not to persist in bringing me to misery and want in my old days."

"Were I to do so it would be no more than a just punishment for the crimes you have committed," returned the inexorable young man; "but we have talked enough on this subject. You will find that Raymond Middleton, your *dear* nephew, is a man of his word. The gold, the gold!"

"No, no, recollect it is a large sum—a very large sum, one thousand guineas!"

"Aye, not a coin less."

"Consider, dear Raymond, consider."

"I have considered, and once for all I tell you, that if you dare refuse to fulfil your oath, before another hour has passed over your head, you shall be the inmate of a gaol."

Sir Horace groaned, and writhed his body in agony, and again he looked imploringly in his nephew's face, as he ejaculated,—

"Oh, Raymond, and can you forget that it is the brother of your own father whom you thus threaten? Can you have entirely steeled your heart to every feeling of pity ?"

" It is not Sir Horace Middleton who should expect pity from his fellow creatures," answered Raymond. " Think of your crimes, old man, and then ask for compassion if you dare."

" From you, at least, I should expect it, Raymond. Spare me."

" What a waste of time is this," said Raymond, impatiently. " Do you refuse?"

" No, no—but ——"

" The money then."

" And must it indeed be so ? Will nothing move you to relent ?"

" Nothing."

" Hard-hearted youth," cried the baronet, rising from his knees, " you will repent this, depend upon it you will."

" Well, I am willing to run the risk of that," replied Raymond, recklessly ; " however, every iota of our agreement I am determined to have fulfilled."

The old man again groaned, and then slowly advancing to the cabinet, he brought forth the bags containing the money, one by one, and placed them on the table before Raymond, who counted them over to see that they were correct.

" And these bags each contain a hundred guineas ?" he demanded.

" Alas, alas !" sighed Sir Horace, " and of these you are about to rob me."

" Well, be it so," returned Raymond, " I am not very particular about terms at present."

He untied the bags one by one, and inspected their contents to satisfy himself there was no deception, and while he was doing this, Sir Horace swayed his body to and fro in his chair, in a state of the greatest mental excitement and despair.

" Ah !" said Raymond, unable to conceal his exultation, " here is the gold, and now for the agreement."

"The agreement ?"

" Ay, for the annuity ; you cannot have forgotten that was a part of the bargain which you swore to fulfill."

" Raymond, Raymond !" cried the distracted baronet, " you will not persist in this ; I cannot, and will not believe that you will."

"Psha! no more trifling ; a bargain's a bargain, and I am determined that you shall not escape from the fulfilment of your's to the very letter."

" Wretch !" exclaimed the old man, unable to contain his rage, " I will grant you no more, you shall not force it from me."

" Are you mad ?" demanded Raymond.

" Yes, your villany—your monstrous extortions, drive me mad. I have already given you a fortune—a splendid fortune, and I will not submit to be further plundered."

" Very well," returned Raymond, with the most hardened coolness, " since you prefer the gallows, e'en take your choice. I go this moment to denounce you as a murderer."

He moved towards the door as he spoke when Sir Horace, worked up to a pitch of frenzy, rushed after him, and laying his hand on his arm to arrest him in his purpose, while his face exhibited the utmost terror, he cried,—

" No, hold—hold ! Raymond, nephew, forbear ! you cannot—will not do this. You would not have the blood of your own relation upon your head. Oh, for the love of Christ ! relinquish your cruel purpose."

" Think you I am to be foiled ?" demanded Raymond, sternly.

" But, Raymond ——"

" Here are writing materials, do you consent to sign the deed ?"

" I—I would, but ——"

" No equivocation ; the word yes or no."

" Yes—yes, I—I do consent ; Heaven help me !"

" Heaven help you ! ha, ha, ha !" laughed Raymond, scornfully, " you are a worthy being to appeal to Heaven."

" Oh, do not mock me."

" Write as I shall dictate to you," said Raymond, impatiently, placing the materials before him ; " this task accomplished, the business is settled."

The miser took up the pen, but his hand trembled so violently, that for a moment or two he could not guide it on the paper. Raymond commenced, and Sir Horace, with much difficulty, wrote as he dictated, and when he had completed the arduous task, he sank back in his chair quite exhausted and overcome by his emotions, and the wretched old man sobbed as if his very heart would break.

A sardonic smile of triumph overspread the countenance of Raymond, as he took up the paper, and read the contents, then, carefully folding it, and placing it in his bosom, he exclaimed,—

" 'Tis well; by this you agree to allow me annually the sum of five hundred guineas, Sir Horace, on the condition that I keep inviolable certain secrets that have come to my knowledge. Thus the business is settled, and you are safe."

" Safe—safe !" repeated the baronet, with a ghastly look ; " villain! robber ! have you not brought me to ruin ? Of what value now is life to me ?"

" Well," coolly returned Raymond, " if you are tired of it, you can easily rid yourself of it; for my own part, I mean to enjoy mine, so I will just take the liberty of placing the money in this empty box, and then I will bid you farewell, *dear* uncle, for one year, at least."

Having thus ironically and scornfully addressed himself to the trembling old man, Raymond proceeded to place the bags of gold in a small empty box which stood on the side-board, and locking it, said,—

" There, that is all secure, and now, Sir Horace, our interview is at an end, for which I dare say you are not sorry. I am obliged to you for your generosity, and depend upon it, I shall make the most liberal use of it. In less than another hour I shall depart from the Manor-house, and leave you to enjoy yourself in your own peculiar way."

Every word that Raymond uttered went to his uncle's heart ; never had he felt so truly miserable and degraded as he did at that moment, for he saw the scorn and detestation in which his profligate nephew held him, and he pictured to himself a long series of annoyances and threats, and dangers that were in store for him from him alone. He bit his lips, and the rage and emotion he experienced for some moments choked his utterance.

" Raymond, ungrateful boy," he said at length, " most assuredly a bitter curse will pursue you for this. The gold you have thus extorted from me by intimidation will do you no good, it ——"

" At any rate," interrupted Raymond, " I have obtained it in as honest a way as yourself, and I have not committed murder to ——"

" Raymond, Raymond !" gasped forth the agitated Sir Horace, shuddering with conscious guilt, and his face becoming as livid as that of a corpse, " oh, forbear, forbear, you have obtained your demands, do not torture me thus."

" Why do you provoke me to it, old man ? But before I go, I once more warn you to remember your oath, dare not to attempt to remove one article from the cavern, for although I may be far away from you your every action will be known to me, and should you venture to break your compact in the slightest degree, so sure will I denounce you to the world in your true character. You are now acquainted with my mind, and from my present conduct you may feel convinced that I am determined. Adieu. When we next meet, you will see me in a different character to that you have hitherto known me."

" No pity, no mercy !" groaned the miser.

" You deserve neither.'

" And this from a boy that I have cherished as if he were my own son."

" Ay," returned Raymond, with the utmost coolness.

" Raymond," said the baronet, who began to feel more alarmed than ever at his manner, " tell me, whither are you going, and what are your intentions ?"

" That is my business, and I do not choose to make you acquainted with it," answered the former. " No doubt you will hear from me quite as soon you wish."

" There is a strange, a fearful ambiguity in your words which I cannot unravel."

"Possibly not. Adieu."

"Stay, stay, Raymond, do not leave me in this dreadful state of doubt and suspense."

"I have told you all that I intend for the present; it depends entirely upon yourself as to what shall be my future course."

"Upon me, Raymond?"

"Yes, upon the manner in which you keep your oath. Recollect that."

"The curse of hell has fallen upon me!" said the old man, wringing his hands, and with a shudder of horror.

"Well, I leave you to draw your own conclusions upon that subject," replied Raymond; "once more I bid you farewell, until we meet again."

"May that never be," muttered Sir Horace to himself, and he sank back in his chair, quite overcome by the power of his emotions. Raymond took up the box, and fixing a mingled look of scorn and triumph upon the miser, he pointed to the room door, to which his uncle tottered and unlocked it, and he then departed.

Sir Horace sank on his knees with clasped hands, and for some time his bosom, heaved with the most convulsive sobs, whilst the tears trickled fast down his aged and furrowed cheeks. Oh, there is something truly melancholy in seeing an old man weep, and it must surely have melted any heart to pity, guilty even as he was to have beheld the venerable baronet at that moment. But the poor wretch wept in terror and vexation, not in remorse. For some minutes he continued in this manner, and unable to articulate a syllable; but at last, still remaining on his knees, he exclaimed, in the most piteous accents,—

"Gone—gone—and taken my gold—my bright, my beautiful, and precious gold. One thousand bright guineas; oh, each one of those guineas of which he has thus mercilessly plundered me, is a drop of blood from the old man's heart. Oh, agony agony! He mocked me, too; he holds me in his power as well as the rest, and when the sources are dried up, when he and they have exhausted them—impoverished me—drained them dry, when I can no longer pander to their avarice, when they have robbed me of all it has cost me so much care and anxiety, they—they will resign me to the gallows! They will leave my old bones to blanch on the gibbet, and laugh to the unearthly music of the frame that contains my mouldering remains, as it swings and rattles in the midnight wind."

He paused, for a chill like that of death came over his frame; a thousand fiends seemed worrying at his bewildered brain, grinning and rendering more vivid the horrible anticipation his distempered imagination had conjured up. A mist rolled before his eyes, which burned in their sockets, and he could see nothing but the grim phantoms created by his conscience. His wrinkled, withered hands ploughed the air as if they would grasp at something which still was not tangible; then he covered his face with them, and the wretched old man sobbed such heavy, hollow sobs, that seemed as if they could emanate from a breaking heart, from such a heart as has experienced unmerited wrong, and would court release from further oppression in the cold, yet tranquil grave. But were, on the contrary, those sobs those of remorse, of repentance—of one who sincerely feels the weight of his crimes, and would fain make all the atonement in his power to his fellow-creatures, and still live to become a better man? No; they sprang alone from sordid regret, from mortified avarice, and the demon was still reigning uppermost in that old man's breast which for so many years had been his idol, and had plunged him so deeply in guilt.

A short interval of silence ensued, only interrupted by the hollow moans and sobs of the miserable baronet, and during which time drops of perspiration and emotion chased each other down his furrowed cheeks, and his whole frame was convulsed with the same agony as the wretched culprit experiences on the point of execution; at length he suddenly started to his feet in a delirium of despair, and gazing vacantly around him, with clenched hands and quivering brow, he ejaculated,—

"He will betray me!—I marked the deep meaning in his countenance; and when he has gone, I know not whither, he will denounce me as a murderer, and bring me to condign punishment. Oh, fool, weak fool that I was, not to bury my knife in his heart when he lay helpless, unconscious, at my mercy. But he has not yet left the mansion; cannot I recall him to my presence and induce him, under some specious pretext, to remain? But another night, if he stayed here, and let whatever might be the consequences that followed, it should be his last; and I might gain the restitution of my money as well as silencing him for ever. Ha!—I I—I will recall him; I—I will coax him, wheedle him, and—nephew! dear nephew! good Raymond, come back, and ——"

He half advanced to the door of the chamber as he spoke, but returned again to the spot he had quitted in despair.

"Fool! fool!" he cried, "of what avail would be my arts, my entreaties, my promises? He would only mock at me the more, for have I not tried him and found him inflexible? He is going I know not whither; he has heard me acknowledge myself a murderer; he has got the proof in his charge, and I dare not remove them, for he has said that he shall have constant spies upon my actions, and should I do so, he will immediately reveal my guilt to the world; nor can I, dare I, doubt that he will keep his word. Would that I had some trusty friend who would track his footsteps and perform my bidding; he would not long live to triumph. Martin Trevors—no, I fear that man, and dare not confide to him my wishes. Oh! I am foiled every way. And this is the viper I have cherished for so many years to sting me at last. This is he my charity has supported, whom I snatched from misery and starvation in infancy, and warmed, and nurtured him into life and manhood, to pursue me in my old days, as a demon, to destruction. May lightnings blast the being I have reared!"

He gnashed his teeth, and compressed his lips, while every feature was distorted, and the expression of his livid countenance was truly unearthly and frightful to look upon. The hurricane of his passion was at its full height, and overwhelmed him with its violence. He staggered to a chair, into which he sank as feeble and powerless as an infant.

He was suddenly aroused by hearing the clattering of horses' hoofs on the pavement of the yard in front of the mansion, and starting from his seat at the sound, the meaning of which he immediately anticipated, he staggered to the window, which he dashed open hastily, and looked out, and no sooner had he done so than he beheld Raymond on horseback, and about to depart.

"Raymond—nephew—dear Raymond!" he almost shrieked.

Raymond looked up at the sound of his uncle's voice, but his countenance betrayed the utmost malignity and exultation, and he urged on his horse to depart.

"Raymond! Raymond!" shouted the baronet, in still more frenzied accents than before; "stay!—stay!—but a moment—just to speak one word in kindness, dear nephew; but a single word."

Raymond laughed aloud in mockery of his supplications, and waving his hand derisively, galloped off, and dashing through the open gates, was immediately hidden from the distracted baronet's sight.

For a few moments the old man clang to the window unable to move, and his eyes glaring wildly in the direction his nephew had taken; then staggering from it, he once more sank in his seat, and became completely lost in the distraction of his thoughts.

"'Tis all over," he at length said, in a subdued tone of the most abject despair; "the ingrate, the villain, has triumphed completely, and I am left alone to misery and all the horrors of anticipation. Is there no one to pursue him, and force him to return? No, no, I'm mad. Bar the doors—let no one enter—there are officers—I will not be taken—bring back my gold! Ha! ha! ha!"

Nature could support no more; the wretched man's feelings had been put to a trial beyond their strength, and with an hysterical laugh that resounded through the building, he fell prostrate and insensible upon the floor.

CHAPTER VII.

THE PIRATES' RETREAT.—MARTIN TREVORS.—THE PLOT.

THE darkness of night had fallen upon the earth, and the piercing cold and fast falling snow rendered it such a night as would make the comforts of a blazing fire still more duly appreciated, and must bring despair and death to the wretched wanderer, who unfortunately should be exposed to the inclemency of the weather.

The scene was a spacious cavern, apparently hewn out of the solid rock, and so, in fact, it was, but communicated by a secret way with a small pot-house, kept by a sturdy-looking fellow, commonly called Red Ralph, from the fiery hue of his hair, and the general cast of whose features was of that repulsive and ominous description that rendered him a gentleman whom very few travellers would feel much inclined to meet with in the dark.

Now what the real character of a hostelry on that lonely part of the sea-coast was likely to be, it would require no great stretch of imagination to conjecture; in fact, it was well known; but although Red Ralph had received frequent visits from the revenue officers, they had never been able to detect him in any contraband traffic, the reason of which was that they were so keen sighted to their own peculiar interests, that they were necessarily blind to the faults of certain individuals who in secret supported them.

But it is not at present with the house we have to do, but with the cavern to which we have alluded, and which was so artfully contrived that it might very easily escape suspicion, while it afforded every facility for the transactions which were carried on in it. It was wide and lofty, and at the further end was a secret aperture which communicated immediately to the sea-shore, but was concealed from observation by several old chests being piled against it. The cavern received light and air from several natural fissures. Kegs, chests, powder casks, and various articles of apparel, were strewn promiscuously about; nor was the place deficient of arms of every description, which was a plain proof, if any were wanting, that the persons who frequented the cavernous abode were prepared to defend themselves, should their secret congregations be intruded upon by any impertinent customers.

At night the place received light from several lamps, that were hung about in different directions, and a stove of ample dimensions afforded warmth in the winter.

This extraordinary place had, doubtless, existed for many, many years, but in what manner Red Ralph became acquainted with it, we have no means of showing; but probably the secret had been imparted to him by some of his former associates, and certainly a more efficient proprietor could not possibly have been appointed.

On the night of which we are writing the scene in the cavern presented a singularly characteristic appearance. In the centre was a table, rudely formed, at which several men were seated, whose countenances displayed anything but the more amiable qualities of human nature; but who seemed determined to enjoy themselves, if a person might judge from the profuse display of jugs and glasses that were spread before them, and the rude mirth which animated their hardy features. At each end of the table was a keg of Hollands, to which each man applied to replenish his glass when it was empty, and when the said kegs, or, rather, the contents of them, were exhausted, they were quickly replaced by others, which were fully qualified to render the same service.

Other men were lolling carelessly and indolently about in various parts of the cavern, some on chests, others seated on casks, smoking and drinking at their leisure. All seemed bent upon hilarity, and loud peals of the most boisterous and hearty laughter frequently shook the cavern. Red Ralph was seated at the head of the table, and was one of the most prominent in promoting the mirth, and in assisting to dispatch the exhilarating beverage with which they were so well supplied.

"Ha! ha! ha!" he laughed, in reply to some observation that had been made by one of his companions, "you say right, Dick Scud; I never hear the wind rattle, as it does now around this old cavern, but I consider it the bosun's whistle piping all hands to splice the main brace, and you know we are never willing to disobey orders; so off with the grog, my lads, for thanks to the daring fellows with whom we are connected, we have a sea of good stuff at our command which can never be exhausted. So toss it off, boys, and d—n the fellow who first cries avast!"

"A toast—a toast!" shouted two or three of the men.

"Ay, a toast; I'll give you one, my lads, with all my heart," answered Red Ralph; "here's

"To the rovers of the sea,
Unshackled and free,
Wherever they be!"

Every glass was raised in an instant, and every tongue responded to the toast in the most vociferous manner.

" Bravo, Ralph," exclaimed the man who had been designated Dick Scud ; " a capital toast, and I respond to it with all my heart. Lor', how little do the swabs who talk about enjoyment, and pay taxes, and all that sort of thing, dream about such a snug little cabooce as this. I must give you another toast ; here's ' Success to the Reckless, and all her daring crew!' "

" Bravo! bravo!" shouted every voice. " Success to the Reckless and her daring crew !"

This toast was done full honours to, the same as the preceding one.

" A better craft never ploughed the ocean," continued Dick Scud. " I say, what would the land swabs give to know her real character now, as she rides at anchor in the offing?"

" Right, right," coincided two or three of the men.

" Ay, Dick." said Red Ralph ; " but I am much mistaken if she will not spread her character far and wide on the ocean, and even prove a rival to that Davy s craft, the Death Ship."

" Avast, there, mate," interposed one of the fellows ; " compliments are very well, but it's no use talking about rivalling the Death Ship, which sets all power at defiance, and to which any other vessel is no more to be compared than a cock boat to a seventy-four."

" Well, well, you may be right, Joe Hatchway," said Dick Scud ; " and perhaps you know something more about her than we do, so ——"

" I !" exclaimed Joe, starting to his feet, and looking enraged at his companion ; " d—n it, you don't mean to say that I ——"

" Come, come ; belay, belay," interposed Red Ralph ; " we must have no quarrelling. And what if you should know more about her than any of us ? what's the odds ? Is she not of the same trade as your craft ? and, therefore, there is no occasion to grumble about superiority. Come, follow my example, and drink away ; there's nothing like grog ; why, it has been mother's milk to me ; I was nursed at a keg, and I took it so natural, and was so fond of it, that I have never been weaned ever since, and do not expect that I shall for the rest of my days."

" Well said, Ralph," observed two or three of the men.

" And now," resumed Ralph, " perhaps Dick Scud will give us a song, a regular rattling one, in which we can all join chorus."

" Ay, ay," answered Dick, " with all my heart;" and then, in a voice far more noisy than melodious, he sang the following words :—

" Spread the broad sails, and away, away,
 Far over the boundless deep ;
Wealth is our goal ; then, on for our prey,
 And a wary look-out we'll keep.
She's as brave a bark as ever was launched
 O'er the ocean waves to skip ;
Her guns are true, and her men are staunch ;
 What can match with the Pirate Ship ?

CHORUS.
" Drink, drink, drink ! with shout and with glee,
To the bonny wild rover of the sea !

" Through breaker and tempest, see how she rides,
 And battles the furious wind ;
Plunder her aim ; all fear she derides,
 In seeking that gold to find.
A sail, a sail ! ha, ha ! my boys !
 Bear down ! how we'll make 'em skip ;
For there is not a vessel afloat, my boys,
 That can conquer the Pirate Ship !

CHORUS.
" On, on ! more than devils, indeed, they must be,
That can match the wild Rover of the Sea !

" We gain, we gain ! in vain she tries
     To elude the destined fray ;
Over the billows our bark she flies ;
     On, on, away and away !
Ha, ha ! my lads, we near her now,
     She cannot give us the slip ;
A broadside ! the quality just to show
     Of the daring Pirate Ship !

CHORUS.
" We have her ! we board her so bold and free !
Hurrah ! for the Rover of the Sea !

" ' Quarter ! quarter !' they shriek in vain ;
     Of mercy we are bereft ;
At 'em, my bloodhounds, again and again,
     'Till there is not a lubber left !
She's ours ! and sure such a noble prize
     Were worthy a twelvemonth's trip.
Scuttle her, sink her ; in spite their cries,
     She's a prey to the Pirate Ship !

CHORUS.
" Drink, drink, drink ! with shout and with glee,
To the bonny wild Rover of the Sea !

The most boisterous acclamations followed this song, which made the cavern resound again.

" Bravo, Dick !" said Red Ralph ; " a capital song, a capital song. But when do you expect the young skipper ?"

" Why, to night," answered Dick ; " it is the time he promised to rejoin us, and I don't care how soon, for it might be dangerous for us to remain here much longer."

" Oh, there is no fear of that," returned Ralph ; " the land sharks have not the least suspicion. This will be the first trip he will have made with you, will it not ?"

" Yes, and we have yet to try his mettle ; but I think he is one of the right sort, and that we shall have no reason to complain of him. Our late captain would not have appointed him as his successor had he thought so."

" True," coincided Ralph ; " but it was rather extraordinary that the captain should leave the command of the vessel to so young a man, and who was a stranger to you all."

" It is," returned Dick ; " but it was his dying wish, and we must not disobey it. I believe this Raymond Middleton had rendered him some service, or he was somehow connected with him ; but I do not know the particulars."

" It is strange that he should leave the regular service to take the command of a pirate, especially when he might have lived like a prince at that rich old shark, his uncle's expense."

" Ay, so it is," observed Dick Scud ; " and therefore we ought to think all the better of him ; besides, he may still enrich us from the old swab's coffers, and that is something to be considered."

" Considered, be d—d !" cried Joe Hatchway, with a dissatisfied look. " I should think that the captain might have thought of one of those who had shared with him in every danger throughout so many years before this youngster."

" Grumbling again, Joe ; avast, avast," said Dick.

" Avast yourself, Dick," growled Joe ; " why should I put my jawing tackle under hatches any more than yourself ? I say we have cause to grumble."

" Ay, ay," responded two or three voices.

" Who had so much right to the ship as ourselves ?" demanded Joe.

" True, true," again shouted several of the pirates.

" Beware, beware, messmates !" said Dick ; " this mutinous language may do us harm."

" Mutinous !" repeated Joe, with a sneer.

" Yes," returned Dick ; " have we not acknowledged him for our commander?"

" You may."

" And you have."

" Perhaps I might contradict you. I do not much fancy owning as a commander a beardless boy."

" Avast, avast," again remonstrated Dick Scud ; " it would be madness for us to quarrel about this matter."

" Perhaps it would," growled Joe, sulkily.

" Besides, it is only right that we should give him a fair trial," added Scud.

" True," coincided Red Ralph.

" And what then ?" demanded Joe.

" Why," returned Dick, " if he should not turn out all that we have a right to expect, we have then the power in our own hands to dispossess him."

" Ay, that is reasonable enough," observed Ralph. " Besides, he may bring you wealth extorted from the coffers of his miserly uncle."

" Well," returned Joe Hatchway, in the same dissatisfied tones, " do as you please ; I have still my opinion, and we shall soon see which is right."

" Well, let the matter drop for the present," advised Ralph ; " the wind continues to blow smartly, and I do not think we shall have the young skipper here to-night."

" And a very pretty skipper he will make, if he is afraid of a capfull of wind," sneered Joe.

" Psha !" returned Scud, " it seems you are determined to be contrary to-night, Joe. But come, we will talk no more about this ; let us have some more grog, Ralph, and if Raymond do not shortly arrive, we must return to the vessel, for the lads in whose charge she is left, will not be very well pleased at our lengthened absence."

They replenished their glasses, and were preparing to drink, when a shrill whistle was heard outside the cavern.

" Ah !" exclaimed Dick, " the signal—it is he."

The signal was repeated, and then the pirates took away the chests that closed the aperture, and a man entered, whose person was enveloped in a long cloak.

" Ah ! who have we here?" demanded the pirates, fiercely, drawing their swords, and instantly surrounding the intruder with the most threatening gestures.

" Hold !" cried the man, throwing off his cloak ; " what would you do ?"

" Martin Trevors !" cried the pirates, in a breath.

" Ay," returned Martin, with a satirical grin ; " one of your best friends."

" One of our best friends," repeated Dick Scud ; " I know not that."

" But I do," said Martin, " and so does Red Ralph here. Is he come yet ?'

" Who do you mean?"

" Who should I mean ? Your new captain, Raymond Middleton."

" He has not," answered Dick.

" 'Tis well," remarked Trevors ; " I have ridden fast, but he will be here shortly."

" How know you that ?"

" Because I heard from old Scrapegold, his uncle, that he had left the Manorhouse some hours since. He was on horseback, and I must have taken the shortest cut, or I could never have outstripped him."

" Well ; what were you in such a hurry for to get here before him ?" demanded Scud.

" I will tell you," answered Trevors ; " but first of all I must inform you, that he brings money with him."

" Ah !"

"Yes, a thousand guineas out of which he has frightened his uncle. Is not that good news for you?"

"What difference can it make to us?" inquired Dick.

"Well, if you do not know the value of it," said Trevors, "it is no fault of mine."

"Now, what would you?"

"As Martin Trevors," replied several of the men.

"Ay, as Martin Trevors, be it so; but as one also who has peculiar power which ye have all ere now felt. As one who holds ye and many more at his will and mercy, and yet whose power is of that mysterious character, that while you are compelled to own it, and obey it, you cannot penetrate the source from whence it springs. Do I not speak the truth?"

As Martin Trevors thus spoke, he hastily glanced round upon them all, and assumed an air of command and conscious dignity, which awed even the stoutest hearts amongst them.

"Well, well," at length said Dick Scud, "to the purpose; what brought you here?"

"A glass of grog, Ralph." said Trevors, taking a seat.

"Now then to business," he added, after having quaffed a portion of the contents of the glass. "Raymond Middleton, perhaps you are aware, wishes to get the girl, Rosetta Belford, in his power."

"True."

"And will employ you to attempt to seize and convey her on board your vessel."

"Well?"

"She must not be taken there."

"Not taken there?"

"No."

"Would you have us disobey our captain's orders?" demanded Dick Scud.

"Not so far as the seizure of the girl goes," answered Trevors; "but in the rest you must."

"How, must?" repeated two or three of the pirates, in an angry tone.

"Yes, I say must—I command you," returned Martin.

"D——n!" shouted Dick Scud, "are we to endure this, lads?"

"Nay, now, be cool" said Trevors; "be cool, and listen to what I say. You must endeavour to persuade Raymond Middleton to keep on board the vessel, and instead of conveying the girl to him, bring her to this place, where she must be concealed, and the captain must be informed that you have failed in your attempt. See that she is kept in safe custody, but let no injury be done to her, and then await my further orders."

"Well," said Dick Scud, with a laugh, "may I never see salt water again if this ain't as cool and as modest as anything I ever heard. Disobey the skipper, and await your further orders. Do you hear this, messmates?"

"Yes," returned Martin Trevors, "they all hear it; and they not only hear it, but must obey it."

"And what if we should refuse?" demanded one of the pirates.

"Why, not one of your lives would be worth a rope's end," replied Trevors, rising, and erecting his form to its full height.

"By h—ll, this is too much!" exclaimed Scud, drawing his sword, and the others following his example.

"You are but one man, and think you to bully us all into obedience to your will?"

"I will compel ye to do my bidding, even were it to give me the command of your ship, and toss your captain to the sharks," returned Trevors, with a look that completely astounded the whole of the ruffians.

"And what if we never suffered you to depart hence, but sacrificed your life upon the spot?" interrogated another of the pirates.

"Do it, if ye dare, and take the consequences," said Martin Trevors; "my fate, rest assured, could not be concealed, and there are those of terrible power on the ocean as well as on land, who would avenge my death in such a way as you can little imagine. Nay, mock not my words, but brave the danger I threaten if you dare."

The pirates stared upon each other, and then upon Martin Trevors, with the most unspeakable amazement.

" But, Martin," interrupted Red Ralph.

" Psha !" impatiently cried Trevors, " I have no time to waste in idle words. Do you promise, all of you, to do as I bid ?"

" And what should we gain by it ?" inquired Dick Scud.

" At any rate you have nothing to lose," returned Martin. " Come, the word, will you make me a friend or a foe ?"

The pirates were bewildered, and consulted one with another for a few moments, and seemed uncertain how to act. At length Dick Scud, turning to the singular and mysterious intruder, said, —

" Martin Trevors, we know not whether we should heed your words, neither can we understand the power you boast of possessing, but ——"

" Know you not one mighty monarch that rules the waves," interrupted Trevors, " and who holds you and all other marauders in terror and subjection—the pirate ship of death ?"

" Ah !" ejaculated the ruffians in a breath, and fixing their eyes earnestly upon his countenance.

" And fear its power ?"

" We do."

" 'Tis the fearful crew of that ship who would avenge the death of Martin Trevors, and who would not fail to learn to whom he owed his fate."

The pirates started, and gazed at the mysterious man with more astonishment than ever.

" Nay," he said, rising, and folding his cloak around him, " spare your surprise, I speak the truth. Now, are you prepared to do as I have instructed you ?"

" We are as well as we are able ; but should we fail ——"

" Why, then the fault will not be your's, if you are faithful. Red Ralph, you will see to the security of the girl till you behold me again. You know I am a man of my word."

" Well, well, I consent," said Ralph ; " but should Raymond Middleton suspect ?"

" And what have you to fear from him ? He will be safe on board the vessel, and in the power of his crew. Hark ye, too, ye may not go unrewarded if I find that you perform your task faithfully."

" Well," said Dick Scud, " we have made up our minds."

" And you consent ?" said Trevors.

" We do."

" Enough. But still I have other injunctions for your ears."

" Name them," said Scud.

" Never to reveal a word of this to Raymond Middleton, or to any one else. Nor must you mention my visit here this night."

" Your wishes shall be complied with," said Dick. " Is that all you have to require ?"

" It is," answered Trevors ; " remember my words—good night."

With these remarks Martin Trevors folded his cloak around him, and left the cavern, the pirates gazing after him with stupified amazement.

It was not till some minutes after his departure that the silence was broken, when one of them observed,—

" Well, I think we have been altogether most infernal fools to suffer ourselves to be thus bullied and frightened into obedience to the commands of one man."

" Perhaps not," observed Joe Hatchway, who had hitherto remained silent.

" How ! what do you know of the business ?" demanded Dick Scud.

" Nothing more than that I consider we should be imprudent if we attempted to deceive him. He made no empty boast, or he could not have conducted himself with so much confidence."

" Think you, then, that he is connected with that devil's craft the Death Ship?"

" Yes," answered Joe; " at any rate it would not be well to run the risk."

" What can he want with the girl?" said Scud.

" That's his business. Probably he only wants to foil the designs of Raymond Middleton; and if it was only for that, I, for one, would willingly assist him."

" Why should you have such a bad feeling towards the skipper?"

" Because he is promoted to a berth that he has no right to," answered Joe. " Have we not all of us toiled hard enough, and long enough, and been placed in every danger, to have had the preference to him?"

" But it was the will of our late captain," observed Dick Scud, " and therefore we have no right to grumble at it."

" He must have been mad when he uttered such a wish," returned Joe. " What service could this Raymond Middleton have rendered him, that he should meet with such a reward, and be made the commander over our daring crew?"

" With that we have nothing to do."

" We have everything to do," rejoined Joe Hatchway, obstinately; " I say that we were all a set of fools to submit to it."

" You had better tell the captain so," remarked Dick Scud.

" And I should not care much about doing that."

" And what would you have had us done, Joe?" asked one of his companions.

" Become our own masters," answered Hatchway.

" Ah! what, have taken possession of the vessel?"

" Yes, who had a better right to it?"

" But," interposed Red Ralph, " if Raymond Middleton acts as he ought to do, and he seems to be a young fellow of some mettle, I don't see what you have to complain of."

" I have told you what I have to complain of," answered Joe; " I like not to be under the command of a stripling boy, whom we know nothing about. How do we know whether or not he may intend to deceive us, and, after all, betray us into the hands of the government sharks?"

" Psha!" ejaculated Scud; " you are talking nonsense, Joe."

" Well, you may think it so, if you please; and I only hope that you may not find yourself deceived."

" Shall we not have him completely in our power?"

" And the enemy may overhaul us before we are at all prepared to resist. What then would be the use of repenting, even though we might have the opportunity of revenging ourselves upon the skipper?"

" You suffer your apprehensions to get the weather-gage of your reason, Joe."

" You would not think so, when a dozen or so of us were strung to the yard-arm, or shot like dogs," retorted Hatchway. " A pretty captain of a pirate cruiser he will make, who only thinks of overhauling a petticoat. Bah! had he thought of bearing down upon his old miserly uncle's overloaded coffers, and adding their contents to our store, he would have been much better employed, and I should have thought more of him."

" Why, there is something in that, to be sure," remarked Dick Scud.

" A knife," added the villain, Hatchway, " would have settled all the business, and once on board our gallant craft he would have been secure."

" Well, that may yet be done," remarked Scud; " but we understand from Martin Trevors that he has already extorted a thousand guineas from the old nunks."

" Of which we must take care to secure a share," added one of the pirates.

" Yes," coincided Dick Scud, " and, after all, I cannot help thinking that Raymond Middleton will prove no lubberly churl. At any rate, let us try him, and we have the remedy in our own hands should he attempt to deceive us. But I know not what to think of this Martin Trevors."

" I believe him to possess the power he has boasted of, and should not like to offend him; we all know what it is to incur the vengeance of the crew of the Death Ship."

"Ay, ay," coincided one of the men, "and at any rate this Martin Trevors is a daring fellow. Now if we had such a man as him for our captain."

"And are there not plenty of stout and reckless hearts amongst our own crew to take that post?" demanded Hatchway.

"Why, for the matter of that," answered the man, "I dare say there is; but, come, messmates, it is getting late, and as the captain does not seem likely to arrive, we had better finish our grog, weigh anchor, and make all sail to the vessel."

See page 99.

"But Trevors said that he would be here presently," observed Dick Scud, "as he had started from the Manor-house some hours before. We had better wait a little longer."

"What can have detained him?" said Red Ralph.

"Can anything have happened to him on the way?" said Scud; "having so large a sum of money about him, his ife ——"

"Hark!" interrupted one of the men, "there is the signal."

The whistle was again heard, and Ralph then went to the secret entrance, and inquired in a cautious voice,—

"Who's there?"

"A friend!" was the reply.

"The password."

"Steady!" answered the person outside.

"'Tis the captain's voice," said Scud.

"Curses on him!" growled Hatchway, between his teeth.

The chests were again removed, and Raymond Middleton entered.

"All hail to our captain!" shouted several voices, but Joe Hatchway remained silent, and eyed Raymond with looks of malice, which were not unobserved by several of his companions.

"Thanks, my brave lads," returned Raymond Middleton, throwing off his cloak, and taking a seat; "I made all sail from the mansion, and should have been here before, but I lost my way in the storm, and was forced to put in at the nearest port to get refreshments. But here I am among ye, and greet ye all; in a few days we shall commence our cruise, and I may career as your captain, and if you do not find me firm and staunch from stem to stern, ready for action as a twenty-four pounder, and reckless of danger as the captain of the Death Ship, why, string me up to the yard-arm, or throw me overboard as food for the sharks!"

"Bravo! bravo!" cried all but Joe Hatchway, who sat moodily in one corner of the cavern, and continued to mutter unintelligible sounds to himself.

"Now, Ralph," resumed Raymond, "how stands the grog? We must have a jorum or two, and then to the craft."

The glasses were quickly refilled, and Raymond, taking one in his hand, rose and said,—

"Here's to the dare-devil hearts of the Reckless!"

The most uproarious acclamations followed this toast, and every one, with the exception of Hatchway, drank it most heartily.

"To Raymond Middleton, captain of the pirate crew!" cried Dick Scud.

"Hurrah! to Raymond Middleton, captain of the pirate crew!" responded the men, and when silence was restored, Raymond observed,—

"My lads, on becoming your skipper, I acted partly in unison with my own roving disposition, and a feeling of hatred against the service in which I have met with many insults. I would be free, unshackled by the restraint of rascally laws, which give riches to a chosen few, and slavery to thousands! I would be free, free as the breeze that wafts the vessel over the billows, and what so free as the life of a rover of the seas? These are my wishes, these are the thoughts I know you all entertain, and to obtain their gratification, you will find Raymond Middleton prepared to brave every danger, to exert every energy, and to smile even at death itself."

The loudest acclamations shook the cavern at the conclusion of this speech, but Hatchway still remained silent, and a sardonic and contemptuous grin overspread his forbidding features.

"Another thing I have to say," continued Raymond, "I shall bring to you all the power of riches to help you on your daring course. My uncle's coffers have already been levied upon by me; I hold him in my power, and it will be strange, indeed, if I do not empty them before long. One thousand guineas I bring with me this night, which shall be equally shared among my gallant crew, to enable them enjoy themselves when they may venture on shore in a foreign land."

"Bravo!" once more shouted the pirates, "long life to our new captain, Raymond Middleton."

"Before we quit this coast, however," continued Raymond, "there is one service I wish to engage you in. I have before informed you that the charms of a certain girl, Rosetta Belford, have excited my admiration, and my most ardent passion. She must be mine! She must be the fair mistress of the pirate captain. Do you swear to assist me in obtaining possession of this fair prize?"

" We swear !"

" Enough ; I know I may depend upon you, and her seizure can be easily effected. To-morrow I will arrange with you my plans. Now to the vessel !"

" Ay, ay, to the vessel," exclaimed several voices, and the pirates arose from their seats, and having hastily finished their grog, prepared to depart, Hatchway, however, still retaining his seat.

" Did you not hear the commands of our captain, Joe ?" said Dick Scud, advancing towards him.

" I did," sulkily returned the former.

" Then why do you loiter ?"

" Ah !" growled Hatchway, slowly arising from his seat, and casting a strange and impatient glance around him.

At this moment a strange and confused noise was heard, apparently proceeding from the house connected with the secret cavern.

———

CHAPTER VIII.

THE ATTACK BY THE COAST-GUARD.—THE DEATH OF JOE HATCHWAY.—THE EXPLOSION.—ENGAGEMENT ON THE SEA.—THE ESCAPE OF THE RECKLESS.

" WHAT's that ?" demanded several of the pirates, looking at Red Ralph for an explanation.

" Oh, it is only some of the fellows in the house, I suppose, got a little too groggy," answered Ralph.

The noise increased, and seemed to be approaching towards the cavern.

" There is something more in this than you suspect," said Raymond Middleton, drawing his sword ; " are all the doors leading from the house to the cavern secured ?"

" To be sure they are," replied Ralph ; " what have we to fear ?"

" By h—l !" exclaimed Dick Scud, as the sounds grew louder, and the knocking against and forcing of doors could plainly be heard, " we must be upon our guard ; there is danger at hand ; some treachery has been at work."

" Treachery !" repeated Ralph ; " what infernal rascal would dare ——"

Before he could finish the sentence, voices were heard outside the secret door which opened immediately upon the cavern, and heavy blows, as if with a crow-bar, were dealt upon it.

" We are betrayed !" cried Raymond ; " some infernal villain has done this. Stand firm, my lads, and let the rascals see what metal we are made of !"

He had scarcely uttered the words, when the door gave way with a loud crash, and several revenue officers appeared on the top of the steps which descended into the cavern.

A dozen pistols were discharged at them in an instant, and one or two of them fell wounded, the remainder leaping into the cavern sword in hand and commencing the deadly combat with the boldest determination.

Joe Hatchway instantly flew to join the officers, and taking a pistol from his belt discharged its contents at the head of Raymond, but he missed his deadly aim, and the next moment Dick Scud had closed with him sword to sword.

" Infernal, treacherous swab ?" cried Scud, " it is you that have done this."

" Ha ! ha ! ha !" laughed the pirate, triumphantly ; " it is, and I glory in the deed. Down with them ; they cannot escape, they ——"

Before he could finish the sentence, the sword of Scud was buried in his heart, and he fell a ghastly corpse at his feet.

The combat now raged with terrific fury, Raymond and his companions fighting like lions, but their party was small compared with that of the officers, and defeat appeared certain, Red Ralph and another of the fellows having already fallen.

" Yield, Captain Middleton," said the leader of the officers ; " you find it is useless to resist,"

" Yield !" exclaimed Raymond; " never ! We are prepared to die, but never like cowards to yield."

The combat was continued with increased determination, and the confusion that prevailed, the shouts of the officers, the curses of the pirates, and the groans of the wounded, were truly terrific. Several of the officers were wounded, and two of them were killed; the pirates fighting their way towards the secret entrance of the cavern, which one of them had opened. But here more of the coast-guard appeared, and it seemed as if the fate of the pirates was inevitable, for their retreat on every side was cut off. Raymond, however, cheered on his men, and those who were engaged with the coast-guard at the entrance having succeeded in driving them on to the beach, Raymond and his party made towards it, the officers in the cavern following, and fighting desperately. Raymond and most of his companions succeeded in retreating from the cavern, and encountered the coast-guard on the beach, but before the unfortunate officers could follow, Dick Scud, who was the last of the pirates that left, seized one of the lamps, and with a terrific oath, before any one could offer to prevent him, threw it into a large cask of gunpowder, and sprang upon the beach, where Raymond and the other pirates were still engaged with the coast-guard.

Instantly a dreadful explosion took place, which caused a convulsion for some distance like that of an earthquake; a dense black smoke filled the atmosphere; huge masses of rock, mingled with the shattered limbs of the unfortunate persons who had not time to escape from the cavern, were hurled into the air, and sounds far more deafening than the most terrific peals of thunder reverberated for miles around. In a moment, and almost every vestige of the cavern and the house attached to it was destroyed; and so sudden and so unexpected was the shock, that all who felt it stood appalled, uncertain from what cause it proceeded.

Not so, however, Raymond and his companions; for, taking advantage of the confusion and horror into which their antagonists were thrown, they discharged their pistols at them, and then made a precipitate retreat towards the place where their boats were concealed, and, much to their surprise, found them secure, as they expected nothing less than that the coast-guard, by the instructions of Joe Hatchway, would have taken possession of them.

" Hurrah ! my brave lads," exclaimed Raymond, as he sprang into one of them, " fortune, although she has frowned, has not yet quite deserted us. We must pull like devils to the ship, for we have not a moment to lose, depend on it. We shall have a revenue cutter or two after us presently. 'Tis a cursed disaster, but it cannot be helped."

Quickly the pirates were in their boats, and pulling with all their might towards the Reckless, which could be seen, by the reflection of the fire, riding at anchor at no great distance. It was but the work of a few minutes for them to reach her, and they beheld most of the crew gathered upon the deck, and gazing in consternation and surprise towards the scene of the late explosion. In an instant they were on board.

" Weigh anchor, my lads, spread every stitch of canvas, and away, or the land sharks will be down upon us in a few minutes," commanded Raymond, who was perfectly cool and collected, notwithstanding the disappointment he had experienced.

" Ay, ay, captain," replied the men ; and, with the promptitude usual to them in such cases of emergency, they hastened to obey his orders, but before they could complete them a revenue cutter appeared in sight, making quickly towards them.

" The wind is in our favour," said Raymond; " and they will have a hard chase to overtake us."

" They near us, captain," said Dick Scud, the mate of the pirate ; " we shall not get over this unfortunate business without another tussle with the swabs."

" Be ready, then, to give them a royal salute, my lads, at the guns," returned Raymond ; " and fear not but we shall be able soon to make them cry peccavi.

Ha! they come! I see plain enough there is no chance of escaping them; but they are no match for us; they have had a taste of our quality on shore, and if we do not send them all to the devil, as we have done their friends, my name is not Raymond Middleton!"

Raymond Middleton, animated by the excitement of the moment, seemed quite another man to what he was when we first introduced him to the reader. Naturally bold and intrepid, he now appeared even to surpass himself, no doubt stimulated by the desire to ingratiate himself into the good opinion of the daring crew of which he had become the commander, and certainly, if that was his object, he succeeded, for the men looked upon him with admiration, and hurried to obey his commands.

The enemy bore towards them with all speed, and they could hear the shouts of the men aboard, as they were carried far across the ocean by the midnight air. The pirates replied to them by a cry of defiance equally loud, and prepared for the action, which they now saw was inevitable.

" Lay to, lay to, my lads," commanded Raymond, as the cutter approached, " and give them a pill or two, by way of a beginning."

His orders were obeyed, and the enemy soon came within gun-shot.

" They must be fool-hardy lubbers to venture that cockle shell against us," said Raymond. " Now's the time, my brave fellows; fire! fire!"

Two twelve-pounders were immediately discharged at the cutter, but apparently without effect, and, after returning the compliment, she came riding on amid the shouts of her men, which were returned with tenfold interest by the pirates. In spite of a heavy fire from the Reckless, the gallant vessel still came on, pouring a broadside into the pirate ship, which did it some little injury, and, being now fairly alongside of her, the combat commenced with the most determined skill and bravery on both sides.

It was soon, however, evident that the pirate ship must prove too powerful an enemy for her to cope with, with any chance of success; notwithstanding, the crew of the cutter had the hardihood to attempt to board her, and dreadful was the slaughter they suffered in consequence, the pirates fighting with the most savage fury, and seeming determined to sacrifice the lives of all their gallant antagonists, their cannon keeping up a heavy fire all the time.

The scene was one of the most exciting description, and Raymond performed such acts of cruelty as showed him well fitted for the desperate course of life upon which he had entered.

Several of the crew of the cutter were slain, and the captain, perceiving that the case was hopeless, and that, if they continued the combat, every soul must perish, gave the word of command for a retreat, disengaged the vessel from the Reckless, and sheered off, amid the shouts of triumph from the pirate crew.

" Ha! ha! ha!" laughed Raymond, as he watched the progress of his departing enemy; " poor devils, let them e'en escape with the dressing they have got. They will have something to talk about for a few months to come. Now, my lads, we must pursue our course with all the speed we can while the wind favours us, for a more powerful enemy may be sent in pursuit of us than we could very well conquer; we have had enough of fighting to-night, and before daylight we must be far away from this coast."

It was found that the Reckless had received but very little damage, and only three of the pirates were wounded, and that but slightly, so that the combat was considered a most signal triumph altogether, and the crew augured well of their new captain from the consummate skill and intrepidity he had evinced throughout.

Everything on board assumed an appearance as if nothing had happened, and the pirate vessel, propelled by a forwarding breeze, was soon far away from the scene of the late action.

" The rascal Hatchway to betray us!" said Raymond to Dick Scud, as they were pacing the deck together. " It was next to a miracle that we escaped from our retreat."

" Ay, captain," replied Scud; " he expressed dissatisfaction this night in the cavern, but I never suspected that the fellow would have acted in this manner. However, he has paid for his treachery with his life."

"Yes, thanks to you, Dick," returned Raymond; "and had it not been for your blowing up the cavern, we should all have been taken prisoners, or perished by the hands of the superior enemy we had to contend against. We are all greatly indebted to you, and depend upon it I shall not forget you."

"Oh, I want no thanks, captain," answered Dick; "you will never find Dick Scud flinch from doing his duty."

"Well said," returned Raymond, "well said. Now, let a sharp look-out be kept, and then we will have the grog afloat, and have a little revelry after our triumph."

This announcement was hailed with acclamation by the pirate crew; and they gave themselves up to the most riotous mirth, in which Raymond heartily joined.

But when Raymond retired to his cabin, he gave himself up to the feelings of vexation and disappointment which agitated his bosom.

"Curses light upon the memory of the traitor who caused this misfortune!" he soliloquised, "and has thus, for the present, at any rate, defeated my plans. I had hoped ere to-morrow's sun had set to have had Rosetta in my power, and there was no risk I was not prepared to run to obtain possession of so fair a prize. What a lovely companion would she have formed for me in my perilous adventures; but now she is lost to me probably for ever. Frank Trevors loves her, and, perhaps, ere I can venture to return to England, will have made her his wife. D——n! I would that I had secured him on board, I would have taken care to have spoilt his courtship for ever. It has been an unlucky affair altogether, when everything promised so well. I wished it to have remained concealed that I had taken to this course of life, then I could have carried on my schemes with greater advantage; but now it will become known to all, and I must not venture into the neighbourhood of the Manor-house again unless it is in secret and disguise, and even then I may be discarded. My uncle, too, may threaten to denounce me. But no, he dare not; I hold him too much in my power for him to venture to do so. But Rosetta shall not yet escape me; no, I will devise some means to get her in my hands, in spite of all obstacles; she has constantly occupied my thoughts for many a year, and I am determined not so easily to relinquish the gratification of my wishes, even though dangers, almost insurmountable, stand in my way.

"But away with these thoughts; I have now other business to occupy my mind for the present. I have entered upon a bold life, and I must not disgrace the character I have assumed. No, no, they shall find that Raymond Middleton is a pirate captain in every sense of the word.

"Well, let my name become known; what matters it to me? At any rate it shall be my care that it shall never be mentioned without striking terror and dismay into the breasts of all who hear it. I have chosen a life of freedom, of reckless daring, and I will enjoy it to its fullest extent. Oh, it is a much merrier, a more unshackled life than the one I have quitted, though, forsooth, it is not so *honourable!*

"Ha! ha! ha! what care I for honour? It is only a bugbear that fools labour for and rogues enjoy. I will be content to be the pirate chief, the bold marauder of the seas, without the *honour!* My uncle, too, I know him to be in some way connected with the Death Ship; could I but encounter that much dreaded and mysterious vessel (in spite of all the danger, I wish it), I might ascertain a few more particulars that might be of use to me. I do not forget the scene in the vault, and there are some circumstances connected with that which require elucidation. The original of the portrait in the chest must be discovered. Yes, yes, I have much to do; plenty of business marked out for some time to come.

"The idiot boy, saved from the burning vessel, has also excited my curiosity and anxiety, and the observations I heard Sir Horace make use of render me more curious upon the subject. It appeared that his features had struck him, and I could not help remarking that they bore a great resemblance to the portrait of the female. I must endeavour, at the first opportunity, to learn more about this."

Thus meditating he continued for some time, before he thought of retiring to rest.

CHAPTER XI.

THE REFLECTIONS OF MARTIN TREVORS.—HIS VISIT TO THE MANOR-HOUSE.— THE FEARS OF THE MISER.

WHETHER the statement which Martin Trevors had made in the cavern respecting his power and connection with the mysterious crew of the Death Ship, be true or not, we cannot at present undertake to say, but certain it is, that he was a man whose real motives and thoughts no one could penetrate, not even his son, who had frequently endeavoured, but in vain, to solve the ambiguity of his father's character, and often feared that either his past or present secret actions were such as would not bear scrutiny.

As Martin rode from his cavern towards his home, he frequently gave utterance to strange expressions, which, had any person overheard, they would have taken him to be a madman. Then he would chuckle and laugh with a sort of wild delight, but frequently cast his eyes around him to see that no one was at hand who might overhear him.

"Ha!" he ejaculated, "my plans work admirably; all goes as well as I could wish, and I see the course clear before me. The fools! how readily I awed them into obedience by even my bare assertions. But it was no empty boast; no, no, Martin Trevors never makes empty boasts, and so some persons will find out by-and-bye. The girl in my power, my plans will be in a fair way of operation. Ha! ha! so, Raymond Middleton has turned pirate. 'Tis well, 'tis well,—all in favour of the success of my deep-laid schemes. Old Middleton is more than ever in my power, and I will so entangle him in my meshes that he cannot escape from them. He believes he knows Martin Trevors; ha! ha! ha! the old fool, he will never know him till it is to breathe a death knell in his ear."

Again he laughed in the exultation of his thoughts, and then relapsing into silence, urged on his horse, for the snow was falling fast, and the wind was still howling keenly around.

He had got within a mile of his dwelling, when he was startled by a noise resembling a heavy clap of thunder, and looking up he beheld the sky redly illuminated in the direction from whence he had come. He paused, and gazed at this apparent phenomena for a moment or two in surprise.

"What can be the meaning of this?" he exclaimed. "Ah!" he added, "it is evidently a violent explosion, and a fierce fire appears to be raging in the very direction of the cavern. Can anything have happened there? But no, no; why should such an idea occur to me? Some accident at sea merely, I dare say. Well, that is nothing to me."

The coolness with which he uttered these words was truly characteristic of his nature, and he again proceeded on his way, and shortly afterwards arrived at home. Frank was awaiting his arrival, but he did not even condescend to utter a word in reply to his greeting, and throwing himself into a chair he became lost in meditation.

"You are late, father," said Frank.

"What of that?" was the surly reply.

"Nothing but ——"

"Bah! go to bed, boy," interrupted Martin, and taking up a lamp, he stalked from the room, and retired to his chamber.

"Strange man!" said Frank, when he was gone; "what can be the meaning of his conduct? Who can fathom his actions? Stern and forbidding, and yet

I cannot believe him to be unkind. Oh, no, I should be ungrateful were I to think so; but, alas! his repulsive manners, and the ambiguity of his behaviour, I fear, will prove an impenetrable bar to my happiness. Mr. Belford, I already begin to think, looks coldly upon me, and Rosetta—oh, my lips falter as I repeat the name of that fair being to whom my affections have been devoted from childhood, and I fondly hoped that our sentiments were reciprocal, although we had never ventured to breathe our passion to each other. But I can no longer deceive myself; she loves me not; it is only friendship that reigns in her breast towards me, and I see nothing but the prospect of misery before me. Since Julio has been an inmate of the house also, I have marked a more than usual coldness in her demeanour towards me. Oh, what would I not give to receive the smiles of affection she bestows upon him. But no, by Heaven I do her wrong; it is but the sympathy and pity which forms a part of her nature for that poor desolate lad which calls forth those expressions. This uncertainty, this doubt, however, is agonizing, and I cannot much longer endure it. I will acknowledge to her the passion that glows within my breast, and learn at once my fate from her lips. Oh, Rosetta, most beautiful in person and mind of all created beings, if you frown upon my love, then indeed my doom is sealed, my hopes entirely annihilated, and I must never more hope to know happiness."

He sighed deeply as he gave utterance to these words, and then with a heavy heart sought his chamber. Unfortunate youth! he was indeed destined to experience innumerable troubles and disappointments; his lot was cast in a gloomy mould, and clouds were at that time impending o'er his head, which were shortly destined to burst and overwhelm him.

In the morning Martin Trevors walked forth towards the beach, as was his usual custom, and he then heard from some fishermen the particulars of the destruction of the cavern, and the escape of Raymond Middleton and his companions. His astonishment and emotion on receiving this intelligence may be readily imagined, and he hastily bent his steps from the spot in order that his violent agitation might not excite the attention of idle curiosity.

"Now, by all my hopes," he muttered to himself, as he walked away, "this is most unfortunate. It has baulked me in my plans. The cavern destroyed; what infernal hand has been the author of this treachery? I must see Sir Horace immediately. Oh, curses on this occurrence!"

His features were distorted with rage as he spoke, and he walked hastily towards the Manor-house, revolving in his mind the remarkable events that had taken place within the last few hours, and forming the most strange and evil projects for the future.

"But why should I feel regret at what has taken place?" he muttered to himself; "Raymond is safely removed out of the way, and now that his character is known, he must not venture to this neighbourhood again, and, therefore, the coast is clear before me, and there is no one to obstruct me in my designs. If the parsimonious old dotard was before in my power, he is more securely so now than ever, and I will not fail to take advantage of it to carry into effect my deep laid schemes. The old villain imagines he knows me, but he is not half acquainted with me yet. He little imagines the spirit of revenge which guides me in all my actions towards him. I could immediately gratify it to the fullest extent; I could crush him, place him in the hands of the public executioner, but it would not answer my purpose to do so yet. No, no; it must be my aim to rack and torture his mind with mingled hopes and fears; and thus will I gratify the implacable hatred I bear towards him. Oh, how little do the fools who have courted my friendship know the real character of Martin Trevors. *Martin Trevors*, ha! ha! ha!"

He laughed aloud in the exultation of his dark thoughts, and still proceeded on his way.

"But yet," he resumed, "it is unfortunate that the secret cavern is destroyed, for it has deprived me of one means of carrying my designs into effect. Curses light upon the traitor who has done this! I trust that he has met the fate he deserved, if not I will pursue him to destruction. It shall not, however, thwart my plans against the girl, Rosetta Belford. No, no, they are too artfully contrived for anything to frustrate them; and then that idiot boy; ha! it must be my after care to secure him, and make him the instrument of my plans. I feel more certain than ever, the longer I reflect on it, that it is he I suspect, and, therefore, he must be secured, or should his senses return he might be able to divulge more than it would be pleasant or convenient for the world to be made acquainted with. It is strange he was suffered to escape by those who held him in their power."

See page 111.

Thus soliloquizing, the mysterious man at last arrived at the Manor-house, and immediately demanded an audience of Sir Horace Middleton.

"My dear master is in his study, sir," said Simon Snipe, "and has given strict orders that he should not be disturbed, upon any pretext whatever."

"But I must and will see him," said Martin Trevors, in an authoritative tone of voice, that made Simon start; "these excuses will not do for me; tell him I am here, and be quick."

Simon departed to obey the commands of Trevors, and quickly returned, and desired Martin to follow him. He did, and was ushered into the room where Sir Horace was seated, and who viewed him with a tremulous and suspicious glance as he entered.

"How now, good Martin Trevors?" he faltered out, when Simon had departed, and he closed the door.

"Good Martin Trevors!" repeated his visitor, with a scornful laugh; "how long is it since you have discovered my peculiar virtues, good Sir Horace Middleton?"

"Do not mock me, Trevors," said the old man; "I always feel a strange dread creeping through my veins, for which I cannot account, when I see you assume that air of sarcastic irony and impenetrable meaning."

"Do you?" returned Trevors, "and so you should; you have more reason to do so than you perhaps imagine. You have good cause to fear me, Horace Middleton."

"Alas! alas! I feel I have," said the baronet; "you—you know me too well; you know all my secrets, and ——"

"I do," interrupted Martin Trevors, with a look of exultation; "there is not a thought that is unknown to me."

"But I may depend upon you, Martin; you—you are my friend?"

"Your friend!"

"Yes, yes; my adviser, my, my ——"

"Your keeper," added Trevors, with a look of malice, that made the wretched old man groan with agony.

"But—but you will not betray me, Martin?" he faltered out.

"It would not answer my purpose to do so at present."

"At present! But you will not betray me?"

"I have before told you I will not while you keep faith with me; but let me only discover, by a single word or action, that you have attempted to deceive me, and you know the consequences. I would have a deep, a terrible, and an overwhelming revenge."

"I will not deceive you, Martin; I—I have never attempted to do so," stammered out the trembling old man. "But what would you now? I have given you the gold you demanded; you do not seek to extort more from me. I—I ——"

"Bah!" interrupted Martin Trevors; "I came not for that purpose at present; I need it not just now, when I do I will have it; your gold is mine, and you dare not refuse my demands."

"Alas! alas!" groaned Sir Horace. "But what brings you here this morning, Martin?"

"To bring you more news."

"More news?"

"Ay," answered Trevors; "and of such a nature as you little expect to hear."

"Ah! but of what character is the intelligence you have to impart, good or bad?"

"Both."

"Name it; quick, quick."

"Your nephew, Raymond Middleton."

"Ah! what of him? the villain, the robber, the profligate! What of him, Martin? Have you discovered whither he has gone?"

"Ay; think you that his designs could long be concealed from me?"

"No, no; I know your penetration, Trevors; but do not keep me in suspense; where is he?"

"Far across the ocean by this time, no doubt," answered Trevors.

"And may that ocean be his grave," exclaimed Sir Horace; "but how know you this?"

"It matters not, I do know it; and more, I know that Raymond Middleton is at this time the captain of a pirate vessel."

"The captain of a pirate vessel!" repeated the old man, with a look of astonishment and incredulity. "Raymond Middleton turned pirate?—impossible."

"It is true ; and as such he is now known to the public," answered Trevors.

"Oh, 'tis well, 'tis well," cried Sir Horace, with an expression of exultation. "Denounced as a pirate ! oh, this is glorious ; he has himself broken the laws of his country, and I have nothing more to fear from him. He will not, dare not, again approach me, and my gold will be secure. Thanks, thanks, good Martin Trevors for this intelligence ; it is the best that has been imparted to me for years."

"Nay, old man," returned Martin ; "do not exult too soon. You may behold Raymond again, and it is only I to whom you must look to release you from his power."

"And you will do so, Martin ; you will not suffer the villain, the ingrate, whom I have so long cherished, the boy whom I snatched from death, to ——"

"And more fool you, and you are justly rewarded for your mad benevolence, if such a name can be given to any action of your life."

"Well, well, Martin, I acknowledge it ; I—I do indeed ; but you will not suffer him to triumph over me? Say you will not."

"No," replied Martin Trevors, with an emphatic look ; "because the whole of that triumph I reserve to myself."

"Ah! Martin, still I fear you."

"And so you should ; so you must ; and did you but know all, you have but little esteem or friendship to expect from me."

"No more of this, Trevors," said the trembling baronet ; "but, tell me all the particulars you have ascertained."

"Listen then," said Martin, taking a seat closer to Sir Horace Middleton, and he then detailed to him those facts with which the reader is already acquainted. It would be impossible to describe the surprise and emotion of Sir Horace as he proceeded, and when he had concluded, he exclaimed,—

"It is true then, it is true ! Raymond is known as a pirate ; he is denounced as the outrager of the laws of his country, and I am safe !"

"You flatter yourself, Sir Horace Middleton," returned Trevors, with a scornful sneer; "but beware ! mind that you are not deceived."

"Would that he had perished in the combat," ejaculated the old man.

"Indeed !" said Martin ; "but I say not so."

"And why, why, Martin ?" eagerly demanded the baronet.

"Because he must serve as an instrument to my future plans."

"I cannot understand you."

"No doubt ; and I do not intend you shall."

"Why do you ever maintain this air of mystery towards me, Martin ?"

"That is my business, old man," returned Trevors ; "you will understand it soon enough, when you know me better."

"And do I not know you ?"

"Yes, as Martin Trevors—as the agent, the secret agent of the Death Ship."

"And the secret spy upon my actions," added the old man, with a groan.

"Ay, be it so," answered Martin ; "you flatter yourself with having got rid of your nephew, whom you were idiot enough to suffer to become acquainted with many of your secrets ; but is Raymond Middleton the only one whom you have cause to fear ?"

"Alas! too well you know he is not," answered Sir Horace ; "do I not fear you ?"

"And the commander and crew of the Death Ship."

"Yes, yes ; oh, agony !"

"And is there no one else whom you have reason to dread ?" demanded Trevors.

"No, no ; there is no one else."

"Bethink yourself, Sir Horace Middleton ; recall the past to your memory, endeavour to remember whether or not there was any one whom you formerly injured, and whose hatred and vengeance you should now apprehend, if that one particular individual should happen to exist."

"What mean you? you torture me."

"Answer my question."

"No, no; I cannot recollect any one."

"You have a very convenient memory, Sir Horace Middleton," said Martin Trevors, with a sardonic grin. "You cannot then recall the actions of five-and-thirty years since?"

"No, no; how should I? It is a long time, and I am an old man."

"Shall I then remind you?"

"You!"

"Yes; my recollection is not quite so shallow as yours, and I can, perhaps, serve to brighten it."

"You—you cannot," answered Sir Horace, fixing upon him a keen look, and trembling involuntarily. "How should you be able?"

"That you will learn."

"I have not known you so many years, Martin Trevors."

"Not as Martin Trevors; and time it seems has greatly changed my features, or you have become so hardened in guilt, that the voice of conscience cannot reach your flinty heart."

"I would forget the past," groaned the old man; "oh, that I could bury it for ever in oblivion."

"No doubt of it," returned Trevors, with a sneer; "it is not calculated to give rise to many very pleasant reflections."

"Cease, cease," said Sir Horace, with much agitation.

"Oh, no," answered Martin; "I have not done yet. I say again, I would recall to your memory the events that took place five-and-thirty years since."

"You cannot know them," said the baronet.

"But I will prove that you are a liar, Sir Horace Middleton," exclaimed Martin, sternly, and fixing upon the old man a look which made him tremble more violently than before; "I will show you that Martin Trevor's knowledge is far more extensive than you seem to imagine. Five-and-thirty years ago, Horace Middleton was a plain and simple clerk in a commercial house, in the city of London; is not that the truth?"

The baronet started, and once more fixed a penetrating look upon his interrogator.

"It is, it is," he faltered out; "but how know you this?'

"Ha, ha, ha! I told you that you would find my knowledge more extensive than you expected. Now, Sir Horace, does not your memory recall any particular events that occurred during the time of your *honest* servitude?"

"Forbear, forbear!"

"Oh, no, I must fulfil my promise; you must hear me out, for it is a subject I have long wished to talk to you upon, and I cannot have a better opportunity of doing so than the present."

"Mysterious man! how could you have acquired this knowledge of me?"

"Oh, you and I are much older friends than you have hitherto supposed."

"*Friends!*"

"Ay, or acquaintances; which you please. Well then, you have admitted that you were a poor clerk in the commercial house of which I speak?"

"I have," answered Sir Horace; "but what of that, Martin?—what of that?"

"What of that?" repeated Trevors; "and you were always remarkable for honesty and integrity, while you held that situation, were you not?"

"Honest! Martin. Who can deny that?"

"No, no; of course," interrupted Martin, with a bitter sneer; "who can deny that you were most honest, most faithful, most prudent? It was always the character of Horace Middleton; he had too great a contempt for filthy lucre to covet it, or endeavour to obtain it by any but the most fair and praiseworthy means."

"Why do you thus taunt and mock me?" demanded the agitated old man,— "what is it you aim at?"

"You shall hear. It was Leonard Gresham, who was the rogue, the thief, the villain!"

"Leonard Gresham!" cried the baronet; "oh, why do you repeat that name I had hoped never to hear mentioned again?"

"Oh, you do remember him, then?"

"Oh, yes, yes; unfortunate, injured youth."

"Unfortunate, injured!" repeated Martin, with a look which struck terror into his guilty soul. "Was he not then justly punished? Did not the young villain rob the master who had been so kind to him? Were you not the principal witness against him on his trial, and could any one doubt the truth of your evidence, it was so clear, so consistent, so conclusive?"

"Spare me, spare me, Martin."

"Nay, you must not suffer your modesty to prevent you listening to the repetition of your good actions, Sir Horace Middleton."

"Martin Trevors," observed the baronet, "by what means you acquired your knowledge I know not; but—but I do confess that Leonard Gresham was innocent of the crime for which he was so cruelly punished. I was the villain, I ——"

"But there must be some mistake in this, Sir Horace," interrupted Martin, sarcastically; "you do yourself an injustice; but it is all owing to your bad memory, I presume. However, let me proceed. Leonard Gresham was a junior clerk in the same house, I believe, and, at the time of which I am speaking, he was not more than seventeen years of age."

"True, true; ill-starred lad!"

"It was very young to be so deeply skilled in crime."

"He was not guilty—I repeat that he was not."

"But I must proceed with the facts as they occurred. For some time Mr. Luttrel, your master, had found himself robbed to a considerable extent, but he could not discover the thief. That task was left for you, Sir Horace Middleton, to accomplish; and, most faithful, most trustworthy servant! you did it, and in a manner that reflects eternal credit on your character. You detected the villain; saw him take the cash, and deposit it in his chest, where it was afterwards found. What could be more clear? what could be more conclusive?"

"Martin Trevors, it was a villanous invention of my own altogether," gasped forth the baronet. "I was the absolute thief; I do confess it all to you now. I stole the money, and to screen myself, placed the cash in the box of the unfortunate Leonard, which condemned him."

"But I have not finished my story yet, Sir Horace," said Trevors, who evidently exulted in the powerful emotion which the baronet evinced. "Leonard Gresham being thus proved, beyond all possibility of a doubt, to be the thief, was forthwith committed to prison, tried on your evidence—your evidence only—Sir Horace Middleton, convicted, and sentenced to death."

"Alas!" groaned the old man; "it is too true. But they did not hang him."

"No, they did not hang him; the young villain received too much clemency. His sentence was most mercifully commuted to perpetual banishment, and you were promoted to the entire confidence of your master, and ultimately became his partner. It was only just that real honesty should be so rewarded."

"This bitter sarcasm agonizes me, Trevors," said Sir Horace; "how have you become acquainted with all these guilty particulars?"

"Oh, you will not marvel, when you have heard me out," replied Martin Trevors. "Well, Leonard Gresham was transported for life, and served several years of the most abject misery, when he managed to effect his escape, and got on board a vessel, so disguised, that it would have been impossible for any one to have detected him. That vessel was afterwards captured by the Death Ship, but the life of Leonard Gresham was spared, and he became one of that daring and fearful crew."

"Martin Trevors!" exclaimed the old man, clutching his arm; "can you speak the truth?"

"I do," replied Trevors, sternly, and fixing upon the baronet such a look as made him shrink aghast. "Moreover, I tell you, that Leonard still lives."

"Still lives?"

" Yes ; and now, Sir Horace Middleton, since you have heard my story, and acknowledged the truth of it—since you have confessed that Leonard Gresham was innocent of the crime of which he was convicted, and for which he was punished, say, have you nothing to fear from his vengeance ?"

" Oh, yes, yes," groaned Sir Horace ; " but where is he now ?"

" His eye is continually upon your actions," returned Trevors; " he is the master of your destiny. You are powerless in his hands, and at his will you swing from the gallows, and no earthly power can save you. Reflect on that, Sir Horace Middleton, and dare not refuse any command that I may think proper to impose upon you."

" Martin, Martin," cried the terrified baronet, " oh, yet reveal more to me. Tell me, how know you these fatal events? Tell me where I may find the deeply injured Leonard, that even now I may make him all the atonement in my power."

" Atonement," laughed Trevors, scornfully ; " what atonement could you make to him ? But reflect, I repeat, upon what I have said, and beware ! Good morning to you, Sir Horace Middleton."

" Do not leave me thus, Trevors, I implore you," said Sir Horace ; " tell me ——"

" I will tell you no more at present," interrupted Martin; " recollect what I have already said to you, as you value your life."

With these words, [Martin Trevors fixing, a look of the most fearful meaning upon the countenance of the alarmed baronet, quitted the room, and left him to his own reflections.

Sir Horace clasped his hands in an agony of despair, and for some moments was unable to speak ; but at length he said,—

" Oh, how the villain has tortured me, by the repetition of this fearful tale ! But how has he become acquainted with that which my lips have never divulged to any one ? And does Leonard Gresham still live ? If he does, what have I not indeed to fear from his vengeance ? But can it be that he has suffered all these years to elapse without seeking to gratify it ? And to have been one of the crew of the Death Ship, too. I am lost in wonder, perplexity, and consternation. Oh, am I never to know rest ?—am I never to be released from this perpetual state of fear and anguish ? No, how can I expect it ?—how do I deserve it, wretch, robber, murderer as I am ? Of what use to me is that gold which I have been at such pains to accumulate, since it cannot procure me happiness or security ? Fool, misguided fool that I have been throughout my life ; had I not better have remained a beggar, than thus to have suffered myself to be plunged by accursed avarice into crime and misery ? Oh, what would I not now give, could I but recall the past ? What sacrifice would I not willingly make to become once more innocent and happy ? My fate is spread before me ; I see it with a clear eye ; there is no deceiving myself ; no buoying myself up by false and delusive hope. The gallows, yes, the gallows is my final doom. Oh, horror, horror ! and when that dreadful day arrives, for come it surely will, how shall I meet the awful fate ?—how endure the shouts and execrations of the gaping and exulting multitude ? My very soul freezes with horror at the thought. These reflections will drive me mad. And he told me to reflect on his words. Alas ! he had no occasion to do that, for never can I erase them from my memory. Oh, torture, most insupportable."

He threw himself into his chair, covered his face with his hands, and swayed his body to and fro in a state of the greatest mental excitement.

" And this news, too, about my nephew," he resumed, after a pause ; " I had hoped it would have relieved me from a great portion of the danger by which I am surrounded; but Martin Trevors has undeceived me, and bids me despair. Oh, that he had perished in the explosion which took place in the cavern, then at least should I have been rid of part of my fears. But he will return to me at the time he has promised, in spite of the danger he will incur by so doing, and I dare not betray him, for he holds me in his power, and would denounce me as a murderer. My brain is distracted; I know not what course to pursue. Weak fool that I was not to take his life when he was at my power and mercy. But could I even then have escaped detection ? Could I have concealed my guilt from the penetrating eye of justice? No, I could not; and thus I should but have hastened my fate. From Martin Trevors I have nothing to hope; he only seeks to accomplish his own dark designs, and will not assist me. Were he dead, I should feel more at rest. I fear him more than ever since this last interview, and the observations he has made use of to me. I cannot penetrate his intentions, but feel convinced they tend to my destruction. And, is it to endure such torture as this that I wish to live? And yet—to die, to have to meet that dread eternity, hidden from mortal eye, oh, horror! horror! I dare not think of it. This, this, mad votaries of avarice, is your reward! this is the harvest of your sordid labours! Oh, eternal curses light upon the hour when I suffered the insidious fiend to take possession of me."

Again the wretched old man groaned, and then paced his room with disordered steps, and in a state of mind which language must fail to pourtray. Throughout the day he continued in the same state of mental anguish and excitement; and, when the darkness of night fell around, it increased to a degree which he found it almost utterly impossible to support. His imagination conjured up all sorts of frightful images, and he trembled to remain alone in his dismal chamber, and at length he rushed forth from the Manor-house into the open air, scarcely knowing whither he was going, or what he was about to do.

The night was piercingly cold, and the keen wind swept in hollow gusts around; but he heeded not that, and he pursued his way, as if he was hunted by a hundred fiends, and laughing wildly in delirious agony. Unconsciously he took the way which led to the cliffs, and had gained the summit of one of the loftiest, before he was aware of where he was. The moon cast a broad, silvery light upon the ocean, upon whose broad waters he gazed with a wild and vacant eye, folding his arms, and traversing the cliff with the air of a maniac.

"All is still around, save the howling wind, in every breath of which a curse seems to be conveyed to my ears," he ejaculated; "there is no eye, save that of Heaven, to watch my actions. No one to arrest the dark purposes of my soul. How peaceful is the ocean! how calm to the rude tempest that rages in my breast, and preys upon my tortured brain! And shall I live to continue to endure this torture? To be continually threatened by those in whose power I am, and to be haunted by the grim phantoms of my murdered victims? The vast and tranquil waters of the deep seem to invite me to death. Death! but will my sufferings terminate with my life? Have I not a dreadful account to render before the judgment seat of Heaven, and can I hope to receive forgiveness for the dreadful crimes I have committed? No, no; eternal torments are in store for me, and I dare not, cannot hope. I fear to die! Still it cannot be worse than the earthly demons that now pursue me, and hiss their curses in my ears. Hark! what sound was that which came howling to my ears in the blast? Again, again! I hear it plainly, it is no delusion—it is the shriek of my murdered victims. It calls aloud for retribution, and it will be heard. I cannot shut it out—I cannot fly from it—it pursues me everywhere and in every hour. Horror, horror! death is preferable to such agony as that I now endure. And they will have my life, should not my own hands deprive me of it. They will consign me to the gallows—they will doom me to the death of a dog, and mock and exult as I struggle in my dying convulsions. One plunge, and I shall escape it all! one plunge, and my earthly misery will be over. Desperation nerves me—madness urges me, and thus I rush into the presence of that Almighty Judge, whose laws I have so savagely broken."

As the wretched man thus spoke, he extended his arms above his head, and was about to leap from the cliff into the dark waters that washed its base, when his arm was suddenly arrested by some person behind him.

"Ah!" he cried, for he had not heard any one approach, so fully occupied had he been by his own fearful thoughts; "who seeks to frustrate my purpose? release your hold, fiend, and let me end a life that is worse than the torments of hell to me."

"Fool!" exclaimed a stern voice, and Sir Horace then saw by the light of the moon, that it was Martin Trevors who held him.

"Ah, Trevors!" he cried; "you here? Why have you followed my steps?

Why are you thus constantly watching my actions? Do not detain me—let me end a life which I can no longer endure."

"Fool!" repeated Trevors, forcing him from the spot; "and think you that death would terminate your tortures? Think you that the murderer is ever permitted to rest in peace in that eternity upon which you would madly rush? Come away, I command, this is not the spot for you at this hour of the night."

"You command, Martin Trevors?"

"Yes, I command, and you dare not disobey me. To the Manor-house, I say, and endeavour to learn reason."

"Oh, that my reason had fled for ever—that I could drown the voice of conscience in everlasting forgetfulness."

"Bah!" exclaimed Trevors, still forcing him from the spot.

"Oh, why will you not suffer me to die?" implored the wretched man.

"Because it would not answer my purpose for the present," answered Martin, with a look that froze the very soul of the baronet with horror. "Come, come; home with you, and try and sleep away this paroxysm of insanity."

"Sleep," repeated Sir Horace; "and think you that a wretch like me can sleep?"

"What's the use of all this whining cant?" demanded Trevors, sternly; "it is too late to repent now."

"Repent! oh, I cannot repent, I ——"

"No more, but attend me."

"Leave me, Trevors."

"Not till I have seen you safe within the walls of the Manor-house," answered the latter; and, forcing him from the spot, he hurried him down the side of the cliff, into the path which led towards his gloomy dwelling, regardless of the groans of anguish and regret that escaped the baronet's bosom.

"Oh, Trevors," he exclaimed, "but for you, my body would at this moment have been buried in the waters of the deep. What is your purpose with me, that you will not suffer me to end that life which has become an earthly purgatory to me?"

"Sir Horace Middleton must not be food for sharks," returned Martin Trevors, with peculiar emphasis. "There is much left for him to do yet."

"Mysterious man, what mean you? What would you with me?"

"Time will show, never fear."

"You take pleasure in torturing me."

"Perhaps I do."

"You pursue me with a feeling of revenge, and for why I know not."

"And it is my will that you should for the present remain in ignorance. The truth will come upon you quite soon enough, no doubt."

"I never did you harm, Martin Trevors."

"So you think."

"In what have I injured you?" demanded Sir Horace; "let me know, and I will readily make you all the compensation in my power."

"Compensation!" repeated Martin, with a look of the most ineffable scorn; "what compensation can the old dotard, Sir Horace Middleton, make to me? But I will talk no more of this; I tell you that you are the slave of my will, and must not, shall not disobey it."

"Heaven help me!"

"Heaven! hypocrite, villain, what have you to do with Heaven? Is not your soul eternally damned? Dare you hope for mercy?"

Sir Horace groaned, but could make no other reply; and Trevors, still retaining his hold of his arm, hurried him on towards the Manor-house, at which they shortly afterwards arrived, and the door being quickly opened by Simon Snipe, Martin attended the wretched old man to his chamber, where he sank into a chair, and pressing his burning temples, gave utterance to the most violent sobs of anguish.

"Come, arouse yourself from this worse than childish weakness, old man," said Martin Trevors; "of what avail is it? You have plunged too deeply in crime to repent now. Retire to your bed, and I will see you again in the morning, when I expect not to find you the madman that you are at present."

" Mad!" repeated Sir Horace ; " yes, yes, you say true—very, very true ; I am, indeed, mad ; the voice of conscience ——"

" Psha! seek rest, old man, seek rest."

" Rest, there is none for a wretch like me. Oh, Trevors, when the darkness of night sets in, and I am wrapped in the gloom and solitude of my chamber, hideous noises vibrate in my ears, ghastly forms arise to my imagination, and ——"

S e page 119.

" And does the form of Leonard Graham ever arise to your imagination, Sir Horace Middleton ?" demanded Trevors, with a look that penetrated to, and appalled the very soul of the trembling baronet.

" Forbear, forbear, Trevors," he gasped forth ; " I—I have acknowledged the treacherous, the villanous part I acted towards that unfortunate youth, and willingly would I make reparation ; but he lives not."

" I tell you again that he does," returned Martin, " I say that he not only lives, but that he constantly watches your actions; that it is food to his revenge to witness your misery, and to know that at any time one word of his would consign you to an ignominious death."

" Oh, horror—horror! can this be true? But tell me, Martin, where is he?"

" You would not dare to meet his revengeful eye, Sir Horace Middleton."

" Oh, tell me where I can find him, and even though he strike me dead at his feet, I will seek his presence, and implore his forgiveness."

" Not all the gold you possess could purchase his pardon for the irreparable injuries you have inflicted upon him," said Martin Trevors; " nothing whatever could induce him to abandon those deep and terrible designs he has so long cherished. Ask yourself what atonement you could possibly make to him? Was he not young and guiltless? You blasted his prospects, defamed his character, and branded him with the name of felon. Through your base means he was doomed to drag the convict's chain, and the very current of his nature became changed, and he became a man of crime; you have been the author of all this, and yet you would seek forgiveness from the wretched victim whom you have thus irretrievably ruined. Bah! to bed with you, and seek to regain that reason you have so long lost."

" Oh, Trevors, did you but know the agony which now racks my mind, even you, stern and insensible to commiseration as you are, would pity me."

" Pity you!"

" Yes, yes, yes, I am an old man, Martin, a very old man, and—and I feel that I shall never know happiness again."

" What!" cried Trevors, with an expression of the most bitter irony, " not know happiness, when you have got all the means to render you so? Have you not your gold, Sir Horace, your precious gold, for which you have laboured so hard in the field of crime? Oh, you must be a very happy man; very happy indeed. Ha, ha, ha!"

" Mercy—mercy! do not mock me thus! Oh, Martin, at what a price have I not purchased that gold! Would that I could recall the past."

" Enough of this cant, old man," returned Trevors, " it sickens me to hear it."

" Oh, why did you arrest me in my deadly purpose? Why did you not permit me to end at once this dreadful, this perpetual torment?"

" Because it is my will that you should live. But no more of this. Be calm yourself, and reflect upon the madness of your designs, and thank me for having interfered to save you from the perpetration of the rash act. Think you that death would have terminated your tortures?"

" Ah, no!" groaned the baronet. " and—and, oh, I know not how to act, what to do—I am a wretched old man."

" Will you endeavour to be composed?" demanded Trevors, " or I will not leave you."

" Yes, yes, I will try," eagerly replied Sir Horace, alarmed at the idea of Martin Trevors remaining with him all night. " I will seek to conquer my emotions, and to forget the awful past. You may leave me, Martin; I will be calm; I will seek my couch, and try in sleep to banish these dreadful thoughts. Good night—good night!"

" Good night," responded Trevors, as he moved towards the door; " I shall visit you again in the morning."

Having uttered these words, Martin Trevors left the room, and retired from the Manor-house. Sir Horace stood for a few moments after he was gone, and with clasped hands gazed vacantly towards the door. A stormy sea of racking thoughts rolled across his brain, and a weight of lead seemed to press upon his heart.

" He is gone," he said, at length; " he is gone, thank Heaven. Oh, how I tremble in that man's presence, for I feel myself involuntarily the slave of his austere will, and dare not disobey him. His words penetrate my very heart like a dagger, and yet in vain I try to fathom his thoughts, to unravel the mystery of his dark designs, while I feel convinced that they tend towards my ultimate destruction. He is gone, and I am alone; what shall now prevent me from ending at once this wretched existence? But one blow, and all is over; but, no—no—would it be over? Would my anguish end with existence? Oh, no—my soul, appalled, acknowledges that there is a terrible futurity. The tortures of the damned arise to my imagination; flames of fire blaze around me—I struggle in the grasp of fiends, who mock my agony! The awful, the eternal doom of the murderer is presented to my sight. Vultures are gnawing at my heart—a liquid fire scorches my brain! Off—off! demons! hurl me not into that burning gulf; I will struggle with you—I will grapple with you, with the strength of a giant! Ah! my feet totter on the edge of that fearful precipice! I sink! I fall! Save me—save me—save me! oh!"

With a groan so awful that it would have appalled the stoutest heart to have heard it, the wretched, guilty man clasped his burning temples with the frenzy of despair, staggered from the spot on which he had been standing, and sank insensible upon the couch. Nature was completely exhausted, and for a time Sir Horace received a respite to the agony of his mind in unconsciousness.

CHAPTER X.

THE CONFESSION OF LOVE.—THE REJECTION.—THE DESPAIR AND DISAPPEARANCE OF FRANK TREVORS.

THE extraordinary events that had taken place at the secret cavern of the rocks, and the discovery of the real character of Raymond Middleton, caused the greatest sensation in the neighbourhood, and afforded subject for much conversation, but to none did it cause more surprise than Michael Belford and his family.

"I always suspected the character of Raymond Middleton," observed Michael; "I could see plain enough, notwithstanding the specious mask he assumed, that the blackest vice found a ready asylum in his breast."

"But who could have imagined that a young man, who had gained distinction in the service of his king and country, and who had such brilliant prospects before him, would have turned the lawless captain of a crew of pirates?" said Mrs. Belford.

"True, dame," returned her husband; "it is most extraordinary; but it is fortunate that the neighbourhood has got rid of the unprincipled young libertine on any terms, and if his avaricious old uncle were to follow him, it would be no great loss."

"It would not, indeed, Michael, for most certainly do I believe Sir Horace Middleton to be a bad man."

"No doubt of it, and the mystery of his actions, to say the least of them, is sufficient to excite suspicion."

"He has proved a curse to the neighbourhood ever since he resided here," observed the dame.

"He has," coincided Michael, "and the poor whom he has been the means of banishing from the homes of their forefathers have no reason to bear him any good will. I look upon him with greater suspicion than ever since the remarkable emotion he betrayed on beholding Julio, and the strange observations he made use of."

"Ah!" ejaculated Mrs. Belford, "it was, indeed, most wonderful. It was evident that the poor boy's features struck him as resembling some particular individual, the recollection of whom caused him such violent emotion."

"True," said Michael; "I have often thought of it since, and have been unable to form any reasonable conjecture upon the subject; but I must keep a watchful eye over Julio, for even here his secret enemies may lurk, and try to do him harm."

"Heaven forbid," said Mrs. Belford, "for I love the poor maniac boy as if he were my own child, and should anything happen to him, I verily believe it would break my heart."

"Poor lad—poor lad," remarked Michael; "he is, indeed, worthy of every compassion. It is a sad thing to see one so young, so fair, and so innocent, deprived of reason; but I trust that the time will come when the Almighty will restore him to his senses, and when His just retribution will overtake the wretches from whom he has suffered such fearful and irreparable injuries."

"Most heartily do I respond to that wish, Michael," said his wife. "And then the poor child is so gentle, and so affectionate, and it is enough to break one's heart to hear him talk of his unfortunate mother, and repeat the sweet and plaintive ballads she used to sing to him. Oh, surely they must have been monsters of the blackest die who could have been guilty of such atrocities."

"They must; but what surprises me more than all is, that they should not have sacrificed the life of Julio as well as that of his mother."

"It is a mystery which time only may explain," returned Mrs. Belford.

"Ay, right, dame, right," said Michael, " and I trust that Heaven will enable us to protect poor Julio from danger till that time arrives. I cannot, however, again help expressing my satisfaction at the departure of Raymond Middleton from this place, for I liked not the looks which he bestowed upon the boy when he visited us on the afternoon of the storm ; and I have often thought that that was merely an excuse, in order that he might gratify his curiosity, and once more behold Rosetta."

"Ah! Michael," exclaimed Mrs. Belford, " surely you do not think that Raymond Middleton had dared to raise his thoughts towards our daughter ?"

"I do, dame," answered Michael, " and the more I reflect upon his conduct on the occasion of which I have spoken, the more I am convinced that my suspicions are correct; and had he remained in the neighbourhood, we should have had cause to dread him. Was he not, even from a lad, a reckless libertine ?"

"True, true."

"And, therefore, it is not surprising that the charms and innocence of our dear Rosetta should have excited his passions. Besides, do you not remember the boldness of his remarks, when I so sharply reproved him for his fulsome and empty flattery ?"

"I do, Michael," answered the old woman, " and I also recollect the impassioned looks he bestowed upon the blushing countenance of our child when she entered the room, and the air of disappointment he evinced before she made her appearance. Ah! Michael, Rosetta is a treasure we must guard with a watchful eye."

"Fear not, wife," returned Michael, " the virtues of Rosetta will always be able to resist temptation, and to frustrate the designs of the insidious deceiver. But she tarries at the cottage of old Dame Henslowe longer than I expected."

"The poor old woman is very ill, you know," said Mrs. Belford, " and Rosetta, no doubt, is anxious to remain as long as she can with her, to keep her company, and administer to her wants. She cannot be engaged in a more amiable or benevolent office."

"True, dame, and in performing such deeds of humanity and charity she finds her principal delight. Heaven bless her, for never had parents a child of whom they should feel more proud."

"Ah, Michael !" ejaculated his wife, " Providence has been very good to us to provide us with such a comfort in our old days, and we ought to feel most grateful for it."

"We ought indeed, dame," said Michael. "But how quiet poor Julio is ; I have scarcely heard him move in the room where we left him, since Rosetta departed on her benevolent mission."

"Ah, the poor child was sadly grieved because we did not think it prudent to suffer him to accompany Rosetta, for he is never happy when she is out of his sight."

"No, he loves her as fondly, I believe, as if she were his own sister ; but who could help becoming attached to so gentle and affectionate a being ?"

"No," coincided the dame, " they must be insensible to all feelings of tenderness who could. But, hark ! I hear him stirring now ; and now again, he's singing one of those wild and plaintive ballads which make such an impressive appeal to the feelings."

The sweet, but melancholy voice of the maniac was now heard singing the following words,—

" No funeral shroud enclosed her form,
There was but one to weep,
And mid the fury of the storm
They cast her in the deep.
But loud was heard one fearful scream,
Above the thunder's roar,
' Julio !' the winds re-echoed back,
And mother was no more !
Poor mother !"

As he uttered the last words in accents of thrilling emphasis, Julio entered the room in which Michael and his wife were seated, with melancholy step, and his eyes cast to the ground.

"No more, no more," he sighed—"poor mother is no more, and poor Julio is left alone —they have all deserted him. I thought I had one, too, whom I was permitted to call sister, and I sought to be happy, and to forget the past ; but she has left me also—gone away, and Julio has no mother—no sister, now."

"Julio," said Mrs. Belford, in a kind and compassionate voice, and gently approaching the poor wandering boy. He looked up, and uttering a cry of recognition and delight, rushed to the arms of the affectionate old woman.

" Ah !" he cried, "you, then, have not left me ; I thought that all had abandoned me, and I wanted to seek the ocean grave of my poor mother, that I might weep my sorrows to her silent shade. But it was cruel to take poor sister Rosetta from me."

"Be calm, Julio," said Mrs. Belford ; " Rosetta has not left us, only for a short time ; she will soon return, and then you will be happy."

"Happy !" repeated Julio, his fine eyes sparkling ; " oh, yes, Julio is always happy when pretty sister Rosetta is near him ; for she is so kind to him, and ever smiles so sweetly upon him. Ah, me ! there are not many who will pity Julio."

" But we pity you, my poor boy ; we love you, and will do all we can to make you happy," said Michael.

"Oh, yes, I know you do," eagerly replied the maniac ; "you are so good, but I fear that Julio is unworthy of your kindness ; but yet indeed, indeed, he would be very grateful."

" We know you would," said Mr. Belford, fervently, and pressing the poor boy's hand ; "we know you are grateful, and we are sufficiently rewarded for all that we can do for you."

" And Rosetta has not left me altogether," said the maniac, with a wild and earnest gaze ; " I have not offended her, have I, that she should thus abandon me ?"

" No, no, Julio," answered Mrs Belford, " she will soon return, fear not."

"Oh, I should break my heart if she were not," said the hapless boy ; " for who would talk so kind to me as sister Rosetta ?"

Michael and his wife endeavoured to soothe him into composure, and at last succeeded much better than they had at first expected, and he seated himself between them at the fire, and proceeded to give utterance to his usual wild and melancholy wanderings.

Occupied in acts of benevolence at the cottage of old dame Henslowe, Rosetta heeded not the lapse of time, and twilight had set in before she arose to depart. The cottage was, however, no great distance from her home, and she therefore apprehended no danger from any one whom she might meet with on the road.

The moon shone beautifully bright, and myriads of stars twinkled in the clear hemisphere. The air was frosty, but invigorating, and Rosetta proceeded on her way with a light and buoyant step.

She had come in sight of the hill, upon whose summit the residence of her parents stood, when she suddenly heard footsteps behind her, and directly afterwards her name was repeated in a man's voice, with a request for her to stop.

She turned round with some astonishment and alarm, but they were banished when she perceived that it was Fiank Trevors who had spoken, and who was hastily advancing towards her.

She stopped immediately, but still she felt a strange palpitation at her heart, for which she was at a loss to account. It was several days since she had before seen Frank, and she now experienced a feeling of confusion and restraint in his presence which she could not conquer. When he had come up to her, she perceived by the moonbeams that his face was pale, and there was a melancholy expression in his eyes as he fixed them upon her, which particularly attracted her attention and excited her curiosity.

" Are you not well, Frank?" she inquired, in a timid voice ; " you look pale, and ——"

" Yes—yes," interrupted Frank, " no doubt I do look pale and sad—for I am sick, sick at heart, Rosetta."

" Sick at heart, Frank," repeated our heroine ; " has anything, then, occurred to disturb you?"

" No, no," answered Frank, in a faltering voice ; " and perhaps it was foolish of me to say anything about it, but I wished to see you, Rosetta."

" To see me, Frank ?"

" Yes ; but why do you look so surprised, Rosetta ? Ah ! there was a time when I thought it afforded equal happiness to both when we met. But a melancholy change has taken place ; Rosetta looks not on me as she was wont to do, and Frank Trevors is no longer the welcome companion that he formerly was."

" Your words are strange, Frank," said the damsel, with emotion ; " I do not understand you."

" And yet methought that Rosetta was not so dull of comprehension," returned Frank Trevors. " Rosetta, for some days my breast has been a raging sea of distracting passions, of torturing doubts, of hopes, of fears ; but I can no longer endure to keep my thought confined to my own bosom ; my fate rests upon the decision of your lips, Rosetta, and this night shall decide it."

" For Heaven's sake, be more explicit, Frank," said the agitated Rosetta ; " I cannot understand your meaning."

Frank paused for a moment or two, and seemed to be endeavouring to acquire firmness to accomplish the task he had imposed upon himself, then at the same time fixing upon the blushing countenance of our trembling heroine a look of the most inexpressible affection and anxiety, he said,—

" Rosetta, from the earliest days of our childhood we have been companions ; we have deposited our every thought in each other's bosom, and studied most carefully one another's wishes. We strolled the same fields, and climbed the same hills together, and we gained knowledge from the same page. As I grew older, I looked around upon the other damsels that came within the sphere of my friendship and acquaintance, but I saw none that I could admire like Rosetta Belford. Her beauties, her virtues, were ever present to my thoughts ; they haunted my imagination in my waking moments, and accompanied me to my pillow in my dreams. The delusions of boyhood were banished beneath their increasing influence ; I could no longer be mistaken ; the sentiment which I had ever believed to be merely that of friendship, I found to be love, ardent, sincere, pure, unquenchable love ! Ah ! you frown upon me ; the coldness of your looks seals my fate, and tells me I have only to despair."

" Let me return home, Mr. Trevors," said the blushing damsel, with increasing agitation ; " I must not, dare not listen to this."

" Nay, Rosetta," exclaimed Frank, gently detaining her, " you must not leave me thus ; end at once my anxiety—tell me whether to hope or despair."

" In my esteem," faintly replied Rosetta, " Francis Trevors must ever hold a paramount situation."

" Esteem !" repeated Frank, beating his breast ; " oh ! the word is colder than ice itself ; but, alas ! I see plainly how it is, some other more fortunate youth possesses that heart I so long have worshipped."

" Frank, Frank," ejaculated our heroine, " spare my feelings, and torture me not by these importunities. I am yet too young to think of love, and—but I cannot ; suffer me to return home, and on some future occasion ——"

"No—no," interrupted Frank, eagerly, " let me now, this moment, hear my doom from your lips, and I promise you that if you reject my vows you shall never more be offended by my presence. Death itself would not be half so terrible as this suspense. Speak to me, Rosetta, by the friendship which you own you bear me ; be candid, be explicit, and tell me whether I am to be happy or wretched for ever ?"

" Heaven forbid that I should be the cause of one moment's unhappiness to you, Frank," said the damsel, in a faint voice, while her heart palpitated violently against her side.

" Nay, Rosetta, you torture me."

" Listen to me, then, Mr. Trevors," said Rosetta, with more firmness, " and receive my words with all confidence and patience. You have asked me to be candid, and it would be cruel of me to attempt to deceive you, were it even in my nature to do so. My heart is yet a stranger to love, at least the love which you have described to animate your breast, and for which I assure you I feel grateful. Mr. Trevors, I admire your virtues, I honour you for your noble qualities of head and heart ; I esteem, and always shall esteem you as a friend, as the friend and companion of my earliest days, but I cannot love you as a husband."

Frank Trevors groaned, covered his face with his hands, and for some moments his emotion was so great, that it completely choked his utterance. Rosetta viewed him with the deepest commiseration, and her heart throbbed more violently than ever.

" 'Tis done," he at length said, fixing upon her such a look of intense despair, that she could never forget ; " 'tis done. Rosetta, your words have decided my fate ; may you meet with one who will endeavour to make you as happy as Frank Trevors would have done. Bless you, bless you, Rosetta, and farewell for ever !"

Hastily he snatched her hand, and pressing it again and again vehemently to his lips, with a long groan of the most indescribable agony, he rushed from the spot with the air of a maniac.

" Frank, Frank !" exclaimed the alarmed damsel, as she viewed his receding form. " Oh, what would you do ?"

He heard not her voice, but still rushed heedlessly on, and was in another instant out of sight.

" Poor Frank," ejaculated our heroine, as she slowly moved away from the spot; " how it grieves me thus to be compelled to disappoint your hopes; but I have spoken only the dictates of my heart ; ever must I regard your virtues with the greatest respect, but to love you as a husband ; oh, I feel that that is impossible. And yet there was a time when, methinks, I could have willingly bestowed on you my hand, and should have been content to unite my future destiny with yours. What can be the cause of the change which has come over me ? I have seen no other being who has engaged my affections. What, then, can have wrought this alteration in my mind ?"

The image of Julio arose to her imagination, and deep blushes suffused her cheeks, while her heart experienced a sensation that was quite new to her, but remembering that the evening was now far advanced, and fearing that her parents would feel uneasy at her prolonged absence, she quickened her pace, and soon afterwards arrived at her dwelling.

Frank Trevors hurried on, totally regardless of where he was going. His brain was distracted, and the most fearful thoughts rushed upon his mind. The fiat of his doom was sealed by the declaration of Rosetta, and he cared not what became of him.

At length, breathless with the speed at which he had proceeded, he paused, and looked wildly around him. He found himself on the beach, and the blue waves dashed at his feet, while the low moaning sound that came from the waters vibrated with a melancholy effect in his ears. Not even the keen air that whistled around him, however, could cool the almost insupportable fever of his brain, and one moment he was half tempted to end at once his anguish by plunging into the deep; but an inscrutable power arrested him in his rash purpose, and he viewed with horror the thought which had for the instant occurred to him.

"She loves me not," he cried, "her lips have acknowledged it, and I must no longer flatter myself with the bright hopes that have so long allured and entranced my senses. But can I ever cease to love, to adore her? No, while life still circulates within my veins, her beauteous image must ever be dearest to my heart. Oh, may she be happy; may she meet with one who is worthy of her exalted virtues, and who will love her, worship her as sincerely as I do. She has confessed that I am not the object of her affections, and that decides my destiny. My course is now clearly before me; I have no longer any business here; I have too long remained inactive, and now, proud, swelling ocean, I hail ye as my future mistress. To my king and country I devote my future services, and if a cannon-ball should lay me low, I can resign my breath without regret, since all I love on earth can never be mine."

As he uttered these words, he became more calm, determination sat upon his fine manly brow, and with a sigh he turned from the spot, and retraced his way towards home, resolving before the break of day to quit that home, perhaps, for ever.

On arriving at home, he concealed his agitation from the observation of his father as well as he was able, and having complained of indisposition, he retired to his chamber, but not to rest; no, he busied himself in packing up a few necessary articles for his premeditated journey, and then sat himself down to write a farewell letter to his father, in which he briefly stated, that being tired of the life of inactivity he had hitherto pursued, he had determined to enter as a seaman on board a ship, and requested the forgiveness of his father for not having given him previous notice of his intentions and wishes. He then, without stopping to undress, threw himself on the bed, and endeavoured to snatch an hour or two's sleep; but this he found to be impossible; his mind was in too violent a state of agitation, and no sooner had the clock tolled the hour of three, than he arose, and having first supplicated the protection of Omnipotence in the determination he had come to, he descended the stairs with silent and cautious steps, and quitted the house. He cast one lingering look upon his native home, and then proceeded on his journey to London, which was the place of his destination.

We need not attempt to describe the feelings of poor Frank Trevors as he hurried on his way, yet there was, at the same time, an unaccountable lightness at his heart the farther he left his home in the distance behind him.

At length he reached the hill on which the old stone house was situated, and with slow and melancholy steps he ascended its rugged sides, and at length stood before the dwelling, and gazed with eager eyes up at the different windows.

"In yonder chamber reposes one to whom my whole soul is devoted," he sighed; "all—all that I prize on earth, but whom, perchance, I never may behold again. But a few months, and Frank Trevors, the rejected, may repose in the arms of death. And will she ever think of me, as the companion, the friend of her youth? Will she ever drop a tear to my memory? Oh, yes, I know her gentle heart too well, to believe that she will not remember my evil destiny with pity and regret. Sleep on, fair girl, and may no fearful dreams disturb your rest. Farewell, farewell—a long farewell, and perhaps, for ever. May Heaven and all good angels watch around you, and shield you from every harm, when I am far away."

His voice was choked with convulsive sobs; he cast one ardent parting glance at the window of Rosetta's chamber, then covering his face with his hands, he dashed down the hill, and hastened on his melancholy journey.

CHAPTER XI.

THE ANGUISH AND REGRET OF ROSETTA.—THE RAGE AND DISAPPOINTMENT OF MARTIN TREVORS.—THE INTERVIEW IN THE OLD STONE HOUSE.

THE interview with Frank Trevors had made a melancholy impression upon the mind of Rosetta Belford, which she could not conquer, and she had seldom, if ever, retired to her chamber with such dismal thoughts as she did on that occasion. The uncertainty of what Frank intended to do, and the solemnity with which he had left her, filled her bosom with many painful ideas, and she longed for the arrival of the morning that she might have her doubts and apprehensions removed. The honour and sincerity of Frank's affection, she was thoroughly convinced of, and how bitterly it grieved her to be compelled to impart anguish to his bosom, and to blight the sanguine hopes he had encouraged ; but she had spoken her real sentiments, she could only esteem him as one of her dearest friends, and it would have been cruel, and highly culpable for her to have deceived him. She could not have done so, for her's was the very soul of candour, simplicity, and truth.

But certainly her sentiments had undergone a great change latterly, for there was a time when she might have convinced herself that Frank Trevors possessed more than her esteem, and what had brought about that alteration? certainly no misconduct of his; no, he was ever noble, generous, and enthusiastically affectionate and attentive towards her. His whole study had ever been to please her, and he seemed never so happy as when he was in her society. She was confident that he harboured not a thought in his breast, but such as would redound to his honour, and she could not but admire him for his virtues. She could regard him with all the warm affection of a sister, but she could not become his wife. She was unable properly to unravel her own feelings, and yet when she thought of Julio, she felt a strange emotion stealing through her frame, which filled her with confusion, and caused the deepest blushes to mantle in her cheeks. But why should this be? She could feel no other sentiments towards the poor maniac youth, than those of pity and admiration. And yet his form was constantly before her imagination, and the more she reflected upon him, the more powerful her emotion became. He was so handsome, so simple, so affectionate; and then the cruelty of his fate, all conspired to excite her deepest sympathy and admiration, and to strengthen the impression he had made upon her; but yet she could not help feeling surprised at the power he had gained over her, and at the new feeling he had excited in her breast. But could this be love? Her heart palpitated most violently against her side, as this question suggested itself to her mind, and she found it impossible to answer it to her satisfaction.

Poor Frank Trevors! she feared that he was destined to experience much misfortune, and she would be the indirect cause. She reflected deeply upon every word he had uttered, and she became more uneasy and apprehensive that he would be driven by despair to commit some rash act,—to take some headstrong course. But she trusted that he would, after all, reflect more coolly upon it, before he was induced to do that which might plunge him into future misery, and which could not but be productive of unhappiness to her. She had treated him with candour, and not unkindness, and surely he could not blame her for the sentiments she had expressed, although she deeply regretted the disappointment it had caused to his hopes. Notwithstanding all he had said, she hoped she should again behold him on the following day, when he would have become more calm, and resolved to bear his fate with manly resignation, and endeavour to find some other damsel on whom he might devote his affections, and who should be every way worthy of his numerous merits, his undoubted virtues.

She regretted that they had ever met, since it was likely to bring much unhappiness on them both; and nothing could be more repulsive to her gentle nature than to be even the innocent cause of anguish to any of her fellow-creatures, especially such a youth as Frank Trevors.

"Would that I could have loved him," she sighed; "would that I could have consented to become his wife, what misery it might have saved. But I cannot help my feelings, and never, never, can I bestow my hand upon any man when my heart does not accompany it. May he meet with one who is worthy of him, and cease to remember me but as a friend and the companion of his youth. My esteem, my warmest wishes shall ever be his, and I trust that time will serve to banish his sorrow and regret, and that he may be placed in that position of life his virtues so justly entitle him to."

Those reflections kept her waking for some time, and in spite of all her efforts to the contrary, her emotion gained strength, and she was in a state of the greatest suspense, until she should behold Frank again, and had ascertained to what determination he had come. The hints he had thrown out were quite sufficient to excite her greatest apprehensions, and yet she was unable to come to any satisfactory conclusion upon them. There was a fearful, a melancholy meaning in the expression of his countenance at the time he left her so abruptly, and the words he had given utterance to, which she could not penetrate, but which gave rise to a feeling of alarm in her breast. But surely Frank would never allow his despair so to gain an ascendancy over him, as to tempt him to any rash and impetuous act, and which might involve him in future misery, and likewise those who were connected with him? No, no, he would reflect more dispassionately upon it, and try to become calm, and to conquer the unfortunate passion he had encouraged for her, and to meet with some other female whom he could love as well, and who would return his affection, and render him happy. Such were her fervent hopes, and she prayed to Heaven before she closed her eyes, that they would be realized, and that all would terminate better than could at present be anticipated.

Her imagination was haunted by troublesome dreams, and she was glad when the morning dawned, and she could leave her couch.   But she felt an unconquerable depression of spirits, and doubts and fears continued to disturb her mind.

"And was it not necessary," she reflected, "that she should make her parents acquainted with what had taken place?   It was, and yet she shrank from the task, with a feeling of repugnance that she could not conquer.   Would her parents approve of her conduct?   Were they not favourable to the passion of Frank Trevors?   She was assured that they were, but still she was confident that they would never seek to bias her affections, or wish her to bestow her hand upon any man, whatever his condition in life might be, who could not also possess her heart.

She endeavoured to compose herself before she entered the room in which her parents were; but still she could not banish the heavy melancholy of her looks, and it quickly met their observation, and excited their surprise and anxiety.

"You are not well, Rosetta," said her mother; "you look pale and agitated; tell me, my love, what is the cause of this?"

Rosetta blushed and hesitated.

"Dear Rosetta," said Mrs. Belford, "your ingenuous countenance cannot conceal the truth; something has occurred to disturb you.   I noticed your emotion on your return home last night, but I would not then disturb you with questions; but, indeed, I must now urge you to explain yourself, for you are aware of the anxiety we must always feel in anything that interests you, and I know that my Rosetta can have no secrets she can wish to conceal from her parents; there is not a thought that passes in her mind that she should be ashamed to acknowledge."

"Oh, no, my dear father," returned Rosetta, making a powerful effort to conquer her emotion; "indeed there is not.   But yet I know not whether my conduct in this instance will meet with your approbation, although it has been dictated alone by candour and sincerity."

"Rosetta can do nothing that can call down the censure of her parents," returned Michael. "Proceed, my child, for your observations have increased my anxiety."

"I will, dear father; but where is Julio?" said Rosetta, looking round the apartment.

"He has not yet left his chamber," replied Mrs. Belford.

"'Tis well," remarked Rosetta, in a faltering voice; "it would not be prudent for him to hear what I am about to state, although he might not be able to comprehend its meaning.   It is to the ears of my parents only that I must communicate these delicate facts."

"Then at once commence the task, dear child," said her mother; "and rest assured that whatever it is you may have to state, that we will listen to you with every indulgence."

Rosetta looked her thanks, but still she could not entirely conquer her emotion, and was compelled to pause for a few moments in order to collect herself.

"My dear parents," she at length commenced, "I believe you have ever found me dutiful and affectionate; that it has been my whole study to render myself worthy of your love, and never to entertain a thought contrary to your will."

"Oh, yes, yes, my child," returned Michael; "you have ever been all that the fondest parents could wish.   But why thus preface your statement?"

"I consider it necessary," answered Rosetta; "but—but to the task which I have allotted to myself.   Francis Trevors ——"

"Ah! what of him?" demanded Michael. "He has seldom visited here of late, and I feel surprised at his neglect towards those from whom he has ever met with the warmest friendship."

" It has been from no feeling of disrespect that he has absented himself," said the damsel ; " you must do him the justice to believe that."

" Well, well, I do believe that," remarked Mr. Belford ; " Frank is an honest, warm-hearted lad, and I feel for him the greatest respect. But what of him now ?"

Rosetta sighed and held down her head, as she answered,—

" I met him last night as I was returning home, and it is from what transpired at that interview, that has thus violently agitated me. Oh, my parents, I fear that I shall be the innocent cause of rendering him miserable for ever."

" How so, my child ?" asked Michael ; " compose yourself, and be explicit."

" Better had it been for Frank and myself had we never met."

" What mean you ? Does not Frank Trevors love you ?"

" He does, he does, and that is the cause of my anguish. Last night he confessed his love,—but—but, although as the friend and companion of my youth, I can and must ever esteem him, I cannot return his passion."

" Say you so, my child ?" returned Michael ; " then indeed I do pity poor Frank, and must confess that I feel no little disappointment myself, for he is a worthy lad, and I had hoped that you would feel the same powerful affection for him as he does for you, and that you would one day have become his bride. But Heaven forbid that I should seek to control your affections, confident as I am that they will never be devoted to one who is not worthy of you."

" Oh, thanks, thanks for this kindness and indulgence," ejaculated Rosetta, fervently. " But I could expect nothing less from you, my dear parents. Never, never will I abuse the confidence you place in me ; never act contrary to your will. I feel honoured by the sentiments Mr. Trevors has avowed to me, but I could never willingly become his wife, and, therefore, I was compelled in candour and honesty to reject him. I would have waited until I had consulted with you, but he was so urgent, and I could not flatter him with hopes which my heart told me could never be realized."

" You say right, my Rosetta," said Michael, " and Heaven forbid that I should ever see you united to a man on whom you could not bestow your heart ; although Frank Trevors is a youth whose virtues shine pre-eminent, and who, I am certain would have done all in his power to render you happy."

" True," ejaculated Rosetta ; " I am indeed fully sensible to his merits, and deeply do I regret that I have been compelled to blight his hopes, although I trust that he will be able in time to conquer his ill-fated passion, and to place his affections on some other damsel, who can return his sentiments with equal fervour."

" To that wish I most cordially respond," said Mr. Belford. " Frank deserves to succeed ; but tell me, how did the poor lad bear the disappointment ?"

" Alas ! he was wrought up to the highest pitch of anguish, and I am apprehensive that he will be urged by despair to commit some rash act, which would greatly embitter my future days."

" Oh, no," returned Michael, " I cannot believe that he would do so. No doubt his grief is great, but he will become calm, and endeavour to submit with resignation to his fate. But tell me all the particulars, and then I shall be better able to form an opinion."

Rosetta complied, and Michael and his wife listened with increased interest and attention.

" Poor lad, poor lad," said Mr. Belford ; " it is indeed a sad disappointment to him, but I trust that he will not be induced to do anything wrong. You say he left you in an abrupt manner ?"

" He did," answered Rosetta, " and the emotion he evinced I shall not easily forget. Oh, it is an unfortunate thing that we ever beheld each other."

" I deeply sympathize with him," said Michael, " but cannot blame you for the conduct you have pursued, my child ; although it would have afforded me much pleasure and satisfaction could you have returned his passion. But did he say that you would not behold him again?"

" Yes ; and at the time he uttered the words, he fixed upon me such a look as I shall not be able to efface from my memory."

"What can he mean to do?" said Mrs. Belford; "I hope to Heaven that his reason and fortitude may return, and that he may not be tempted to do that which he may ever afterwards have bitter reason to repent."

"He will think better of it," observed Michael, "but I will visit the house of his father in the course of the day, and advise with him."

"If he is there," said Rosetta.

"There!" repeated her father; "what do you mean? Think you he will leave his home?"

"I scarcely know what to think, but strange apprehensions have tortured my mind ever since our interview."

"My dear child, I trust that you will find they are groundless," said Michael; "but tell me, has love hitherto been a stranger to the breast of my Rosetta? Has she seen one on whom she could place her affections, and who returns her passion?"

Rosetta blushed deeply, and for a few moments could not return any answer, but at length she said,—

"Oh, my father, how delicate is the question you have put to me; but think you if I had I would have kept it a secret from you? Rosetta has not a thought which she has ever had a wish to conceal from her beloved parents."

" I believe you, my child," said Michael, "and confident I am that you will never entertain a passion that is unworthy of you."

"I seek no more than the love of you—of my mother—of—of Julio," faltered out Rosetta.

" Yes, yes, of Julio," returned Michael; "for he, poor lad, deserves the love and sympathy of all, for the deplorable situation in which he is placed, and the cruel misfortunes it has been his hard lot to encounter. I do not marvel that you should love him."

"As a sister should love her only brother," said Rosetta, in a faint voice, whilst she felt a powerful sensation at her heart, which she had neither the will nor the power to conquer. Her parents embraced her affectionately, and now that she had revealed all that had taken place between her and Frank, she felt relieved of a heavy weight, and did endeavour to hope that he would in time be able to obtain tranquillity.

At this moment they heard the voice of Julio, as he descended the stairs, and soon afterwards he entered the apartment. He advanced towards Mr. and Mrs. Belford, whom he embraced, and he then turned his face, glowing with pleasure, on Rosetta, whose fair hand he took, and pressed it vehemently, but with the most modest respect, to his lips. She felt considerable emotion, and could not help the crimson blushes that mantled in her cheeks.

"Sister Rosetta was very unkind last night to leave Julio," he said; "oh, it made me so sad, so very sad, for I thought that I had done something to offend, and it would break my heart if I were to do anything to displease pretty Rosetta."

Our heroine bestowed upon him one of her sweetest smiles, as she said,—

"Julio has done nothing to offend me, and I am sorry that my unavoidable absence from home last night should have caused him any uneasiness."

"Oh, this is kind, 'tis very kind," said the maniac, "but all so like your sweet nature. But you will not leave me again, will you? We will ramble together as we have before done; and I will gather the sweetest of flowers to decorate your hair, and will sing you the songs my mother learnt me. But I have had such a sweet dream, Rosetta, shall I tell it you?"

"A dream, Julio?" said the damsel, with one of her most bewitching looks. "Oh, yes, I shall be delighted to hear it."

" Listen, then," said the maniac, and he seated himself by her side, and then passed his hands across her forehead, as if he was endeavouring to recall his scattered memory. "No," he said, "I cannot for the life of me think of it now; I have got such a bad memory in some things; and yet—ah! I remember now; I dreamed that you and I, Rosetta, were foremost in a gay procession of handsomely dressed youths and maidens, who chanted songs of gladness, and strewed our path with sweet flowers, as we moved on our way towards the distant village church. Yes, Rosetta, we were going to the church, and for what think you? Why—but no, I must not tell you, and yet I will. Yes, Rosetta, I thought that we were going to be united, that you were about to become Julio's wife! Ha! ha! ha! was it not a strange dream?"

We need not attempt to describe the confusion and emotion of Rosetta at the observations of the poor maniac youth, she hid her blushing face, and her bosom throbbed violently.

Mr. and Mrs. Belford looked at one another with amazement, and scarcely knew what observation to make.

"It was indeed a singular dream, Julio," returned Michael, at length, "and one which I do not think it is very probable will be realized."

"Ah! but it was, though," said Julio, eagerly. "Yes, we knelt at the altar, Rosetta became my bride, and the spirit of my poor murdered mother appeared before us, and blessed our union. Oh—but I see that I have offended you and sister Rosetta by relating this vision. I am very bold, and, ah! me, how very, very unfortunate I am to incur your anger."

"We are not angry, my poor lad," said Michael, pressing his hand; "but we will drop this subject, and talk about something else."

"Oh, yes," said the maniac; "and what shall it be? Shall I tell you about the death-ship, that rides through the howling blast like an evil spirit of the waters? But, no, that is too horrible a subject, and it would shock your ears to listen to it. And then it will drive me mad again to think of, and of the fate of my poor mother. No, no, I will not talk of that—I will not talk of that. Ah! me."

He sighed deeply, and covered his face with his hands. Michael and his wife endeavoured to divert his mind from the melancholy thoughts which engrossed it, and at last succeeded, and Rosetta having somewhat recovered from the confusion into which she had been thrown by the relation of Julio's dream, entered into conversation with him, with all that sweetness and gentleness which was so characteristic of her nature. But Frank Trevors still occupied her most anxious thoughts, nor could she divest her mind of the apprehensions that beset it. She was most solicitous for her father to do as he had promised, namely, to hasten to the house of Martin Trevors, to ascertain whether Frank was at home, and whether he had acquainted his father with what had taken place. She also entertained a secret dread of the effect which her rejection of the suit of his son was likely to have upon him, for there was something so mysterious in the manners of Martin, that she was sometimes inclined to entertain no very good opinion of him, and considered that it might be dangerous to offend him.

While this was going forward at the old stone house, Martin Trevors was in a state of the greatest rage and excitement, for, on arising from his bed in the morning, he discovered the absence of Frank, and the letter he had left behind him. He could scarcely believe the evidence of his eyes, and read the letter again and again, before he could convince himself. Then he frowned terribly, and uttering a dreadful oath, he struck the table violently with his clenched first, and for a few moments the power of his rage choked his utterance.

"Now, by the infernal host," he at last exclaimed, "this is the worst news I have heard for many a day, and will retard, if not altogether frustrate my plans. The boy gone I know not whither. Confusion! It will drive me mad. And so Frank Trevors was not good enough for the daughter of Michael Belford, after all the hopes which had been held out to him, and the encouragement he had received. The scornful jilt! But let them beware—they have aroused the wrath and indignation of Martin Trevors, and he will not fail to be revenged. Rash boy! to leave me thus, and all through that prude-faced girl, as vain of the little beauty she possesses as if she were an empress. Oh, but she shall pay dearly for her scorn.

Yes, they do not yet know me, or they would have paused ere they ventured to incur my anger. Whither has the fool gone? What may he not in his despair be tempted to do? But I must find him out, if possible, and endeavour to recall him to his senses. Why had he not consulted with me before he took this precipitate step? I could then have arranged my plans, and have placed him in a position to triumph. This moment I will away to the house of Michael Belford, and make them acquainted with my mind. They shall find that they must not attempt to insult Martin Trevors, or his son, with impunity. They have driven Frank from his home, perhaps to lay violent hands on himself, and they may depend upon it that they shall not be suffered to go unpunished."

Again he swore a dreadful oath, and then, taking up his hat and cloak, he left his home, and with disordered steps bent his way towards the house of Belford. He was not long in arriving there, and, just as he did so, Michael was issuing from the door for the purpose of visiting him. The countenance of Martin plainly evinced the rage and emotion that inhabited his breast; and Michael saw plainly that the interview was not likely to be a very agreeable one.

"Good morning, Mr. Trevors," said Mr. Belford; "I was just about to visit you."

"Indeed!" returned Trevors, with a frown and a bitter sneer; "then you see I have saved you the trouble by calling upon you. I don't know whether or not I shall be more free than welcome."

"Martin Trevors has always been a welcome visitor at my house," replied Michael; "but I see you are ruffled, and guess the cause; however, walk in, and let us discuss this unpleasant business over calmly and dispassionately."

"Ay, calmly and dispassionately," said Martin; "I presume you are aware of what has taken place between your daughter and my son?"

"Rosetta has informed me," said Mr. Belford, "and sincerely do I regret that there should have been any misunderstanding."

"Misunderstanding!" repeated Martin Trevors, with a scornful look; "you put rather a temperate title to it. But, of course, the consequences it has been productive of to me are nothing."

"Mr. Trevors," said Michael, "I beg you to understand me rightly. You know full well that I have ever treated your son with the warmest friendship and regard; nay, more, I viewed his attentions towards Rosetta with satisfaction, and would have been most happy had she been able to return the sentiments he has confessed towards her; but I cannot, and, if I could, I would not, control her affections, and ——"

"Bah!" interrupted Trevors, impatiently; "perhaps, before you proceed any further, you will condescend to peruse this letter."

He put the epistle, which Frank had left behind him, into his hand.

"I like not the coldness and austerity of your manners, Martin Trevors," said Michael, as he took the letter. "Let whatever may have happened, at any rate neither myself or my daughter are to blame."

"Indeed!" sneered Martin; "but peruse the letter, peruse the letter."

Michael did so, and as his eyes glanced over its contents, his countenance exhibited the greatest emotion, while Trevors viewed him with a malicious eye, and it was quite evident that the most vindictive feelings were gathering in his breast.

"Rash young man," exclaimed Michael, when he had read the letter; "most sincerely do I feel for and pity him."

"Pity him!" returned Martin Trevors, with a fierce look. "And is pity the only feeling you should entertain towards him?"

"You surely cannot blame me, Martin?" said Mr. Belford.

"Blame you!" repeated Martin; "have I not reason to blame and censure you?"

"Be cool, Trevors; I seek not to quarrel with you, nor do I see that there is any necessity for so doing. Explain yourself."

"Be cool!—Ha! ha! ha! Excellent advice to a father whom you have robbed of his son."

"Robbed you of him!" repeated Michael, with indignation; "this is language which I did not expect from you, Mr. Trevors, and which I cannot and will not tolerate."

"Nay," returned Martin, with a determined air, "you may tolerate it or not, which you please, it matters little to me; I came here to speak my mind, and it is not Michael Belford, or any one like him, that will prevent my doing so."

"I can scarcely believe my ears," said Michael, looking at the enraged man with astonishment; "but you shall not anger me; proceed—of what is it you accuse me?"

"Of deceiving my son," answered Martin; "of encouraging him with hopes which you never intended to realize; of tampering with his feelings; of cruelly mocking him, and blighting his prospects for ever."

Michael heard him with amazement, and for some moments he was unable to return any answer; but he conquered his resentment, and at length exclaimed,—

"By Heaven, this is false! You do me the greatest injustice, Martin Trevors."

"But I maintain that I do not," replied Trevors; "I repeat my accusation. Did you not for years encourage the intimacy of my son with your daughter? Did you not look with an approving eye upon the attentions he paid her? You could not be blind to the real nature of his sentiments towards her, and you flattered his hopes merely to mock his feelings and drive him to ultimate despair."

"Beware, Martin," said the indignant Mr. Belford; "you may try my patience too far, but I cannot believe that you are serious."

"But I am. Martin Trevors is not accustomed to joke, especially upon such subjects as this. I say again, that you have deceived, tampered with the feelings of my son, and driven him from his home. Rosetta, your daughter, I also accuse of coquetry and deception."

"By all my hopes, I will not tamely endure this, Martin Trevors," exclaimed Michael Belford, his cheeks flushed with resentment. "Accuse my child of coquetry and deception—she who is all candour, truth, and innocence!"

"Ha! ha! ha!" laughed Martin; "she is the very paragon of perfection."

"Dare not to cast an aspersion upon her unblemished character, Martin Trevors, or, by Heaven, notwithstanding the friendship that has existed between us for years, you may dearly repent it."

"You do well to threaten, Michael Belford, but I heed it not; it is not you who can alarm Martin Trevors by an angry look, or a few empty, bombastic words."

"Martin," said Mr. Belford, "you have suffered rage and disappointment to overcome your reason on this occasion; it is better that this interview should terminate, and I will see you again when you are more cool and collected."

"Oh, indeed!" returned Trevors, with a malicious look; "but I am perfectly cool and collected now, and I will speak my mind, however unpleasant it may be to your ears, Mr. Belford."

"This conduct is not to be endured; I will not be insulted in my own house."

"Then we will walk into the open air, if you please," replied Martin, with the most bitter sarcasm.

"Martin Trevors," said Michael, struggling hard to control his feelings of resentment, "I did not expect this from you."

"No doubt of it. You thought I was a weak fool, that would submit to injustice without a murmur, I suppose."

"No man could ever accuse Michael Belford of acting unjustly towards him."

"But I do."

"Hear me, Martin Trevors," said Michael, "and let my answer satisfy you, and convince you of the wrong you do me and my daughter, by these aspersions. It is true that I have ever encouraged the visits of your son to my house, and approved of the attentions he paid to Rosetta, for no one is more fully sensible to his merits than I am, and most happy should I have been for him to become my son-in-law; but great as the esteem which my daughter I know bears him, she has confessed that she cannot love him with the affection that a wife should bestow upon her husband; she has spoken with candour and truth, and never would I seek to urge her to bestow her hand upon any one who did not also possess her heart."

See page 135.

"Oh, of course, Frank Trevors is not good enough for such a pattern of excellence as Rosetta Belford," returned Martin, with the most malicious irony.

"Mr. Trevors," said Michael, "it is evident that you have come here with a determination to quarrel; but I will not engage in any angry discussion with you. You will think better of this, and I must request that the present interview may end."

"Oh, but I have not done yet," said Trevors; "you shall hear me out, however unpleasant it may be to you. Martin Trevors is not the man to be cajoled and insulted without resenting it."

"Cajoled! insulted!"

"Ay, those are the words, and what I mean."

"Are you mad, Martin? you surely must be, or you never would talk thus."

"Mad! Ha, ha, ha! when a man speaks a few unpleasant truths, you deem him mad. Eh, Michael Belford?"

"I beg of you to retire, for I would not that this meeting should terminate in the way it is likely to do, if you persist in such language as that you have already made use of."

"So then, Michael Belford orders me from his house. Oh, this is an extraordinary proof, indeed, of the friendship you have so much boasted of."

"I am willing to hear you, Martin, if you are prepared to discuss this unfortunate business in a proper temper ; but I will not submit to have myself or my daughter calumniated."

"Calumniated !" repeated Martin, with a sneer; "but 'tis well, no doubt some other youth of more pretensions has supplanted Frank in the affections of your daughter, and I wish her joy of her conquest."

"Cease, Martin," exclaimed Michael, his bosom swelling with indignation ; "you may try my patience too far."

"And what if I do?" demanded Trevors, fiercely ; "think you that I will shrink from the consequences ? But I will be cool ; oh, yes, I will be very cool ; you will invite me to your daughter's wedding, Michael, will you not ? If it is only out of old *friendship's* sake."

"Leave the house, sir, I will brook this no longer."

"Oh, but I am not going yet, notwithstanding you command me ; and you may tell your coquette, and jilt of a daughter ——"

"Coquette ! jilt !" exclaimed Mr. Belford, furiously, and clenching his fists ; "have I lived to hear my innocent child thus basely calumniated ? But you are not serious ; you cannot be."

"I am. I repeat that Rosetta, in her behaviour to my son, has shown herself to be a coquette and a jilt !"

"Villain ! recall your words, or ——"

"Villain, in your teeth !" cried Trevors ; "I repeat every word, every accusation that I have uttered."

"Then thus do I resent the foul calumny," exclaimed the now infuriated Michael, springing upon Martin Trevors, and seizing him by the collar. But he forbore to strike him, although he endeavoured to force him towards the door.

"Take your hand off my collar, Michael Belford !" cried Trevors ; "or by hell it shall be worse for you !"

"You have grossly, basely insulted me," said Mr. Belford, "and I insist that you leave my house !"

"Forcibly ejected, and by you !" cried Martin, fiercely ; "never !"

He grappled with Michael, and they struggled violently together for some moments, but Martin Trevors was much the more powerful man of the two, and at length succeeded in shaking Mr. Belford off, and hurling him violently to the floor, and he was proceeding to follow up his advantage by a blow, when the door of an adjoining room was suddenly thrown open, and Rosetta, pale and trembling, rushed into the apartment, and darted in between them. Martin Trevors, when he beheld her, shrank back a few paces, and eyed her with a look of malice, which was perfectly demoniacal.

"Rash, passionate man, what would you do?" she exclaimed ; "what is the meaning of this daring outrage ?"

"You here, girl," said Martin Trevors, in a voice hoarse with rage ; "'tis well, for to your face I accuse you of hypocrisy and deception. I charge you with having sported with the feelings of my son, but to blight all his future hopes, and to leave him to despair. Hear me ; you have aroused the wrath of Martin Trevors, and he will not fail to have revenge. I will make this once happy home desolate, and wring the hearts of you and your parents to distraction. You will not become the wife of Frank Trevors ; no, no, but you shall be made the mistress of one who is sunk in the lowest depths of degradation. Good day, Mr. Belford, and *Miss* Rosetta. Reflect on my words and tremble !"

Thus saying, the ruffian shook his clenched fist at them, and fixing upon them a look of the most fiendish meaning, quitted the house, and closed the door violently after him. Rosetta was overpowered by her feelings of terror, and sank insensible in the arms of her father, just as Mrs. Belford and Julio entered the room. The scene of consternation that ensued, we must leave to the imagination of the reader, while the mingled feelings of rage and emotion which Michael experienced, were almost insupportable.

CHAPTER XII.

THE FEARS OF ROSETTA.—THE SCENE BETWEEN TREVORS AND SIR HORACE MIDDLETON.—THE DISAPPEARANCE.

"GOOD God! what is the matter?" cried Mrs. Belford, as she beheld the insensible state of her daughter; "what violence has Martin Trevors attempted, that it should thus alarm my poor child? Speak, Michael, and tell me all about it."

"Martin Trevors is a scoundrel!" replied Michael; "he has calumniated us and our dear Rosetta, and had it not been for her sudden arrival, the ruffian would have dealt me a blow."

"A blow!" repeated the old woman; "could he indeed have been so violent and unjust? Oh, surely there must be some misunderstanding in this."

"He has grossly misrepresented our motives," returned Michael; "accuses Rosetta of having played the jilt towards Frank, who has absconded from home, without stating whither he has gone, or what are his intentions."

"Accuse Rosetta of being a jilt!" said Mrs. Belford, her cheeks flushed with indignation. "Has he, indeed been so base? Cruel, ungenerous man, what has she done to deserve this?"

"It all originates, as you may imagine, in Rosetta having rejected the suit of Frank Trevors, and he taxes her and us with having shamefully deceived him, and tampered with his feelings."

"Headstrong man, how little has the friendship we have ever evinced towards him and his son, merited such a return as this! From this time then, we may consider him as our enemy?"

"Yes, and our most implacable one," answered Michael. "He has vowed a terrible revenge."

"But he will think better of this," said Mrs. Belford; "and if not, Providence will not fail to frustrate his plans. My poor Rosetta, this will be a terrible shock to your feelings. But how little deserved has it been. It would, indeed, have been a fortunate job for you both, had neither you nor Frank ever have met each other."

"It would most certainly," coincided Michael; "and yet do I pity the young man from my very heart."

"And so do I," remarked the old woman; "but little did I anticipate that such would have been the result of the intimacy between him and our daughter."

"Sister Rosetta, sister Rosetta," said Julio, approaching nearer to our heroine, with much emotion in his demeanour, and taking her hand; "why do you not look up and smile upon Julio as you always do? Oh, how pale, how very pale she is. Who has dared to frighten Rosetta? Let Julio know, and although he is young, he will find more than the strength of a man to punish those who have injured her."

"Do not fear, my poor boy," said Michael; "Rosetta has only fainted, and will soon recover again. See, she even now opens her eyes. Rosetta, my love."

"Oh, joy, joy!" ejaculated the maniac; "sister Rosetta, oh, tell me, are you better? What has happened to cause this?"

Rosetta faintly smiled upon him, and he took her hand, and pressed it with wild transport to his lips. Then she looked around the apartment, and in a tremulous voice, ejaculated,—

"Where is he, is he gone? Oh, how terrible were the words he uttered; and he would have struck you, my father, had I not interposed."

"Fear nothing, Rosetta," said her father; "he is no longer present, and in spite of all his threats, we have nothing to apprehend from him."

"I trust to Heaven that we have not," sighed Rosetta; "but Frank Trevors; oh, what has become of him?"

"He has left his home, and gone I know not where," answered Michael ; "for he did not inform his father in the note he left behind him."

"Unfortunate young man !" said Rosetta ; "how deeply do I regret that I have been compelled to disappoint the hopes you had so fatally formed ; but surely I was not to blame for speaking the truth, and indeed, indeed I could not love him."

"Love him !" repeated Julio, hastily, and fixing upon her a look of the most touching expression, while his bosom seemed to throb with more than ordinary emotion ; "who—who ? Rosetta must not love any one but Julio."

"And her parents," added Mrs. Belford, soothingly and persuasively.

"Yes, yes," returned the maniac, "Julio and her parents."

He then seated himself by her side, and gazed intently up in her face, without apparently being able to comprehend the conversation that ensued.

Rosetta, having now become more composed, requested her father to relate all that had passed between him and Martin Trevors previous to her interposition, which he did, and our heroine and her mother listened to him with mingled feelings of astonishment, fear, and disgust.

"Never could I have believed that such was the character of Mr. Trevors," observed Rosetta ; "or that he could have suffered his rage and disappointment to carry him to such fierce extremes. Heaven knows that I have ever entertained the warmest esteem for his son, and no one can feel deeper regret at the rash course he has taken than I do."

"I know it, my child," returned Michael ; "and I trust that he will yet conquer his feelings, and, returning home, endeavour to reconcile himself to his fate. But never can I forgive the base aspersions which his father has cast upon us."

"Oh, it was most cruel and unjust," said Mrs. Belford.

"And he called me hypocrite, deceiver," ejaculated Rosetta ; "oh, what have I ever done to merit such opprobrious epithets ?"

"Nothing, my child," said her father ; "but let it not disturb you, I beg of you."

"I fain would banish it from my memory, but cannot," said the damsel ; "and then the threats which Mr. Trevors held out, still ring in my ears, and never shall I be able to forget the expression of his countenance, as he gave utterance to them."

"They are not worth heeding, my love," remarked Michael ; "for if it is even his will, he never can have the power of putting them into execution."

"I trust not," said Rosetta ; "but alas ! there seems to me to be more terrible meaning in those words than we can at present imagine."

"You must try to banish all such ideas from your mind, Rosetta, and I have no doubt that all will yet be well."

"Heaven send that it may, and that poor Frank Trevors may not be tempted to do anything, which he may afterwards have reason to repent, and which would cause me the deepest regret, as I should look upon myself as the indirect and innocent occasion of his troubles."

"You cannot have anything to reproach yourself with, Rosetta," observed Michael ; "so do not let that thought again trouble you."

"Would that Mr. Trevors would remove from the neighbourhood, for I shall never consider that you, my dear parents, are safe for a moment while he continues to reside in it."

"Oh, I fear him not," answered Michael ; "and do believe that he only made use of the threats in order to give vent to his unfounded rage. I am an old sailor, and not used to be frightened at trifles. Besides, there is the strong arm of the law to prevent him from the perpetration of any outrage, and he would find me more than a match for him."

"You remember what he said about the secret power he possesses, my dear father," said Rosetta ; "and I cannot help thinking that he did not speak entirely false."

"Mere empty boast, my child ; it was nothing more, depend on it."

"But when we reflect upon the mystery of his manners," remarked Mrs. Belford, "and many other circumstances connected with him, it is enough to induce us to place more confidence in his assertions."

"Yes," rejoined Rosetta, "and my father cannot have forgotten his strange behaviour on the night of the appearance of the Death Ship; his emotions, and the observations he made use of when he beheld Julio; oh, should he be in any way connected with that dreadful and mysterious vessel, what may we not have to fear from him."

"Nay, Rosetta," said Michael, "you surely alarm yourself without sufficient cause. I cannot help thinking that the idea you have just expressed is preposterous."

"Who talks about the Death Ship and mentions the name of Julio?" ejaculated the maniac, starting to his feet, and gazing vacantly around him. "They shall not have me again in their power. No, no, I defy them, monsters, murderers as they are, to tear me away from hence. They know not where I am, and therefore what have I to fear?"

"Nothing, Julio," answered Michael, "under this roof, with the blessing of Heaven, you are perfectly safe, and shall never more fall into the power of your cruel enemies."

"Oh, thanks, thanks!" returned the poor boy, with looks of the most unbounded delight; "and shall I never more be separated from you, from sister Rosetta, until I rejoin my mother in Heaven? Then, indeed, shall I be most happy."

Michael Belford and his wife smiled kindly on the unfortunate lad, and he then relapsed into silence, and seemed to take no notice of the conversation which followed between Rosetta and her parents.

"And he would have struck you, my father," again observed our heroine, "had I not made my appearance. That shows to what extreme lengths he will suffer his passion and revenge to go."

"It would have cost him dear had he done so, Rosetta," replied Michael.

"Headstrong, unreasonable man, to do us such base injustice, by attributing to us motives which could never, under any circumstances, have entered our thoughts."

"True, and it shows at once that his character is mean and despicable."

"But you will not seek another interview with him, dear father?" inquired the damsel, anxiously.

"No," replied Michael, "I will leave him to his own thoughts, and only hope that he may never again cross my path, at any rate till he has seen the injustice he has done us, and may repent of his conduct. I bear him no animosity, although I have ample cause for doing so."

"I am certain you do not, Michael," said his wife; "for it is foreign to your nature to do so; and I fervently hope that this affair will not be attended with any more unfavourable results. Did poor Frank but know what has taken place, I am confident that he would feel the greatest regret and disgust at the conduct of his father; for disappointed though he has been, he would sooner suffer a thousand deaths, than utter a word, or entertain a thought derogatory to Rosetta or to us."

"You do the poor lad no more than justice by such an opinion, dame," returned Michael; "and I hope that fortune may yet shower her favours upon him, and that he may return a happier man than he has hitherto been. He is every way deserving of a better destiny, and in the course of time he may be able to triumph over the passion that at present predominates in his breast."

"But surely it was most hasty and imprudent of him to abandon his home," observed our heroine; "and I cannot but feel most anxious to know whither he has gone, and what are his future intentions."

"And so am I," said Michael; "but I have a strong suspicion of what are his designs."

"Indeed!" ejaculated Rosetta, eagerly; "oh, name them, for I cannot divest my mind of the fearful doubts which beset it."

"I have always heard Frank express a great predilection for the sea," remarked Mr. Belford.

"Ah! true, true!"

"War is now raging fiercely," continued Michael; "the government wants seamen, and it is not at all improbable that Frank has determined to enter upon the service."

"Yes, it may be so," said Rosetta; "it is indeed most likely. And, if it be so, may Heaven guard him safely through all the dangers it may be his lot to encounter."

To this wish both Mr. and Mrs. Belford most heartily responded, and after a short time the conversation ceased, and Rosetta tried to become more tranquil, though when she thought of all the painful circumstances of the morning, she found this a task that was indeed most difficult to accomplish. The fearful observations and threatening looks of Martin Trevors continued to haunt her imagination, and, when she was alone, she gave herself up to all the anxiety of meditation.

That Trevors was a desperate and determined man, she was fully persuaded, and his conduct on this occasion was sufficient to satisfy her to what lengths he would suffer his jealous suspicions to go. She could not divest her mind of the belief that both herself and her parents had much to apprehend from him, and again she lamented that she and Frank had ever become acquainted, since it was likely to be productive of so much misery to them both. Deeply, too, she regretted that she had not been able to return his passion, and had thus been compelled to blight the hopes and prospects of a young man, who was so well calculated, from the intrinsic merits he possessed, to render any woman, who could reciprocate his vows, happy. She fervently prayed that time might work a revolution in his sentiments, and that, if ever they should meet again, he might be able to view her with a feeling not more powerful than that of friendship. There were times when she could not bring her mind to believe that Frank was the son of Martin Trevors, they were so unlike in disposition and manners; but that was a question which could not be of any momentous interest to her, and she therefore quickly dismissed it from her thoughts.

She trembled lest her father should accidentally encounter Martin, for, from the violence of the latter's disposition, and the malicious feelings he had evinced towards him on the last interview, she apprehended the most dangerous results to them both, if such a meeting should unfortunately take place.

When Martin Trevors quitted the house of Michael Belford, as he retraced his way towards his home, he gave vent to curses loud and deep, and his mind brooded over the most diabolical designs.

"The old hound!" he cried; "to lay violent hands upon me, and try to force me from his dwelling. By hell, my blood broils when I think of it, and, had not the girl interposed, I would have fully retaliated upon him for his boldness. But, if they think to escape my vengeance, they are much mistaken. They know not Martin Trevors yet, or they would see the danger of incurring my wrath. They may think my threats are mere empty boastings, but they will find out that they are not so, when it is too late. Oh, how my taunts seemed to gall him! but I will have my revenge in a much more satisfactory way, and they shall have reason to curse the hour when they first beheld me, but more especially when they incurred my hatred. They will not be the first who have fallen victims to my wrath. Oh, no; were I known in my real character, how would many shudder in my presence. The girl Rosetta, if she has placed her affections on another, which I strongly suspect she has, shall never have the opportunity of gratifying them. No; before many weeks, probably before many days have elapsed, she shall be in my power, and then shall the bitter punishment of her scorn commence. Oh, it will be glorious sport for me to witness her agony, and to taunt her with the rejection of the love of Frank! Already has my prolific mind, stimulated by hatred and revenge, formed a plan of torture most exquisite for them all, and I will not rest until it is in full operation. So Frank Trevors was not good enough for you, my dainty damsel, eh? 'Tis well; you shall be compelled to become the mistress of one whom you most loathe, and whose path is that of the most abominable crime. Oh, I have always the most excellent methods at command of lowering the pride of upstart beauty, and so you shall find to your cost. It is not your rejection of the suit of Frank that I regret, for I never intended that you should become his wife, only I interfered not with it for a time, lest it should frustrate the other plans I had in contemplation. Curses on the foolish boy for abandoning his home so abruptly, and thus retarding the progress of my plans! But it is no use to repine now, for it cannot be helped, and I will leave no scheme untried to discover him, and bring him to his senses. Had he been acquainted with the extraordinary and secret particulars connected with him, he would not have been so mad as to act in the manner he has done, and I question much if it would not have changed his sentiments towards Rosetta. Bah! he should not have acted in the manner he has, for, notwithstanding the austerity of my manners, I have ever treated him with the care and attention of a parent. No matter; I have no doubt I shall be able to settle everything to my satisfaction by-and-bye. That maniac boy, too, I must keep a sharp eye on him also, and consider how he shall be disposed of. I have plenty of business to perform, but I dare say I shall be able to accomplish it with my usual ability."

Thus soliloquizing, he arrived at home, and throwing himself into a chair, ruminated deeply upon all that had taken place, and the course it would be necessary for him in future to pursue.

"It will not be prudent for me to remain in this neighbourhood much longer," he observed, "and yet I must not retire far from it. No; I must be near Sir Horace Middleton, to keep the same careful eye upon his actions that I have hitherto done. There is much for me to accomplish with the old wretch yet, and I must not suffer any opportunity to pass me, of ripening my plans. But no one shall know whither I have gone, and then they cannot entertain any suspicions against me, nor prove any obstacle to the completion of my wishes. But why should I dread suspicion, when I have for so many years escaped it? Ha! ha! ha! I have played my cards well, and yet see a rich game before me."

An expression of exultation passed over his features as he gave utterance to these words, and he remained for some moments silent; then he arose, and once more putting on his hat and cloak, as some sudden thought appeared to strike him, he again left his dwelling, and bent his steps towards the Manor-house, determined on having an interview with the baronet.

In the course of a quarter of an hour he arrived there, and, in his usual authoritative manner, commanded to be shown immediately into the presence of Sir Horace. He was obeyed, and the baronet greeted him in his usual tremulous manner, though his care-worn features were more pale than they even ordinarily were, and showed how agonizing had been his thoughts since he and Trevors had last met.

Martin viewed him with his invariable look of scorn, but Sir Horace could perceive very plainly, in addition, that he had experienced something which agitated his mind, and he was most anxious, yet fearful, to know what it was, for his guilty soul always anticipated something in connection with himself, some fresh danger at hand, to add to the load of care which already distracted his brain. He felt the power which Martin Trevors had over him; he knew that he must be the mere creature of his will; that his life was in his hand; that he was indeed the secret spy upon his actions which he had represented himself to be; and it will not be wondered, therefore, that the wretched miser should tremble in his presence, and shrink appalled from the sinister expression of his eyes, which was always more powerful whenever they were fixed upon him.

The baronet, however, managed to rise, and, with a faltering air, handed Martin a chair, on which he unceremoniously seated himself, and then fixed upon his companion a more stern and stedfast look than before.

"Well, Martin Trevors," at length said the baronet, in a querulous voice, "what is the purport of your visit to me now?"

"You will know that anon," answered Trevors; "what are you looking so scared about? Have you not recovered from your mad fit yet? But, psha! you are always mad; I ought to know that."

"Would that I were, Martin," returned Sir Horace; "would that I were indeed always mad, then should I not be troubled with the dreadful, the racking thoughts, which constantly oppress me."

"It is the enjoyment you have taken such particular pains to purchase, Sir Horace," returned Martin, with a sneer.

" Enough of this, Trevors," ejaculated the miser; " it can do you no good to add to my tortures by these bitter taunts."

" Oh ! but it does though," remarked Martin ; " it is glorious food to me, and every pang they cause you, affords most ample satisfaction."

" Why should it do so, Martin ? Why should it do so ?"

" No matter; I come here now upon another errand than merely to exult in your misery."

" Ah ! what mean you ?" demanded the trembling old man ; " you do not seek more gold, do you ?"

" Not at present—when I want it I shall command it," replied Martin Trevors, " and you dare not refuse me."

The baronet groaned, and, after much difficulty, observed,—

" You have something to communicate, Martin, have you not ? you never come here but you are the harbinger of bad tidings."

" Indeed ! but, however, this time the bad tidings, unfortunately, principally concern myself."

A faint expression of satisfaction glowed in the haggard countenance of Sir Horace, and he awaited with impatience to hear what it was that Martin had to impart.

" Ah !" continued Trevors, " I see the difference in the expression of your features on that intimation."

" No, no, Martin ; you mistake me ; I ——"

" No matter," interrupted Martin Trevors ; " but, perhaps, you may not have so much cause for gratification as you seem to anticipate. I suppose you will not be sorry to hear that I intend to quit this neighbourhood shortly."

" Ah !" ejaculated Sir Horace, with a feeling of hope and pleasure which he could not conceal.

" Only the immediate neighbourhood," added Trevors ; " only the place which I have for so long a time inhabited ; for circumstances have within the last few hours occurred, which render it necessary that the place of my locality should not be known."

The brow of Sir Horace Middleton again loured.

" I do not understand you, Martin," he observed.

" I dare say not ; but it is my intention to be perfectly explicit. You must not imagine for a moment that I am going to leave you to yourself. No, no ; I must continue to be the constant spy upon your actions. You must not have a thought that shall remain unrevealed to me."

The miser again groaned, and looked at Martin with anxiety.

" Proceed, Trevors," he said, in a faltering voice ; " do not keep me in suspense ; what is it that has caused you to come to this sudden determination ?"

" The thirst for vengeance, and the more speedy accomplishment of my wishes."

" But I, Martin ; I ——"

" Oh ! you have not much to do in this matter ; I have you safe enough, whenever it pleases me to put my final plans into effect."

" You torture me !"

" Well, I cannot help that. However, I will at once to the business. I suppose you are aware that my son had fixed his affections upon the girl, Rosetta Belford ?"

" Yes, yes ; and that my graceless nephew also ——"

" Ay, I know all about that ; but don't interrupt me."

" I will not, Trevors—proceed, proceed."

" All along Frank has flattered himself with the idea that Rosetta returned his love."

" And did she not ?"

" No ; yesterday evening he formally confessed his love, and received a scornful rejection."

" Well, well."

" Driven to despair," continued Martin, " by this disappointment of his hopes (more fool he, I say), he has left me, absconded from his home, and gone I know not whither."

"Ah! and you seek revenge against the girl and her parents?" said Sir Horace.

"I do, and will have it. What's more, I must have possession of her person."

"Well," demanded the baronet, "and what has this to do with me?"

"Oh! I intend that it shall have something to do with you, though," answered Trevors.

"How so? In what way? I am too old to have any hand in such stratagems."

"Hark ye; I have already matured my plans with respect to the girl, and, in order that I may carry them into effect with less danger, I intend to leave my present habitation, and to keep concealed somewhere near the spot. The first opportunity I have of seizing Rosetta, she must be brought hither, where she can be kept a close prisoner, until the opportunity presents itself of completing my designs."

Sir Horace started, and trembled on hearing this.

"Trevors," he said, "you cannot mean what you say?"

"But I do, though," answered Martin.

"Would you bring destruction upon me? What can I do with the girl in this place? I fancy that the eye of suspicion is turned upon me whichsoever way I direct my gaze, and ——"

"And so it is," interrupted Martin, with a malicious look of exultation; "you are known for a miserable old niggard, one who has amassed wealth but to oppress; and people have long asked each other by what means you have obtained it, and what it is that presses upon your conscience, and makes you shun the light of heaven. What I propose—nay, command—will not strengthen the dark surmises already cast upon your character."

"But—but the excitement the abduction of the girl, Rosetta, will cause in the neighbourhood, Martin! The strict search that will be made after her, the ——"

"Pshaw! what will that concern you? They will never suspect that you, the old miser, the miserable, drivelling old hunks of the Red Manor-house, could entertain any designs against a damsel so young and beautiful. Your amorous days are gone by, Sir Horace Middleton; all is winter, chilling frost, now, if ever anything like spring or summer could possibly have formed a portion of your icy nature. Oh, you are perfectly safe from any suspicion of amatory intrigue—ha! ha! ha!"

"Oh, Martin," gasped forth the tortured old man, "why will you persist in this bitter irony? Think better of it."

"I have thought enough, and decided," returned Martin Trevors, sternly; "the girl must be brought here."

"And why here, Martin, why here?"

"Because it is the most convenient place, and answers the designs I have in contemplation."

"Alas! alas! you are bent to ruin me."

"I am determined to make you the entire subject of my will," replied Martin, with a look which made the wretched Sir Horace shudder. "It is worse than madness to attempt to defy me, or to resist my commands; though I think you know that by this time, Sir Horace Middleton."

"And should it be discovered that Rosetta Belford is confined here, my destruction is certain."

"But I will take good care that it is not discovered," returned Martin.

"And what are your ultimate designs against the girl?"

"That it does not suit me to reveal at present. She probably will not remain here long, for it is my intention to dispose of her another way."

"And how is she to be attended to?" demanded the trembling miser.

"Leave that to me; it is sufficient for you to know that she is to be brought here. It is no use for you to murmur, my determination is fixed."

The old man clasped his forehead, and swayed his body to and fro, with convulsive agony. Martin Trevors viewed his emotion with a sardonic grin of scorn and triumph.

"Oh, horror!" groaned Sir Horace; "surely death would be preferable to this!"

"Perhaps it might," said Martin Trevors; "but that will come to you soon enough. It is at my will that you live or die. Your gold cannot save you when I give the word."

Again the wretched old man groaned, and looked at his unwelcome and mysterious visitor with a piteous glance. But Martin was insensible to commiseration, and therefore he appealed in vain.

"Oh, Trevors," he ejaculated, "why do you continue to haunt me like a fiend? Why did you not suffer me to end my wretched existence this morning, when my mind was wound up to the highest pitch of determination by despair?"

"Because it was not my will," answered Martin. "Oh, no; I have much more for you to do yet. Besides, you should feel a pleasure in being revenged against Michael Belford, and all his family, if you knew all."

"Why so, Martin?" eagerly demanded Sir Horace.

"Because he has saved one from death whom you have cause to dread."

"What mean you, Trevors?—what mean you?"

" That boy, that maniac boy, whom he rescued from the burning vessel, and whom you encountered with him and his daughter on the cliffs."

" Ah! what of him?" asked the old man, with a terrified look.

" Why," replied Martin, " I am now more than ever convinced, that maniac boy is the son of ——"

" No more, no more, Trevors; mention not her name," gasped forth the baronet, with a ghastly look. " You—you told me they were both no more."

" And so I believed they were," returned Martin; " but I am now certain that at least *he* lives, and that the boy Julio, whom Michael has saved, and now has under his protection is he."

" More torture! more torture!" ejaculated the miser, smiting his breast. " But if you are convinced of the truth of what you assert, why is not he the object of your vengeance? Why is he not secured, and—and disposed of?"

" Oh, then," exclaimed Martin Trevors, with a sarcastic look, " you are not so penitent, after all, Sir Horace Middleton; you would not hesitate to commit more murder."

" Spare me! spare me! again I implore."

" Well, I will not talk any more upon that subject. According as you act, so will my conduct be guided. You will have nothing to fear from the boy, or any one else, while you do not offend me. Nay, more; I may, perhaps, ere long place him in your power."

" No, no," groaned Sir Horace, with a look of terror; " not for worlds—not for worlds! I cannot bear to gaze upon his features. Ever since I beheld them they have continually haunted my imagination, and froze my soul with horror."

" You are a very coward, Sir Horace," said Martin Trevors, with a look of contempt.

" I—I am an old man, Martin."

" You are an old villain."

" I know it, Martin, too well I know it; but it is not you that should upbraid me."

" And who has more right to do so, or to triumph in your sufferings?"

" Why, what have I done to you that you should entertain such feelings of hatred and animosity towards me?"

" What have you done?—ha! ha! ha!" laughed Trevors, maliciously. " But this is not the time for explanation. I reserve it for a much more fitting period. You have heard my designs."

" Alas! alas! and will nothing persuade you to abandon them?"

" Nothing. It is useless for you to remonstrate with me. You dare not refuse obedience to them."

" Too well I feel that I dare not," replied Sir Horace.

" 'Tis well that you do," returned Martin.

" But how can you bear the damsel away from her home without being detected?" asked the baronet.

" Leave that to me; I have formed all my plans, and what I have fixed my mind upon has seldom yet failed of success. Who is to know, or even suspect that she is confined here? Besides, it may only be for a short time, and then you will be released from all your fears."

" And whither do you intend to convey her ultimately?" interrogated Sir Horace.

" Far across the ocean," answered Trevors. " Oh, I will have such a revenge against her and her parents, as they little dream of."

" Martin," observed the old man, " you had better reflect before you venture to perform anything rashly, and which may involve you in ruin."

" Bah!" exclaimed Martin, impatiently; " I have reflected enough; I have only now to act, which I shall lose no time in doing."

" And why are you resolved to leave your place of residence?"

" To quiet suspicion, and to further my plans."

" And whither do you intend going?" again asked Sir Horace.

"Oh, I shall not be far from you, depend upon it," answered Trevors; "I shall know and observe all that passes here, and shall very frequently honour you with my company."

"Alas! alas!" sighed the miser.

"Ay, you may sigh and whine," said Martin with a sneer, "but it is all to no purpose. Such old friends and acquaintances as you and I are not to be separated upon easy terms. Besides, you may need my assistance when you least expect it."

"In what way, Martin?"

"Your nephew, Raymond Middleton, may return—nay, I am sure he will, if he escape the dangers of the desperate life he has entered upon."

"Eternal curses light upon him!" exclaimed the old man, passionately; "and may the angry waves hide his hated form for ever from my sight."

"And this you say of the nephew, the dear nephew to whom you have ever behaved so kindly?" returned Trevors, sarcastically.

"Ay, fool—fool that I have been. But you will stand my friend, Martin, should the ungrateful dog venture to return to me, will you not?"

"Your friend!"

"Yes, yes; you will not suffer him to triumph over me?"

"That depends entirely upon yourself, as I have before told you."

"You have me in your power, Martin, and you know too well that I must act in obedience to your wishes."

"I am glad that you acknowledge it," said Trevors; "and it will be well for you if you always bear that in mind."

"Alas! how am I to forget? But you will not give Raymond the power to denounce me?"

"He dares not do so, while I exist."

"Oh, thanks, thanks for that assurance."

"Perhaps you may not have so much cause for self-congratulation as you seem to think," returned Martin, with a peculiar look.

"You speak in problems, Trevors," said the baronet; "I cannot understand you."

"Those problems may be solved by-and-by, though I know not whether it will be exactly to your satisfaction. Raymond Middleton, I repeat, shall not harm you, while you remain faithful to me."

"I will, I will, Martin."

"That's enough," answered Trevors; "and so now our interview is at an end."

"But, answer me, Martin," said Sir Horace; "what do you purpose to do to protect me from my graceless nephew, should he dare again to visit me, as he has threatened to do?"

"Wait till the time arrives, and then you will see," answered Martin.

"You will not suffer him to rob me of more gold?"

"No."

"Good Martin, that promise inspires me with confidence."

"Psha! no more of your good Martins," said Trevors, with a frown. "I do not attempt to deceive you, I owe you no good will, and it is only to answer my purpose that I permit you to live."

"Mysterious man! you fill my soul with a secret and nameless horror, when you speak to me and look on me as you do now."

"No doubt of it," returned Trevors; "and it is meet that you should tremble with dread, when you are in my presence."

"And yet I know not why I should do so."

"Ask your own conscience."

"I have never harmed you!"

"Never harmed me!" repeated Martin Trevors, with a fiendish look; "oh, liar, liar!"

The wretched old man shrank appalled from him, and trembled all over.

"We will talk no more of this, Martin," he at last gasped forth; "we will talk no more of this. But, for the love of mercy, spare me, and do not do anything which may involve me in ruin."

" Oh, certainly not," replied Martin, ironically ; " You have a right to expect that I shall be very careful of your safety."

" But your son, Martin," said the old miser, endeavouring to change the subject which was so agonizing to him ; " what do you intend to do with respect to him ?"

" Discover him, if I can," answered Martin ; " the rash boy, had he but known all the circumstances which are connected with him, he would not have acted so precipitately. He would have learned to have scorned the love of Rosetta Belford, and to have exulted in the prospects that were before him. You do not know Frank Trevors, Sir Horace Middleton."

" As your son, I do," answered the baronet.

" As *my son* !—ha, ha, ha !" laughed Trevors, with a peculiar look ; " you may know him in another character, by-and-by."

" Again your words are inexplicable to me," ejaculated Sir Horace. " He, of course, can have no business with me."

" Perhaps you may find yourself mistaken, Sir Horace."

" You surely have not made him the confidant of our secrets ?" said the baronet, with a look of terror.

" No, I have not," replied Martin ; " let that suffice you. Good day, Sir Horace ; do not forget what I have told you, and be prepared to receive the girl, Rosetta, whenever I may bring her here."

" Would that you would change your mind, Martin," said Sir Horace ; " surely you might find some other place to conceal her."

" But I do not intend to seek for one," returned Martin Trevors, sternly. " I can meet with no place to answer my purpose so well as the Red Manor-house."

" But when do you intend to put your designs into execution, since you will have it so ?" inquired Sir Horace.

" As soon as opportunity presents itself, which I dare say will not be long first."

" Shall I see you again before you leave your present residence ?"

" Probably you may," answered Trevors ; " but that can matter little to you, and I have no doubt you are not over anxious to see me too often. Remember, that I shall still be close at hand, and a close observer of your actions, so that it would be madness on your part to attempt to deceive me."

" I will not, Martin, I will not," said the baronet, with a shudder.

" Mark me ; no more mad attempts on your life. You surely would not leave your darling gold yet, and rush upon that perdition which inevitably is in store for you."

" Forbear ! forbear ! oh, horror !" groaned the guilty man.

" Weak fool !" exclaimed the ruffian ; " coward in heart with all your guilt. Oh, what a contemptible wretch are you !"

" Alas ! I know it too well ; but, Martin —— "

" Bah !" interrupted the latter, with a fierce look, and he stalked from the room, and closed the door after him with a loud bang.

Sir Horace Middleton sank, overpowered by the violence of his conflicting emotions, in his chair, and for some time was unable to give vent to his feelings only by convulsive sobs.

" More trouble, more terrors," he at length groaned forth, beating his breast, and large drops of agony standing upon his quivering temples. " Every way this fearful, this mysterious man, seeks to annoy me, and I dare not offer any resistance to his will. He possesses an influence over me which I cannot understand, and gold will not prevail upon him to relent. Oh, that some kind friend would release me from him ; then might I experience something like a ray of peace. Peace !—fool ! wretch ! peace is not for me ! It can never more be mine. I, who have committed such hideous crimes, dare not to hope for it. And can I think of procuring it by the shedding of more human blood ? Oh, horror ! how deep is my wretched soul steeped in guilt. With what galling fetters of misery have I not bound myself—fetters which must at last bear me down to everlasting torment ! . And he will bring hither that girl ; she will be left in my charge ; the miser, the murderer, who dread to meet the gaze of my fellow creatures. And she will know me, and should she ever escape from the power of Trevors, she will denounce me ; bring me to the punishment,—perhaps to the gallows. Another one to dread ! Oh, torture inexpressible ! May some lucky accident foil the designs of Trevors, and convey the girl beyond his power."

He paused, and gave himself up entirely to the agony which these thoughts created.

"That maniac boy, too," he continued ; "if Martin Trevors speaks the truth, my worst fears are confirmed, and it is he I have so much cause to dread. Accursed fortune that preserved him from death ! But yet why should I fear him ? His senses have fled, and even if they were not, he would not know me, unless, indeed, my name has been revealed to him by his mother. Ah! that thought maddens me. But she would not dare to do so, and—no—no—I will not alarm myself with fears like these ; but may I not behold him again, for I dare not gaze upon his features, so like those of his murdered mother ! Ah! what noise was that ? Methought I heard a dismal voice cry ' murder !' No, it was only my terrified imagination ; and yet the voices of the dead are constantly ringing in my ears. They will not suffer me to rest. Rest—ah ! no, there is no rest for me. Martin Trevors, you are the fiend that tortures me more than all, and my misery but affords you food for exultation. Would that I could fathom your real character ! then might I know better how to act. Who can he be, to know so much of my history, and that portion of it which I thought was long since buried in oblivion, or that no one could be acquainted with but myself. I know him to be the secret spy upon my actions, and, therefore, that alone should be sufficient to make me dread him ; but yet I feel convinced, from his recent observations, that he has more powerful motives for his mysterious conduct than it is possible for me to penetrate. It is evident that he hates and despises me ; he does not hesitate to acknowledge it, and, therefore, what may I not expect from him ? What else but that he will at last bring me to destruction ? Oh, agony insupportable ! Cannot I conceal myself in some remote corner of the earth, where no one may know me, and I may end the few wretched years that are allotted to me unmolested ? Ah ! no, I feel convinced that there is no place to which I can fly where I can remain undiscovered by my secret and dreadful enemies. They possess an almost supernatural power, and would search me out, even though I were buried in the bowels of the earth. And I dare not rush upon death ! No, my soul shrinks appalled at the contemplation of the awful punishment that is in store for me in eternity. There is no hope of mercy for a wretch like me ! Oh! that my lips could give utterance to a prayer !"

He sank back, overwhelmed with agony, and covered his face with his hands, and in that posture he remained, fixed like a statue, for some time, until, at length, in order to relieve in some measure the harrowing torments of his distracted brain, he walked forth into the open air, avoiding all those places where he was likely to encounter the gaze of his fellow creatures.

"Ah !" ejaculated Martin Trevors, as he quitted the Manor-house, and retraced his steps towards his residence, which he had resolved so soon to quit ; "contemptible wretch I justly designated you, but yet will I make you the help- less tool and victim of my deep laid plans. Oh, what rare food it is to me to gloat over your anguish and your fears, and to know that when you have served my purpose to the utmost, I can complete my vengeance by consigning you to the death of a dog. Your gold! ha! ha! ha! you are but the treasurer. Every coin of it is mine, whenever I like to claim it. Now, scornful beauty! fair Rosetta Belford, my designs are in a fair way to triumph, and I will wring the hearts of your parents to the core. Frank Trevors will not become your husband ; you have rejected him ; good ; I never intended that you should become *his* bride ; but you shall be the mistress of one degraded by crime, and who will sufficiently punish you for your coquetry and deception. Would, however, that I could trace the footsteps of Frank. I must exert all my energies to do so, and to bring him to his senses. Foolish, headstrong boy, I thought he would have had more consideration of me than to have acted in the manner he has done."

By this time he had arrived at the foot of the hill, on the summit of which the house of Michael Belford stood. He looked up towards it with a scowling brow, and for a few moments he was half determined to again visit him, but upon reflection he thought it was best to avoid another encounter, as it might only lead to something that would retard the progress of his plans, and he therefore walked on.

"Ay," he exclaimed, as he proceeded, "for awhile triumph in your imagined security; the storm will burst upon you soon enough, and then it will be my turn to laugh. You have excited the wrath of Martin Trevors, and his vengeance never fails to descend upon the heads of those who offend him. It will be my care to make that now happy home desolate before many weeks, or probably days, have elapsed."

With these words the villain hurried on his way, deliberating his dark laid designs in his head as he proceeded, and, firmly fixed in his diabolical resolves, he sat himself down to contrive fresh schemes of vengeance against those who had excited his unjust indignation.

CHAPTER XIII.

THE ATTEMPTED SEIZURE OF JULIO.—THE SECOND APPEARANCE OF THE DEATH SHIP.

SEVERAL days passed away, and the inmates of the old stone house neither saw nor heard any more of Martin Trevors, but the excitement which had been caused in their breasts by his visit to Michael Belford, his ruffianly behaviour, and the threats he had held out on that occasion, was not at all abated.

Michael treated them with scorn, but his wife and daughter were far from being disposed to do the same, and they were in a state of the greatest alarm whenever Michael left home, lest he should encounter Martin Trevors, and some outrage be committed.

Rosetta, too, could not banish the unfortunate Frank from her thoughts, and most anxious was she to know what had become of him, although she was inclined to believe that the supposition of her father was correct, namely, that he had come to the resolution of entering upon a sea-faring life, and she sincerely wished that he might be preserved from all danger, and enabled to banish her image from his memory, unless it was in the character of a friend; for, notwithstanding the faults of his father, she felt that she must ever esteem him as such, while he continued to deserve it.

Could she have loved him, she would have been most happy to become his wife, but fate had apparently ordained it otherwise, and she felt it to be her duty to bow to its will. Poor girl, had she been aware of half the anguish to which she had subjected the unfortunate Frank, and the many vicissitudes he was destined to encounter in consequence, how much more poignantly would her gentle heart have been wrung. But a circumstance was about to occur which, for a time, would divert her thoughts from that melancholy subject.

About a fortnight after the visit of Martin Trevors to the old stone house, Michael returned home rather late in the evening from a visit which he had been paying to old Kit, and Rosetta and her mother could see from the animated expression of his countenance that he had something to impart.

"I have news for you," he observed, after having doffed his hat, and taken his usual seat by the fireside.

"News, father," said Rosetta, eagerly; "have you, then, heard of poor Frank Trevors?"

"No, my lass," answered her father, "I have heard nothing of the poor lad; I wish I had; but I have something to tell you of his father."

"His father!" repeated Mrs. Belford and his daughter, in a breath; "have you, then, seen him?"

"No, no, I have not," returned Michael, "and I hope I shall not for some time, although I bear him no animosity.   The fact is, Martin Trevors has left the house he has inhabited for so many years."

" Left his house!" exclaimed Rosetta and her mother, in astonishment; " where then has he gone?"

"That I know not," answered Michael, " neither do any of his neighbours. His house was found to be entirely deserted only yesterday, and no one, as far as I have been able to ascertain, saw him remove."

" It is most strange !" remarked Mrs. Belford.

" And most fortunate," added Rosetta ; " not that, as the father of Frank Trevors, I cease to respect him, but I fear that his malice was deeply rooted, and should my father have encountered him, I am fearful of what the consequences might have been.   It is certainly very remarkable that he should have been induced to abandon his home."

" It is," coincided her father ; " but Martin Trevors is a man of mystery, whcm it is impossible for any one to fathom.   I have often reflected upon his singular and unfeeling conduct on the night of the appearance of the Death Ship, and the destruction of the vessel from which I preserved poor Julio.   He was first aware of the presence of that terrible craft, and from the remarks he made appeared to be prepared for its arrival.   I have often since thought (but I hope Heaven will pardon me if I do him an injustice by the supposition), that he is in some way connected with that awful marauder of the seas !"

" Oh, God forbid that your surmises should be correct, my dear father," ejaculated our heroine, " for, if they are, what may we not still have to dread from his vengeance ?"

" Do not alarm yourself, my dear child," said Michael, " for, after all, my surmises may be erroneous, and I hope they are, and Trevors may have convinced himself that he has done us wrong by the foul aspersions he cast upon us, but is ashamed to see us to apologize."

" Poor Frank !" ejaculated Rosetta ; " and no intelligence has been obtained as to what has become of him ?"

" None," answered Michael ; " but I firmly believe that the opinion I first formed is correct, and that he has become a seaman."

" May fortune favour him wherever he goes, and guard him from every peril," said our heroine, fervently.

" Well spoken, Rosetta," said Mr. Belford, " and to that wish, I need not say I most heartily respond.   And it is not at all improbable that his father has gone in search of him."

" It must have been some very powerful motive that could induce him to abandon that house in which he has for so many years resided," observed Mrs. Belford.

" It must, indeed," coincided Rosetta ; " but still I cannot but feel more satisfied since he has left the neighbourhood, for I cannot forget the terrible threats he made use of towards us, and Martin Trevors appears to be a man who is always determined to carry any designs he may have formed into execution."

" In this instance I trust it is not so," remarked Mr. Belford, " and if he should be bold enough to attempt any outrage, we must always be prepared to resist him.   I fear him not."

" But how shall we be able to guard against him, my father, should he really intend us wrong ?" inquired Rosetta.

" Of that we will talk hereafter," replied Michael ; " but, for the present, rest yourself contented, and do not anticipate dangers that may never threaten us."

" May not his retirement from his house only be a scheme to further his plans, to quiet our suspicions ? and may he not still be concealed in some other part of the neighbourhood ?" suggested Rosetta.

" Ah !" ejaculated her mother, with a look of alarm, " that is not at all improbable.   Martin Trevors is well known to be a frequent visitor to the Manor-house, and to be on terms of mysterious intimacy with Sir Horace Middleton ; may he not there be concealed ?"

"That is most unlikely, dame," returned Michael; "although I have often felt astonishment at the intimacy between him and the wretched old baronet, whom every one looks upon with suspicion, and views with disgust, if not with hatred."

"I fear that Sir Horace Middleton is indeed a bad man," observed our heroine.

"His actions prove him to be so," said Mrs. Belford; "he shuns the light of day, can never look any one, like an honest man, in the face, and I am no judge of countenances if he suffers not from a guilty conscience. I fear that he has never amassed the large wealth he is said to possess by fair means."

"I shall never forget the terror he evinced, and the observations he made use of, when he beheld poor Julio," said Rosetta.

"Ah! his conduct on that occasion was most extraordinary," remarked Michael, "and I have often reflected upon it. The features of Julio seemed to make a remarkable impression upon him, and to call up the recollection of some person whom he wished to forget."

"And the unfeeling remarks which Martin Trevors made in respect to him, on his visit to our house," said Rosetta ; "they were worthy of attention, and perfectly corresponded with the behaviour of Sir Horace Middleton."

"True," coincided Michael ; "and it would appear, also, that he was most forcibly struck with the features of the unfortunate boy. We must guard him with the most jealous care. Would to Heaven that his reason were restored to him ; that might explain the terrible mystery connected with him."

"Alas !" sighed Rosetta, while a powerful feeling, much more than sympathy, throbbed at her heart ; "alas ! I fear that his reason is fled for ever."

"Say not so, my dear child," remarked her father ; "God is good, and will not suffer one so young and guiltless ever to remain a wreck. At times, indeed, his recollection seems for a few moments to return, and I am strongly of opinion that it only requires care and attention to enable reason, in the course of time, to resume her seat."

"Oh, may your hopes be realized, my father," said Rosetta ; "for poor Julio is certainly worthy of a better fate."

"He is," said Michael ; "but it was most fortunate for him that he has fallen under the protection of those who will be as watchful of his happiness as if he were their own son."

"Oh, yes," ejaculated our heroine ; "and should Julio recover his senses, I feel convinced that he will never repay your kindness with ingratitude."

"I am sure he will not," said Mrs. Belford ; "for it is evident that his nature is kind, gentle, and generous ; and already the innocent affection he evinces towards us more than amply repays us for our care."

"Could we but elicit from him the name of his parents, we might obtain some elucidation of the mystery," said Rosetta.

"True," replied her father ; "but that is a subject, which, in his present state of mind, we dare not venture to touch upon, for it always drives him frantic. Poor boy, his is indeed a hard destiny, and no wonder that such atrocities as he has evidently witnessed, the barbarous murder of his mother, and all the accompanying horrors, should have turned his brain."

"It is not," said Mrs. Belford ; "unfortunate child, I wonder that he could at all survive them—but see, he comes. We must not talk upon this subject before him."

Julio now entered the room, and the conversation dropped.

When Rosetta was alone, she reflected upon the information which her father had given them, and although she felt more satisfied at the departure of Martin Trevors from the neighbourhood, she could not succeed in banishing the apprehension from her breast that he would not abandon his designs of vengeance, and that he was only waiting until he could more securely put them into execution. She believed him to be a desperate and determined man, and one who would not hesitate to commit any crime in order to accomplish his wishes and to gratify his malice against any one who had excited his wrath ; melancholy forebodings came over her mind that many troubles were in store for her and her parents, and the more she endeavoured to dissipate these ideas the stronger became the influence they obtained over her. Again and again she regretted that she and Frank had ever become acquainted, for then much of the misery she now anticipated would have been saved, and Frank might have been happy and prosperous. Sincerely did she pray for his safety, in whatever course of life he might have embarked ; and most anxious was she to learn what had indeed become of him, innocent cause, as she was, of his misfortunes ; and she felt that he had at least acted with unkindness in not having forwarded to them some information as to his future intentions, which friendship alone ought to have prompted him to do.

Days passed on, and still no information was obtained as to where Martin Trevors had gone, or what had become of him. The circumstance created some sensation in the neighbourhood, and various were the conjectures that were formed upon it— many of them to the prejudice of Martin, for his mysterious habits, and other incidents connected with him, had given rise to many strange speculations ; and they now considered that he must have had some very powerful motives indeed for thus so abruptly abandoning his home. There were many, also, who even ventured to hint their suspicions that he had been for years engaged in some secret and unlawful pursuits, and that it was the fear of detection that caused him to fly the neighbourhood, in part of which suspicions, as it has been shown, they were far from incorrect.

But the disappearance of Frank Trevors created the deepest interest in the breasts of every one; for the general urbanity of his manners, and his numerous intrinsic merits, had gained for him the sincere respect of all who were acquainted with him, and they could not but feel the greatest anxiety for his fate. The real cause of his sudden departure from his home was, of course, unknown to them, or it might have given rise to many unpleasant animadversions on the conduct of Rosetta Belford, though no one could justly have blamed her for what she had done.

Rosetta and her parents became more confident that Martin Trevors had indeed quitted the neighbourhood altogether, as the time elapsed without their seeing or hearing anything of him, and the fears of our heroine gradually abated, and she resumed her walks as usual, not being apprehensive of any danger ; but a circum-stance was about to take place, which was calculated to resume them with tenfold force.

The maniac boy had been absent from their society for two or three hours, but it did not at first excite any surprise in their breasts, for they supposed that he was only amusing himself, as he was accustomed to do, in his own apartment; but at length Mrs. Belford observed,—

" Julio has been alone longer than usual, and I have not heard him moving for some time ; what can have induced him to remain so long from us ?"

" Probably the poor boy is brooding over his sorrows, dame," returned Michael ; " but I will go and arouse him, for such lonely meditation may have the most fatal effect upon his bereaved mind. I see that Rosetta, by her looks, is most anxious to behold her unfortunate companion again."

Rosetta blushed, and an unaccountable feeling of apprehension came over her. Michael left the room, and she and her mother waited with impatience till his return. He was not gone many minutes, and, on coming back, his countenance exhibited symptoms of alarm.

" Julio is not in his apartment," he said, " nor can I see him in any other part of the house."

" Good God !" exclaimed Rosetta and Mrs. Belford in a breath, and starting to their feet in a state of the greatest consternation ; " what can have become of him ? He surely cannot have left the house."

" I fear he has," answered Michael ; " but do not alarm yourselves, he may not have strayed far, and I will immediately go in search of him. It is the first time he has ventured to go forth alone."

" Alas ! alas !" ejaculated Rosetta, her countenance becoming ghastly pale, and her bosom throbbing violently ; " some danger may have befallen him. Oh, hasten, my dear father, while I and my mother will go contrary ways in search of him."

" No, no, remain where you are till I come back," said Michael, " and fear not that I will return without him. Perhaps he may have strayed to the cliffs, which you know is his favourite place."

" Gracious Heaven !" cried Rosetta, " in the wild frenzy of his madness, what may he not be tempted to do ?"

" Compose yourself, my child," said Michael, as he seized his hat and stick, " I will bring him safe back again, depend upon it."

Neither Rosetta or her mother made any reply, and Mr. Belford hastened from the house, and, descending the hill, immediately took his way towards the cliffs, his mind filled with considerable apprehensions, although he had endeavoured to conceal them from his wife and daughter.

The maniac boy had for some time amused himself in his own room, in the simple way he was accustomed to do, conjuring up the form of his murdered mother, and talking in wild and touching language to her image, then singing the songs she had taught him, until he was worked up to a pitch of extraordinary delirium, and the thought suddenly suggested itself to him, that he would wander to the sea-side, where he imagined he should behold her spirit.

" But Julio must be alone," said the poor boy to himself; " he must have no one to interrupt him in his devotions—no, not even pretty sister Rosetta. I will haste to where the wild waves sweep over the pebbly beach, and the dolphins gambol in the sun's golden beams. Mother, dear sainted mother, I come to you. But, hush! hush! they must not hear me, or they will stop Julio in his sacred task. Hush! hush!"

Then with the cunning not unnatural in maniacs, he cautiously opened his room door, and silently stole down the stairs, and reaching the back door, unfastened it without noise, and darted from the house. He laughed aloud with wild delight when he found himself in the open air, and felt the fresh breeze upon his cheeks. The wretched prisoner, released from long confinement, could not have felt greater ecstasy than did the poor maniac boy as he bounded with almost supernatural speed down the steep side of the hill, on the summit of which the house was situated, and made his way towards the cliffs. His hair flowed wildly but grace- fully in the wind, and any one to have beheld him at that moment could scarcely have believed it was an earthly being they gazed upon.

He continued to run on, laughing and shouting aloud, and clapping his hands, in a perfect frenzy of delight; he felt himself free as the air which fanned his cheeks, and for a time the hapless youth gained a respite from the gloom and horror of his fate. He met no one on his way, and in a very short time, such was the rapidity of his speed, he gained the cliffs, up which he bounded, and gazed with outstretched hands and the most inexpressible transport upon the deep.

The sun was just sinking to rest in the bosom of the western ocean, and the waters were bright and red with its golden rays.

" 'Tis there! 'tis there! my home, all so calm and beautiful!" cried the maniac; " the home of my mother is there. Oh, is it not a bright and sunny place? Hark! how the waves gently murmur; they are breathing a solemn requiem to the re- pose of her spirit. Mother! dear mother! your child kneels before your ocean grave, and beseeches you to appear to him!"

He knelt as he spoke, and clasped his hands vehemently together, while his countenance exhibited an expression it would be impossible to describe in adequate language.

" Mother! dear mother!" he once more exclaimed, " again I call upon you; will you not listen to the supplications of your poor bereaved boy? She heeds me not! What have I done, that her sainted spirit should now abandon me? Oh! I must have been very, very wicked, or she would not thus leave me to despair. Mother! mother! No, no, she will not come! she will not come. Ah, me, poor Julio is now indeed most wretched!"

He covered his face with his hands, and sobbed most bitterly, and in this attitude he remained for several minutes; but at length he suddenly again started to his feet, and gazed earnestly across the ocean. The waves, tinged with the last red glare of the sun's departing rays, had now a perfectly ensanguined hue, and when the maniac beheld it, he uttered a loud shriek of terror, and his eyes flashed with more than even their usual wildness.

" Ah!" he cried, " 'tis changed to blood! all blood. It is the blood of my mur- dered mother! And now, methinks, I see her mangled form struggling with the crimson waves. Ah! see, she is there. Her ghastly eyes are fixed upon me; her blood-stained hands are stretched towards me, as if to invite me to come to her. Mother, mother, I obey you! You shall not plead in vain. I come, I come to join you in your ocean home!"

At that moment, when he was about in his madness to spring from the cliff on which he stood, into the ocean beneath, his arm was grasped by a powerful hand, and at the same time a hoarse and savage voice exclaimed,—

" Hated brat, there is one at hand to arrest you in your purpose, whom you have cause to fear. You must not die yet; no, no, Martin Trevors requires you for another end. You must with me, while there is no one to observe us."

It was indeed Martin Trevors who held him, and when the unfortunate maniac turned round and gazed upon him, he uttered a loud scream, and struggled violently to release himself from his grasp, while Trevors gazed upon his features with mingled feelings of hatred and triumph.

" Ah !" cried the poor boy, " who are you that would prevent Julio from joining his murdered mother beneath yon sea of blood? Let me go, monster, for I know you now—you are one of the assassins of her who gave me being. I see the name of murderer stamped upon your brow. Release me ! release me !"

" Babbling idiot !" exclaimed Martin, " and yet there is some reason in your madness. Silence ! and with me, for it is useless to resist."

As he thus spoke, Martin Trevors tried to force him from the cliff, but the maniac still struggled desperately, with all the strength of madness, and his wild cries pierced the air. Martin Trevors uttered a dreadful oath, and looked around him, but he could perceive no one near, and again he exerted himself to the utmost to drag Julio from the spot. The strength of the unfortunate boy was now almost exhausted, and it was comparatively nothing when opposed to that of Martin, but he still rent the air with his cries, and Trevors became alarmed, lest they should reach the ears of some one who might be passing by, and who would probably fly to his assistance ; still he was so bent on securing his person, that he persisted in his efforts, and endeavoured all that he could to stifle his cries, but all to no purpose.

He had dragged him half way down the cliff, when he perceived several fishermen approaching, and he then knew that his brutal design was frustrated, and that it would be more prudent for him to endeavour to make his escape, before he should be recognised; he, therefore, with an oath hurled the maniac from him to the earth, and he then dashed forward, endeavouring to avoid the men who were approaching, but he could not do so until they had distinguished his features, and shouted aloud his name. Overwhelmed with confusion and alarm, he hurried on with the speed of lightning, and was quickly out of sight.

The fishermen approached the spot where Julio was lying insensible, and raised him from the ground.

" Why, it is the poor maniac boy, whom honest Michael Belford rescued from the burning vessel," observed one of them; " what could that rascal, Martin Trevors, whom every one thought had left the neighbourhood, want with him, I should like to know ?"

" Poor lad," said another of the fishermen; " he has, no doubt, strayed from home unknown to Michael, who will be in a great state of alarm when he misses him, for I know that he is as fond of him as if he were his own son. Let us convey him to Mr. Belford's house without delay."

" See, here comes Michael," said the first speaker ; " and if one may judge from his appearance, alarmed enough he is. It is a fortunate job the poor lad is not hurt."

Michael now hastened to the spot, and his delight on beholding Julio may be better imagined than described, but when he saw the insensible condition he was in, he was alarmed lest something serious had happened to him. He hastily inquired of the men, whom he knew, what had taken place, and they informed him ; but when he heard that it was Martin Trevors who had committed the outrage, his indignation and astonishment increased.

" The villain, then, is still lurking somewhere in the neighbourhood, bent upon the accomplishment of some evil designs," he said.

" It does, indeed, look like it, Master Belford," said one of the fishermen, " and it is lucky that we happened to be attracted to the spot by the lad's cries, or he would probably have committed some desperate act. He must be an infernal rascal, or he would never seek to injure a poor maniac boy like this."

" What his motives can be, I know not," observed Michael ; " but it is evident that he knows this unfortunate boy, and has some reason for wishing to get rid of him. I must keep a strict look out for him, and endeavour to foil him in his villanous designs if possible."

Julio now slowly recovered, and, opening his eyes, stared vacantly upon the persons who surrounded him.

"Where is he?" he cried; "where is that bad man who tried to prevent poor Julio from joining his mother in her watery grave? But no, it is not water now; it is blood. Hark! do you not hear how it gurgles and hisses, boiling hot from the veins of the murdered victim?"

"Julio," ejaculated Mr. Belford, in his kindest accents, "do you not know me?"

"Ah! my more than father, the father of Rosetta," exclaimed the maniac, flying towards him with the greatest delight; "but, no, no," he added, passing his hands across his forehead; "I must be dreaming. You are not he I mentioned. He did not accompany me here, and ——"

"Come, come, Julio," interrupted Mr. Belford, taking his arm, with a persuasive look, "let us return home; Rosetta has been so uneasy at your absence."

"Rosetta unhappy," said Julio; "and I the cause; oh, I must have been very wicked, very cruel to make poor Rosetta unhappy. Come, come, let us go, and I will kneel for pardon at her feet."

Michael having warmly thanked the fishermen for their kindness, took the arm of Julio once more within his, and led him from the spot.

On the way home, the maniac appeared very melancholy, and frequently upbraided himself for having made Rosetta unhappy; but Michael did all he could to tranquillize him, and he at last succeeded, and they arrived at home; Julio bounding into the house with eager impatience, and throwing himself at the feet of Rosetta.

The delight of our heroine and her mother, on beholding the interesting object of their anxiety again, may be readily imagined, while Julio laughed and wept by turns, and called upon Rosetta to forgive him for having made her unhappy. She took his hand in the kindest manner, and smiled sweetly upon him. That smile was Heaven to the maniac's soul, and his countenance brightened.

"I will never, never leave Rosetta again," he said; "and, indeed, it was very cruel of me to do so now. We will wander forth together, and we will be so happy, for no harm can come to Julio while sister Rosetta is by his side. But—but I wished to join my mother, when that cruel man prevented me. Oh, had you but seen him, Rosetta, how he would have shocked you. He looked so frightful, just as those wretches looked who slew my poor mother."

"Whom do you mean?" asked Rosetta and her mother, whose anxiety to know what had happened to Julio during the time he had been away from the house was most intense. Michael, however, looked at them significantly, and they forbore to urge the question.

"Who do I mean?" ejaculated the maniac, passing his hands across his forehead, as if he was trying to recall some recollection to his mind; "I know not; but —but he looked so fearfully upon me, and uttered such dreadful words, and he would have torn me from you, Rosetta. Yes, he would have murdered Julio, and I wonder he did not."

Rosetta and her mother shuddered with horror, and their curiosity momentarily increased.

"Julio will not leave his home again without he is attended by Rosetta or myself, will you, my good boy?" said Michael.

"Oh, no, no," eagerly answered the maniac; "and it was wrong, very wrong of me to do so now; but you will forgive me, won't you?"

"Yes, Julio," returned Mrs. Belford, kindly; "we do forgive you, for we know you love us, and would not do anything that would cause us pain."

"No, that I would not," answered Julio, fervently. "But we must visit my poor mother's ocean home, and listen to the mournful billows as they sing their requiem to her departed spirit. I heard them to-day; but then the waters became blood red, blood red. Oh, had you but seen them as I did!"

Michael and the others tried to soothe him, and to divert his mind from these sad thoughts; and they at last succeeded, and the poor boy became calm, and looked at Rosetta with an expression of admiration and delight which went to her heart.

"Ah, me!" said the maniac, at last, "I am very tired. I have been a long journey to-day, a very long journey, and I want rest."

Michael was glad to hear him speak thus, for he was anxious to gratify the curiosity of his wife and daughter; and he, therefore, requested Julio to retire to his chamber, hoping that by the morning he would have sufficiently recovered from the shock he had received, and would again become calm and contented.

"Yes," said Julio, "I will go and dream of my poor mother, and offer up my prayers to her sainted spirit. Good night, Rosetta; Julio will never again make you unhappy. Good night, good night."

He bent his knee to the ground before Rosetta, and, raising her fair hand to his lips with the greatest respect, kissed it vehemently. Then he embraced Mrs. Belford, and giving his hand to Michael, suffered him to lead him from the room, and to conduct him to his chamber.

Rosetta and her mother impatiently awaited the return of Michael, and he did not long keep them in suspense.

"Poor boy," he said, on his return, "he has had enough to alarm him, and I cannot be too grateful for his preservation from the power of one whom I am now thoroughly convinced is a villain, capable of any crime. We must be watchful and wary, for there is no knowing what danger may threaten us. Our enemy is at work, and it must be our task to adopt such measures as may effectually frustrate his plans."

"Of whom do you speak?" eagerly demanded our heroine and her mother in a breath.

"Martin Trevors," replied Michael.

"Ah!" ejaculated Rosetta, trembling; "is he then still in the neighbourhood?"

"He is; and I know not how close he may be to us. He it was of whom Julio spoke. He seized him on the cliffs, and attempted to drag him away, and had it not been for the fortunate arrival of some honest fishermen, attracted by his cries to the spot, he would have succeeded in his villanous object."

"Gracious Heaven!" exclaimed Rosetta and her mother. "What could have been his purpose with the poor maniac boy?"

"To get him in his power, and, perhaps, to take his life," answered Michael. "This outrage proves that he knows who the boy really is, and is connected with the wretches who murdered his unfortunate mother."

"Alas!" said Rosetta, "never could I have believed that Martin Trevors was such a miscreant. How fortunate it is that Julio was rescued from him; but what have we now to fear from him, determined as he seems upon revenge?"

"We know him sufficiently now," observed Michael, "and must, therefore, be on our guard against him. I must endeavour to find out the place where he is concealed."

"That will be difficult to do," said Mrs. Belford, "and may be attended with the greatest danger. Would that we were out of this neighbourhood altogether, since we have now an enemy whom we have so much cause to dread, and whose designs, or the power he has to carry them into execution, we cannot penetrate."

"No, dame," returned her husband; "we must not quit the home in which we have been happy for so many years. Martin Trevors will surely not have the daring to attempt any further outrage?"

"Should he, indeed, be connected with those wretches, the pirates, which it seems too probable that he is," said Mrs. Belford, "his power may be greater than we can now imagine, and he will not rest until he has accomplished the whole of his evil designs. I tremble to reflect upon what the consequences may be."

"Would to Heaven that we had never known him!" ejaculated Rosetta.

"Why, it would have been better had we not," remarked Michael; "but do not give way to alarm; Martin has now shown himself in his true character; he has unmasked himself, and probably will not venture to appear here again, lest he should be brought to justice."

"I fear that he knows his own security too well to apprehend that," replied Mrs. Belford; "where can he be concealed?"

"I cannot form even the least conjecture," answered Michael, "unless he be, indeed, secreted in the Manor-house; and if that is the case, Sir Horace Middleton must be as bad as he."

"There can be little doubt of that," said Mrs. Belford, "from the intimacy that has ever existed between them. Poor Julio then, it is evident, is known to Trevors, and his behaviour on the night that you rescued him from death, and the observations he made use of when he beheld the poor boy, are sufficiently accounted for."

"They are," observed Michael; "and he must be a villain of the blackest dye, or he would never seek the life of a poor defenceless boy, who could never, by any possibility, have injured him."

"He could not," observed Rosetta. "May Heaven protect Julio from his power!"

"I will see the magistrates upon the subject," said Michael; "and they may, probably, devise some means to protect us from his vengeance."

"Unfortunate Frank!" ejaculated our heroine, "to have such a father! He is amiable and good, and could never have been aware of the real character of his parent."

"He could not," coincided Mr. Belford, "or he would have abandoned his name, in horror and disgust, long since. It is most surprising that Martin Trevors did not attempt to corrupt the mind of his son, so that he might have made him a fitting instrument towards the furtherance of his guilty plans."

"It is," said Mrs. Belford; "but, instead of that, he has bestowed the utmost care upon his education, and in the cultivation of his mind, as if he intended him to fill a far higher station in society than that to which he seemed born. It seems to me almost impossible that one so noble in character as Frank is should be the son of one who is now shown to be such a consummate villain."

"Yes," remarked Rosetta, "it does indeed. And what will be the anguish of poor Frank, should he ever return, to learn the real character of his father? Most sincerely do I feel for him."

"He is, indeed, to be pitied," said Michael; "but I hope he may prosper in what he has undertaken, and become independent of his misguided father. I shall ever esteem him for his noble qualities, although I cannot now but feel gratified that he did not become my son-in-law, notwithstanding he could not be accountable for the faults of his parent. I plainly see that the connection would have brought much misery upon us all."

"Yes, it could not have done otherwise, when we discovered the guilt of Martin Trevors," said Mrs. Belford. "It would have brought shame upon us, and blighted the happiness of Rosetta and Frank for ever."

"I tremble to think of what the consequences might have been," observed our heroine. "May Heaven reform the guilty Mr. Trevors, if only for the sake of his son."

"That wish is well worthy of you, my child," said Mr. Belford; "but it is now getting late, and we must separate for the night."

Rosetta embraced her parents affectionately, and, taking up a lamp, retired from the room. When she had gained her own chamber, she threw herself on her knees, and most fervently poured forth her gratitude to the throne of grace for the preservation of Julio, and supplicated its protection for his future safety, and that of her beloved parents. The event had given rise to the greatest apprehensions in her bosom, which she found it impossible to conquer. It was evident that Martin Trevors was determined upon having a terrible revenge, for the disappointment he had experienced in her rejection of the suit of his son, and she saw no means by which they could guard themselves against his evil designs. She remembered the fearful threats he had given utterance to, and she had every reason to fear that he would make every villanous effort to put them into execution, and, if he even failed, he would keep them in a constant state of dread. That he knew Julio, and was determined to destroy him, or to secure him in his power, was now quite evident, and she could not but entertain the greatest apprehensions for the safety of that unfortunate lad, in whose fate she now felt a greater interest than ever, for she looked upon him with the same ardent affection as if he were her own brother—a sentiment which, even unknown to herself, was fast strengthening into a feeling of a much more tender nature. She would, indeed, feel most happy if her father could be prevailed upon to leave the neighbourhood altogether, as her mother had suggested, and retire to some place where they might remain undiscovered by Martin Trevors, and live in security from his malicious and diabolical machinations. In-

deed, she had not felt happy in the old stone house since her father had related the story of Hugh Clifton, and she had learned that he had formerly inhabited it; nor could she imagine any reason why her father should be so attached to it, notwithstanding the many years he had resided in it; but she felt convinced, from the observations he had frequently made use of, that nothing would induce him to abandon it.

She now felt more anxious than ever to unravel the mystery connected with Julio, and to see him placed in a position of entire security from his enemies, but still she saw no greater prospect of its being elucidated than ever. She prayed to the Almighty to restore him to his senses, and then, indeed, all would be explained, and the guilty brought to condign punishment for the atrocious crimes they had perpetrated, more especially in the sanguinary and cowardly assassination of Julio's ill-fated mother.

During the night Rosetta slept but little, for these thoughts continually crowded upon her brain, and filled her breast with the most agonizing doubts and apprehensions.

She arose at her accustomed hour, and, on descending into the parlour, she found her parents and Julio already there. The latter hastened to meet her, and the smiles which gladdened his handsome countenance showed plainly that all the events of the previous day were banished from his mind ; and most happy was our heroine to observe it, although she could not participate in his serenity.

After the morning repast was over, Michael departed to the house of the magistrate, having previously cautioned Rosetta by no means to venture to stir from the house, or to suffer Julio to do so, during his absence.

Michael having imparted the facts to the magistrate, and received that gentleman's advice upon the subject, and his promise of assistance, returned home, and the remainder of the day passed over without anything particular worth mentioning taking place.

Several days elapsed without their being able to hear anything more of Martin Trevors, and their fears gradually subsided, and they began to hope that he had now, indeed, quitted that part of the country, although they could not bring their minds to believe that he had so readily relinquished his base designs. But, when weeks, and even months, vanished without anything occurring to create their apprehensions, they did, indeed, become more confident, and imagined that Martin Trevors had abandoned his intentions, and would not again molest them, fearful of the consequences which might result to himself should he make any such attempt.

Sir Horace Middleton had not been seen out during the whole of that time, and it might almost be imagined that he had likewise quitted the neighbourhood, had it not been for the appearance of his trusty servant, Simon Snipe, who now and then quitted the house to procure provisions.

But Sir Horace was still there ; and, in the gloom of his spacious mansion, continued to suffer the greatest misery from the stings of his guilty conscience, and the constant fears of detection that assailed him.

Martin Trevors visited him every night, his person so disguised that it would have been impossible for even those who knew him well to recognise him ; but the baronet could never elicit from him the place of his concealment, although he could see no reason why he should be so resolute in refusing to reveal it to him.

So long a time had now elapsed since Martin had made him acquainted with the designs he had in contemplation against Rosetta, that he began to hope he had abandoned them ; but Trevors quickly undeceived him, and bade him prepare himself for the reception of Rosetta, for, although he had delayed her seizure until his plans were more matured, he was fully determined that nothing should prevent him from putting them into execution, and that his thirst for revenge was still as insatiable as ever.

Sir Horace heard him with alarm, and in vain remonstrated with him upon the subject.

" Why will you persist in a design which cannot afford you any commensurate gratification for the trouble and danger you will incur, and which may bring destruction upon me ?" he said.

" Bah !" impatiently replied Martin ; " have I not repeatedly told you that my determination is unalterably fixed, and why then will you thus annoy me ? Think you I will so readily abandon the idea of vengeance, because the accomplishment of it may be attended with a little danger ? Martin Trevors is unused to fear ; as for you, what danger can you incur by the girl being confined here ? No one will suspect where she is, and certainly not that she is concealed in the house of the wretched miser, Sir Horace Middleton."

"But you cannot accomplish your plot without assistance," said the baronet.

"No; and it is for that only that I am waiting," answered Trevors.

"And who will you employ?"

"That matters not to you."

"But it does, Martin, it does," returned the old man, with a look of terror. "They may betray us, and then ——"

"Psha! you are an old fool as well as a coward," interrupted Martin; "I shall employ none but those on whom I can depend, and who know you well."

"Know me, Trevors?"

"Yes; know you for one of their own sort—a villain."

"Oh, Martin, why will you thus torture me?"

"You torture yourself. But all your arguments are useless; the girl must be brought here a prisoner, and that most likely in a day or two."

"Alas! I see you are bent on my destruction," groaned the baronet.

"I am bent on the gratification of my wishes," returned Trevors; "and I will brave the consequences."

"But I cannot, Trevors. I am an old man, and unfit to bear a part in such designs."

"Nevertheless, you must, in spite of your objections. What have you to fear from the girl? She will be powerless, and I will take good care that she shall not escape the fate that I intend for her. She will not long be a prisoner here, and will not have the opportunity of betraying you afterwards, depend on it."

"Would that I could think so."

"But you must. I am tired of listening to your worse than childish fears; let me hear no more of them."

"Alas, has it then come to this, that I am not allowed to be the master of my own place?"

"You never were," replied Martin Trevors. "I am your master, and consequently the master of your house, and all that belongs to you."

"Martin Trevors," exclaimed the miserable old man, "forbear! I cannot, I will not endure these bitter torments."

"But you must. How can you help yourself, slave as you are of my will, and completely in my power? Does not your very life hang upon my word?"

"Alas! alas!"

"Then why obstinately endeavour to dissuade me from my purpose?" demanded Martin. "You know it is useless, and can only serve to excite my wrath."

"Well, well, Martin, I will not," said Sir Horace; "but pray be careful how you act, for the least mismanagement might end in our utter ruin."

"Oh, leave that to me. Think you that this is the first time that I have been engaged in such affairs?"

"Oh, no; I am well assured that it is not," answered the baronet.

"Well, then, why need you caution me?"

"But you failed in your attempt to seize the boy, you know, and that might have been productive of the most fatal results."

"Ay, if I had not been too nimble for the officious rascals," returned Trevors.

"But they recognised you."

"Yes; that was unfortunate, for it showed that I had not quitted the neighbourhood as it was supposed I had, and has doubtless put Michael Belford on his guard; but all his care and precaution will not save his daughter from my power, nor shall the boy escape me either. He shall shortly be a prisoner in this house, or my name is not Martin Trevors."

"No, no," hastily ejaculated Sir Horace, with a look of alarm; "not in this house, Martin, not in this house. I could not dare to look upon the features of that boy again even for the universe."

"You have become a greater coward than ever," said Martin, with a frown. "Would you have the boy remain at liberty, when, should he recover his senses, he may be able to disclose such facts as would place us both in a most awkward situation ?"

"No, no," said the baronet; "would that he had perished in the flames; then would my fears have been greatly diminished."

"And you would not care if he was disposed of now ?"

"Oh, Martin, would you but do that—would you but secure him so that I might never more behold him, you would indeed be rendering me a service."

"What, would you have me shed his blood ?"

"Hush, Trevors," gasped forth the trembling old man; "do not speak so loud; we might be overheard. I—I would have you rid me of him. You understand me ?"

"Oh, yes, I understand you," said Trevors, with a malicious grin; "and this is the remorse that you cant so much about. Bah! but we will talk more of this anon."

And with these words Martin Trevors abruptly quitted the room, and left the guilty Sir Horace to his own gloomy reflections.

We must now return to the house of Michael Belford. Winter had now again approached, and nearly a twelvemonth had expired since the attempted seizure of the maniac, by Martin Trevors, of whom, as we have said before, they had not heard anything, and they therefore at last concluded that he had quitted that part of the country altogether, and consequently abandoned his designs, and they became more assured and contented. But Rosetta frequently thought of Frank, and was anxious to ascertain his fate, though she feared that she would never be able to do so now, and sometimes she even feared that he was no more, so great was the despair he had evinced on their last interview.

Julio grew apace, and no one could gaze on the manly beauty of his countenance, and the graces of his form, without admiration. But no change had taken place in his mind; there all was as dark and hopeless as ever, and his kind friends began to fear that his reason had indeed fled for ever.

Many were the pangs this sad reflection cost our heroine, for she could not help now acknowledging to herself that Julio had inspired in her breast a sentiment of a far more tender nature than that of pity or sympathy, and at times she even ventured to encourage hopes, which, in the present situation of the unfortunate youth, could never be realized. Her parents read her thoughts, and deeply sympathised in her feelings, while at the same time they hoped that she might be able to conquer her passion, for they saw but little prospect of Julio ever becoming her husband, even if his senses were restored to him.

It was such another tempestuous night as that with which we commenced our narrative, and about the same time of the year. The wind howled fearfully around the old stone house, and the rain descended in torrents. Rosetta and her mother felt very uneasy, for Michael was from home, and had been absent the whole of the afternoon.

"The storm still rages with unabated fury," said Rosetta, going to the window; "how will my poor father ever be able to reach home ?"

"I know not," answered her mother; "it is unfortunate that he did not delay the business he has gone upon till another day, especially as the weather was so unpromising."

"Yes," observed Rosetta; "I wish indeed that he had done so. Besides, it is now getting late, and I begin to feel alarmed at his protracted absence."

"Oh, he is doubtless staying at some house until the storm has a little abated," said Mrs. Belford; "he could never venture forth in such weather as this."

"It does not seem likely to abate to-night," said our heroine; "how frightfully the wind bellows around this old house. Ah, mother, it was just such a night as this when the Death Ship last made its appearance, and poor Julio was rescued by my father from the burning vessel."

"Ah!" exclaimed her mother, with a look of terror; "why do you remind me of that dreadful night, my dear child? And now I recollect, this is the very day of the month on which that occurrence took place."

" It is," said Rosetta. " Oh! how I wish my father would return. I begin to feel a most unconquerable sensation of fear steal over me."

" Do not give way to it, Rosetta," said Mrs. Belford, though she was, in fact, as much alarmed as her daughter. " Nothing will, I trust, happen to disturb us to-night. Ah! gracious Heaven! what was that?"

They both heard it, and appalling was the sound, so unearthly, so indescribable. They clung fearfully to each other.

" It was that terrible warning cry," gasped forth Rosetta, " the certain harbinger of approaching calamity."

Their terrors increased, as the raging storm continued with unabated fury, and the wind shook the windows, and howled in terrific gusts through every avenue of the building. Julio had felt indisposed during the afternoon, and had retired at an early hour to his chamber.

Rosetta and her mother continued fixed near the window, and endeavoured to conquer their fears, but could not. In this manner another hour passed away, and still Michael did not return. The anxiety and terrors of Mrs. Belford and her daughter became almost insupportable, and their minds were distracted by the most dismal forebodings, which the strange and awful cry they had heard served to strengthen.

They strained their eyes through the window, but the darkness was now impenetrable, and it was impossible for them to distinguish any object beyond. Still Michael came not, and they began to fear that something had happened to him, and that some misfortune was about to befal them, which would be productive of the greatest misery to them, and which they could not by any possibility avert.

They almost feared to look around them, lest they should encounter some fearful form, and when they thought of the mysterious and awful form which they had seen flit past the old house on the night of the tempest, the most superstitious apprehensions filled their breasts.

Faster fell the rain, and the wind, which now blew a perfect hurricane, seemed to shake even the old stone building to the very foundation.

" It is impossible that my father can venture through such a dreadful storm as this," said Rosetta. " How unfortunate it is that he should have not delayed his business until another time, since it was not so very urgent for a day or two, I believe, and portentous clouds hung over the horizon even when he left home."

" Yes," observed her mother; " and I tried to persuade him not to venture forth. But he was determined, although I know not why he should have been so particular for a day or two; but he now, no doubt, regrets that he did not yield to my persuasions, for he must be perfectly aware of the uneasiness of mind we are enduring, and how anxiously we are looking for his return, although it is almost utterly impossible that he should do so in such a tempest."

" And yet, methinks, he will brave it," said Rosetta; " for he knows that we shall be in the greatest state of excitement whilst he remains absent. Where can he find a shelter?"

" Perhaps he has not yet started from the house of the person to whom he has gone upon business," remarked Mrs. Belford; " or he may have reached old Kit's, and, if such is the fact, you know he will be safe enough."

" Oh, yes," answered our heroine; " and if we could but be certain that he had done so, we might be contented. Alas! I cannot help feeling the most dismal forebodings of approaching evil."

" Nay, my dear child," said her mother, who was, however, as much alarmed as herself, " you must endeavour to banish those melancholy ideas from your breast."

" But that dreadful cry, dear mother!—we could not be deceived, for we both distinctly heard it, and even now it seems to ring in my ears. Would to Heaven that my father would be persuaded to quit this neighbourhood, for a fatal spell seems to rest upon it, and the spirit of Hugh Clifton to hover about this old house."

" Hush, hush, Rosetta, for Heaven's sake," said the terrified old woman, casting a fearful glance around her, as if she dreaded yet expected to behold some ghastly object. " Oh, that Michael had never related that awful legend!"

The loud report of a gun was now heard booming through the tempestuous air, from the direction of the sea.

"Ah!" ejaculated Rosetta, "there is some vessel in distress.   Heaven help the unfortunate beings, and rescue them from the dreadful fate with which they are threatened."

"Amen!" solemnly returned Mrs. Belford; "for if Heaven does not help them, they certainly must perish in such a dreadful tempest as that which now rages, spreading universal destruction around.   But who, alas! can venture forth to their assistance?   Inevitable death must be the consequence of any such attempt."

"It must, indeed," said Rosetta; "and it was as violent a storm as the present when my dear father, at the risk of his life, saved Julio from the burning ship. Hark! again!"

Once more the report of a gun was heard, and then all was silent, save the furious howling of the blast, and the loud pattering of the rain against the windows."

"This suspense is insupportable," said Rosetta; "the storm continues to rage with unabated fury, as if in mockery of our anxiety.   All merciful God, preserve my poor father, and bring him safe back to us."

"Depend upon it, he is under shelter, my dear child," said her mother; "for, had he ventured to proceed on his journey, he must have been home before this."

"It is getting late," said our heroine; "it is now past ten o'clock, and my father is seldom absent from home at such an hour."

"But it is easily accounted for on such a night as this," returned Mrs. Belford; "we must try to dismiss these fears from our minds, and pray to Heaven that the tempest may abate in fury, when Michael will, no doubt, soon return, and in perfect safety.   What harm can befall him?"

"Martin Trevors," suggested Rosetta.

"Oh, we have nothing to fear from him now," answered her mother, "for it is quite evident that he has quitted this part of the country altogether, and has probably abandoned his evil designs, knowing the great risk he would himself run in endeavouring to accomplish them."

"I would that I could think so," said our heroine; "but when I remember the terrible threats of Martin Trevors, and the outrage he committed upon poor Julio, I cannot help apprehending that he is only awaiting any opportunity that may present itself of more securely gratifying his diabolical vengeance."

"Consider the many months which have elapsed since we have heard or seen anything of him."

"True; but this may be only a deep-laid scheme of his to drown our suspicions, and throw us off our guard.   Martin Trevors, I fear, is not the man to easily abandon any designs upon which he may have fixed his mind.   It is very unfornate that we ever became acquainted with him."

"It is.   But who could have thought that Martin Trevors, in spite of his mysterious manners, was the vindictive character it now seems he is?"

"No," said Rosetta; "and yet, notwithstanding all my efforts to the contrary, I could not help always looking upon him with a feeling of suspicion and dread. Poor Frank! it seems almost impossible that you should be the son of such a father."

"Ah, poor lad!" remarked Mrs. Belford, compassionately; "I wonder what has become of him."

"I should be more satisfied did I but know," said our heroine; "but I fear that we shall never learn any more of him.   How great would be his regret and anguish, did he but know the manner in which his father has committed himself—the disgrace which he has brought upon his name."

"He would, indeed," coincided Mrs. Belford; "unfortunate young man, I fear that his will be a melancholy destiny; but yet he cannot be responsible for the actions of his father."

"Oh, no," returned Rosetta; "Frank's virtues entitle him to every esteem, and no one can more cordially wish him prosperity and happiness than I do."

"I know it, my child; I am sure of it," said the mother.

"Oh, my mother," sighed Rosetta; "when I reflect upon the foul aspersio ns which Martin Trevors cast upon my character, the blush of shame and indignation mantles in my cheeks."

"Think no more of it, Rosetta; the calumnies of the guilty cannot injure you, and deserve to be treated only with the utmost scorn. Base, indeed, must have been the mind of Trevors, to suffer him to give utterance to such language to one whom he knew so ill-deserved it. Ah! thank Heaven, the wind is going down; the rain descends not so heavily; the storm will presently subside, and your father will then speedily return."

"I hope so, dear mother," ejaculated Rosetta, "for I can no longer endure this state of suspense with any degree of patience."

The tempest had, indeed, greatly abated, and Mrs. Belford and her daughter continued to watch at the window, with the hope of beholding the approach of Michael. But their hopes were still doomed to be disappointed, and their uneasiness increased every moment.

In the meantime Michael, for more than two hours, had put up at an inn, on the way from the place where he had been to; but at length, tired of waiting any longer, and knowing the state of alarm and anxiety his wife and daughter would be in at his protracted absence, he determined to brave the inclemency of the weather, and, buttoning his great coat closer around him, he sallied forth into the open air, and hurried on his way as fast as he could.

It was indeed a dreadful night, and Michael was soon wet to the skin, while the wind blew so violently that he could not, without the greatest difficulty, keep his feet. He remembered that this was the anniversary of the night of horror, on which he rescued Julio from death, and, in spite of himself, he could not help strange and dismal presentiments besetting his mind.

He proceeded on, through the raging tempest, without meeting any individual; but he was still a long way from home, and he deeply regretted that he had not deferred the business he had been upon till another day, when the weather might have been more favourable. He was completely drenched to the skin, and therefore it would be useless to put up at any other place, especially as the storm did not appear likely to subside during the night. To remain from home, he could not think of, for he knew well what the terrors of Rosetta and her mother would be, should he do so. They would make sure that some accident had befallen him, and besides, he could not, for a moment, bear the idea of leaving them alone all night.

He increased his speed, and had arrived near the cliffs, when the loud report of a gun thundered in his ears, which he had no doubt proceeded from some ship in distress, and soon afterwards he perceived the glare of several lights emitted by the torches carried by the persons who, no doubt, had been attracted to the spot with the hope of being able to render some assistance to the unfortunate mariners.

"Heaven help the poor creatures!" said the humane Mr. Belford; "but, alas! I fear that no mortal power can render them the least assistance in their dreadful extremity. It must be a miracle indeed that can save them in such a storm as this."

Again Michael increased his speed, and, notwithstanding the fury of the tempest, the miserable condition he was in, and his anxiety to arrive at home, he could not help hastening towards the cliffs, in order that he might ascertain the extent of the danger which threatened the unfortunate vessel. Once more he heard the report of the signal of distress, and his anxiety every moment gained fresh strength.

"Alas! my poor fellows," he ejaculated, "you appeal, I fear, for help in vain. The awful fate that awaits you is inevitable, unless the Almighty commander of all interpose to save you. May His mercy be extended to you, and quell the fury of the remorseless waves which are now fast dashing you to destruction."

By this time Michael had advanced so far that he could hear the shouts of the men upon the cliffs, as they hurried to and fro, apparently with the useless design of attempting to afford assistance. The next moment one simultaneous, appalling shriek reverberated far around, and then all was deathlike silent, with the exception of the voice of the wind, which seemed to howl in exultation over the destruction that had just taken place.

"It is all over," said Michael, as he ran hastily towards the cliffs ; "the poor fellows are hurled into eternity ; may Heaven receive their souls."

He had now reached the cliffs, and joined the persons who were there assembled, who, in reply to his anxious inquiries, informed him that the unfortunate vessel (to the assistance of which no one had dared to go) had but a few minutes before gone to pieces, and no doubt that every one on board of her had perished. Portions of the wreck were tossed about on the waves, and two or three human bodies were dashed upon the beach, and from their clothes, and other articles found upon them, it would seem that she was an English trading vessel called the Dexterous, but this was all the information they were able to obtain.

Michael gazed with a melancholy feeling across the angry ocean, and reflected upon the awful sacrifice of life which had just taken place. The sight, even to him, who had been used to such scenes, was a most appalling one, and he could not contemplate it without a shudder of terror. The darkness was almost impenetrable, and the lurid glare emitted by the torches which were carried by several of the persons assembled, added impressiveness to the scene.

"We can do no good here," said one of the men ; "the poor fellows have all gone to Davy Jones, and as the storm continues without any prospect of abating, I think we should be much better in our cabins. Ah! Master Michael, this is just such another night as it was this time last year, when the devil's craft (for such it certainly is) made its appearance, and you saved the poor maniac boy from the burning ship."

"It is Gerald," answered Michael ; "and may Providence shield us from any further calamity."

"So I say, Mr. Belford," observed Gerald. "But, ah! what is that?"

Michael and the others looked in the direction to which Gerald pointed, and beheld a strange blue supernatural light flickering in the distant horizon.

"What can this mean?" exclaimed Michael ; "it must proceed from the mast head of some vessel. It approaches nearer, and now—ah! by Heaven! do you not see, my friends?"

The strange light now became stronger, until the whole of that portion of the horizon was illumined by its unearthly beams ; and then the dark outline of a vessel was plainly discernible, as it was tossed about on the billows, and seemed to bid defiance to their power. Amazement and terror rivetted the attention of every person on the cliffs, and they watched the vessel with fearful expectation. It became more and more distinct, yet it did not appear to be approaching them, until at length the majestic and mysterious ship became clearly revealed like a gigantic phantom in the midst of the troubled ocean. Another moment, and the light gleamed full upon the black flag, which fluttered from her mast-head, and displayed its ghastly and well-known emblems.

"Gracious Heaven!" exclaimed Michael, "it is—it is the Death Ship!"

"The Death Ship! the Death Ship!" repeated every one in a breath, and they strained their eyes towards the direction where that awful bark was proudly riding, as if in defiance of the fury of the raging elements. A shudder of horror thrilled through every breast, and they exchanged ghastly looks of fearful foreboding.

But a few moments, and the light vanished, and the Death Ship disappeared as if by magic.

CHAPTER XIV.

THE CONFLAGRATION.—THE SEIZURE OF ROSETTA.

"Strange, fearful mystery!" exclaimed Michael, turning to his companions, "surely no human beings can man that dreadful craft! When will this be unravelled?"

"Never, I fear, Master Belford," replied Gerald. "If this is not Lucifer's own ship, my name's not Gerald Wetherby. Heaven save us from falling into the clutches of its awful crew!"

The storm had now greatly abated, and Mr. Belford, filled with strange and harassing thoughts, walked away a few paces, in order to return home, when he was suddenly startled by several of the men, exclaiming,—

"A fire! a fire on land! Behold!"

Michael looked up, and beheld flames ascending into the air, apparently from some lofty eminence, at no great distance from the spot on which he was standing.

"Good God!" he cried, in a voice of distraction! "it is in the direction of my dwelling! Oh, can it be? Forbid it, Heaven! Follow me, I implore you, my friends, and render your assistance. My wife! my child, Julio!"

With the delirious air of a madman, Michael Belford rushed from the spot with the speed of lightning, and followed by the men. The nearer they approached, the more convinced did the agonized Michael become that it was indeed his house which was falling a prey to the devouring element. The flames raged with increased fury, and illumined the sky with their lurid glare for miles around.

"Oh, God! oh, God!" cried the frenzied old man; "what a terrible calamity is this. My wife! my Rosetta, I shall be too late to save ye. Horror, horror! and must I indeed be deprived of ye in this dreadful manner?"

They reached the foot of the hill, and then beheld the house in flames from the basement to the roof, out of which they were pouring with a hissing and frightful noise.

Up the rugged side of the hill Michael rushed with delirious haste, and giving vent to his despair in the most fearful shouts. His companions followed close at his heels, but when they reached the burning pile, all hope appeared to be entirely at an end, for the fire had spread to such an alarming extent that it seemed totally impossible to enter the building.

"My wife, my child!" exclaimed Michael; "I will save them, or perish with them!"

Without uttering another word, he dashed through the flames and smoke, which was so dense that he was almost suffocated. Although he was considerably burnt, nothing could stay him in his progress, notwithstanding the ruins were falling about him in every direction. He gained one of the inner apartments, just as Mrs. Belford, forced along by Julio, entered it, and sought to make their way to the outer door. Michael uttered an exclamation of frantic delight, for he imagined that Rosetta was also with them, and with much difficulty he succeeded in forcing them through the flames into the open air.

"Oh, my child! my Rosetta!" he cried; "she is not here; speak, wife, where is our daughter?"

"Lost, lost!" groaned the wretched old woman, clasping her hands with the most indescribable agony.

"Lost, lost!" repeated the horror-struck Michael; "my darling, my only one, my Rosetta fallen a victim to the devouring element. Oh, God! oh, God! this is too much for a wretched father to bear."

"No, no, Michael," returned Mrs. Belford, in a voice half choked with the violence of her intense agony. "Not in the flames, not in the flames has she perished. The ruffians who are the cause of this calamity forced her from the house, and have borne her away!"

"Rosetta torn away from me!" cried Michael; "my home destroyed. Oh, may the vengeance of Heaven fall heavily upon the inhuman perpetrators of this monstrous act."

"Yes, yes," exclaimed the poor maniac youth; "pretty sister Rosetta is taken away; the monsters! the fiends! But Julio will find them out, and force her from their power, or perish with her!"

Mrs. Belford, completely exhausted, had now become insensible, and Michael stood over her in a state of complete stupefaction. The flames had now nearly exhausted their fury, the roof of the old stone house fell in with a terrific crash, and the dense clouds of black smoke that followed completely darkened the air.

"My daughter!" exclaimed Michael; "oh, where shall I seek my daughter?"

"Be calm, Mr. Belford," said Gerald; "this is a dreadful calamity, but Providence may yet befriend you, and restore your daughter to your arms."

"Oh, never, never," cried the despairing man; "she is taken from me for ever. Who are the miscreants that have done this? Oh, God! this is indeed my death blow."

"Come, come, Michael," said Gerald, kindly, "you must not take on so, poor man. We will all assist you to recover your child, and Heaven will assist us in our efforts,"

"They rushed into the place," said Julio; "there were three, four, five, six of them. They were masked and armed. I tried to protect Rosetta, but they tore her from me, and having kindled these frightful flames, they bore her screaming from the house. Her shrieks even now ring in my ears! Rosetta, Rosetta! Julio will find you, or die in the attempt."

"Wretched man," ejaculated Michael, "what have I done that Heaven should visit me with such a calamity as this? I have now no home, no child! Oh, horror, horror!"

"Let us assist you to convey your poor wife to the nearest habitation, which is old Kit Hayward's," said Gerald; "and when she recovers, she may be enabled to give us such information as may assist us in discovering your daughter, and of releasing her from the power of the atrocious ruffians who have committed this outrage."

"Oh, no, it is too late," said Mr. Belford; "the wretches have succeeded in their villainous designs, and have doubtless borne my poor child to a place of security. I shall never more behold her! I shall never more behold her!"

It is needless to attempt to describe the anguish of Michael; his brain was tortured to distraction, and he was scarcely conscious of what was going forward. He offered no resistance to Gerald and his companions, however, who raised his wife in their arms, and he passively followed them down the hill, Julio having taken his hand, and giving utterance to the wildest expressions of grief.

When they had gained the foot of the hill, they met old Hayward coming hastily towards them. He had also been from home, and it was not until some time after his return, that he became aware of the fire that was raging in the dwelling of his unfortunate friend. We need not attempt to describe his emotion when he now beheld Michael, and was make acquainted with all that had taken place.

"The miscreants," he exclaimed; "who can they be? Poor Rosetta! But do not despair, my good old friend, for she will be discovered, depend on it, and restored to you uninjured. The magistrates must be made acquainted with this dreadful outrage immediately, and an instant pursuit set on foot after them."

"Alas, it is all useless," groaned Michael; "my poor child, my darling Rosetta is lost to me for ever. Oh, it was wrong in me to leave them so long alone."

"Nay, Michael," said Mr. Hayward, "you reproach yourself unjustly. It is, indeed, a melancholy catastrophe, but you are not to blame."

"Not to blame! not to blame!" repeated Mr. Belford, in wild accents; "oh, God! oh, God! what will become of me? Wretched, lost for ever."

"Cheer up, cheer up, my dear friend," said the compassionate Mr. Hayward, in the most soothing accents, "all will yet be well, all will yet be well, depend on it. Providence will not permit the guilty thus to triumph in their iniquity, and your daughter will be restored to you."

"Oh, never! never!" sighed Michael; "she is gone for ever, my innocent child; she who was the only comfort of mine and her poor mother's declining years. Oh! it will break her mother's heart. Alas! what desolation in a few minutes have the heartless miscreants caused. My home destroyed, my child torn from me; monsters! what have I done that they should take this terrible revenge against me? Ah! Martin Trevors! he it was who threatened me with a fearful vengeance; to destroy all my happiness, to ruin the prospects of my daughter. He it is who has done this."

"Can he possibly have become such a villain?" said old Kit.

"Oh, yes," returned Michael; "his observations, his base aspersions when we last met, and afterwards the outrage he committed on this poor lad, prove him to be a man capable of committing any atrocious crime. Heaven pardon me if I judge him wrongfully, but I firmly believe that he is the author of this atrocity."

"He must indeed be a heartless miscreant, if your suspicions are correct," observed Mr. Hayward; "but come, come, let us hasten to my house, so that everything may be promptly done towards the restoration of your wife. I need not say that there you will find a welcome home."

"Home! home!" groaned the unfortunate old man, beating his breast, and with a look which filled every one who beheld him with the greatest pity and grief; "I have no home, now; no home, no child. Almighty God! this visitation is too severe, far too severe—I shall go mad!"

"Be calm, I beseech you," said Kit.

"Calm!" repeated Michael, with a wild and vacant look; "I am not more than man, and how can I be calm under such dreadful circumstances as these? Oh, Kit! you know not what it is to lose so fair a child as she who is mercilessly snatched away from me, to become the victim of what I shudder to think upon. Oh! she was so affectionate, so innocent, so dutiful! What can ever replace her loss?"

"But she will be restored to you, Michael; indeed she will," said Kit. "My good friend," he continued, addressing himself to Gerald, "will you hasten to the magistrate's house, and inform him of what has taken place? He will, promptly, I know, adopt means to endeavour to rescue the poor girl from the wretches who now hold her in their power, and to bring them to punishment for the dreadful outrage they have committed."

"Yes," answered the willing and humane-hearted fisherman; "I will hasten there immediately, and I earnestly hope that ere many hours have elapsed, some intelligence will be obtained of the route the villains have taken, and the poor damsel be restored to her unhappy parents. For my own part, I will exert myself to the utmost, and I know that my friends here will do the same. Alas! I feared that some dreadful calamity was about to happen, when that terrible devil's craft made its appearance again this night."

"Alas! alas!" ejaculated Mr. Belford; "hasten, my good Gerald; and, for the kindness and sympathy which you show me, may my eternal blessings light upon your head. But, alas! where can we search for the miscreants? where find a clue to them?"

"Let us no longer delay," observed Kit; "every moment is precious, and will give the villains an opportunity to escape. Away, good Gerald, so that the pursuit may be immediately commenced."

Gerald bowed significantly, and instantly departed in the direction of the magistrate's house. Michael Belford then turned a melancholy gaze towards the smouldering ruins of that house in which he had passed so many days, so many years of happiness; and then with a heart ready to burst, followed Kit Hayward and the others, who were supporting the insensible form of his wife to the dwelling of his friend, which was only a short distance off.

The news of what had happened soon spread around the neighbourhood, and caused the greatest excitement and indignation against the heartless perpetrators of so diabolical an outrage. Every one deeply commiserated with Michael Belford in the heart-rending calamity which had befallen him, for no man was more universally respected than he was, and they determined all to exert themselves to the utmost to discover Rosetta, and to bring the wretches who had been guilty of so abominable a crime to that punishment which they so justly merited. But the task was a most difficult one, for it was impossible for any person to form the least conjecture as to the direction which the ruffians had taken.

A medical man was promptly in attendance at the house of Kit Hayward; and, after some exertion, he succeeded in restoring Mrs. Belford to her senses, Michael and Julio watching over her at the same time, in a state of the greatest anxiety and distraction. On her recovery, she looked vacantly around her, and beholding her husband, she uttered an exclamation of agony. He flew to her side and embraced her affectionately, while tears of the bitterest anguish chased each other down his aged cheeks.

"Ah!" she exclaimed; "where am I? This is not our home, Michael. Home —home!—oh, horror!—we have no home, now—it is destroyed. But, my child— my own fond and innocent Rosetta—where is she? She is stolen from us—monsters hold her in their power. We shall never behold her again! Oh, God!—oh,

God! What a mercy it would be to us, Michael, were we this hour to be deprived of life!"

"My heart will break!" groaned Michael, beating his breast, and his voice almost stifled by the insupportable violence of his emotion. "My child—my sweet, blooming girl—oh, where are you?—where have the atrocious villains borne you? and what are their designs against you?"

"Murder, Michael, murder!" returned Mrs. Belford, in accents which smote all who heard her with pity and horror. "Oh, my poor husband, it is Martin Trevors who has, too certainly, perpetrated this fiendish act."

"Martin Trevors!" ejaculated Mr. Hayward, with astonishment and disgust. "Can it be possible that he has been guilty of such a hideous crime? But endeavour to collect yourself, I pray you, Mrs. Belford, and inform us briefly of all the particulars, so that we may be the better prepared to take proper steps towards the recovery of your daughter."

"Yes, yes," exclaimed Michael, eagerly, and with a look of the most unspeakable agony; "let us know everything, that not a moment may be lost. I will pursue the wretches even to the most remote corner of the earth, and recover my child, or perish in the attempt. Speak, my dear wife, and tell us all, for the love of Heaven."

Mrs. Belford struggled violently with her feelings, but it was some moments ere she could give utterance to a syllable; however, at last she said,—

"Myself and poor Rosetta, Michael, had been most anxiously awaiting your return, and many were the agonizing fears we entertained that some accident had befallen you in the storm."

"Yes, yes," ejaculated Michael, with frenzied impatience. "Proceed—proceed."

"At length we heard a knock at the door," continued Mrs. Belford; "and thinking it was you, Michael, that had returned, I flew gladly to the door to open it; but no sooner had I done so, than six men, wearing black masks, and armed with swords and pistols, rushed into the house, and seized upon Rosetta. We both screamed loudly; and poor Julio, who, it seems, had only thrown himself on his bed, undressed, rushed into the room, and endeavoured to release our child from their hold, but in vain. One of the miscreants discharged the contents of a pistol at him, which, fortunately, missed him; and, having set fire to some of the furniture in the room, they darted from the house with their precious prize, whose futile shrieks for help rang in my ears for several moments, in tones which I can never forget. We tried to follow them, but the flames, which, fanned by the wind, quickly spread, prevented us. The rest you know; I can explain no further. Oh, God!—oh, God! spare my brain, or I shall certainly go mad."

"Horrible!—horrible!" gasped forth Mr. Belford, beating his breast. "Then you saw not the direction which the monsters took?"

"I could not," answered Mrs. Belford. "The flames, as I have before said, prevented me. Would to Heaven that I had perished in them. What is now to become of us, Michael, deprived of all that we held dear in life?"

"My heart will certainly break with agony," exclaimed her wretched husband. "Oh, my beloved wife, what a fearful calamity is this!"

"Do not give way entirely to despair," remonstrated Mr. Hayward, compassionately; "for it may not yet be too late to save her. But what reason have you to suspect that Martin Trevors is the author of this dreadful outrage, Mrs. Belford?"

"One of the villains spoke," replied the old woman; "he appeared to be the leader, and I am certain that it was the voice of Trevors."

"The miscreant!" cried the distracted Michael; "it is too certainly he. He threatened us with his vengeance, and he has now most awfully kept his word. But I will pursue the monster to destruction. Let me immediately forth, and endeavour to find him."

"Pray become more calm," said Kit; "for it is only by that means that we may hope to succeed. The magistrates are by this time acquainted with all the fearful particulars, and doubtless will not lose a moment in instituting a pursuit after the ruffians."

"But, alas! what chance is there of gaining any clue to them?" ejaculated Michael.

Gerald now returned, and informed them that he had made the magistrates acquainted with all that had happened, and they had expressed their most earnest sympathy with Michael and his wife in the shocking calamity that had befallen them, and had immediately despatched persons in every direction in pursuit of the villains, which they trusted would be attended with success.

It would be impossible adequately to describe the sufferings of Michael and his wife during that night. Sleep, of course, they could not think of attempting, and it was more than Mr. Hayward could accomplish to bring them to anything like a state of tranquillity. Poor Julio, too, he could not be prevailed upon to retire to rest, and his lamentations at the loss of Rosetta were pitiful to hear. The morning came, and still there was no intelligence of Rosetta, or the villains by whom she had been seized. Michael could contain himself no longer, and, in spite of the remonstrances of Kit, he started forth, accompanied by two or three of his neighbours, in search of his lost child, although he was perfectly at a loss which course to take.

That Martin Trevors was the author of this atrocious outrage, they all now entertained but very little doubt, and Michael made his way to the magistrates, and informed them of his suspicions, and they immediately instituted a strict inquiry to ascertain whether he was lurking anywhere in the neighbourhood, and offered a reward to any one who could give them information concerning him; although they entertained but little hopes that their praiseworthy efforts would be rewarded with success.

Michael then suggested to them the probability of his being concealed in the Manor-house, in consequence of his intimacy with Sir Horace Middleton, and although the magistrates could not believe that the baronet would take a part in any deed of such enormity, they sent to make all the necessary inquiry.

How Sir Horace received them, the reader may more easily conceive than we can describe; but they could elicit no intelligence whatever of the villain, and nothing to corroborate their suspicions that the baronet knew anything as to what had become of him, and poor Michael, after wandering about the whole of the day to no purpose, returned to the house of Mr. Hayward in despair, where he found his wife in a state of mind bordering upon distraction, and deaf to every remonstrance that was made use of to console her.

"Alas!" exclaimed Michael, "the wretches have too well succeeded in their diabolical designs. They have destroyed our once happy home, and torn our unfortunate and innocent child from us for ever! Death would now be a mercy to us, since all our hopes of future peace are entirely annihilated. Oh, my Rosetta, what is now your situation!—what your sufferings!"

"Horror! horror!" groaned Mrs. Belford. "My brain burns to madness when I think of it; better, better had they deprived us both of life, my husband, than thus have robbed us of our darling child. Who could have imagined that such fiends in human shape were in existence?"

"May the curses of offended Heaven pursue them to destruction!" ejaculated Michael, vehemently clasping his burning temples. "Little did I imagine that in our old age, we should have been visited with such a frightful calamity as this."

"Cheer up, my dear friend," said old Kit Hayward, "cheer up, and endeavour to hope for the best. The vengeance of Heaven will undoubtedly overtake the monsters, be they who they may, and I sincerely trust that your daughter will be returned uninjured to your arms. They cannot long escape the vigilance of their pursuers."

"Alas! how futile are such hopes," replied Michael Belford; "where can the pursuers direct their course? Even now, too, my unfortunate daughter may be no more. She could not possibly long survive this cruel outrage."

"Rosetta, dead!" ejaculated Julio, in tones of the most touching agony; "have they then murdered her, as they did my poor mother? Would that they had slain Julio also, for, deprived of his pretty, his kind sister Rosetta, what has he now to live for? But let me go forth in search of her. I will find her out, or seek at once my silent grave in the ocean deep. Rosetta! Rosetta!"

With these words, the poor youth was rushing towards the door, when he was arrested by Mr. Hayward.

"Stay, Julio," he said, persuasively; "you must not be permitted thus to wander forth alone. Pray to Heaven, and Rosetta will be restored to you, depend on it."

"Pray! pray!" repeated the maniac; "oh, yes; I will heartily offer up my supplications to the Almighty; and I will implore my mother's sainted spirit to intercede for me, for what can repay Julio for the loss of Rosetta? Oh, she was so fair, so innocent, so affectionate!"

"She was indeed, my good boy," said Michael. "Oh, my bursting heart! This blow will prove my death, and Heaven knows I care not how soon."

"You weep," said the maniac, with a look of intense compassion, "but you must not, for Julio will search for her all over the world, and restore her to you. No power shall keep her from me. Let me go, for still do I hear her frantic shrieks calling upon me for help, and who shall dare to prevent me from flying to her assistance. 'Julio!' she cries; There, again! Let me go, I say!"

Mr. Hayward had the greatest difficulty to detain the unfortunate youth, and it was not until after considerable trouble that he was in the least degree pacified.

Hour after hour passed away in the same wretched manner, and still without their being able to obtain the least information of Rosetta, and Mrs. Belford was so completely worn out with anxiety and grief, that she was compelled to retire to bed, to which it seemed most likely that she would be confined for some time to come.

We need not attempt to describe the state of mind to which Michael was reduced, for the reader can much more readily conceive it. Mr. Hayward exerted himself to the utmost to console them, and to lead them to hope, but with very little or no success; and, indeed, under the very painful and peculiar circumstances, he had no argument to offer.

They had received frequent communications from the magistrates, but none that were at all calculated to banish their despair. Not the least information had been obtained of Rosetta, or the wretches that held her in their power, and it was a matter of astonishment and perplexity to imagine how they had managed to escape from the country without detection; for it seemed now positively certain that they were no where concealed in the neighbourhood, and it could not be reasonably imagined that they would have remained there. Another day, another night now passed away, and still nothing occurred to inspire them with the least ray of hope. They were, in fact, driven to a state bordering upon madness, and were deaf to all the expostulations that were made use of to tranquillize them.

Everything that the house had contained was consumed, and Michael and his wife were left in a manner destitute, although he fortunately had an annuity that was amply sufficient to support them. Every one who knew them felt the greatest pity for their misfortunes, and exerted themselves to the utmost to endeavour to discover their lost daughter, but with scarcely any prospect at all of success; and when day after day elapsed without their being able to gain any information, they gave up the attempt in absolute despair.

And it was pitiable to behold the sufferings of Julio, and to hear him constantly calling upon the name of Rosetta. He resisted every effort that was made to tranquillize him, and it seemed but too likely to have the most fatal effect upon his already deranged intellect, while it showed the real strength of the affection he bore towards the unfortunate damsel.

CHAPTER XV.

THE ABDUCTION OF ROSETA.—THE ENCOUNTER.—THE DEFEAT OF MARTIN TREVORS.—
THE PIRATE SHIP.—ROSETTA A PRISONER.

THE ruffians bore the hapless Rosetta, screaming in their arms down the hill, towards a neighbouring wood, and in vain tried to stop her cries. She saw flames ascending from the house; she thought she could hear the frantic cries of her mother and Julio, and it is a wonder that her senses did not immediately leave her.

"Miscreants! monsters! fiends in human shape!" she exclaimed, "release me! Oh! see the flames consume my once peaceful dwelling! Mother! Julio! Oh! who will save you from the devouring element?"

"Let them perish in the flames; at any rate we have you safe in our power," said one of the villains, in accents of exultation.

"Ah!" ejaculated our heroine, with the utmost horror and alarm; "that voice! Martin Trevors!"

"Yes," returned the ruffian; "it is, indeed, Martin Trevors. Thus does he avenge himself for your scorn and deception."

"Monstrous, brutal man," cried Rosetta, "why do you use me thus? I never injured you. Oh! for the love of God! spare me! save me!"

"I have secured you," returned Martin Trevors, in tones of exultation; "that is enough for me. Before many hours have elapsed, my scornful damsel, you shall be inclosed in the arms of one who views you with no other sentiments than such as have their origin in sensuality. Oh! fear not, he ———"

"Mercy! mercy!" shrieked the appalled Rosetta, unable to endure any more; "oh, God! and shall this heartless man be thus permitted to triumph? Mother, Julio. Oh! Martin, Martin, you surely cannot be insensible to every feeling of pity? You will not thus ———"

"Cease your cries, girl," interrupted Martin, in accents which plainly showed that any appeal our heroine might make to him was completely useless; "you and your parents have dared to offer insult to Martin Trevors, and he never yet submitted to it. Those who presume to offend him, powerless even as he may appear to be, never yet escaped without experiencing his vengeance. Ha! ha! ha! ha! see the flames ascend to the clouds! They cannot escape! Oh! this is glorious! This is indeed ample satisfaction for the part you have acted; but it is only a prelude to that which you have yet to suffer. Away with her, comrades! Heed not her cries! there is no one here who will venture to interrupt us."

Again the unfortunate damsel screamed aloud, whilst the ruffians bore her with the greatest rapidity from the scene of conflagration, obeying to the very letter the commands of Martin Trevors, and taking the direction of the wood, where they were most unlikely to meet with any obstruction, and in which Martin had taken the precaution to have a vehicle in waiting, in order to convey his unfortunate victim to the place of her destination. She fixed upon him one more look of agonizing supplication, she then endeavoured to speak, but could not; and nature was unable any longer to support the feelings of horror which pressed upon her brain; she turned her eyes towards the blazing ruins of her home, and quite overpowered, she became insensible.

"My triumph is complete," exclaimed Martin; "there is no one at hand to attempt to interrupt us. Quick, quick, my lads; once let us gain the wood, and we may set pursuit at defiance. Oh, see how the red flames from the once happy home of Michael Belford ascend into the air. Ha! ha! ha! it will be a rare thing for the old man to talk of. He will now find that Martin Trevor made no empty boast when he said that he would have ample vengeance for the wrongs that have been inflicted upon him. Away, away, boys; the coast is clear before us, and Rosetta Belford is now entirely at the mercy of him whom she and her parents affected to despise."

Again the villain laughed in fiendish exultation, and his ruffian colleagues, obedient to his commands, hurried on their way towards the wood, with their insensible burden in their arms, and completely invulnerable to every sentiment of pity and remorse.

They gained the wood, and, plunging into its deepest recesses, made towards the spot where they had left the carriage in the charge of several of their infamous associates. But, as they approached it, they heard the cries of tumult, and the clashing of arms, and it was quite evident that some desperate conflict was going forward, which they were unprepared to meet with.

"D——n!" exclaimed Martin Trevors, as he glanced towards the direction from whence the sounds proceeded; "there has been treachery at work. What mean those sounds? Quick! quick! our assistance may be needed; but keep firm by me, and resign the girl only with your lives."

The clamour of the contending parties, whoever they were, increased, and, dashing through the most confined part of the wood, they arrived at the open space in wnich they had left the vehicle, and there beheld the men they had left behind them fiercely engaged with a number of individuals dressed like sailors, and who had surrounded the carriage, and seemed determined to take possession of it at all risks. They far outnumbered the party of Martin Trevors, and the whole of the affair assumed the most desperate aspect.

"By all the infernal host!" exclaimed Martin, as he drew forth his sword, "there has been some treachery in this. Some dastard knave has betrayed us; but be firm, my lads, and we shall yet triumph. Keep close to the girl, and do not suffer them to bear her from your power. You know me well, and as you act in this unexpected emergency, so shall you be rewarded. You are aware that I have the means to fulfil my promises. On to them, and death to all those that dare to oppose us."

Several of the ruffians kept back and guarded their fair prize, whilst the rest, with Martin Trevors at their head, rushed to the assistance of their comrades. Their antagonists met them with a determined front, and repulsed them on all sides, and, from their numbers, it seemed but too evident to Martin Trevors that they must overpower them, and that his diabolical designs were frustrated. With a fiendish shout of wrath and ferocious determination, he rushed upon the man who seemed to be the leader of the party, and aimed a deadly blow at his head with his cutlass; but the man warded it off with great skill, and immediately taking a pistol from his belt, discharged its contents at Martin, wounding him in the right arm. He gave utterance to a dreadful malediction, and instantly was seized upon by two or three of the men, and rendered powerless, being disarmed, and his own companions were too deeply engaged with those who were more than a match for them, to render him any assistance.

Two or three of Martin's party were desperately wounded, and their antagonists, having now gained possession of the vehicle, turned their principal attention to Rosetta, who, after a short but severe struggle, they tore from the grasp of those who held her, and put them to flight in all directions.

"Ha! ha! ha!" laughed the leader of these determined men; "Martin Trevors, I wish not to take your life. You see the game is up; this time, at any rate, the triumph is mine. To the carriage with her, and follow me as speedily as you can. Before many hours have elapsed, Rosetta Belford shall be far away from this neighbourhood—thanks to Martin Trevors, who has so materially, but unknowingly to himself, assisted me in the furtherance of my well-formed designs."

"Dog! dog!" growled Martin, vehemently, between his teeth, addressing himself to the man who had spoken to him, and was masked, although his person appeared to be most familiar to Trevors; "who are you, that should thus seek to foil me in my stratagems? Unmask yourself, if you dare!"

"If I dare!" repeated the unknown, in a tone of scorn, and spurning Martin violently from him. "However, it is not worth my while to take the trouble to answer you. Your fellows have wisely fled, and, if you think your life worth preserving, you will not fail to follow their example. We shall meet again, fear not, and probably you may then find it quite soon enough to know who I am. Rosetta Belford is mine, and no means whatever shall wrest her again from my power."

The men had now placed the insensible form of Rosetta in the carriage, and the stranger having thus spoken to Martin Trevors, who was too much confounded and enraged to make any reply, pointing a couple of pistols at his head, followed, and stepping into the carriage, it was driven off at a rapid rate, the men, who were all supplied with horses, following.

Martin Trevors gazed after the vehicle in a state of furious rage, which it would be a difficult task to give any adequate idea of; and he was so bewildered at his unexpected defeat, that for a few seconds he could scarcely believe in its reality."

"Am I awake?" he at length exclaimed; "or is this only some torturing dream? At the very moment when I imagined my triumph complete to be so defeated! Oh! by all my hopes, this is more, much more than I can patiently endure. Who is he that thus has triumphed over me? And who is the traitor that has thus aided him in his plans? Where are all those upon whose courage and fidelity I thought I could depend? Fled! fled! like dastard knaves as they are. Oh, curses, infernal curses light on th's misfortune. Rosetta gone, torn from me, and at the very moment when I thought I had her securely within my grasp! I shall go mad! And such is the termination of all my deep-laid schemes."

He bit his lips in the fury of his wrath, and scarcely knew what course to adopt. All his infamous colleagues had deserted him, and he found himself completely foiled on every side. He had thought that he had so deeply laid his plot, that nothing whatever could frustrate it, and therefore his rage and disappointment were altogether the more insupportable.

The sky was still illumined with the ensanguined glare from the conflagration which had been the villanous work of his hands, but as Martin Trevors now gazed upon it, he could not help feeling a sensation of remorse, which was most probably caused more from the unexpected disappointment he had experienced in the non accomplishment of his diabolical designs, than from any sincere feeling of compunction for the ruin and misery he had occasioned. He had no doubt that Mrs. Belford and Julio had perished in the flames, and so far, at any rate, his spirit of deadly revenge against Michael Belford was gratified; but the principal object of his wishes was torn from him; she had fallen into the power of some unknown individual, and thus indeed did he feel himself most signally defeated, and he considered that nearly all the trouble he had been at was thrown away.

"May every infernal curse light upon those who have done this," he cried, gnashing his teeth, and his eyes completely bloodshot with the uncontrollable fury of his rage; "but shall they thus escape me? Shall I allow them to triumph over me, and to laugh my indignation and disappointment to scorn? I will pursue them! but whither? They have so far succeeded, they have so well and so secretly contrived their plot, that they may safely bid defiance to all my efforts. Oh! there has been some base treachery at work here. Those on whom I thought I could depend have deceived me. And yet they struggled with their unknown foes to the utmost. They were overpowered by numbers, and no blame can attach to them. But why did they desert me in the manner they have done? Whither have they fled? One of them must have been in this plot, or those who have seized upon the girl could not have been so well prepared. The person of the man who led them on is familiar to me; would that I could have seen his features. Fool that I was not to make a desperate effort to discover them; then might I have known better what course to adopt. But it is too late now, and I am completely thwarted on every side. Sir Horace Middleton, too, he will exult in my defeat, for he will imagine that he shall escape the danger in which the capture of the girl would have involved him. But he must not congratulate him too soon, lest, after all, he should be disappointed. He cannot surely have dared to betray me! No, no; the old reptile has too great a regard for his own safety to attempt to do so. But I will find out the real traitor, and wreak my vengeance upon his head, or perish in the attempt."

He clinched his fists as he thus spoke, and his whole demeanour sufficiently expressed the feelings of insupportable wrath that raged within his bosom. Suddenly the footsteps and voices of several persons approaching smote his ears, and aroused him to a full sense of the probable danger in which he was placed. The fire had most likely alarmed the inhabitants of the neighbourhood, and it might be that these were persons who were sent in pursuit of the perpetrators of the awful outrage. He was alone—he had but slight means of defending himself, and he saw the absolute necessity of taking to immediate flight. He dashed through the wood, muttering curses to himself as he proceeded, and took the direction which led to the Manor House, knowing that there alone he might hope to remain in secret for the present.

He soon outstripped the sound of those whom he imagined to be his pursuers, and he then ventured to pause to take breath, believing himself to be out of the reach of danger. Again his rage found vent in the most savage expressions, and he beat his breast in the fury of his indignation.

" Rosetta," he ejaculated, " is by this time borne far away from my power, and he who holds possession of her will laugh at the triumph he has achieved, and I have not the means of gaining the least clue as to who he is. I had hoped by this time to have had the girl secure, and then the full accomplishment of my designs must have followed. But some cursed spell hangs over me, and all my hopes and wishes appear to be entirely annihilated. What course can I now adopt? What schemes devise to discover her, and to wreak my vengeance upon the head of him who has thus unexpectedly torn her from me? To judge from his appearance, and that of those who aided him, he is a seafaring man, and therefore am I the more confounded and bewildered. Ah! Raymond Middleton! Can it be he who has done this? No, no; he cannot have been so daring; and yet the voice and person were the same. By all my hopes, I will discover the truth or falsehood of this, or perish in the effort. Should it indeed be he, I will, with the assistance of the crew of the Death Ship, pursue him to destruction. My suspicions every moment gain strength, and I will not rest until I have, by some means or the other, satisfied myself on this important point."

He now once more moved on his way, and soon the old Manor House appeared in sight, and Martin Trevors, having made his way round to a private door, rang the bell violently, and it was quickly answered by Simon Snipe, who always evinced the greatest terror on seeing this unwelcome visiter, and the sternness of his brow on this occasion added not a little to his alarm.

" Sir Horace is in his chamber," he faltered out.

" What of that, fool?" demanded Martin; " I must see him directly; stand out of the way."

He pushed the trembling domestic aside as he spoke, and rushed past him up the stairs to the apartment in which Sir Horace was.

The baronet started on beholding him, and at the agitation of his manner; but Martin unceremoniously took a chair, and gazed at him vehemently, and with a look of penetrating suspicion.

" Now, Martin," he demanded, in faltering accents, " what is the matter? You look disturbed, and ——"

" Disturbed!" interrupted Martin, with a savage growl; " ay, I am enraged—maddened; but, no doubt, you will be much gratified when you learn what has happened?"

" I, Martin!" said Sir Horace; " why should I feel glad at that which seems to have caused you so much disappointment? Explain yourself; I do not understand you."

" The house of Michael Belford is burned to the ground!" ejaculated Martin Trevors, and a momentary expression of triumph passed over his features. " Rosetta was in my power, and, ere this, I had hoped to have had her in security within these walls; but I have been foiled, defeated; some villain has betrayed me, and strangers have torn her from my grasp, even on the very eve of my triumph. Oh, curses light on this unforeseen event!"

" Trevors!" exclaimed Sir Horace, with a look of satisfaction which he could not conceal; " can this, indeed, be true? Is the girl, Rosetta, really ——"

" Have I not said so?" fiercely interrupted Trevors; " and think you, old man, that I should feel disposed to joke upon such a subject? Oh, no doubt you are mightily gratified to think that I have been thus thwarted in my schemes, and that the girl will not be placed for the present beneath your roof; but do not congratulate yourself too soon, for, if all turns out as I suspect, you will have but little cause."

" You suspect, Martin!" said Sir Horace, with a look of astonishment; " what mean you? What are your suspicions?"

" That he who has robbed me of Rosetta, is no other than your nephew, Raymond Middleton."

" Nay, Martin," exclaimed Sir Horace, starting to his feet, and gazing at him narrowly; " you cannot mean what you say. My nephew would not venture near this place now that his character is known, and certainly would never attempt to put such a design as this into execution. What reason have you to suspect that it is him?"

"I saw not his features, for he was masked," replied Trevors; "but his voice and person all but convinced me it was him. Oh, I will not rest until I have discovered the truth of this, and deadly is the revenge that I will have."

"You will think better of this, Martin," said the baronet; "it is impossible that your surmises can be correct. Alas! would that you had been able to abandon your designs before you had proceeded to such fearful lengths. What a terrible sensation will this cruel destruction of the home of Michael Belford, and the loss of his daughter, create in the neighbourhood. And that boy, too, what has become of him?"

"Doubtless, he has perished in the flames," said Trevors, "and I dare say you will not be sorry to hear that."

"Ah!" cried Sir Horace, "should he, indeed, be no more! But no, I dare not think so, for, in spite of all my fears, I would not have him meet with so terrible a fate."

"You are an old coward," said Martin; "but I have not patience or the will to argue this point with you now."

"And what has become of the men who assisted you in this plot?" inquired Sir Horace.

"Flown!" answered Martin Trevors; "they were entirely dispersed by the fellows who attacked us, and who by far outnumbered them. The fellows had all the appearance of sailors, and they must have been thoroughly acquainted with my designs, or they would not have been able so effectively to frustrate them. But I will discover the rascal who has done this, or lose my life in the attempt."

"Be cautious, Martin," suggested Sir Horace, with a look of alarm, "or you may plunge us both into the greatest danger. Even now, should any of your colleagues betray you, the consequences might be most dreadful to us both."

"You will, then, still suffer your cowardly fears to prevail over every other consideration?" said Martin Trevors, with a look of the most supreme contempt; "but you may be certain that whatever fate may befall me, you shall participate in it."

"Oh, Martin," said the timid old man, "forbear—forbear; why should you seek to involve me as well as yourself, in such dangers?"

"Because it affords me a feeling of intense gratification which you cannot understand."

"Mysterious, fearful man," said Sir Horace; "would that our connexion were at an end; for I fear that it will terminate in my destruction."

"Probably it may," returned Martin, with a look of triumph. "I do not seek to disguise from you that I owe you no good will. I only refrain from sacrificing you altogether, in order that I may render you the instrument to work out my designs. But I am in no humour to talk to you on this subject. My brain is on fire with rage and disappointment. Let me have wine, to endeavour to allay, in some measure, the anguish of my mind."

"Subdue this excitement, Martin," ejaculated Sir Horace; "wine will but serve to add to the fever of your brain, and ——"

"Bah!" interrupted Martin Trevors, impatiently; "no more of this nonsense. Will you comply with my demand or not?"

"Well—well—Martin; be not angry," said the old man, trembling at his looks; "I did but speak for your good. There is wine upon the sideboard; help yourself."

Martin took up the decanter, and pouring out a glass, swallowed the contents with avidity.

"And now, Trevors," demanded Sir Horace, "what do you purpose doing under all these peculiar and alarming circumstances?"

"What do I mean doing?" repeated Trevors; "why, exerting myself to the utmost to trace out the rascals who have been the means of thus for the present defeating me, and of not only getting the girl in my power, but of wreaking my most deadly vengeance on their heads."

" It is madness to talk thus," said the baronet ; " the whole neighbourhood is by this time, no doubt, alarmed, and any such attempt on your part would only be attended with the most fatal results. You must make your escape from this part of the country as quick as possible, for every moment of delay is fraught with the greatest danger."

" Indeeed !" sneered Martin ; " but indeed I shall do nothing of the kind, though no doubt you would be very glad if you could get rid of me in that manner."

" What then do you intend ?"

" To remain here. I cannot have a better place of security."

" Remain here, Trevors ? Oh, no, you surely cannot mean that."

" But indeed I do. I shall take up my future residence here, until I have devised some plan to accomplish my wishes."

" Think better of it, Martin," ejaculated Sir Horace ; " should any of your associates denounce you, search might be made for you here, and the destruction of both yourself and me would be sure to follow."

" Well, you must e'en take the chance of that," returned Trevors ; " you know it is useless to raise any objection to my determination."

" I will give you gold, anything, Martin, if you will but leave me, and abandon your present designs."

" You will give me gold ; psha ! I seek not your gifts ; I will demand what I require. Your gold is mine, and you dare not refuse me. I have made up my mind, and, therefore, you may as well rest contented. It is no use your grumbling about it, or seeking to oppose me. This must be my future residence, or until such times as I have gained some information of the girl, and once more got her within my power. It is not likely that I will submit to be so easily foiled. My suspicions become stronger that Raymond Middleton is the author of this, and I will never cease in my efforts to find out the truth or erroneousness of my conjectures ; should they prove to be correct, I will have such a revenge, such a glorious revenge as shall make the human heart shudder, when it is afterwards related."

Sir Horace Middleton looked more ghastly pale than before, and sinking back in his chair, he stared at Martin Trevors vacantly, but forebore to give utterance to the feelings of terror which agitated his bosom.

Martin gazed at him for a moment or two with his usual expression of hatred and contempt, and then arising from his seat, traversed the room with uneven footsteps, and muttering inarticulate curses to himself. He then poured himself out another glass of wine, which he quaffed, and once more turned his gaze upon the baronet.

" You tremble, old man," he said ; " I can well read the dastard fears that inhabit your bosom ; but you may as well save yourself this emotion, for whatever dangers I become involved in, you must share, and you ought to know by this time that I am not the man to be moved from my determination."

" Alas ! I do too well, Martin," replied the baronet ; " but I am an old man, and need you wonder that I do not possess the same nerve as yourself ?"

" You have possessed nerve enough ere now to become a villain ; but when the least shadow of danger seems to threaten you, you tremble with all the weakness of an infant."

" Oh ! Martin, would that the fearful crime you have this night committed could be recalled !"

" You will have more reason to quake, Sir Horace Middleton, should I discover that it is indeed your nephew who has thus so far foiled me in my well laid schemes."

" But that cannot be, Trevors ; you must have been mistaken."

" But I feel all but convinced that I was not," answered Martin ; " the cur was not bold enough to unmask his features, but his voice and person struck conviction to me. But I will find out the truth or fallacy of my conjectures, and ——"

"How—how?" interrupted Sir Horace.

"My plans are not yet formed, but I will not rest until I have hit upon some means of accomplishing my wishes."

"It cannot be Raymond, or he would have visited me, knowing that he holds me in his power, and have demanded the fulfilment of his bond. Oh, Martin, I cannot rest while you remain here."

"Well, it matters not to me," said Trevors, "you must put up with it; this is my place of security, and I shall not fail to avail myself of it, so you might as well make up your mind contented."

"Take gold, Martin," said the deeply agonized baronet, "anything; I will submit entirely to your demands;—quit the country, which you may do in such a disguise that it may be impossible for any one to recognize you. Do not delay, or it may be too late."

"Oh! no doubt, Sir Horace Middleton," said Trevors, with a sneer, "you would be mighty glad to get rid of me in that way; but you are greatly mistaken if you think I am to be so easily persuaded to abandon my schemes. No, no, although the girl is at present taken from me, I do not despair of being yet enabled to get her in my power."

"And your son, Martin?"

"Ah! it is the thought of him that goads me on. Oh! shall I rest satisfied until I have had an ample revenge?"

"And have you not had it?" demanded the baronet; "surely the destruction of the house of Michael Belford, and the loss of his daughter, if even he and his wife have not perished in the flames, ought to be sufficient to gratify the most fiendish malice."

"But it will not appease my deadly feeling of hatred," fiercely returned Trevors; "oh, I had hoped, ere this, to have had the girl, Rosetta, in my power, that I might have exulted over her sufferings, and have shown her what it is to excite the wrath of Martin Trevors."

"Fearful man!"

"No more of this. Are the doors all secured?"

"Yes, yes, they always are, especially at this hour of the night. But do you not fear, Martin?"

"Fear! what?"

"Pursuit."

"Psha!"

"Are you not known to be the perpetrator of this terrible outrage?" interrogated Sir Horace, eagerly.

"Yes, to those who aided me in my plot, and who did not take to flight until they had made a bold resistance, and were overpowered by numbers."

"But one of your colleagues must have deceived you, or how could they who snatched the girl from you, have been so well prepared to frustrate your plans?"

"Bah! I am in no humour to discuss that part of the subject now. I do not fear that any one will betray me; besides, it will never be suspected that I have sought refuge here, so near the scene of the outrage. You need not alarm yourself, for I shall probably not long remain here. My busy mind cannot long remain in inactivity."

"Your obstinate determination, I feel convinced, will bring us both to destruction, Trevors."

"Well, perhaps it may," returned the latter, coolly; "but we must take the chance of that. However, I am worn out with fatigue and vexation, and I must therefore endeavour to snatch a few hours rest. I shall sleep in the chamber adjoining your's, Sir Horace."

"So near, Martin?"

"Ay, why not? you are not afraid of me, Sir Horace, are you?" said Trevors, with a look of bitter sarcasm.

The old man made no answer, and Trevors coolly took up the lamp, and motioned to him, with an air of command.

"Come," he observed, "it is late; we will to rest, Sir Horace."

"To rest," repeated the baronet, with a fearful look; "alas! rest is never doomed to be my portion."

"Come, come," impatiently ejaculated Trevors, and Sir Horace reluctantly arose from his chair, and with trembling steps followed him from the room towards the chamber in which he slept. Martin opened the door and entered, and the baronet tottered in after him, and sank in a chair by the side of the bed.

" I dare say you did not anticipate having me so soon for a guest, Sir Horace," said Trevors, with a sneer.

"Martin," returned Sir Horace, "do not mock me; my mind is distracted with the different thoughts and terrors which steal over it. Every moment that you remain here is fraught with danger, and I cannot but apprehend the worst. Oh, why did you not restrain your feelings of revenge, at any rate, till some better opportunity presented itself?"

" You talk like an old idiot as you are," answered Martin; "but enough of this; give me the key of the adjoining chamber, and I will retire to rest, and leave you to your own meditations. No doubt they will be of their usual agreeable nature."

Sir Horace, with a faltering hand, presented him with the key, and Martin having lighted another lamp, opened the door, and with a look of mingled scorn and menace, disappeared from the terrified baronet's sight.

Sir Horace clasped his burning temples, and gave himself up to all the agony of his feelings. Nothing but the certainty of inevitable destruction presented itself to his imagination, he had no means of escaping from it while he was in the power of such a villain as Trevors, who seemed determined to make him the dupe and instrument in all his diabolical schemes, and he dared not set him at defiance, so completely did he hold him in his trammels. Instant death, so long that it was not a death of shame and ignominy (and from the bare contemplation of that, his guilty soul sank appalled), surely would be preferable to this state of horror and suspense.

The fearful outrage that Martin Trevors had that night been guilty of, shook his frame with an indescribable sensation of dread, and he listened with breathless attention to catch the least sound, lest the footsteps of Martin should have been traced to the Manor-house, and the officers should appear to drag them both to punishment. Then in his disordered imagination, he almost fancied he heard the crackling of the burning ruins of Michael Belford's house, and the appalling shrieks of the unfortunate inmates for help. He thought he beheld the form of the poor maniac boy struggling in the midst of the raging element, and calling upon the name of one that was imprinted upon his memory in characters of blood! Horror thrilled through all his veins, and he groaned aloud.

Then he tottered from his seat, and going to the door, which opened into the chamber of Martin Trevors, he listened; but all was silent, and he, therefore, concluded that he had retired to rest. Rest! could such a miscreant, after the perpetration of such a dreadful deed, sleep? Oh, yes; he was insensible to every feeling of remorse; the voice of conscience troubled not his hardened soul.

But now another thought rushed upon his brain; it was a dreadful one, but for a moment he encouraged it. The sleeping man was now in his power, and at one blow he might rid himself for ever of his greatest foe, and no one would know who had committed the deed, or what had become of him. It would surely be no sin to rid the world of such a villain. Thus the old man argued, and in the impulse of the moment, he took up a knife that happened to be lying on the table, and again approached the door. There was a deadly chill upon his heart; but every nerve was for an instant wound up to desperation, and he clinched the knife with a firmer grasp.

" He is my greatest enemy," he muttered to himself; " he delights to torture me, and would ultimately consign me to a death of shame. Why, then, should

I hesitate to rid myself and society at large of such a master? No one is at hand to witness the deed; and who is there that will take the trouble to inquire after him? Suspicion cannot light upon me, for it is known only to my two faithful domestics that he has sought a refuge in my house. All is now still, and—the deed shall be done; he dies!'

As Sir Horace Middleton thus spoke he cautiously tried the chamber door, but Martin Trevors had fastened it, and thus the desperate designs of the guilty old man were defeated, and he was saved from the perpetration of another crime to add to the dark catalogue that already pressed upon his conscience.

The wretched baronet's reason, in some measure returned, and he shuddered with horror at the dreadful and bloody thoughts which had but the minute before suggested themselves to his brain. He dashed the knife from him, and sinking in his chair, again gave free indulgence to the poignant anguish of his emotions.

"Wretch," he muttered to himself, " wretch that I am! shall I add another murder to those which already press so heavily upon my guilty soul? Villain although he is, could I expect to escape the just retribution of offended Heaven, for the hideous deed? Oh, no, my doom is sealed, and it is not by adding to my crimes that I can hope to escape from it. Martin Trevors, miscreant as you are, and much as I dread you, I cannot take your life. Oh, that mine had been sacrificed long ere I had known you!"

For some time he remained silent, and totally unconscious to everything but the horror of his own thoughts, which increased by the solemnity of the hour, and the silence which reigned around. All the fearful deeds of the past rushed upon his memory with insupportable violence, and he could imagine that he saw the grim spectres of the victims of his cruelty scowling upon him, and heard their curses howling in his ears. Flames of fire seemed to flash before his eyes, and he feared to move or speak.

And thus did the wretched old man continue for more than an hour after Martin Trevors had retired to rest, and feared to move or speak. He longed for morning, yet dreaded the results of it, for he was perfectly well aware of the excitement which would be created in the neighbourhood by the awful conflagration of the house of Michael Belford (who was so much respected), and the disappearance of his daughter. He was perfectly at a loss to conjecture who the men could be that had rescued the unfortunate damsel from the power of Martin Trevors; but he could not believe that it was, as he suspected, his nephew, who he did not think would make any such attempt, when, by so doing, he would run so great a risk, and, moreover, would render his appearance at the Manor-house, to further his other designs not only dangerous, but impossible. And yet Martin Trevors appeared positive as to his voice and person, and he had therefore every reason to remain in a state of doubt and suspense.

At length he threw himself on his couch, and tried to stifle his thoughts in sleep; but a long while was it before it descended upon his aching eyelids, and, even when it did, the horrors of the dreams that occurred to his disordered imagination were, if possible, greater than his waking moments.

At length the morning dawned, and the baronet started from his couch, and a feeling of terror came over him, when he beheld Martin Trevors seated in the room, and watching him with a penetrating and malicious look.

"So, you have awoke at last," said Trevors; "I hope you have had pleasant dreams."

"Pleasant dreams, Martin?" gasped forth Sir Horace, with a shudder. "Oh! how can you talk to me thus? But you have changed your mind, have you not?"

"Changed my mind!" repeated Trevors, with a scornful laugh; "think you, then, I change like the weathercock? What mean you?"

"You will not remain here, Trevors?"

"Indeed, but I shall, while it answers my purpose to do so. But, come, arouse yourself; these cowardly apprehensions will answer you no purpose. Even let the worst come to the worst, they can but hang you, you know."

"Hang me, Trevors!" ejaculated the guilty baronet, trembling in every limb; "oh! how can you take delight in torturing me, by talking thus?"

"And if that should be your fate," continued Martin Trevors, ironically, "you may console yourself by the reflection that it has been that of many a better man before you; and that you have not been idle in the world of crime, but have done plenty to entitle you to the distinction."

"Alas! alas!" groaned Sir Horace, "I have indeed been most cruel, most guilty; and you would plunge me still deeper into crime."

"And what have I to do with your conscience?" demanded the hardened villain; "I dare say I shall find enough to do with my own, if ever it begins to trouble me, which I do not see much probability of its doing at present."

"Martin Trevors," said the baronet, "indifferent as you may now appear, I fear that you will ere long have reason to repent of this reckless and inhuman feeling. It will not remain long a secret as to who has been the author of this dreadful outrage, and a strict search will be made after you."

" Let them search, they will find it a more difficult matter than they perhaps imagine to discover me. Fool! what have you to fear? They will never, at any rate, suspect that I have sought refuge here. But I am not going to rest quietly, in spite of all the danger. I will try every means to discover who are my secret foes, and to wreak my vengeance on their heads."

" Oh! beware, beware, Trevors."

" Psha! think you I am to be so easily daunted? But, come, it is time the morning repast should be ready, and I must get you to despatch that extraordinary animal of a servant of yours to the town, to see what news he can gather of the business last night, then I shall be better prepared how to act. You can depend upon him, I believe."

" Yes, yes," answered Sir Horace, falteringly; " Snipe is a faithful fellow, but ——"

" There, no objections," interrupted Trevors, impatiently; " I will send him direct, and it will be well for him, if he uses caution in his inquiries."

Sir Horace Middleton returned no answer, for he was afraid of exasperating his determined companion, and they walked to the breakfast-room, where Simon Snipe was summoned into their presence, and instructed how to act.

Snipe eyed Martin Trevors with looks of alarm and suspicion, but he promised to use the greatest precaution, and took his departure from the Manor-house immediately.

Both Trevors and Sir Horace waited with the greatest anxiety and impatience his return, but did not enter into much conversation, and Martin sat gloomily brooding over all that happened to him during the last few months, and muttering curses upon the several disappointments he had experienced. At length, however, Snipe came back, and Martin Trevors hastily interrogated him as to the information he had been enabled to obtain.

Snipe made him acquainted with all the particulars which have been related respecting the entire destruction of Michael Belford's house by the hands of incendiaries; the miraculous preservation of Mrs. Belford and the maniac boy, and the disappearance of Rosetta. He added, that the whole of the dreadful circumstances had caused the greatest sensation in the neighbourhood, and that the utmost exertions were being made to discover the miscreants who had been guilty of the abominable crime.

" You can leave the room," said Martin, addressing himself to Simon, who very readily obeyed the mandate, and Trevors and Sir Horace were left alone.

" So," said Martin, " the boy has then escaped the flames."

" Thank Heaven!" ejaculated the baronet.

" And why should you congratulate yourself on his preservation?" demanded Trevors, fiercely. " You may repent that you did not get rid of one whom you have so much reason to dread. But he shall not escape me, depend on it."

" What would you do with him?" said the baronet; " I would not have him harmed, and why should I fear him, maniac as he is, and ——"

" Should he ever recover his senses, Horace Middleton, would you have no reason to fear him then? Might he not be able to divulge certain facts, which it would not be altogether agreeable to you to have made known. He must be secured."

" Oh! forbear, Trevors," exclaimed Sir Horace; " already has the poor boy suffered too much, and I do repent me of ——"

" Repent!" interrupted Trevors, with a look of scorn; " oh, you do well to whine about repentance now, after all the evil is done."

" For mercy's sake, do not bring that boy into my presence; I shall think that the ghastly countenance of her whom I should have loved and cherished, but whom I left to misery and an untimely death, was glaring upon me, and that her hollow voice invoked the vengeance of offended Heaven upon my head. Pity me, Trevors, and abandon any designs you may have formed. Surely your vengeance has been already sufficiently satiated. You have destroyed the once peaceful home of Michael Belford, and driven him and his wife forth upon the world to mourn the loss of their only child: this—this, at any rate, should satisfy you!"

"Very pathetic!" ejaculated Martin Trevors, with a sarcastic grin. "How long have you learned to moralize, Sir Horace Middleton? It certainly is a novelty to hear the devil preaching a sermon."

The baronet groaned, and covered his face with his hands.

"Martin Trevors," he at length said, "you have heard from Simon the sensation that is caused by the awful events of last night. It may soon be known that you are the guilty party, and the strictest search will then be made after you."

"And what would you have me do?"

"As I suggested last night," replied Sir Horace. "Disguise yourself in a manner that may defy detection, and make your escape with all possible despatch from this part of the country."

"Indeed!" returned Martin; "but you will not get rid of me in that manner, I again assure you. No! here, where I am secure, I will remain, or, at any rate, until I have discovered who the fellow is that has dared to obstruct me in my plans, and who at present holds the girl in his power."

"You must be convinced by this time that Raymond Middleton is not that individual," observed the baronet.

"I am not," answered Martin Trevors; "and I will not be contented until I have satisfied my doubts."

"In what way can you do so?" demanded Sir Horace.

"Oh, fear not," answered Martin Trevors, "but I will find the means. As for Michael Belford, and all connected with him, my revenge is not yet half complete against him, while Rosetta is in the power of another. No, no, my brain must be busy in concocting fresh schemes. I must not—I cannot remain inactive."

Sir Horace returned no answer, for indeed he was in no mood to discuss a subject that was so painful to him, and which had so greatly excited his apprehensions. He knew well that it was no use to expostulate with Martin Trevors, who, indeed, evidently, as he admitted, exulted in his misery; and he looked forward to the consequences that would result from the desperate villany of that bad man with the most gloomy forebodings. He could not extricate himself from his trammels; he dared not resent his conduct towards him; for he felt that, with all his ill-gotten treasures, he was completely powerless,—and torturing, maddening, indeed, were the thoughts that this gave rise to.

The day passed on in the same gloomy manner, Martin Trevors never for an instant quitting the baronet, and ever and anon giving vent to his feelings of rage and disappointment, in the most violent and fearful language.

The fears of Sir Horace Middleton every moment increased, but he dared not to give expression to them in the presence of Trevors, who he well knew would heap upon him his heaviest maledictions, should he venture to do so; and seldom had the wretched old man felt greater anguish of mind than he did at that moment.

Night arrived; darkness reigned around; and Martin Trevors started up from his seat, as a sudden thought seemed to flash across his mind, and exclaimed,—

"My cloak! I can endure this suspense no longer; 'tis more intolerable than the tortures of the damned. I will go forth."

"Go forth, Martin!" said Sir Horace. "You surely will not venture; consider the danger. Should you be seen, you ——"

"Oh, I dare say you are very anxious about my safety," interrupted Trevors; "not long since you were urging my departure from hence."

"But you are not going for good, are you, Martin?" interrogated the baronet, eagerly.

"Oh, then you would not care if you were certain that I was going to leave you altogether?" sneered Martin. "However, I do not intend to gratify your wish just yet. I shall come back again, never fear."

"But shou'd you be seen by any one who might know you, on your going out or on your return, it would then be known that I have harboured you here, and you would thus involve me in destruction as well as yourself."

"So, it is only the fears you entertain for your own safety that cause you to be so very solicitous about mine. But it matters not; as I have before told you, our fates are both mixed up together, and if I fall you must fall also. This is my determination, and, therefore, you had need be careful of my safety."

"Oh, Martin, why should you thus seek to torture me?" said Sir Horace.

"Why put the question, since I have answered it so many times before?" returned Trevors. "It is because I hate you, old man, and the more unhappy you are, the more do I exult."

"I know not what I have done to you, at any rate, that you should pursue me with such a deadly spirit of revenge."

"The time may come when you will be enlightened upon that point," said Martin Trevors; "the day of reckoning will come, depend on it. But the hour waxes late, and I must be gone."

He threw a large mantle around his shoulders as he spoke, and, slouching his hat over his brows, in order to conceal his features as much as possible, he prepared to depart.

"Whither are you going, Trevors?" eagerly inquired Sir Horace.

"It suits me not to tell you," answered the former. "But I am determined, come what may, to endeavour to satisfy the doubts and suspicions which at present occupy my mind. Give me the key of the private door, and I can let myself in; but I do not expect to find that you have retired to rest on my return. I may have business for you to do."

"Business for me, Trevors! What mean you?"

"That will be explained in good time," replied Martin. And, having received the key from Sir Horace, he stalked from the room, and departed from the house by the private door. He looked eagerly around him before he emerged from the threshold, and, observing that the coast was quite clear, he hurried on his way towards the place of his destination.

CHAPTER XVI.

ROSETTA IN THE PIRATE SHIP.—THE IMPORTUNITIES OF RAYMOND MIDDLE-
TON.—HER VAIN APPEAL TO HIM.

ROSETTA must have remained in a state of insensibility for some time, for she had felt nothing of the motion of the vehicle, although it had travelled a considerable distance; and when she recovered, so strange was the scene which surrounded her, that she could not for a second or two understand it.

The murmuring of the waves as they dashed against the rocky cavern in which she now found herself, aroused her, and looking up with terror and amazement, she saw that she was surrounded by several men, whose ferocious looks filled her with terror, and she screamed aloud as all the horrors of the night returned to her recollection.

"God of heaven!" she cried, "where am I? Oh, cruel man, restore me to my parents, if they have not perished in the flames that were kindled by your inhuman hands. Ah! my poor mother! Julio! horror! horror! Martin Trevors, 'tis you that have done this! Alas! how fearfully have you fulfilled your threats."

"Martin Trevors no longer holds you in his power," said one of the men, who, from his dress, and the air which he assumed, seemed to be superior to the rest; "beauteous Rosetta, you are now the valued, the inestimable prize of Raymond Middleton. Behold!"

He tore off his mask as he thus spoke, threw aside the large cloak that enveloped his person, and Raymond Middleton, indeed, stood before her. Poor Rosetta stared at him aghast, and for a short time her astonishment and fears were so great, that she could not utter a word.

Raymond advanced towards her, and assumed a tone of tenderness and admiration, as he said,—

"Lovely girl, the power of that love with which you have long inflamed my bosom, has urged me to this determined act. I would have wooed you with an honourable love, but I saw that you would reject me with scorn. Seas have since divided us; but your image has ever been present to my fancy, and I could not banish from my mind the blissful hope of one day possessing you. That hope, thanks to fortune, is realized; you are mine, mine for ever. Yonder rides my gallant bark, and in a few minutes we shall be on board; come, then, my love, my chosen bride, and ——"

"Villain!" interrupted the indignant and disgusted damsel, repelling his advances; "hold! shock not mine ears with your odious vows; but you will not, you cannot dare to persist in his atrocious outrage. Will you not pity my youth, my innocence, and abandon your cruel designs? Oh, think of the horrors I have this night endured in the destruction of my home, and probably the loss of all that is dear to me! Mercy, mercy, Raymond Middleton, as you hope for mercy from on high."

"Sweet Rosetta," replied Raymond, in the most tender accents he could assume, "from me you shall experience nothing but the most ardent devotion. You shall reign mistress of my heart; no wish that you can express shall remain ungratified; but I can never, never again resign you. Shall another become the master of those charms I prize far more than my life? By all my hopes, never! And see, the boat intended to convey us on board my gallant vessel now approaches; but a few moments, and we shall be on board, and my happiness will be complete."

"Save me, save me! oh, Heaven!" shrieked Rosetta, with frantic despair, as she beheld through an opening in the rocky cavern, by the light of the moon, which was now shining brightly, a boat approaching; and quite overpowered by her fears, she sank back in the arms of Raymond, and once more became insensible.

When she again recovered, she found herself reclining on a kind of ottoman, in what was but too evident the cabin of a ship, and feeling the motion of the vessel as it skimmed over the waves, she started to her feet, and gazed with horror and a bursting heart around her. She then, for the first time, perceived that a female of rather decent appearance, and about the middle age, was in the cabin. She felt some relief on finding herself in the presence of one of her own sex, and with streaming eyes, and supplicating looks, she appealed to her for pity.

"It is not in my power to assist you, my poor girl," said the woman, compassionately; "but do not give way to such an excess of terror, for, after all, perilous even as your situation is, you may yet be protected from danger."

"Oh, God!" exclaimed Rosetta, wringing her hands, and otherwise evincing the almost insupportable horror of her feelings; "where am I? Tell me, I beseech you?"

"You are on board the pirate vessel, of which Raymond Middleton is the captain," answered the female.

"A pirate vessel! in the power of Raymond Middleton! torn from my friends!" ejaculated the distracted Rosetta; "then Heaven help me! or I am, indeed, lost. Oh, my parents; Julio, where are ye, now? Methinks I see my aged mother struggling in the flames that were kindled by the miscreant, Martin Trevors and his colleagues. I hear my poor father's cries of despair! God! God! this is more than my brain can support!"

"Endeavour to calm the violent agitation of your feelings, my dear young lady," said the female, evidently viewing the unfortunate girl with the deepest commiseration; "critical as your situation at present is, Providence may yet preserve you from danger."

"Calm my feelings!" repeated the distracted Rosetta, groaning with agony,

"Oh, I must be formed of adamant, could I be calm under such horrible circumstances. Where are my parents? Where is Julio? Gracious Heaven! this trial is more than human fortitude can sustain; I shall go mad!"

"Would that I could assist you, miss," said her companion; "how willingly would I do so. But, indeed, I am here as powerless as yourself."

"Your words are those of kindness and sympathy," ejaculated our heroine; "oh, think of the agony I must be enduring, when I think of the dreadful fate my poor mother has experienced, when I reflect upon the misery of my aged father at this overwhelming calamity."

"I do, indeed, pity you, miss; but that, unfortunately, is all I have the power to offer you."

"And who are you, and what has placed you in this degrading situation?"

"I am the victim of an untoward destiny, and have not the power to help myself," answered the woman, with a sigh. "I am the wife of one of the crew of this lawless vessel, and have not the means of escaping from it, or Heaven knows how willingly I would do so. Ah! young lady, my heart is not depraved, although I am a pirate's wife, and compelled to do his bidding. I was once happy, but I shall never be so again. How often have I prayed for death, for life has long been a misery, an insupportable burthen to me. But come, my poor girl, partake of a little wine, which may serve to revive you."

Rosetta did just sip the glass which Martha (for that was the name of the woman) presented to her, and then burst into a violent paroxysm of sobs and tears, and was completely deaf to all the remonstrances and attempts at consolation offered by her companion.

"'Tis all in vain," she sighed, and wringing her hands at the same time. "What arguments can soothe my anguish? In the power of Raymond Middleton! borne far away over the boundless deep, surrounded by heartless miscreants, without the least hope of escape, and with the dreadful reflection upon my mind of the fearful fate of my poor mother; oh! would it be wonderful if frenzy were to seize upon my brain? Better would it have been had I perished in the flames, then at least my misery would have been at an end. And where is the villain, Raymond? Oh! you will not suffer him to approach me! You will not permit him to pollute my ears by his hated, his unholy vows?"

"My poor girl," said Martha, "what power have I to prevent him? But do not give way to this excessive terror; I do hope that Raymond Middleton will take compassion on your present painful situation, and at least be persuaded to act with forbearance."

"Forbearance!" repeated Rosetta, with a look of despair; "alas! what forbearance can I expect from one who could be guilty of this cruel, this monstrous outrage? My heart sinks within me, and I cannot but anticipate the worst. But I am faint,—dreadful feelings come over me. Mother, father, Julio! Oh, that this horrible sensation may be that of approaching death! I—I——"

The poor girl could utter no more, a paleness like that of approaching dissolution overspread her features; her eyes closed, and she became insensible.

Martha was much alarmed, for she thought that the vital spark had fled for ever, and she uttered a loud exclamation of terror, which reached the ears of Raymond, who was in the adjoining cabin, and he immediately rushed in to inquire the cause. When he beheld the deplorable state of his unfortunate victim, his alarm was as great as that of Martha, and he hastily approached her, and placed his hand upon her heart.

"It still throbs," he ejaculated; "she has only fainted from exhaustion and terror. I could not but expect this. Desire Hawkesly to come here immediately. His skill in these matters, no doubt, will soon restore her, and then she must be kept as quietly as possible for a day or two, until the violence of her anguish shall have somewhat abated. Quick! quick!"

Martha hastened from the cabin, after having fixed a look of supplication upon Raymond, which he repelled with a frown.

Raymond Middleton hung over the inanimate form of our heroine with mingled feelings of fear and admiration. Even pale and careworn as she was, he thought she looked incomparably lovely, and the villain even dared to imprint a fervent kiss upon her lips, while his bosom glowed with the most fierce and unruly passions.

"Beauteous Rosetta!" he ejaculated, "oh! it would, indeed, drive me to madness to lose you thus, after all the trouble it has cost me to get you in my power. But my hopes must not, will not thus be frustrated. I dare not think of it. I have secured my prize, and even death shall not yet snatch it from me, until my triumph is complete. No wonder that she should endure this suffering. It is no more than I had a right to expect. But I will conquer her emotions and abhorrence, or my name is not Raymond Middleton."

At this moment Martha returned, accompanied by Hawkesly, who, having at one time been in the medical profession, was found to be of great use on board the ship. He felt the pulse of Rosetta, and then, in answer to the eager inquiries of Raymond, said she was not in any imminent danger, but was overpowered by the strength of her mental sufferings, and the effects of sea-sickness, but that with care, she would shortly recover.

"Thanks, thanks, Hawkesly," said Raymond; "you have removed a weight of fear from my mind. Let every attention be paid her, and give me immediate notice of the different changes which may take place in her."

"Ay, ay, captain," said Hawkesly, "I will see to the fair craft; but you must keep your distance for the present; for should she behold you, it will do anything but tend towards her recovery."

"I will obey, since I see the necessity of it," said Raymond Middleton; "but by all my hopes I shall find no rest until I have had the felicity of an interview with her, and have once more listened to the music of her voice."

"It is not very likely to breathe very musical tones to you, captain," said Hawkesly, with a significant grin.

Raymond frowned, but returned no answer, and walking from the cabin, left our unfortunate heroine to the care of Martha and Hawkesly.

He walked upon deck, wrapped in deep meditation. The sun was fast rising from the broad bosom of the eastern ocean, and all was calm and beautiful. The vessel steered on its course, wafted by propitious gales, and the coast of England was left many, many miles behind.

"She is mine," soliloquized Raymond, as with folded arms he paced the deck, —"she is mine, far beyond the reach of pursuit; and ere long my triumph will be complete. Yes, Rosetta Belford, the fair, the innocent, is destined to fill the arms of the pirate captain. Oh, I have managed my plot well, and may set detection at defiance. Martin Trevors, you have unconsciously become the instrument of my plans, and rendered my success complete. You little expected to be so foiled, or you would have been better prepared to resist me. Great as your secret power may be, you may yet find Raymond Middleton more than a match for you. And that sordid old miscreant, my uncle, he must not flatter himself with the idea that he has got rid of me altogether. No, no, he shall fulfil the articles of the compact entered into between us to the very letter. I hold him in my power, notwithstanding the course of life to which I have taken, and should he hesitate to comply with the smallest even of my demands, when we meet again he shall swing, ay, even though I mount the same gallows the moment afterwards."

Thus he continued to mutter to himself for some time, and to pace the deck, until he was joined by Hawkesly, who informed him that Rosetta was restored to sensibility, but was in a state of mind bordering on distraction, and that she must not be seen by any one but Martha, or the consequences to be apprehended would be of the most fatal description.

"Well, well, I will obey," said Raymond; "but a few days will exhaust my patience, and I must then see her at all hazards."

"You had better be cautious, captain," remarked Hawkesly; "if you act with any undue impetuosity you may lose the fair prize you have been at so much trouble to obtain, altogether."

See p. 182.

"By all my hopes," ejaculated Raymond, vehemently, "I would sooner lose my gallant craft, much as I value her, and all my daring men on board of her."

"Indeed," observed Hawkesly, with a significant look; "but I would have you be cautious, captain, for a pirate's life, you know, should be one of plunder, and not of love-sick dallying."

"Ah!" cried Raymond, hastily, and with a look of anger, "what means this boldness! Do you venture to overhaul my conduct, Hawkesly?"

"Not I, captain," returned Hawkesly, coolly; "but I merely took the liberty of reminding you that pirates are sometimes apt to become dissatisfied when they imagine that their interests are in any way neglected by the individual they have chosen to command them."

"By the infernal host!" exclaimed Raymond, passionately, and fixing a penetrating look upon Hawkesly, "there is something more in this than you think proper to reveal. Have I in any way neglected the interests of my crew since I have been the captain of this vessel?"

"I do not say that you have," answered Hawkesly; "but we have not had much business to do lately; the lads do not like an inactive life, and I have already fancied that I observed signs of discontent amongst many of them."

"Signs of discontent!" repeated Raymond, passionately; "who are the rascals that have dared to murmur? Reveal them to me, Hawkesly, and they shall find that I can at least act with promptitude and determination where it is required."

"Oh, I cannot point out any of them particularly, captain," said Hawkesly; "but I thought I would merely take the liberty of putting you on your guard."

"Hawkesly, can I depend upon you?"

"You may; I, at any rate, am your friend."

"Then you will keep a sharp look out, and give me timely notice should any danger threaten."

"I will."

"Mutiny!" cried Raymond, in tones of indignation; "will they dare to contemplate such a thing?"

"I do not say that they will, captain," returned Hawkesly; "but it will be as well not to give them any cause of complaint."

"And have I ever done so, Hawkesly?" demanded Raymond; "have they not always found me studious of their interests, and ever foremost in danger?"

"They have," answered Hawkesly.

"What more would they have?"

"Well, I do not say positively that it is as I suspect; but you cannot blame me for communicating to you my thoughts."

"I do not, Hawkesly; but I will not believe this of the lads, until I have had some strong proof of it."

"You will not intimate a word of what I have said, to any of the crew?" said Hawkesly.

"Certainly not," said Raymond; "for that would only cause an open rupture, when perhaps, after all, there may be no cause for it."

Hawkesly now quitted Raymond, who continued to pace the deck for some time longer, and his mind was very much disturbed after the hints which Hawkesly had thrown out to him, although he could not exactly persuade himself that there was any foundation for them.

"The fellows would not dare to turn traitors against me, when I have always done everything to promote their welfare and conciliate their favour," he said. "Hawkesly must have been mistaken in the surmises he has formed. But should they indeed prove to be correct, my situation will be a most critical one; for what could I do to oppose them? I must, indeed, as Hawkesly has advised, be watchful; and should I see anything to confirm his suspicions, I must use the readiest means to suppress the mutiny, and to take care of my own security and that of Rosetta. Upon Hawkesly and Dick Scud, I feel certain that I can depend, and therefore, after all, the danger may not be so great as I at present anticipate. I will be firm, and show the crew under my command that I have the skill and courage to resent any act of treachery on their part."

We must now return once more to our unfortunate heroine, who, upon being again restored to a state of consciousness, looked timidly around her, and at once all the horrors of her situation arising to her memory, she exclaimed, in tones of the bitterest anguish,—

"Mother! father! oh, where are ye? The villains have torn me heartlessly away from you; you will never behold your poor girl again. God of heaven! what have I done to merit this? I am in the power of a miscreant who will not shrink from the perpetration of any crime, however hideous, for the gratification of his inhuman wishes. I am upon the wide ocean, being borne I know not whither, and where I may in vain seek for one pitying being to interpose between me and destruction. Why am I thus selected to be the victim of continual persecution? Death would surely be far better than this. And see, the red flames ascend to the clouds from the burning ruins of my once peaceful dwelling, and my poor mother and Julio are still within the blazing walls. Horror, horror,

horror! Will no one stretch forth a pitying hand to save them? Are you all so cold and heartless that ye can stand coolly by and look on with indifference? Hark! how their frantic shrieks rend the air! Great Heaven! and must they, then, meet with so dreadful, so untimely a fate? Hold me not; if no one will fly to their rescue, at least I will, and an all just Providence will give me strength to accomplish the hazardous task. Monsters! ye mock me! Ye laugh at my sufferings; oh, I appeal in vain! Lost! lost! lost!"

The poor girl sank back quite exhausted, and was quite unconscious of the presence of Martha, who, greatly moved by compassion for her melancholy condition, did all that humanity could suggest to ameliorate her anguish, but with little chance of success. She, however, was enabled to administer a cordial to her which served in some measure to revive her, and her agony found considerable relief in a copious flood of tears, in which Martha suffered her to indulge without interruption.

After some time had elapsed in this manner, Rosetta clasped her hands vehemently together, and with a bursting heart implored the protection of Heaven; but when she looked around her and found where she was, and felt the motion of the vessel as it bounded over the deep, she gave herself up to the most abject despair, and groaned aloud in the bitterness of her uncontrollable agony. Martha continued by her side, and her looks told much more than words could have expressed, the commiseration she felt for her, and the pleasure she would have felt in being able to afford her any relief; but, alas! situated as she herself was, that was impossible.

"Do not, I pray you, my dear young lady," she said, "give way to this violent grief; for melancholy as your situation even is at present, something may yet occur to save you from the danger with which you are threatened, and restore you to liberty."

Rosetta stared at her vacantly for a moment, as if she scarcely comprehended what she had been saying, and then, in a voice half choked with emotion, she ejaculated,—

"Who are you that would thus inspire me with false hopes? Am I not in the power of the villain Raymond Middleton, who has threatened me with destruction? Am I not being borne across the perilous deep, far, far away from my native land, and where no one will interpose to save me? Is not my home, my once happy home, destroyed? Has not my aged mother perished in the flames, and yet you would bid me hope! Oh, 'tis cruel mockery!"

"Heaven forbid, miss, that I should attempt to mock you," replied Martha; "on the contrary, most sincere and fervent is the compassion I feel for you, and most happy should I feel were it in my power to render you any assistance, or to mitigate the sufferings you are enduring. But after all, many of the fears you now entertain may be without foundation. Your poor mother may have been saved, and ——"

"Saved! saved!" interrupted Rosetta; "oh, no, I dare not hope so; did I not behold her and Julio struggling with the devouring element when the monsters bore me away? They are lost, lost; and even if they are saved from that awful fate, will not their hearts be broken at the loss of Rosetta? Oh, my unfortunate parents, I feel for you even more than myself."

"May Heaven watch over them and preserve them for your sake," observed Martha.

"Ah!" exclaimed Rosetta, looking at her with astonishment and incredulity; "and do you indeed pity me? Am I not entirely abandoned by every one, and left to the mercy of that cruel man, who has dared to insult my ears with his odious vows?"

"Believe me, miss," answered Martha, "that in me, at any rate, you shall find an ardent and sincere, though humble friend."

"A friend," repeated our heroine; "oh, how welcome is the word to mine ears. But, alas! you are, you say, as powerless as myself, and have nothing to offer me save your commiseration."

"Would that I had," returned Martha; "how freely would I award it to you. But let me endeavour, at least, to tranquillize your feelings, since it is by fortitude alone that you can hope to resist the many trials to which you may be put, and to awe Raymond Middleton into forbearance."

"Alas!" sighed our heroine, "nothing will, I fear, awe a man of Raymond's hardened and determined character into forbearance. He has made up his mind to make me his victim; and how can I hope to avoid the dreadful, the revolting fate, when he holds me completely in his power? My God! my senses will surely sink under this fearful shock. Poor Frank Trevors, better would it have been for me even had I consented to become your bride. Then might this calamity, probably have been avoided."

She covered her face with her hands, and sobbed in the most violent manner, Martha exerting all her efforts to no purpose to console her, and to lead her to hope that something would occur when she least expected it, to rescue her from the danger by which she was at present surrounded.

"And whither is he conveying me?" asked Rosetta, in melancholy accents; "what is the place of our destination?"

"That I know not, miss," answered Martha; "Raymond always keeps his designs a profound secret from every one but such of his crew as he can place the most implicit confidence in."

"Great Heaven!" groaned Rosetta, "what will become of me? Would that the waves would swallow me up in their friendly bosom, for death would now be a mercy to me, in my present fearful situation."

Throughout the day our unfortunate heroine continued in the same state of anguish, and at times her feelings so overpowered her that her senses wandered, and she gave expression to her grief in the most wild and piteous accents.

When her reason returned her sufferings were even more acute; and how dreadful were her reflections. What was the fate of her mother and Julio? The blood congealed with horror in her veins at the thought, and she could scarcely support her feelings with any degree of patience. The most frightful images were conjured up to her imagination. She again fancied she saw them struggling in the flames, and heard their appalling shrieks, and nothing could divest her mind of the terrible thought that they had both perished.

And what must be the torture that her poor father must now be enduring? Could he ever support so frightful a calamity, bereaved as he was of all that was dear to him at one fell blow, and universal was the desolation which these cruel enemies had caused.

As night approached, her anguish, if possible, increased, and she listened with nameless fears to every sound that stirred in the pirate ship, and apprehended every moment, notwithstanding the assurances of Martha to the contrary, that Raymond would venture to obtrude himself upon her.

The murmuring of the waves, as they dashed against the sides of the vessel, seemed to breathe despair to her senses, and the torture of her mind became insupportable.

Martha scarcely ever left her for one instant, but watched by her with the most anxious solicitude, and exerted herself to the utmost to tranquillize her feelings. This was, however, a task that was almost hopeless, and Martha began to fear that Rosetta's feelings had received a blow from which it would be long ere she would recover, and that indeed it was more than her strength of mind would be able to withstand.

"Good Heaven!" exclaimed Rosetta, "I must be insensible to all feeling, I must be something more than human, if I could long survive these accumulated misfortunes. Raymond Middleton, your cruel, your diabolical schemes will, I trust, yet be defeated, and I shall hail death as a blessing and relief. But must I never behold my parents again? Oh, could I but have been permitted to see them once more, and to be convinced that they had not perished, if it were the will of Heaven, I should be contented to die in their arms, and the Almighty would reconcile them to my fate since they would know what had befallen me, and that I had, at least, escaped the pollution of the destroyer. Oh, what a monster he must be who could thus be the author of all this misery!"

"Do not despair yet, my dear young lady," said Martha; "Raymond Middleton may repent; he surely, bad as he is, cannot resist your anguish and innocence."

"Alas! what have I to hope from one who could even contemplate so fearful an outrage as this?" sighed the damsel. "Repent! oh, he must be totally insensible to every feeling of remorse. May Heaven in mercy take me to itself rather than suffer me to experience dishonour."

"Raymond Middleton surely can never proceed to such fearful extremities as that," remarked Martha, who still endeavoured to inspire her unfortunate companion with those hopes which she was herself far from encouraging; "he has said that it is his intention to make you his wife.

"His wife!" repeated Rosetta, with a look of horror and disgust; "oh, what a hideous mockery is this! His wife, the wife of Raymond Middleton, the villain, the pirate! Never! never! by all that is sacred; the murderer's knife would be far more welcome, and I should even consider it a merciful hand that would inflict the blow. But oh, will that Almighty Power, whose laws I have never wilfully offended, suffer the miscreant to succeed in his atrocious designs?"

"He will not, Rosetta," replied her attendant; "and with that assurance, suffer hope to gain ascendancy in your mind. Something will yet occur, depend upon it, to rescue you from his power. But endeavour to gain a few hours sleep, for after all that you have undergone for so many hours, you must be completely exhausted."

"Sleep!" repeated our heroine; "oh, how can I expect to do so, with these dreadful thoughts crowding upon my brain? Would that my cares were hushed for ever in the sleep of death, since it seems that I am destined to endure perpetual misfortune."

"Your lot at present appears a dismal one, miss," observed Martha; "but I can never believe that an all-merciful Providence will suffer one so young and innocent to fall a victim to the inhuman designs of villany."

Rosetta shook her head and groaned, and it was quite evident that despair had taken full possession of her bosom. And under all the circumstances, was it at all wonderful that the poor girl endured the most indescribable agony? It was indeed surprising that her senses did not sink completely under the shock.

Sleep never once closed her eyelids during that melancholy night, and Martha never ventured to leave her, for she knew not what she might not in the frenzy of her despair be tempted to do. Her lamentations, and the manner in which she at intervals called upon the names of her parents, and of Julio, were truly pitiable to hear, and most deeply did Martha commiserate with her, and pray to Heaven to protect her, although she had now no arguments to offer by which she could hope to ameliorate the violence of her grief.

Whenever the coarse voices of the pirates reached the ears of Rosetta, her heart throbbed with tenfold terror, and the danger of her situation was presented more vividly to her imagination, and Martha had the greatest difficulty to keep the anguish of her mind within the bounds of reason.

Raymond had frequently sent to inquire after her condition, and whenever a fresh message arrived, it filled her with additional alarm, which her companion found it utterly impossible for her to subdue; although it was not at all likely that he would be bold enough to obtrude upon her for the present, when he must be aware that such a step would be certain to be attended with fatal and immediate consequences.

Raymond Middleton passed the dreary hours of the night in his own cabin, in a state of great uneasiness.

"Should this trial prove too much for her strength to support," he said, "all my plans will be rendered abortive, and I shall have been at all this trouble and anxiety for nothing. But why should I marvel at her anguish? Could I expect anything else? Assuredly not; but a day or two may bring about a favourable change, and then I shall be enabled to prosecute those designs for which I have ventured so much. I must expect that she will make an obstinate resistance, but of what avail will it be? She is powerless to assist herself, and must, therefore, ultimately yield to my importunities, or I must use force to accomplish my wishes. It would be worse than weakness on my part were I to yield to her entreaties or reproaches, after having proceeded so far, and now that I have her entirely at my mercy. Oh, no, Raymond Middleton is not the man to abandon so easily any design upon which he may have fixed his mind; and Rosetta Belford is a treasure it is worth any risk to gain possession of. Oh! how anxiously do I look forward to that moment of felicity, when I can call her mine, mine beyond all redemption. Never did I dare to hope altogether that such unutterable bliss would have befallen me. Fortune, you have been most kind to me, and I owe you gratitude for your many gifts, but for this more, much more than all. But I would much rather that the destruction of Rosetta's home, and probably the sacrifice of her parents, had not taken place; for her agonizing reflections upon that calamity may retard her recovery, and prove an insurmountable obstacle to the consummation of my wishes. It was a bold deed of Martin Trevors, and it was well that I was made aware of his intentions, or Rosetta might not so easily have fallen into my power. I wonder what could have been his designs against the girl? I have in vain racked my brain to form any conjecture as to the cause, but doubtless he was goaded on by feelings of revenge, as I have been given to understand that Rosetta rejected the suit of Frank Trevors, who afterwards suddenly disappeared from his home, and no one could form any idea as to what had become of him. Had the heart of the damsel not been devoted to another, methinks she would never have declined the companion of her youth, and who I thought she had always viewed with favour. Ah! that maniac boy. Can he have inspired her with any other sentiments than those of pity and sympathy for his forlorn condition? The idea seems almost improbable, and yet with impressive meaning did she call upon his name. There is a mystery, too, connected with that boy, which I would fain unravel, and the circumstances under which he was saved by Michael Belford, increase my curiosity. I regret that I did not also get him in my power. But it is most likely from what Rosetta said, that he perished in the flames. No matter, I have much more important thoughts to occupy my mind without troubling myself about him."

Thus did Raymond Middleton continue to ruminate, and anxiously did he look forward to the morning, when he hoped to hear that Rosetta had become more calm, and that it might not be long before he was permitted to seek an interview with her.

The observations which Hawkesly had made use of in the morning, annoyed him considerably, and he reflected upon them maturely, and not without some feelings of apprehension, for should the surmises of Hawkesly prove to be correct, he would be placed in a position of considerable difficulty, and it might defy all his efforts to quell the bad feeling which might have engendered itself in the minds of his daring and desperate crew.

He had observed them narrowly; he had marked their conduct closely; but still he had not yet observed anything in it to justify the suspicions of Hawkesly, although he firmly believed that he had not encouraged them without having sufficient reason for doing so; and he, therefore, determined to remain on his guard, and to be ready to act with promptitude and decision, should occasion require.

As for poor Rosetta, she continued in the same state of suffering, and the agonizing thoughts which crowded upon her brain, rendered her completely insensible to all the humane efforts at consolation which Martha endeavoured to impart to her. Had she been certain of the preservation of her mother and of Julio, she might have been able to have assumed some degree of fortitude. She now freely acknowledged to herself the strength of the sentiments with which Julio had inspired her; and, therefore, did she the more acutely feel their separation, and the uncertainty of the fate that had befallen him.

Throughout the whole of that day and night, Rosetta's feelings were at times worked up to so violent a pitch, that she was in a state bordering on distraction, and raved in a manner that was truly pitiable to hear. She was in a state of the greatest dread, lest Raymond should obtrude himself upon her; but Martha endeavoured to quiet her apprehensions in that respect, and at length she succeeded, and our heroine exerted herself to the utmost to become more calm, and to put her trust in Providence, which surely would protect her from the guilty intentions of Raymond Middleton, and, hopeless even as her case at present appeared, would, she endeavoured to believe, rescue her from his power.

It was some relief to her that she had one of her own sex, in the person of Martha, who could commiserate with her, and had it not been for her society, and the sympathy she expressed towards her in her misfortunes, she must have sunk beneath the power of despair and apprehension.

Often, in the course of the day, did Rosetta offer up her prayers to Heaven, and invoke its protection for her parents and Julio, should they still survive, and she tried all that was in her power to persuade herself that something would yet occur to restore her to them, in which hope Martha did all that she could to encourage her, and to persuade her that Raymond would relent when he saw that she was firm ; but on the latter point Rosetta had the most gloomy doubts and forebodings. Raymond Middleton was certainly a man of the most determined character, or he would never have taken to the course of life he had, and have been guilty of such an outrage, and, therefore, she could not think it likely, she could not flatter herself with the hope, that he would abandon his nefarious designs after he had been at so much trouble to put them into execution. She was completely at his mercy, and what forbearance could she expect from him, urged on as he was by the violence of his evil passion ? She might resist him all that was in her power, but what would it avail ?—undoubtedly he would resort to violence, when he found that he could not accomplish his diabolical wishes by any other means, and she would be degraded, lost for ever ! How the poor girl shuddered at the thought. Even the bare contemplation of such a probable fate was worse than death, and she prayed to Heaven to interpose to prevent such a dreadful calamity taking place. But the idea of being on board a pirate vessel, and at the mercy of such wretches, was of itself sufficient to inspire her with the greatest terror, and to fill her bosom with the most dreadful apprehensions. These thoughts crowding with the most overwhelming rapidity upon her brain, increased rather than abated her illness, and she was quite unable to arise, and Raymond, from the accounts he heard of her, had yet good reason to entertain the most serious fears as to the consequences ; and his impatience increased at the delay which was unavoidably caused to the interview he was so anxious to obtain with her. Still he could not but have expected that the shock her feelings had sustained would have the most alarming effect upon her mind ; and it would most likely be some considerable time before he would be able to consummate his infamous designs against her, whom he had resolved to sacrifice to his brutal passions.

In this manner two or three days elapsed, without any material change for the better taking place in the condition of Rosetta, although every attention was paid her, and Raymond could scarcely restrain his vexation within the bounds of reason.

"And must I," he observed, as he paced his cabin with disordered steps, "must I, after all the trouble I have been at, and the risks I have run to get Rosetta in my power, be doomed after all to be disappointed in the accomplishment of my wishes? By all my hopes, I cannot bear even to encourage such a thought."

But in spite of all, he was compelled to admit that the prospect before him was of a very doubtful description, and that he must act with the greatest caution and forbearance for the present, or he might have reason to apprehend the most fatal results. He strictly enjoined Martha to use all her exertions to restore her fair charge to some degree of composure ; but he had no occasion to do that, for the sympathy of Martha was sufficiently excited in behalf of our heroine to urge her to do all that humanity could suggest to alleviate her sufferings. But under all the terrible circumstances, what relief to the poignant anguish of her feelings could Rosetta be expected to find ? When she reflected upon the probable fate of her mother and Julio, and the misery of her father, she was almost distracted, and she fervently prayed to Heaven to release her, since no other prospect than shame and constant suffering was before her. The villain Raymond would most undoubtedly persist in his base designs, and what, then, would become of her? Must she not inevitably fall a victim to him, and could she survive an hour after she had been so degraded and dishonoured? Oh, no, she could not, and, therefore, the sooner her miseries were terminated by death the better. She shrank from the thought of beholding Raymond with a feeling of the most unbounded horror and disgust, and yet she could not hope that he would much longer delay obtruding himself upon her.

The pirate vessel proceeded on its way, and the impatience of Raymond Middleton increased at the unfavourable state in which Rosetta remained; but he was often inclined to suspect that much of her indisposition was assumed, in order that she might retard the meeting with him she had so much cause to dread. His mind was also far from easy after the hints which Hawkesly had given him respecting the supposed discontent of some portion of the crew, and he watched their actions narrowly, but saw nothing to strengthen these surmises; and he was at last inclined to think that Hawkesly had been mistaken, for what cause had he given them to entertain any mutinous spirit against him? None, that he could think of; on the contrary, he had ever done all that he could to conciliate their favour, and to promote their interests since he had been their captain.

At length, the youth and naturally strong constitution of Rosetta triumphed over her illness in a great measure, and she was enabled to leave her pallet. But still the tortures of her mind were not the least abated, and it was not likely that they should be, since there was not the least prospect of her being released from the danger by which she was surrounded, and nothing could save her from the diabolical designs of her cruel persecutor.

Raymond heard of the favourable change in the health of his intended victim with much satisfaction; but he made up his mind not to seek an interview with her for a day or two, fearful that she might not yet have sufficient strength to support such a trial, and, if she suffered a relapse, it would again retard the accomplishment of his wishes, and, perhaps, frustrate them altogether. He was, however, fully prepared to meet with her reproaches, and must use a cautious game, or, notwithstanding, she was in his power, she might yet escape him, and all the trouble he had been at would prove to no purpose.

The fears of Rosetta increased, as she was now certain that Raymond would shortly annoy her by his presence, and disgust her ears by his odious importunities; and what could she do, poor defenceless girl that she was, in opposition to his advances? He would be unmoved by her supplications; her tears, her entreaties would have no effect on him, for he was insensible to pity; and it was not likely that he would abandon those designs it had cost him so much trouble to put into execution, and when she was entirely in his power, and there was no one who would interpose to frustrate him in his inhuman purpose.

"My God!" she exclaimed, "how utterly hopeless is my situation! Nothing but inevitable shame and misery stare me in the face. There is no pitying hand to snatch me from it. And it is to meet with so horrible a fate as this that I have been reserved? Wretched, wretched girl, why were you ever born, since you are thus doomed to disgrace and infamy. Oh! my poor parents, where are you now? And if ye still live, how unspeakably horrible must be the sufferings you are enduring at the uncertainty of my fate. These thoughts will drive me mad. Oh! Martha, what will become of me?"

"Indeed, miss," answered Martha, "no one can more deeply sympathise with your misfortunes than I do; and it would afford me the greatest delight were it in my power to assist you; but, alas! it is not, and all that I can offer you is hope and consolation."

"Hope, consolation," repeated our heroine, wringing her hands; "oh! how can I venture to indulge in either, situated as I am? The miscreant has me

completely at his mercy, and he will not fail to take every advantage of it. Of what use will it be for me to appeal to him, hardened in guilt as he is, and insensible to every feeling of pity? Oh! Heaven protect me! save me, or I am indeed lost!"

"And yet he surely cannot be so monstrous as to persist in his cruel designs," said Martha; "especially in your present situation. He cannot possibly resist the tears and supplications of one so young and innocent."

"Alas! what sense of feeling can that man possess who could have acted as he has done?" sighed Rosetta. "Has he not torn me from my native land, from every hope of happiness, and think you that he will now pause in the execution of his vile purpose? Oh, no! it would be madness to entertain such an idea; there is no hope, no chance of escape for me; the triumph of my cruel oppressor is but too certain. But shall I live to experience such a fate? Have I not the means of saving myself? You—you, Martha, will not refuse to assist me. Oh!

for some friendly draught to terminate my wretched existence. Death is not half so terrible as dishonour."

"My dear young lady," said Martha, "do not talk in this manner, for it greatly distresses me to hear you. Providence, depend on it, will not desert you in the hour of emergency, and will never suffer the guilty to triumph in the accomplishment of their nefarious plans. Something will yet occur to save you; but much will depend upon your own firmness, which, notwithstanding he holds you at present in his power, may render all his designs abortive."

"Ah!" ejaculated Rosetta, "how can I meet with any degree of fortitude that villain who has doomed me to destruction? Even the sight of him will strike me with horror; but, to have my ears shocked by his disgusting and unholy vows, oh, I can never support it."

"Raymond will surely have some compassion for your innocence," said Martha, "and will act with some degree of forbearance."

"How can I expect it, knowing his base and heartless character? Oh, my situation is indeed most fearful. But you will not leave me, Martha?"

"Not while I am permitted to remain with you; but it is not likely that Raymond will suffer me to be present at your interview."

"My God! and must I be left alone with him?" cried our heroine. "But no, you will not leave me to his mercy. While you remain with me, I might be safe; but, if no one is present to obstruct him, to what lengths may not his evil passions urge him?"

"And what could I do to prevent him, should his determination be fixed?" demanded Martha, with a look of regret. "As I have before told you, I am completely powerless, and dare not disobey the orders of the captain, however anxious I may be to act to the contrary."

"Ah! then there is no hope for me. There is no one on board this lawless vessel that will interpose to save me from the cruel designs of the miscreant. Despair, despair!"

"Do not give way to it entirely at present, miss," observed Martha; "you will be better able to judge of the prospect before you, after the interview you so much dread, is over."

"Alas! I can never support it. How can I listen to the bold and heartless asseverations of that man who, fiend-like, has made his mind up to my destruction? He will not relent, for his bosom must be a stranger to every feeling of remorse. It would be a mercy were he to sacrifice my life at once, since by his cruelty he has annihilated my every hope of happiness."

Martha still made use of every argument she could conceive to console her, but the task was a fruitless one, and indeed she was at a complete loss to find words to inspire her with hope. She well knew the determined character of Raymond Middleton, and it was not at all to be supposed that, now he had succeeded so far, he would be induced to abandon his intentions. She saw plain enough that the destruction of Rosetta was inevitable, unless, indeed, something particular should transpire, and most sincerely did she pity her, and would have been most happy to have rendered her any assistance, had it been in her power.

"Ah! Martha," sighed our heroine, after a pause, "would that I were even like you! I should be more contented than I am at present."

"Like me, miss," repeated her companion; "ah! you know not all my melancholy history, or you would find that you could gain but little by the change. I am indeed a wretched woman, unfortunately united to a man of crime, and forced to lead a life that is most abhorrent to my feelings. Tell me, then, can you think that I am happy?"

"Your destiny is sad enough," returned Rosetta; "but still you may entertain some hope of being released from it, while I can have none."

"Indeed, miss, my situation is almost as hopeless as your own."

"And you say that your husband is one of the lawless crew of this vessel?"

"He is. He keeps a narrow watch over my actions, and I dare not disobey his orders, or I should be sure to incur his vengeance."

" And how was it that you were so unfortunate as to become united to this man ?"

" He was not always guilty," answered Martha, " and he won my affections when he was worthy of them."

They were interrupted in this conversation by a message from Raymond Middleton, who desired to see Martha immediately. Rosetta trembled, for she feared that he had come to the resolution of seeking an interview with her without delay, and in vain did she endeavour to prepare herself for the trying occasion.

She endured a few minutes of the greatest suspense and anguish during the absence of Martha, and every footstep she heard, imagined that it was Raymond approaching. She raised her tearful eyes towards Heaven, and, clasping her hands vehemently together, invoked its protection. At length her mind was somewhat relieved when Martha re-entered the cabin, and she eagerly inquired what was the purpose of Raymond in sending for her.

" To inquire after your health," replied Martha.

" And you told him," said Rosetta, with a look of emotion.

" I endeavoured to persuade him that you were worse than what you really are, miss," said Martha, " for I thought that it would induce him to defer seeking an interview with you at present."

" Oh! this was most kind, good Martha," said our heroine, " but did it succeed?"

" Alas! no, miss," answered Martha ; " he would not be deceived, and therefore ordered me to prepare you to meet him to-morrow morning."

" To-morrow morning!" ejaculated Rosetta ; " Oh! how I tremble at the thought. What will become of me? Will nothing save me from the terrible designs of the villain?"

" Courage, courage, Rosetta !" ejaculated her companion! " it is only by firmness you can hope to frustrate the plans of Raymond Middleton. But I do not think that he will be bold enough to proceed to extremities for the present ; put your trust in Providence, who will not forsake you in the moment when you so much need its aid."

" And must my ears be insulted by his hateful vows?" sighed Rosetta. " I cannot, dare not meet him."

" Resistance would be useless, since it is his will," said Martha ; " but I do not yet give way entirely to despair, and am not without an idea that something will occur to thwart him in his schemes, and to restore you to liberty."

" Oh! Martha," exclaimed our heroine, " would to Heaven that I could think so! But what reason have you to encourage any such an idea?"

" I know not, but the impression has taken most forcible hold on my mind."

" I see no cause for hope," said Rosetta ; " indeed, powerless as I am, and surrounded by such heartless miscreants, to encourage such a thought would, I believe, be most absurd. I am a poor, wretched girl, and cruelly and unmeritedly have all my prospects in this world been blighted. My unfortunate parents, never, never again shall we meet in this world, and ere long I may have met with that disgrace which would render life insupportably hateful to me."

She sobbed aloud in the violent anguish of her feelings, and it was some time ere Martha could succeed in the least degree to pacify her. Dismally that day passed away, and Rosetta anticipated the approaching morrow with an emotion of dread, which she found it impossible, notwithstanding all her efforts, to conquer.

Martha did all in her power to inspire her with resolution, but in vain, and she feared that the interview of the following day would be more than she would be able to find strength to support.

Rosetta passed a sleepless night, for her mind was distracted with the most torturing thoughts and melancholy forebodings, and she was even glad when daylight beamed over the ocean.

Martha entered her cabin at an early hour, and inquired anxiously after her health. Rosetta shook her head, and her pale and careworn countenance fully showed the sufferings she had experienced during the night, and the dismal apprehensions which at present tormented her bosom. She could only be prevailed upon to partake sparingly of the morning repast, for she felt heart-sick and spiritless, and she looked forward to the events of the day with the most melancholy anticipations. The breakfast was scarcely concluded, when they heard footsteps approaching towards the cabin. Rosetta trembled, and clung to Martha, but was unable to utter a syllable, and the next moment the door was thrown unceremoniously open, and Raymond Middleton stood before them. Rosetta could not help uttering a scream of terror when she beheld him, and she clung still closer to Martha.

Raymond fixed a look of mingled admiration and triumph upon the pale countenance of the damsel, and then motioned to Martha to leave the cabin; but our heroine gazed at the captain imploringly, and Martha hesitated.

"Did you not understand me, woman?" demanded Raymond, sternly. "Leave the cabin, I say; the observations I have to make use of are for the ears of Rosetta Belford alone."

"Oh, spare me—spare me, Raymond Middleton!" gasped forth Rosetta. "Has not your cruelty already gone far enough, in tearing me from my native land, and in leaving me in a dreadful state of uncertainty as to the fate which has befallen my unfortunate parents? Suffer Martha to remain here; I cannot, dare not be alone with you."

"Psha!" exclaimed Raymond, impatiently, "you must learn to conquer this diffidence and repugnance, beauteous Rosetta. I have too long delayed this interview, but now I will not permit it to be interrupted. Leave the cabin, Martha."

The latter fixed one look of pity and encouragement upon our heroine, and then, fearing the wrath of Raymond, she obeyed his commands.

Rosetta sank upon a seat, and covered her face with her hands, while despair and terror wrung her heart. Raymond gazed at her for a few moments in silence, and something like a feeling of pity entered his breast. But he then advanced towards her, and, venturing to take her hand, he said,—

"Fair Rosetta, you shrink from me as if I were something hideous, instead of one who is prepared to love—to worship you. Ay, I speak the truth, although you may not believe me. Raymond Middleton has for years been your most devoted slave; and even though many miles separated us, and other damsels smiled upon me, your beauteous image was ever present to my thoughts, and I was wretched until I again beheld you. Fain would I have sought your love in an honourable manner, but you treated me with scorn; and, as I could not bear the idea of seeing you become the bride of another, you left me no other resource than to take the desperate step I have done. But, hear me, dearest Rosetta, while I swear ——"

"Oh, cease, cease!" interrupted Rosetta, her bosom swelling with disgust and shame. "Can you, who have torn me from all that was dear to me in life, dare to insult my ears thus? Have you no sense of shame, or remorse for the misery you have caused? Leave me; and suffer me, at least, to indulge in the horror of my own feelings alone."

"Leave you, Rosetta!" repeated Raymond; "oh, never till I have laid my whole soul before you, and breathed my ardent admiration in your ears. You may call me villain, pirate, if you please; but you shall find that the sentiments I entertain for you are sincere, and such as nothing whatever can subdue. Banish, then, your fears; strive to view me without repugnance, and all that I can do to contribute to your happiness ——"

"Happiness!" interrupted Rosetta. "Oh, what a cruel mockery is this—what a base prostitution of language! Have you not proved yourself unworthy the name of a man? and can you expect that I can ever regard you with any other feelings than those of abhorrence and disgust? Do you not now contemplate my shame and destruction? Have you not deprived me of every hope? Oh, had you struck a dagger to my heart, the deed would have been far more merciful than the fate to which you now doom me."

"Rosetta Belford," said Raymond, in tones of as much affection as it was possible for him to assume, "harsh and cruel as my conduct would appear, I love you with a fervour amounting to adoration. I would make you my bride."

"Your bride—the bride of a pirate! Oh, Heaven, rather stretch me a corpse at your feet."

"Nay, scornful beauty, you must live—live to make me the happiest of human beings."

"Merciful God! take pity on me, and release me from this dreadful situation!" exclaimed our heroine. "Raymond Middleton, your triumph will be brief, for the horror of my feelings, at the uncertain fate of my parents, will assuredly shortly break my heart."

"Rosetta," replied Raymond, "learn to view me with indulgence, and I promise you, faithfully promise you, that you shall behold your parents again."

"Behold them again!" repeated Rosetta; "oh, no, no; if they have not already perished, they cannot long survive my loss; and, even if they should, think you that I could dare to meet them again, after I had suffered dishonour and contamination? Oh, God! oh, God! the thought maddens me!"

She groaned aloud with the mental agony these racking ideas created; crimson blushes of shame suffused her cheeks; her bosom heaved with the violence of her emotion; and, once more covering her face with her hands, she swayed her body to and fro in a state of the greatest possible excitement.

Raymond approached still nearer to her, and once more took her hand in his, which she withdrew with a sensation of the most indescribable horror and disgust, while her whole frame trembled so violently that she had the greatest difficulty to sustain herself.

"Beauteous Rosetta," said the hypocrite, "indeed it grieves me to afflict you thus; but I cannot control the passion with which your numerous charms have inspired me, and sooner could I perish than resign my hopes of making you mine. Think not, although you are on board a pirate vessel, that any harm shall befall you; no, the greatest respect shall be paid you; and fearful indeed should be the punishment of any of my crew that dared to offer to insult you. I am devoted to you—to you alone; I would be the slave of your will, and studious alone of your felicity. I have wealth, power—all which you may command; I am ready, I am anxious to lay them at your feet. Reflect, then, upon my proposals, and strive to view me with respect, at least, if you cannot at present bestow upon me your love."

"Respect!" repeated our heroine, with a look of the most ineffable scorn; "can Raymond Middleton be presumptous enough to expect to gain respect from her to whom he has acted with such heartless, such deliberate atrocity? Away! your presence is odious to me, and my heart swells with shame and indignation at your bold and unfeeling observations."

"But you must, fair damsel, learn to conquer these feelings," returned Raymond with a look of offended pride, "for resistance, obstinacy, and reproaches will but serve to provoke me to acts of violence, which I would fain avoid. I am inclined to woo you with gentle persuasion, to lavish upon you all the affection that it is possible for man to bestow, but nothing can intimidate me, or induce me to abandon any designs upon which I have fixed my mind."

"Great Heaven! what will become of me, in the power of such a villain as this?" groaned the terrified damsel; "I am lost, lost. Oh, my unfortunate parent, what would be your sufferings did you but know the situation of your poor child!"

"Why am I thus treated with scorn and hatred?" demanded Raymond, proudly; "I, whose favours have been coveted by damsels of wealth and birth—I, who have heretofore basked in the smiles of the most peerless beauties! Rosetta Belford, if I have acted harshly, if I have been driven to this extremity, to gain possession of you, you may blame yourself. Had you not treated my advances with scorn, and bestowed all your affections upon the drivelling beggar, Frank Trevors, I was prepared to woo you with an honourable love, and to make you my wife. But your coldness drove me to despair and desperation, and, unable to conquer the passion with which you had inspired me, I was determined to risk fortune, life, everything, to obtain you. That I have done so is a proof of the sincerity of the love I bear you; I have you now, and by all my hopes, I will never rest until I have reaped the bright reward of all my trouble. My bride, my empress, I hail you with all the fond transport of adoration! I will yield everything to you and love—Raymond Middleton, the pirate captain, bows your willing slave for ever!"

"Oh, mercy! mercy!" cried Rosetta, frantically, and sinking on her knees, while she looked up in his face with the most piteous supplication. "Think of my youth, my innocence, and abandon your cruel, your monstrous designs. What gratification can you hope to experience in your brutal triumph over a poor, unprotected, broken-hearted girl? Forbear, I implore you, as you would avoid the terrible retribution of offended Heaven; and, even after all the injuries you have inflicted on me, the many sufferings to which you have put me, I will yet endeavour to forgive you, and cease to reproach your memory."

"Rosetta," replied Raymond, "it is impossible; I could sooner sacrifice even life itself than resign the bright hopes I have formed. Strive to esteem me, if you cannot love, and you shall find Raymond Middleton the most devoted, the most affectionate, of your admirers."

"Inhuman man?" ejaculated Rosetta, "will nothing move you to pity? Oh, for the love of Heaven, relent, and spare me a fate than which death would be far more preferable."

"Am I then so hideous," said Raymond, with a frown, "that you view me thus with hatred and terror?"

"What other feelings can I entertain towards one who has treated me as you have done, and who can basely contemplate my shame and misery? But you cannot, you will not persist in your diabolical purpose. You surely cannot, desperate even as is the course of life to which you have taken, be so entirely lost to shame and compunction."

"Rosetta," returned Raymond, "the life I have chosen is one of freedom, and I would make you my fair companion. You deem me cruel, but you wrong me by the supposition, and my future conduct towards you shall prove to you the strength and sincerity of the sentiments I entertain for you. I will give you time to reflect upon my proposals, to show you that I am at least inclined to act with forbearance. When we have arrived at the place of our destination, I shall expect to find you yield compliance with my wishes, or then, however much it may be against my inclinations, I shall be compelled to use force, and demand at once the prize I may by persuasion be unable to win."

"Great Heaven!" exclaimed Rosetta, in a voice of agony, and rising to her feet, "then there is no hope for me! I appeal to one who is insensible alike to pity and shame. Oh, Raymond Middleton, think of the terrible vengeance that will most certainly pursue you, should you persist in your diabolical designs. But think not that you will have me long to triumph over. No, I can never survive such horrible degradation, and your conscience will be loaded with the murder, the cruel murder, of her whom you affect to love."

"Affect to love!" repeated Raymond; "could you read my heart, you would know my sincerity, much as you despise me. I again swear that all the tenderness and indulgence that man can bestow upon her who holds possession of his affections, you shall experience from me. You shall not have a single thought or wish ungratified, and many fair damsels there are who might justly envy the situation of Rosetta Belford."

"Hold! hold! it shocks my ears to listen to you."

"I speak the words of truth and love."

"Forbear! such mockery is monstrous! But think not that you ever make any impression upon my heart; never can I view Raymond Middleton with any other feelings than those of horror and detestation."

"Say you so, scornful girl?" said Raymond, biting his lips; "but this obduracy will not avail you, and you may yet learn to repent of it."

"And is it by threatening me thus that you seek to prove the sincerity of the passion you have avowed for me?" demanded our heroine, in a firm tone, and her bosom swelling with shame and resentment.

"Your observations provoke me to it," returned Raymond. "I am ready to give myself up entirely to you, and to be guided alone by your will; you will find me no harsh and cruel tyrant, but, on the contrary, no man would be more studious of your happiness, no man could bestow upon you more affectionate attention than I would do. Banish, then, this icy coldness from your heart, and view me as your slave and adorer. By all my hopes, the more I gaze upon your transcendent charms, the more powerful does my passion become, and the readier am I to throw myself at your feet, and to worship you as a superior being. Nay, frown not upon me, for I speak the sentiments of my soul, and by this kiss I vow that no other man than me shall possess so inestimable a treasure."

Rosetta shrieked with terror and disgust as he threw his arms around her, and tried to imprint a fervent kiss upon her lips. She struggled violently, and tried to disengage herself from his embrace, but it was all in vain, and again and again did the daring libertine pollute her fair cheek with his odious caresses. Shame and indignation overcame her; she could endure no more, and, with an exclamation of emotion, her senses left her.

Raymond, for a moment or two, feasted his eyes on the beauties of her countenance, and having once more kissed her rapturously, he stamped his foot, and Martha, who had been in waiting close at hand, entered the cabin.

When she beheld the insensible state of our heroine, she was greatly alarmed, fearing that Raymond had committed some outrage upon her, and she looked at him for an explanation.

"She has only fainted," he observed; "see to her recovery, and you may tell her not to be alarmed, for I shall not visit her again to-day."

Martha returned no answer, and Raymond, having resigned the insensible damsel to her care, quitted the cabin.

CHAPTER XVII.

MUTINY ON BOARD THE PIRATE VESSEL.—DEFEAT OF THE CAPTAIN.—HE IS LEFT ON A DESOLATE ISLAND.

"I SHALL have some trouble with this scornful and abdurate girl, I see," said Raymond Middleton to himself, as he retired from the cabin; "but it is no more than I had a right to expect. However, her resistance will be in vain, for she must—she shall be mine, and nothing whatever can rescue her from my power. But still I must use caution, or her strength will sink under it, and I shall thus most likely lose her altogether. But can I endure her scorn? Never! She must learn to view me with something like respect, or I know not what I might be tempted to do, in order to gratify my wishes and my revenge at the same time."

During the remainder of the day Raymond continued in a state of considerable suspense and excitement, more especially as he heard that Rosetta was suffering much from the shock her feelings had sustained, and Hawkesly assured him that he would not be answerable for the consequences if he repeated his visit for the present.

It was some time after the departure of Raymond Middleton before our heroine recovered her senses, but finding that she was supported by Martha, and Raymond had quitted the cabin, she felt somewhat relieved, and became a little more composed.

"Oh, God!" she exclaimed; "how have my ears been insulted. And he dared to contaminate my cheek with his odious caresses. Alas! what will become of me, in the power of such a villain, and after the threats he has held out to me? Providence assist me, or I am lost and degraded for ever."

"Courage, Rosetta, and put your trust in that Providence you have invoked, and which never deserts the innocent in the hour of danger," said Martha. "Hopeless as your situation at present appears, you will yet be saved, depend on it. The evil plans of Raymond Middleton will be rendered abortive, and you will be restored to your friends."

"Ah! Martha," sighed our heroine, "in vain you would endeavour to inspire me with hopes which reason tells me are most unlikely to be realised. What can release me from the power of this bad man, torn as I am far from my native land; and think you that he will ever be induced to abandon his wicked intentions? No, no; he has declared that he will only give me time to decide upon his brutal proposals, until this vessel has reached the place of its destination, and that then if I still remain obstinate, he will use force to make me comply with his wishes. Therefore, what can I anticipate but the most fearful results, for I shall not have a friend at hand, who can have the power or the will to interpose to save me?"

"But something may occur before the completion of our voyage to rescue you," remarked Martha.

"Alas, alas! what can occur?"

"Something that you little expect."

"Ah!" ejaculated Rosetta, with an eager look; "what mean you? Have you heard anything, Martha, that should raise such an idea in your mind?"

"I have," answered the latter, in an under tone.

"For Heaven's sake, what is it? Do not keep me in suspense."

"From hints which my husband inadvertently threw out," said Martha, "I am inclined to believe that most of the crew entertain bad feelings against Raymond, and that a mutiny is not at all unlikely."

"Ah!" exclaimed Rosetta; "but even if they should render Middleton powerless, will not my situation be equally dangerous; for what feeling of pity can I expect from men so inured to crime? Am I not borne far away from my home, and they would never have the mercy to restore me to my friends?"

"At any rate, there would be some hope of their doing so," returned Martha; "for what motive could they have in wishing to detain you in their power?"

"I dare not, indeed I dare not, encourage the flattering idea. May God help me, for my situation is a most deplorable one. And am I to have my feelings again outraged by the disgusting importunities of that heartless man?"

"Fear not, Rosetta," said her companion, "for he has told me to inform you that you will not see him again to-day; and something may yet take place to prevent him from repeating his visit, at any rate, until you have acquired more fortitude to meet him."

"Fortitude!" repeated our heroine, "oh, how can I ever gaze upon him without horror, especially after the threats he has held out to me? He is insensible to every feeling of remorse, and I cannot but apprehend the worst."

She sank on a seat and sobbed bitterly as these ideas occurred to her imagination, and for some time she was completely deaf to all the efforts which were made by the kind-hearted Martha to tranquillise her. She could see no hope of her condition being much amended, even if the power of Raymond Middleton should be destroyed; for she could expect no pity or mercy from the wretches that formed the pirate crew, and who would, perhaps, on the contrary, feel a savage pleasure in adding to her misery, but certainly would not trouble themselves to restore her to her friends. Restore her to them, alas! it was more than probable that it was now too late. She could not get rid of the horrible impression from her mind that her mother and Julio had perished in the flames, and after such a dreadful calamity, it was not likely that her unfortunate father could long survive. How could he endure such a fearful bereavement? and she even felt for his sufferings more than her own.

Her strength was completely exhausted, but still Martha could not prevail upon her to retire to rest, and such was the agitation of her mind, that she could not venture to leave her even for a moment. Her brain was completely distracted, and it was truly melancholy to hear the exclamations she gave utterance to at different intervals during the day.

The weather had hitherto been favourable, but Rosetta suffered much from sea-sickness, combined with the excitement of her mind.

Night at length arrived, but still our heroine was unable to sleep, and she continued to sit up, listening occasionally with feelings of dread to the rude voices of the pirates, as they arose upon her ears in boisterous mirth. But at length they ceased, and a strange silence prevailed in the vessel, nothing being heard save the dashing of the waves against its sides.

Rosetta looked from the cabin window, but all was dark, and it seemed not at all unlikely that a storm was approaching, a circumstance that added to her fears. Martha several times endeavoured to persuade her to retire to rest, but she would not, and a dismal foreboding of some approaching danger appeared to have taken possession of her mind.

Suddenly, about the hour of the midwatch, they were startled by hearing a strange confused noise on deck, succeeded by the hasty treading of several feet, which seemed to be approaching nearer towards the cabin.

"Gracious Heaven! what is that?" exclaimed the affrighted Rosetta; "some danger threatens; persons are evidently approaching this cabin. Should the villain Raymond dare to obtrude himself upon me at this hour, what will become of me."

"Quiet your fears, Rosetta," replied her companion; "Raymond would not venture to commit such an outrage in your present state of mind. The noise probably only proceeds from the crew performing their ordinary duties in the vessel. Hark! all is silent now again; I do not think there is anything to apprehend."

Rosetta trembled violently, and still looked timidly towards the cabin-door, but all was still again for a few moments, and she began to think it was as Martha had suggested. But she was not suffered to entertain this idea long, for suddenly they heard the voices of several men, as if in angry altercation, and followed by a loud scuffling.

"Some disturbance seems to have taken place," said Martha; "the men are quarrelling, and the sounds appear to proceed from the captain's cabin. Ah! perhaps the pirates are about to put their mutinous designs into execution."

"Gracious Heaven preserve us from the rage of such inhuman wretches," cried the terrified Rosetta; "hark! the confusion grows louder! Murder is being committed."

The shouts and execrations of the men, mingled with the clashing of swords and the report of fire-arms, now became louder, and it was quite evident that some desperate and determined contest was going on. Martha would have left the cabin in order to ascertain what was the matter, but Rosetta prevented her, and clinging to her, awaited in awful suspense the result, expecting every moment to see the cabin filled with the mutineers.

A scene of the most terrific nature was all this time being enacted in the captain's cabin. The mutineers had surprised him just as he was about to retire to his berth, and when resistance seemed to be little better than madness. However, Raymond Middleton was not the sort of man to yield tamely, and several of the men who had refused to join in the plot, having rushed to his assistance, a short but fearful combat ensued. The mutineers were, however, too powerful for them, and two or three of their antagonists being killed, and several desperately wounded, Raymond was disarmed, and secured, in spite of his bitter curses and reproaches. They dragged him upon the deck, and he there expected that his life would be immediately sacrificed.

"Rascals!" he exclaimed; "what have I done to exasperate ye to this? Have I not recklessly braved danger with the boldest among ye? and this is the manner ye reward me!"

"We will have no beardless boy to command us," returned one of the fellows; "down with the lubberly skipper, and then the vessel and its contents will become ours. Down with him, lads."

"No, we will not take his life," said two or three of the others; "it will be enough for us to get rid of him. Place him in the old boat and let him take his chance."

"Ay, ay," coincided the mutineers, and Raymond was instantly seized and dragged aft.

"Oh, villains! villains!" cried the captain, in vain struggling in their grasp; "may the curses of hell pursue you for this. May ——"

Before he could finish the sentence, the crazy boat was launched, he was tossed into it, and committed to the mercy of the waves. He clenched his fists, and shook them menacingly at the ruffians, and in a few moments the boat was drifted by the impetuosity of the waves, far out of sight, and the pirates gave utterance to one hideous yell of triumph.

It would be a difficult matter to describe the rage and agony of Raymond Middleton, in the awful situation he now found himself placed, and he watched the fast receding vessel with looks of despair, and was almost tempted to plunge at once into the deep, for the fate that must otherwise await him seemed to be inevitable. And it was awful to gaze at that mountainous sea, upon which the wretched, but guilty Raymond, was tossed about as if he had been the most insignificant atom; and the waves washing over him with the most resistless force, and threatening every instant to swamp the boat, and at once to consign him to his fate. He was almost worn out with fatigue and despair, and he saw nothing but death before him, for how was it possible that so crazy a vessel could long withstand the power of the waters with which it had to struggle. Yet even in the midst of all this danger, and with the almost certain prospect of a speedy and untimely end, Raymond Middleton ever and anon gave vent to the most fearful curses against the mutineers, who had thus, at one fell blow, destroyed all his hopes, even at the very instant when he thought his triumph all but complete. Once more he cast his eyes in the direction of the vessel ; but it was nowhere to be seen, nor could he behold anything as far as his eyes could penetrate but sky and ocean. He threw himself down in the bottom of the boat, for he could no longer support himself, and he then resigned himself to that fate which he had no doubt would overtake him in a very few minutes.

Never had Raymond Middleton experienced such intolerable anguish of mind as he did at that time ; but it arose more from disappointment at the frustration of his plans than any other feeling, and to think that Rosetta was lost to him for ever ; for, should he ever be rescued from his present awful situation, which appeared to be impossible, it was not at all likely that she would ever again be placed in his power, but that she would, before long, fall a victim to the pirates, and who, having gratified their brutal wishes, would consign her to an untimely end.

" May the curses of hell pursue them !" he exclaimed, in a voice of fury. "Oh, they have nicely foiled me in my well-formed plans, and have reason to exult in their triumph. The wretches, what had I ever done while I commanded them to cause them thus to turn traitors against me? Did I not bring them wealth? Did I not grant them every indulgence ; and was I not always foremost in every danger? But the miscreants will have reason to repent the conduct of which they have been guilty, and the fate they have inflicted on me will overtake them. But why should I prolong my sufferings? Am I not surrounded by black despair on every side? Should I even be drifted to land, which, in this frail boat, seems to be utterly impossible, I must die of hunger, unless assistance speedily reach me. Let me at once precipitate my fate, and end my misery by plunging into the deep. Raymond Middleton, must, then, the proud career you had anticipated, be so abruptly terminated? Oh, that reflection is beyond endurance."

He started up in the boat as he thus spoke, and raised his hands above his head with the determination to make the fatal plunge ; but some instinctive power prevented him, and the ocean having become more calm, something like a ray of hope entered his mind, and he resumed his seat in the boat (which had hitherto weathered the rude billows much better than could have been expected), and gazed with anxious eyes across the broad waters of the deep.

For nearly two hours the wretched man continued in this situation, and totally ignorant of the course in which he was being driven, and compelled to resign himself to chance. What would he not have given to behold some friendly vessel? It would have been Heaven to his sight ; but nothing of the kind appeared, and again the most abject despair settled upon his heart.

" I am lost !" he cried ; " no other prospect is before me than that of becoming food for sharks, or to perish from exhaustion and hunger. The villains had better have sacrificed my life at once, for they have taken a dreadful method of gratifying their revenge. Revenge ! for what? What have I done that they should have imbibed any feelings of vengeance and animosity towards me? I was always studious of their welfare, and they will find no better or determined captain than they did in me. But it proves the truth of what I have often heard, namely, that sincere friendship and confidence cannot exist where villany predominates. Rosetta ! what are now your thoughts? No doubt you exult in my defeat ; but methinks you will have no cause to do so, for your situation will be no better than it was before ; on the contrary, you may find that the villains will not have that consideration for your innocence and beauty that Raymond Middleton would have evinced towards you, great even as was the horror with which you viewed his character."

Again he stretched his eyes across the ocean, and the light having now become more distinct, he perceived what appeared to be the outline of land on the distant horizon, and towards which the wind was drifting him. A momentary feeling of hope darted across his mind, and he felt his strength in some measure revived. But it was only of short duration, for should he even he able to reach it, he might find it barren and uninhabited, and his situation would then be equally as deplorable as it was at present. But the old adage, that "Drowning men will catch at a straw," was fully exemplified in his case, and he watched the land towards which he was being carried by a favourable wind, with half-formed hopes and expectations. The land did not appear to be high, and he, therefore, trusted that he should be able to gain it, notwithstanding his strength was so much exhausted. He baled the water out of the boat as well as he could with a leather hat, which one of the pirates had thrown to him, when he was committed to his fate; but this kept him constantly employed, and it was not without the greatest difficulty that the boat was able to ride, so shattered was its condition.

Nearer and nearer the boat approached the land, which now appeared to be a small island; but, as far as Raymond could at present distinguish, it did not exhibit any signs of vegetation. In about half an hour he had come to within a short distance of it, and the wind having again risen, he was fearful that his boat might be dashed with such violence against the shore, as to be shattered to pieces, and hurl him to destruction. Being an excellent swimmer, and the boat now being only a very short distance from the land, he resolved to abandon it, not doubting but he should be able to stem the waves in safety, in spite of the weakness he naturally felt, after the sufferings he had already undergone. He immediately disencumbered himself of his coat, and plunged into the sea, striking out with an energy that could not have been expected, considering his weakness, and made to that part of the land which was evidently the lowest, and most easy of access, and which he gained in a very short time, and clambering by the sides of the rocks, alighted in safety on terra firma; but completely worn out, he sank prostrate upon the sterile ground, and for a short time remained in a state bordering upon unconsciousness.

How long he had continued in this state of comparative apathy, he knew not; at length he raised his head, and gazed around him, but his limbs were so paralysed by cold and the exertions he had undergone, that he felt himself unable to rise. As far as his eyes could stretch, the prospect before him was most cheerless and desolate. The place upon which he was cast appeared to be little more than a barren waste, with scarcely any signs of vegetation, and not the least token of human habitation. The wretched man's heart sickened at the contemplation, and for the time he felt that he might as well have consigned himself to the deep at once; for, unless Providence should send some friendly vessel to his rescue speedily, there seemed to be no other prospect before him than that of perishing of starvation. Notwithstanding the shocking and deplorable situation in which he found himself, he was so completely worn out with the extraordinary exertions he had undergone, that sleep, or a kind of stupor, insensibly stole over him; and he must have continued in that state for some time, for when he recovered his recollection, the sun was pouring scorching hot upon him, and he felt a sensation of burning thirst upon him that was perfectly intolerable. He arose upon his feet with the utmost difficulty, and then once more cast his eyes around him in despair. A few wild shrubs met his gaze; but, in other respects, the island seemed to be completely barren. He struck his forehead with the intensity of his anguish, and then his feelings once more found vent in the most bitter maledictions against those who had consigned him to so horrible a destiny. And now, for the moment, did his conscience upbraid him, and he felt that it was a fearful but just punishment for the crimes of which he had been guilty, and that he could not appeal to that Power, whose sacred laws he had so recklessly and heinously violated, for its mercy and interposition.

"What a fool—what a wretch I have been!" he cried, "to suffer my evil passions to obtain such an ascendancy over me, when I might otherwise have been so happy and prosperous, independent of every care, and honoured by those who knew me. Fortune had placed me in the most favourable position; but I abused her gifts, and became the slave of my vices, when I should have courted honour and virtue as my good geniuses, and worshipped alone at their shrine. But must I, in my prime, my summer of manhood, perish by such a fate as this?

And it was to obtain the possession of one who could never view me with any other feelings than those of scorn and abhorrence that I have thus sinned, and for which I am now suffering this dreadful retribution. Oh! fool, villain that I have been! I that had the opportunity of distinguishing myself in the service of my country, and have met with universal regard! Rosetta Belford, most keenly do I now feel that it was the greatest misfortune that ever happened to me when I met you, or that I should be placed under the protection of a relative, who could instil into my mind nothing but the greatest vice. My brain is distracted, and a burning heat, worse than the fires of hell, consumes my vitals! Oh! for one draught of water to quench this insupportable thirst!"

He beat his breast, and again threw himself upon the earth, in a state of frenzy and despair. He rolled over and over, and beat his head against the sterile ground in the excessive agony of his feelings. Then he suddenly once more started to his feet, with a strength and avidity that could scarcely be believed, and dashed across the island with all the air of a maniac, with his hands clasping his distracted temples, and his eyes protruding from their sockets, and glaring upon vacancy. In his anguish he picked up the wild herbs which he met with on his way, and eagerly devoured them; but these only added to his thirst, and increased the anguish of his feelings. He paused, and looked wildly around him, giving utterance to incoherent expressions, and raving against the horror of his destiny, then he once more proceeded with hasty steps, until he had almost traversed the whole of the island, when suddenly he uttered an exclamation of delirious transport, as a spring of clear pure water met his sight. Eagerly he knelt down, and slaked his burning thirst at the lucid fount. Never had anything appeared half so delicious to him as did that welcome draught, and when he had amply quenched his thirst, he felt himself, as it were, another man, so greatly had it revived him.

Proceeding farther across the island, he found a cluster of wide-spreading trees, beneath the shade of whose umbrageous foliage he threw himself, quite exhausted, and in a short time, notwithstanding the poignant anguish of his thoughts, sleep descended upon his eyelids, and he did not awake again until the day had far advanced.

He now took a circuit of the island, and found a curious kind of wild fruit, of a very agreeable taste, and which grew in considerable abundance. He ate heartily of them, and having once more slaked his thirst at the spring, he felt greatly refreshed, and became more calm in his mind, notwithstanding his situation was still most melancholy and hopeless.

The ocean was now calm, and he determined to make his way down to the sands, with the hope of being able to obtain some fish that might be washed on shore, and in this he was not disappointed, but caught two or three, which at that time seemed to him of most excellent flavour, and he fully satisfied the cravings of his appetite.

Altogether Raymond's situation did not appear to be so bad as it had at first seemed; the prospect of his immediately perishing of want was banished from his mind, and he endeavoured to hope that something would, ere long, occur to rescue him from the island. As night approached, he returned to the trees, under whose shade he stretched himself, and tried to gain a few hours' repose, in which he succeeded, but his imagination was haunted by the most troublesome dreams, and he awoke very little refreshed.

The principal portion of the following day he passed on the sandy beach, gazing anxiously across the ocean, but without beholding anything to raise his hopes. We need not attempt to describe the anguish of his mind; and most fearful were the curses he continued to invoke upon the heads of those who had been the means of placing him in so dreadful a dilemma, and he vowed the most deadly revenge against them, should it ever be in his power to obtain it, but of that there appeared not the least prospect at present, at any rate.

"And they are revelling in their triumph," he ejaculated, "while I am reduced to this horrible state of loneliness and suffering, and probably shall be here left to perish, unless some vessel should pass this way, the captain of which may feel disposed to take me on board ; but which he would not do, should he have any suspicion of my real character. And what account can I give of myself?—and what course of life would it be in my power to adopt? I dare not show myself again in England, or my destruction would be almost sure to follow. These thoughts are enough to madden me, and yet they are prompted alone by reason. Idiot that I have been to suffer my evil passions thus to ruin all my prospects ; but it is too late to repent now. A brand, a damning mark, is set upon me ; and I see no way of evading the fate that some time or the other awaits me. Rosetta, too, she has escaped me, and I can never more hope to gain possession of her, or to venture to approach her, that is, if she escape from the villains who have her in their power, and who will not fail to make her the victim of their nefarious wishes ; and this, too, at the very time when I thought she was all secure, and that nothing whatever could rescue her from my will. What pains have I taken to work my own ruin and disappointment, and I feel that I am only duly punished for the vices of which I have been guilty ! The miscreants have got possession of my vessel and my wealth, and even should I escape from hence, all my future prospects are annihilated, and I shall become no better than a hunted wandering outcast, pursued by the officers of the law, and afraid to expose my face to public scrutiny, lest I should be detected, and the vengeance of man should overtake me."

He paced the beach with the most disordered steps, soliloquising in a similar manner at intervals, and unable to obtain any tranquillity of mind. That day passed away as the others had done, and still no prospect of deliverance dawned upon the wretched Raymond Middleton. He had been able to procure a sufficient quantity of shell and other fish to satisfy the cravings of his hunger ; but even that could not appease his anguish, when he thought of the utter loneliness of his situation, and of the uncertainty when, if ever it would terminate.

It was on the fourth day that he had been on the island, while he was pacing the sandy beach, with folded arms, that his eyes suddenly rested on a small speck on the distant ocean, which he quickly became convinced was a ship ; but she was so far off that it was utterly impossible for him to distinguish her build, or to form any certain conjecture of the course she was steering.

At the first sight of this, the feelings of Raymond may be readily imagined, and hope sprang up elate in his breast. But, alas, how little cause was there for that ! for it soon became to him but too evident that the vessel was not coming anywhere near the island ; and, after watching her for about an hour, she was completely hidden from his observation, and despair and disappointment settled upon his heart. He left the beach, and wandered about the island with the air of a maniac, and giving free vent to the agony of his thoughts, which were almost too torturing for human endurance.

"No, there is no hope," he exclaimed ; "here must I remain to perish alone, and with the horrors of my guilty conscience. This island is, probably, seldom or never approached, and I shall have no chance of making my situation known. I am lost, lost for ever. Well, I deserve it all, since I could not be contented when fortune smiled upon me, and I was placed in a position to pass through the world with honour and admiration. Oh, if I could but recall the past, and once more regain the situation I have lost, I should be a happy man. But it is useless my relenting now, since I have involved myself in inevitable destruction."

He threw himself on the earth, and gave himself up entirely to the power of his emotions. Consolation he could find none ; for what cause had he to encourage it ? None whatever ; and the more he reflected upon his deplorable situation, the more excruciating became his mental tortures.

At intervals he was half inclined to precipitate himself into the sea, but still that inherent love of life, which often clings to us under the most awful and trying circumstances, prevented him, and he remained a prey to the most abject and overpowering despair. Another night, another day passed, and still there was no alteration in the unhappy condition of Raymond Middleton, nor the smallest prospect whatever of his deliverance.

The weather continued very fine, and the ocean was beautifully calm. With what anxious looks did Raymond pace the beach for hours together, and strain his eyes across it, with the hope of discerning approaching help, but in vain ; and at length he abandoned himself entirely to despair, and looked forward to the ultimate fate that must befall him as inevitable. What would he not then have given had he been engaged in honourably fighting the battles of his country? Indeed, he thought that any destiny would have been preferable to that to which he was now doomed, and again and again he invoked the bitterest curses against those who had betrayed him, and upon whose fidelity he, at one time, thought that he could have placed every reliance. He deeply regretted that he had not taken more prompt and decisive measures to suppress the mutiny, after the warning which Hawkesley had given him ; but even then he should not have been able to defeat them, for the villains were too powerful for him, and they had so well concocted their designs, that they might, with safety, calculate on their success. There were a few among the crew who remained faithful to him, and who were ready to espouse his cause ; but what could they do, when opposed to such a number of determined ruffians, who had made up their minds to succeed in their schemes, or to perish in the attempt !—nothing. It would have been next to madness to have expected such a thing. The only thing that more than all surprised him was that they had not sacrificed his life on the spot ; but, of course, they fully expected that his fall would be certain, for they could not suppose that a boat so shattered as the one in which they had placed him could live an hour.

"And what can be their intentions with regard to Rosetta?" he ejaculated. "I may anticipate the worst ; for it is not likely that such ruffians will have any regard for her situation or sex. No ; they will rather feel a pleasure in triumphing over her innocence ; and, probably, the wish of the leader to gain possession of her, was one of the principal incentives to the mutiny. And am I, indeed, thus foiled, entrapped, caught in my own net, when I thought that everything was secure, and that the person of the lovely Rosetta was mine beyond all earthly power to thwart my wishes ? By the infernal host, the more I ruminate upon it, the more insupportable becomes my rage, and I feel degraded in my own estimation. Sir Horace Middleton has also escaped from my power ; and how great will be his exultation, when the length of my absence shall convince him that he has got rid of me altogether. Martin Trevors is now left at liberty to work his secret plans without interruption ; and, no doubt, he will take good care to possess himself of his wealth, or the greater portion of it, even though he should sacrifice the life of Sir Horace to obtain it. Whichever way I turn my thoughts, nought but rage and disappointment meet them, and add to the misery of my situation.

He beat his breast and bit his lips, in the vehemence of the emotions which these reflections engendered, and it was many hours before he could acquire the least degree of composure.

That night a storm arose, the ocean tossed its white foam to the clouds, and the thunder roared, the lightning flashed, and the rain descended in overwhelming torrents. The earth rocked, as with the powerful shock of an earthquake, and the sea-birds shrieked in frightful concert with the voice of the elements. Dreadful was now the situation of Raymond, having no place of shelter, and being entirely exposed to all the horrors of the storm, every moment expecting to be struck a ghastly corpse by the forked flashes of the lightning, which glared hideously around. He was soon drenched to the skin, and shivering with cold from the effects of his miserable condition, and his limbs were so benumbed, that it was not without the greatest difficulty he could walk about, to keep himself in proper exercise, although it was utterly impossible that he could stretch his weary form upon the deeply saturated earth. Never had the wretched man experienced such an accumulation of horrors as he did on that awful night, and it was only surprising that he could survive them.

The tempest raged with the most frightful violence throughout the night, but towards morning it in some measure abated, the thunder ceased to roar, the lightning no longer darted its forked terrors, and the ocean became more calm. At length he rain entirely ceased, and it seemed as if the storm would in a short time entirely subside, which was the case, and very fine weather succeeded.

Raymond's strength was entirely exhausted, and he was forced to sit himself down on a block of stone, which he had placed underneath the shelter of the trees, and he felt a sensation come over him, as if he were dying. He shook violently in every limb, while his brain burned with fever.

And now all the horrors of approaching death crowded upon his guilty mind, and he shrank appalled at the contemplation. How could he meet that dreaded futurity, which till now he had seldom, if ever, considered! How stand in the presence of that Almighty Judge, whose laws he had frequently so grossly outraged! He shrank from the thought with the same feelings of horror as if he had encountered some hideous spectre, and clung to life with a tenacity which nothing could conquer.

And what was to become of him, alone in this wild place, and without the means of obtaining any remedy in his illness? It seemed to him that death was inevitable, and heavy groans escaped his distracted bosom at the thought. It might be said that Raymond Middleton was truly touched with remorse in that, the hour of his severe trial. He would have prayed, but he knew not how, and his lips refused their office. Then a kind of frenzy seized upon his brain, and he laughed aloud with delirious wildness, swaying his body to and fro, in a state of the most indescribable emotion. Guilty as he had been, it must have excited the pity of even the most insensible being, to have seen him at that moment. It was a shocking sight to behold one so young, and who might have been moving in society honoured and esteemed, reduced to this truly pitiable state by his own vices. Wretched man, he was abandoned both of God and man.

At length he was with difficulty enabled to crawl to the spring, where he quenched the burning and feverish thirst that was upon him, which refreshed him a little, but he found it impossible to support his tottering limbs any longer, and stretching himself upon the still dank earth, he resigned himself to his fate, not doubting but that his dissolution was close at hand.

He continued in a state of delirium for some time, and uttered the most wild and incoherent sentences, and making the very place resound again with the frenzy of his cries. But at length he sank into a kind of torpor, from which he did not arouse for two or three hours, and the fever had then greatly abated, and he felt considerably better, but still he was unable to rise, so much was his strength reduced.

Again he reflected upon the horror of his situation, and the terrors of remorse added strength to the poignancy of his sufferings. To die in a foreign land, without any one near him in his last moments, was, of itself, most dreadful to think upon; but when he recalled to his memory the crimes of which he had already been guilty, his agony increased tenfold.

"Oh! that I were once more at liberty," he cried, "how sincerely would I repent, and endeavour to make atonement to those whom I have injured. Atonement, alas! what reparation would it be in my power to offer for the misery I have caused? Compunction is now too late, for can it save the injured Rosetta from the fate which she has incurred through my villanous means? No, no, it cannot, and I have been the cause of consigning her to shame and degradation more awful even than death. Her parents' hearts, too, have probably been broken by her loss; and I have been the cause of all this. Oh! I am justly, though severely punished for my iniquity, and how dare I presume to look for mercy?"

He beat his breast with the fury of his agitation, and at that moment really felt true penitence for the numerous vices of which he had been guilty, and regretted that he should ever have suffered them to gain so powerful and fatal an ascendancy over him.

During the whole of the day, he continued in the same feeble state, sleeping only at intervals, and then the most torturing dreams flitted before his disordered imagination, and rendered him more harm than good.

The next morning, however, the weather continuing fine, he felt himself much

better, and more settled and composed in his mind, and he was enabled to take a little gentle exercise about the island, which considerably recruited his strength.

He had now been ten days on the island, and still his prospects were as gloomy as at first, and he gave up all hope of ever being rescued from his miserable situation. He obtained a good supply of fish and fruit to satisfy his wants, and, therefore, he at length endeavoured to make his mind more contented, and to leave his deliverance to chance. But that was a task not very easy of accomplishment, and many hours of poignant anguish did the anticipation of the future cost him.

He had no tools, or he could have constructed himself some kind of tent from the timber that the island contained, and then he might have probably felt some small portion of comfort; but there was no possibility of his doing so, and, therefore, it was useless for him to think about it.

His time was principally passed upon the beach, watching the wide ocean which separated him from liberty, and which he despaired of ever being permitted to cross again ; but no signs of a vessel met his sight, and his prospects every day and every hour became more insupportably dismal. The image of Rosetta continually occupied his mind ; and many were the reproaches he heaped upon himself for the manner in which he had behaved towards her; and the miserable fate to which he had, in all probability, been the means of bringing her.

"I shall never behold her again," he cried ; "and if I should, how should I dare to meet the reproachful glances of that much injured girl? Would they not sink me into the earth with shame and confusion? But, alas ! she will never be suffered to escape alive from the wretches in whose power she now is ; and who, like I have ever been, are insensible to pity. Miscreant that I am, I have become a murderer of the blackest dye, and must expect to be pursued by the just retribution of offended Heaven."

But we must now, for awhile, leave Raymond Middleton, and return once more to the pirate vessel, and the sufferings of our heroine.

It has before been stated with what powerful feelings of terror Rosetta listened to the conflict that was going on between the mutineers and the rest of the crew ; and at last, unable longer to restrain her curiosity and anxiety, notwithstanding the consequences which might accrue to herself, and in spite of the endeavours of Martha to prevent her, she rushed from the cabin, the door of which was open, and hastened upon deck, just as the ruffians had committed the unfortunate but guilty Raymond Middleton to the waves, and were shouting aloud in the enthusiasm of their demoniacal exultation.

The singularity and confusion of the scene ; the ferocious looks of the pirates ; their deadly weapons flashing in the partial light, and the several bodies that strewed the deck, formed a combination of horrors that shook every nerve of the damsel's frame ; and, uttering an exclamation of terror, she sank on her knees, and covered her face with her hands.

The attention of the ruffians was now called towards Rosetta, and Martha, who had followed her upon deck, and they were surrounded in a moment.

"Ah ! it is the fair craft," exclaimed one of the pirates, who was called Jack Mizen. "My eyes, but she is a taut, trim-built vessel, any how, and I don't wonder at the skipper taking a fancy to her. However, she must be turned again into her berth ; this is not the place for her."

"Why did you suffer her to come upon deck at such a time as this, Martha?" demanded a tall, dark-whiskered man, who, it appeared afterwards, was her husband. "Conduct her away, and see that you attend to her properly ; we shall see in what manner it will be best to dispose of her by-and-bye."

"Oh, God !" exclaimed Rosetta, her eyes swimming with tears, "if ye are men, spare me, I beseech you, and do not seek to outrage my feelings by any act of violence. Already is my heart nearly broken by the sufferings I have so unjustly endured. Have pity on me, and release me on the first opportunity."

"Why, love ye, my pretty lass," said Mizen, "we would not harm you for the world, rough and uncivilized though we may appear to be. For sticking to a petticoat, at all times and seasons, I will be bound to say that you will not find a truer fellow than Jack Mizen, and to show you that I mean what I say, I will seal my assertion on your lips, and ——"

"Oh, hold ! forbear, bad, bold man !" cried the indignant Rosetta, rising from her knees and retreating to the farther end of the deck. "Oh, Heaven ! what will become of me ?"

"Avast, avast, Jack," interposed the husband of Martha ; "this is not the time to be firing salutes after that fashion. We have other and more important duties to perform now. Come, young lady, you must retire to your cabin. You have no occasion to fear, for you cannot be worse off than you would have been with Raymond Middleton ; but you have nothing more to apprehend from him, he is probably food for sharks by this time, and that ought to afford you some consolation, at any rate."

Rosetta stood in a state of stupefaction, and seemed for the moment to be scarcely conscious of what he said, or what was going forward; but Martha, with a look of the most unaffected pity, took her arm, and entreated her to accompany her back to the cabin. Rosetta did not still seem exactly to understand her, and hesitated when two or three of the pirates approached her, and rudely taking her by the arms, would have forced her into obedience; but this aroused the unfortunate damsel, and, with a look of horror and disgust, she retraced her steps from the deck, followed by Martha.

When she had reached the cabin once more, she sank on her knees, and, with streaming eyes, and fervently clasped hands, she supplicated the protection of the Most High.

"Alas! what will become of me," she ejaculated, "in the power of miscreants, whose chief glory seems to be in the misery of their fellow creatures? Oh! Martha, speak to me—advise me how to act; for you, I know, do sympathise with me in my misfortunes, and would readily assist me all that lies in your power."

"Indeed, indeed I would, miss," returned Martha; "but you see that I am powerless as yourself. However, take comfort, I beg of you, for you have nothing more to fear from Raymond Middleton, and ——"

"Alas!" interrupted our heroine, "and what better is my situation, seeing that I am still in the power of the pirate crew, without any prospect of being released from it? What have I not to dread from such wretches, whose very looks inspire me with horror? Would to Heaven that death would put an end to my sufferings, for I see nothing but shame and degradation before me."

"Something will yet occur to save you, miss, depend upon it," returned Martha. "You heard what was said by my husband; he possesses great influence among the crew, and would, no doubt, be able to restrain them from the perpetration of any outrage."

Rosetta shook her head doubtfully, for, when she took into consideration the character of the pirates, and the crimes to which they were inured, she could not but anticipate the worst.

"Ah! Martha," she ejaculated, "I thank you for the sympathy you express in my welfare, for I am confident that you are sincere; but indeed I cannot entertain the hopes which you would fain inspire me with. The villains are insensible to pity, and my situation is equally as dangerous, if not more so than when Raymond Middleton held the command of the ship. Am I not torn away from my home—my native land, to which I can never expect the pirates will restore me? Oh! my beloved parents—poor Julio, I shall no more behold you! But are they still living? Oh! no; they could never survive their terrible bereavement!"

Her tears flowed fast as these melancholy thoughts crowded upon her brain, and her bosom heaved with convulsive sobs. Martha gazed at her with feelings of the deepest commiseration, but she did not attempt to interrupt her grief, for she thought that the temporary indulgence of it might serve to relieve her mind. When the poor girl remembered the dreadful carnage she had so recently witnessed, and the fierce looks of the daring crew who held her in their power, her very soul shuddered with horror, and she was completely deaf to all the efforts which her kind-hearted companion made to console her.

"Seek rest, my poor girl," said Martha. "A few hours' repose would do you a great deal of good, and might serve to tranquillize your feelings. I will not leave you, and you need not fear that you will receive any interruption."

"Oh! no," answered Rosetta; "my mind is too much agitated to permit me to sleep. Would to Heaven that I could sleep for ever in the arms of death! for what is there left for me but horror and despair? Hark! the wretches are exulting over the crimes they have committed! Their hands yet reeking with the blood of their fellow creatures! Oh, God! protect me! for what have I not to apprehend from monsters such as these?"

The uproarious voices of the pirates now resounded on the air, as they sang their rude chorus of triumph, and, at its conclusion, then loud shouts of mirth, and the ribald observations they made use of, shocked the ears of our heroine and her companion.

The vessel was proceeding on its course, propelled by a favouring breeze, and the daring crew, after having partaken freely of the grog, entered upon the business of choosing their future captain. In order that they might all have an equal chance, and that there should be no cause of complaint or jealousy among them, it was agreed that they should draw lots, and the business was decided in favour of Mizen, who was received with pleasure by his companions; for he was a reckless, daring fellow, and one in whom they could place the greatest confidence, for they knew him to possess the most indomitable courage, as it had been well tried upon many occasions. They all took the oath of fidelity to him, and they then once more proceeded to mirth, in which they indulged to the most boisterous extent.

"And now, my lads," said one of the men, "since the command of the ship has fallen upon Mizen, who is to become the captain of the fair craft? She is a trim built vessel, and——"

"Avast! avast! Dick," interrupted the husband of Martha, "belay your jawing tackle on that point at present. Although we are pirates, we are none of us cowards, and it would be acting like unmanly lubbers for us to bear down upon her in her present condition."

"Right, lad," coincided Mizen; "we must allow the girl a few days to recruit her strength, and then we will see who is to possess her. He will be a lucky fellow to whose share she falls—a mistress that a king might be proud to possess."

"Ay, ay," ejaculated several of the crew. "But there must be no quarrelling over the business. May the best man win her and wear her."

The wish was responded to by the whole of the ruffians, and the most tumultuous mirth succeeded, which the lawless crew kept up till a late, or rather an early, hour.

The terror and anguish of Rosetta increased instead of abating, and she was unable to rise from her pallet, Martha being constantly in attendance upon her, and watching her with the most anxious solicitude. The pirates, however, did not offer to obtrude themselves upon her, and this afforded her some little degree of consolation. How racking were the thoughts that continually crowded upon her brain; how painful were the reflections that constantly suggested themselves to her mind! The horrors of the night on which she had been torn away from her home by Martin Trevors returned to her imagination as vividly as if they had been only just enacted. Again she saw her mother and Julio struggling in the flames, and she groaned in the intensity of her insupportable agony, as she pictured to herself the horrible fate they had most probably met with. And her beloved father, too, what must be his sufferings at the dreadful, the unparalleled calamity that had befallen him? Surely it was greater than he could ever find fortitude to support with any degree of patience. Even now he might have sunk under it; and, if such was the case, what had she to hope for in her restoration to her native land? She would be left alone in the world, without one friend to whom she could look for sympathy and protection. The idea was a dreadful one, and it obtained such a powerful ascendancy over her imagination, that, in spite of all the endeavours of Martha, she abandoned herself entirely to despair.

Poor Julio, too, he was the constant subject of her thoughts, and she could now no longer deny to herself the strength of that love with which he had inspired her, although all hope of its ever being gratified was banished from her mind. Had he not perished in the flames? And even if he had not, what prospect was there of her ever beholding him again? None, none; and therefore was her anguish increased almost to madness.

Several days elapsed in this manner without anything worthy of particular notice taking place. The weather continued pretty favourable, but the pirates began to grow impatient for the want of booty, as they had not met with any prize since the commencement of the voyage.

Towards the evening of the fourth day after the meeting, however, the man on the look out suddenly exclaimed—

"A sail ahead !"

"Ah !" exclaimed Mizen, "can you discern her build ?"

"She seems to be a tolerable sized brig," said the man. "She is steering towards us, with the wind in her favour, and half an hour will bring her within gun-shot. You may see her now clear enough."

"Ay, ay," said the pirate captain; "yonder she comes to a certainty, with every inch of canvas spread. She is a likely looking craft enough; a trading vessel, and of British build. All right, my lads, there will be some sport for us presently. Clear the decks, and prepare for the combat; we will soon let her see the mettle we are made of."

Every man ran to his post with alacrity, and all were busy in preparing for the engagement on board the pirate vessel. The ship came rapidly on, and it soon became quite clear that the idea which Mizen had expressed, of its being a merchant vessel, was correct, and, from its appearance, the villains anticipated an engagement.

In the meantime, the confusion on deck reached the ears of our heroine and Martha, and, from the observations which they overheard, they soon became acquainted with the cause. It is useless to attempt to describe the alarm of Rosetta at the prospect of the scene of horror and carnage that was about to take place, and Martha was in a very little better condition herself; but she did her best to compose her feelings, and they both invoked the protection of Heaven in the approaching struggle.

"It seems to be an English merchant ship, miss," said Martha; "and, should the pirate be defeated by it, you will doubtless be rescued from your present dangerous situation, and once more restored to liberty. Courage, then, and all may yet be well."

"Alas ! I cannot entertain such a hope," returned Rosetta; "my heart misgives me. Oh, never can I support the horrors of this deadly combat. And see, the vessel rapidly approaches; it only hastens to certain destruction."

Martha looked through the cabin window, and saw the vessel almost within gun-shot; and the bustle and noise of the pirates increased every moment, and it was quite certain that they were making every preparation. The ship certainly presented no very formidable appearance, when contrasted with that of the pirate, and there was every reason to apprehend the worst results.

One of the pirate's men came down, and secured the cabin door, to prevent the possibility of their leaving it, and they both awaited the engagement in a state of the most painful and trembling anxiety.

In the meantime, the pirates waited the approach of their anticipated prize with eager impatience, and, from what they were enabled to observe of her, they flattered themselves with the idea of an easy conquest. There were several men on her deck, and no little excitement seemed to prevail among them, they, probably, observing the pirate ship with some degree of suspicion.

The pirate ship now took a tack, and shortly came within hail of her. The merchant vessel then hove to, and directly afterwards the pirate came alongside of her.

"What ship, ho ?" demanded Mizen.

"The Nancy of Liverpool, homeward bound," was the reply. "Your name ?" added the captain of the merchantman.

"Take my answer," returned Mizen, and instantly the black flag was hoisted, and a couple of guns were discharged from the pirate, while the desperate crew gave a terrific and simultaneous shout. The utmost confusion now prevailed on board the merchant vessel; but they seemed determined to resist the pirates to the utmost of their power. They were not backward in returning the fire, and which told with some effect, and the crew, which seemed to consist of about five-and-twenty men, were well armed, so that the pirates saw that they were not likely to find her quite so easy a customer as they had anticipated she would be.

"Ah! my lads," said Mizen, "if that's your temper, I know how to deal with ye. Give the lubbers a warm salute, and let them see how small the chance is that they stand with us."

No sooner was this order given than it was obeyed, and the fire of the pirate did considerable havoc, and threw the crew into some disorder, of which Mizen did not fail to take advantage; the grappling-irons were thrown out, and in a few minutes the pirates boarded her in great numbers, making the air resound again with their terrific shouts. The crew of the Nancy, however, met them with the greatest courage, and seemed resolved to make an unflinching stand, notwithstanding the superiority of the number of their enemies, and the combat was continued with equal intrepidity on both sides, and in which several of the pirates were slain, which only added to their fury and determination; while an incessant fire was kept up by both vessels, the Nancy carrying more metal than her daring foe had at first thought.

"Yield!" shouted Mizen, as he encountered the captain; "your resistance is useless, and, if you remain obstinate, not a soul of ye will be spared."

"Yield, pirate, never!" replied the captain of the Nancy; "there is not a man amongst us that would not sooner die first."

"Give it the dogs, then, my lads," shouted Mizen; "show them no mercy; give them no quarter."

The scene now became awful in the extreme, both parties fighting with fierce resolution, while the shouts and maledictions of the pirates were terrific to hear. The crew of the Nancy, however, remained undaunted, and, being all excellent seamen, the pirates found them a very fair match for them. They were again driven back to their own vessel, and the crew of the Nancy succeeded in releasing her, and at the same time discharged the whole of her guns, which did the most serious damage to the pirate.

"D——n!" shouted Mizen, in a furious voice, "the lubbers will get the better of us now if we do not mind. Give it them as hot as they can sup it; if we do not make them cry 'peccavi' in a few minutes, it will be all up with us."

This order was obeyed, and the Nancy seemed to be hurled nearly out of the water by the violence of the shock. The next moment a terrific explosion was heard; huge black volumes of smoke ascended to the clouds, the ocean seemed one liquid sheet of fire, and, when the smoke gradually evaporated, only a few shattered timbers of the Nancy were to be seen floating on the surface of the deep. The last fire from the pirate ship had communicated with a barrel of gunpowder on board the ill-fated vessel, and in an instant it was destroyed, and every soul on board of her hurled to eternity.

The pirates were completely astounded by this unexpected catastrophe, and at so fearful a disappointment of their hopes, after all the trouble they had had, and the damage their vessel had received, and they gave vent to their rage in the most bitter execrations.

"By all the infernal host," exclaimed Mizen, as he gazed towards that part of the ocean on which the Nancy had only a few minutes before so gallantly rode, "fortune seems to have deserted us entirely. To lose so rich a prize after all the hard fighting we have had, is more than I have patience to endure; but let us only meet with another vessel, and we will have ample satisfaction."

"It is a cursed bad job," said one of the pirates, "and our own vessel is very much crippled, besides all the lives we have lost."

"Well, it cannot be helped," said Mizen, "we did our best, and must only hope for better luck another time. The damage done to the ship, I do not think is so very great after all, and we must see about repairing it as soon as possible. If the weather continues favourable, we shall be able to reach the place of our destination."

The looks of the pirates sufficiently evinced their feelings of rage and dissatisfaction; but there was no one to blame, and therefore it was useless to murmur; and the pirate vessel, proceeding on its course, was soon far away from the scene of the late awful engagement.

CHAPTER XVIII.

THE SHIPWRECK.—THE OPEN BOAT.—THE MIRACULOUS ESCAPE OF ROSETTA.—THE
UNEXPECTED MEETING.

No language could do adequate justice to the terrors of our heroine and Martha
while this terrific combat was going on, and at the dreadful catastrophe which
terminated it. The loading of the cannon, the groans of the wounded, and the wild
shouts of the combatants, froze their very hearts' blood with horror, and it was
wonderful that they retained their senses during that awful struggle, and the torturing uncertainty of the result of it. Every moment they expected death, and although
Rosetta had everything to dread in her present situation, she could not but contemplate so violent and untimely a death with feelings of horror and repugnance.

"Heaven protect the unfortunate crew, and give them power to defeat their
enemies!" she ejaculated. "Oh! Martha, what a dreadful situation is this for
us to be placed in!"

"Be firm, Rosetta," returned her companion, "and put your trust in the
goodness of the Supreme, who will not fail to watch over us, and to protect us
in this hour of trial."

Rosetta clasped her hands together in despair, and sinking on her knees,
solemnly invoked the interposition of the Almighty to save her from the imminent peril by which she was surrounded. But when the terrific explosion took
place, which has been described in the previous chapter, she threw herself on the
floor, overcome with terror, and immediately became insensible. In a few minutes
she recovered, and found herself supported by Martha, who was, however, in a
very little better condition than she was.

"Gracious Heaven! am I still alive?" she exclaimed, looking wildly and incredulously around her; "what fearful catastrophe has taken place?"

"It was the explosion of the unfortunate merchant vessel that you heard," replied Martha; "it is entirely destroyed, and all who were on board of her
must have perished."

"God receive their souls, then," said our heroine, with a shudder; "and I am
then still in the power of the pirates?"

"You are," returned Martha; "but do not despair, for something may yet
occur to release you from it."

"Ah, no," sighed Rosetta, "I see not the most remote chance of it, unless it be
by death. Would that I had perished in this awful hour. I can never support
such scenes of carnage and horror. Surely the vengeance of offended Heaven
will overtake the miscreants for the monstrous crimes they have committed."

"Most certainly it will; and you will not be permitted to fall a sacrifice to
their guilty designs."

Rosetta shook her head and sighed deeply. They were interrupted by the appearance of Martha's husband, who had come to ascertain their situation, and to
see that no accident had befallen them. Having satisfied himself, and given some
injunctions to his wife, he left the cabin, much to the relief of them both; Rosetta
having forborne to appeal to him for pity, as she knew it would be useless, as she
did not expect that he could render her any assistance if he were ever so disposed to do.

It was now late, and as Rosetta was quite worn out with thinking, and the excitement she had undergone, she was persuaded to retire to rest, and it was not
long before sleep came to her pillow. But her imagination was haunted by the
most fearful dreams, and she awoke again before daylight, very little refreshed.
She felt herself too ill, however, to rise, and throughout the day she continued
the same, Martha paying her all the attention that was in her power.

Two days passed away in this manner, without any other circumstances taking
place to alarm her, and nothing transpired to inspire her with hope; the pirates,
however, acted with more forbearance than she had expected they would have
done, and did not obtrude themselves upon her, and that afforded her some little

consolation, although she could not flatter herself with the idea that they would spare her long.

They had now been pretty well a month at sea, and there yet seemed no likelihood of the vessel arriving at the place of its destination, which Martha had at last ascertained was some place on the coast of Africa, when the weather, which had hitherto been tolerably fine, changed, the wind gradually arose, until it blew a perfect hurricane, and our heroine had added to her fears the prospect of all the horrors of shipwreck. The vessel, as has been before observed, had received no inconsiderable amount of damage in the engagement, and was not in a condition to weather a tempest; and, as it increased every hour, the pirates became alarmed, and again gave vent to their rage at the bad fortune that attended them, in language of the most horrible nature. It was ascertained that there were three feet of water in the hold, and all hands were set to work at the pumps, which kept them incessantly employed for hours, without making any visible impression.

The gale increased, and inevitable death seemed to stare them in the face; the breakers washing over the doomed ship with fearful violence, and sweeping several of the crew away. The mainmast at length fell by the board, and great was the consternation that prevailed, even among those hardened men, for they expected every moment that they must perish. The dense darkness of the night increased the horrors of the scene, which baffled all description, and even made the stoutest heart among the pirates quail.

As for Rosetta, she considered that death was certain, and she, therefore, endeavoured to resign herself to her fate, and behaved with much greater calmness than could have been expected on such an awful occasion. She continued on her knees with Martha for some time, and most fervently did they offer up their prayers to Heaven, and await the fate which it seemed likely must shortly overtake them. What a crowd of thoughts flashed across the unfortunate girl in that dreadful moment. The reader may imagine her feelings, but they defy the power of our pen to describe them.

A fearful crash was heard, and then the vessel lurched frightfully, and loud cries of "She sinks! she sinks! To the boats!" smote the ears of the distracted females, who clung to each other with frenzied looks, fully believing that the fatal moment had arrived, for the vessel was going to pieces, and the water rushed with the most alarming impetuosity into the cabin, the door of which was secured on the outside, so that they had no means of escaping.

"The monsters will leave us here to perish," gasped forth Rosetta. "They are quitting the vessel. God of heaven receive our souls!"

At that moment they heard hasty footsteps approaching; the cabin door was burst open, and the husband of Martha presented himself.

"Quick! quick!" he said, seizing them both; "there is not a moment to be lost; the vessel is fast sinking, but it may not yet be too late to save ye. To the boats! to the boats!"

Without saying another word, he forced them from the cabin, and made his way with them to the deck, they almost unconscious of what was taking place; and frightful, indeed, was the scene which there presented itself. All was confusion and horror; the alarmed wretches crowding to get into the boats that were launched, while their dreadful curses and shrieks of despair were mingled with the hoarse voice of the tempest. Rosetta was handed almost insensible into one of the boats, in which were several men, and it was immediately hurried away with the velocity of an arrow, on the bosom of the turbulent billows. She raised her eyes in despair towards the sinking vessel, and called upon the name of Martha, from whom she was thus so suddenly separated. She saw her lifted into the other boat by her husband, who immediately followed himself. It was fearfully crowded, and no sooner was it disengaged than it capsized, and the whole of the unhappy beings were instantly engulphed by the wild waste of waters. Our heroine uttered one piercing shriek of horror, when she beheld the fate of poor Martha; a giddiness seized upon her brain; a mist seemed to float before her eyes, and for a few moments she became insensible to the terrors by which she was surrounded.

It would have been a mercy to her had she remained so longer; but she was quickly aroused by the motion of the boat, the frightful howling of the tempest, and the dreadful imprecations of the men as they struggled with the strength of

madness against the billows. Each wave that swept over them seemed to threaten them with instant destruction, and poor Rosetta, who was completely drenched to the skin, clasped her hands in despair, and committed her soul to the mercy of that Supreme Being in whose presence she expected shortly to be. The fate would, as she believed, be a mercy to her, for even should she escape it, what would not be the horrors of her situation in the power of such wretches as those who were now her companions.

Still the boat was tossed along by the breakers with awful fury, and it was truly miraculous how it could live for a moment, when opposed to such a frightful enemy. But suddenly the wind veered, and abated in violence, so suddenly indeed, that it had all the appearance of magic, and a special Providence seemed to interpose in their favour. The billows no longer swelled in the awful magnitude they had previously done, and the boat having been lightened of the water as speedily as possible, rode more easily. The ponderous black clouds gradually broke away, and everything gave token of an approaching calm. So sudden was the change, that Rosetta could scarcely believe the evidence of her senses; but she was quite exhausted, and sinking to the bottom of the boat, became totally unconscious of everything.

She was suddenly aroused by the loud shouts of the men of " Land! land! we shall yet be saved!"

She looked up; daylight was just beginning to break; and following with her eyes the direction to which the men pointed, she beheld, indeed, what appeared to be land at no great distance. A momentary feeling of delight and gratitude came over her, but it soon vanished, for what had she to hope for in that lone place, and with those guilty and inhuman men for her companions? The awful fate of poor Martha, too, also rushed upon her imagination, and she could not but think it would have been better for her had she perished with her. Mentally she prayed to God to watch over her in this fearful situation, and then she relapsed into a state of apathy, totally regardless of what became of her, since she was deprived of every hope.

The men exerted all their energies to reach the land, and the wind was in their favour. They had arrived within a very short distance of it, when one of the men, in his eagerness to take a more minute survey, started suddenly up; the act was a fatal one, the boat reeled and immediately capsized, and they were all in an instant immersed in the deep.

Rosetta arose again upon the surface of the waters; her senses were bewildered, but yet with the frenzied eagerness of all persons in a similar situation, she struggled for life, and that with a strength which was truly wonderful for one of her sex, and who was so much exhausted by the unexampled sufferings she had undergone. She clutched at something which she saw floating on the waves, which proved to be the boat, and which fortunately righted. With difficulty she drew herself into it, but nature could endure no more; she breathed one heavy sigh, as if her soul was escaping from its mortal tenement, and sunk inanimate in the boat, which was being rapidly drifted towards the land.

But Providence watched over the poor girl, and preserved her life, even though all her companions had perished. She recovered her senses, and opening her eyes, stared with stupified amazement at the situation in which she found herself. She was in a rude tent, and was supported in the arms of a man, whose features the dim light would not at first allow her to distinguish.

" God of Heaven be thanked, she still lives!" exclaimed the man; " Rosetta, dear Rosetta, that we should meet thus."

" Ah!" ejaculated our astonished heroine, " who is it calls upon my name? Speak, where am I, and who are you?"

" Do you not know me, my poor girl?" said the man, in melancholy accents; " but, alas! how should you, since time and intense suffering must have wrought so great a change in me."

" Your voice is familiar to me," said Rosetta, in a faint voice, and disengaging herself from his support; " but the light will not enable me to distinguish your features; again I implore you to keep me not in suspense, but to tell me who you are, and by what strange miracle I have been rescued from a watery grave?"

" I have been made the humble instrument to save you, sweet Rosetta; may Heaven be praised for affording me an opportunity so grateful to my feelings. Rosetta, companion of my boyish days, and whose heart I once flattered myself I possessed, it is Frank Trevors who stands before you!"

" Frank Trevors!" cried Rosetta! " and here!—the preserver of my life! Gracious Heaven! this is surely a dream. I—I——"

She could say no more; a variety of conflicting thoughts crowded tumultuously upon her brain; a death-like sensation came over her, and she fainted in his arms.

CHAPTER XIX.

ROSETTA AND FRANK TREVORS ON THE ISLAND.—MUTUAL EXPLANATIONS.—PAINFUL RETROSPECTIONS.—THE PIRATES.—FRANK AND ROSETTA CONVEYED ON BOARD THE DEATH SHIP.

YES, it was indeed Frank Trevors, the rejected of the unfortunate damsel, whom he now clasped in his arms, and upon whose pale but still lovely countenance he gazed with feelings which cannot be properly described. He had been on the island for more than a month. He had been fortunate enough to be able to recover from the wreck a quantity of provisions and other articles, and had thus been enabled to form himself a tent, and to be as comfortable as the circumstances would admit of. Strange and varied had been the adventures he had met with since he had so abruptly quitted his home; but notwithstanding all his efforts, he had been unable to banish the image of her to whom his heart was so fondly devoted from his mind; and great was the anguish he suffered when he reflected upon her, and knew that all the hopes he had formerly entertained of making her his bride were annihilated. He had never expected to behold her again, but now to meet with her in such an extraordinary manner, and in that part so distant from her native land, was a circumstance so astonishing, that he could scarce believe in its reality. How did his heart throb as he supported her insensible form, and parted the glossy hair from her forehead. Then he gently laid her on a rude couch, that he had formed of leaves, and procuring some rum which he had obtained from the wrecked vessel, he moistened her lips, and chafed her temples.

" Great God !" he cried, " and do I indeed hold to my bosom that lovely being whom I never expected to behold again? Oh, Rosetta, would to Heaven that your valued heart beat responsive with mine own! what happiness would be mine, even though placed in such a melancholy situation! But I must stifle these thoughts, for she has rejected my vows, and I have nothing to hope. I am but too rejoiced to think that I have been made the instrument of saving her from an untimely death. But, still, how dreadful are our prospects; here on this lonely island, should we not meet with assistance, what must not ultimately be our fate? God! preserve but this poor girl, and I care not what becomes of myself. How pale, how very pale, she looks ! Oh, what must she have suffered to undergo so melancholy a change as this! What villany has been at work to tear her from her native land, and expose her to all the perils of the ocean ! I am lost and bewildered in amazement! Her parents, too, what has become of them? The cruel loss of an only daughter, so dear to their very souls, must have broken their hearts. Oh, Rosetta, may you speedily recover, and banish my suspense, for the doubts and fears which haunt my mind are most torturing. Ah! she breathes again more freely. Thank Heaven!"

Rosetta heaved a sigh, and looking up, she gazed steadfastly at Frank, while deep blushes of confusion overspread her cheeks.

" Ah !" she ejaculated, " it was, then, no vision ; I do, indeed, behold you, Mr. Trevors; but to meet in such a place as this, so far away from my native land, and after all the horrors I have suffered. Alas ! what will become of me ?"

" Providence, I trust, Rosetta, will send some assistance to your aid, and restore you to happiness, and your home."

" Happiness ! oh, it will never more be mine. It would have been a mercy to me, had I perished in the deep."

" For Heaven's sake, talk not thus, Rosetta, for it wrings my heart to hear you, and ——"

" Mr. Trevors," interrupted Rosetta, recoiling from him, and fixing upon him a look of suspicion.

" Nay, Rosetta," returned Frank, in the most melancholy accents ; " pardon, I beseech you, the apparent familiarity of my words ; our early friendship gives me some license to address you thus. We are partners in misfortune, and you surely will not at least deny me the privilege of feeling for you the sympathy of a brother. By Heaven, could I harbour one thought towards you which the strictest virtue should blush to hear acknowledged, I should hate myself as one of the most base and despicable of human beings. No, my poor girl, you have decided against my love, and even though my heart should break, I will yield implicit obedience to thy will."

" I will, I do, believe you, Frank," said our heroine ; " but pray drop a subject that is so painful to us both. Is this island uninhabited ?"

" We are the only human beings it contains."

" Alas ! alas ! oh, dreadful fate."

" Do not give way to despair, Rosetta ; some vessel may shortly approach this place, and in the mean time, I have a sufficient supply of provisions to last us for some weeks. Oh, Rosetta, I have encountered many dangers since I last saw you. When I quitted my home, I hastened to London, and immediately engaged myself on board a man of war ; but you are faint ; take some refreshment which will revive you, and then you may seek a few hours' rest in safety ; you will have nothing to fear, my poor girl, while your old friend and play-fellow is at hand. I will watch outside my rude tent, until you permit me to return to your presence."

Rosetta looked her gratitude, and the words of her companion in misfortune inspired her with confidence. She partook, sparingly, of some rum and a biscuit, and she then felt a little more refreshed, although she was very much exhausted by the extraordinary exertions she had undergone, and the dreadful reflections that haunted her distracted mind.

" But, I pray you inform me, who has been the author of your sufferings, and by what means you are thus torn from your native land, and exposed to such a cruel destiny ?" said Frank, who was unable to restrain his curiosity.

" Ah !" exclaimed our heroine, " your questions rekindle all the tortures of recollection in my breast. Your father, Trevors, out of revenge for my having declined your suit, it was who snatched me from my home, that home which he committed to the flames, and left my poor mother and Julio struggling in the devouring element. Oh, God ! can I think of that horrible night, and yet retain my senses ?"

" Powers of mercy, can this be ?" cried Trevors, with a look of the greatest horror. " Is it possible that my father could ever have become such a monster ?"

" I have spoken the truth, Frank ; but spare my feelings."

" Oh ! this is indeed torture ! May curses light upon him who ——"

" Hold ! hold !" interrupted Rosetta ; " cruel though he has been, you must not curse the author of your being."

" Is it not enough to make me do so, after conduct so monstrous as this ? Rosetta, you must look upon me as his son with terror and disgust. I could have endured anything but to have heard this. But he is no more, since the whole of the persons who were in the vessel with you must have perished in the storm. May Heaven have mercy on his guilty soul !"

" Your father was not on board that dreadful pirate vessel with me, Mr. Trevors ; in bearing me away from the scene of the conflagration, he was met by a number of men, who fiercely attacked him, and triumphed, and, on my recovery, I found myself in the power of Raymond Middleton."

" Raymond Middleton !" repeated Frank, with increased astonishment ; " the villain ! And was it then he who conveyed you to the pirate ship ?"

" It was," answered our heroine ; " and of that ship he was the captain."

" The miscreant ! And there was no one at hand to rescue you from his power ?"

" There was not. He has, however, been severely punished for his crimes. But I am exhausted ; by-and-bye I will, if I have strength to do so, give you all the particulars."

"Oh! Rosetta," said Frank, "need I tell you how deep I commiserate with the unexampled sufferings it has been your hard lot to experience? Need I express to you the horror and disgust, the unqualified indignation I feel towards that man whom I dare no longer call my parent? May the Almighty watch over you, and speedily release you, and suffer you to behold your unfortunate parents again."

"In heaven I shall," sighed Rosetta, and the tears flowed fast down her pale cheeks. Frank Trevors was deeply affected, and he gazed at her with the most intense emotion. That they should meet again and under such circumstances seemed scarcely within the range of possibility, and greatly he feared that the unparalleled miseries she had encountered, and the almost utter hopelessness of her present situation, was more than she could have strength to support.

"An hour or two's repose will revive you, Rosetta," he said; "I will retire, and you may rest assured that you will be as safe as if you were once more beneath your own roof. For the present, adieu, and may all good angels guard you."

Inspired with confidence by the words and manner of Frank, Rosetta extended to him her hand, which he pressed with respectful transport to his lips, and then quitted the tent, and walked to some distance in a state of mind it would be a most hopeless task to attempt to pourtray. The event was so remarkable that he could scarcely bring his mind to believe it was not a dream, and most conflicting and bewildering were the thoughts it engendered.

"Poor girl!" he soliloquized, "your's is indeed a most extraordinary and painful destiny. Oh, it seems unjust that Heaven should suffer such miseries to be inflicted on one so amiable, so gentle, so virtuous, so every way lovely. But she will be restored to happiness, and be fully rewarded for all the many severe trials to which she has been so unjustly subjected. Oh, my father, never could I have believed that you would become so heartless a villain. And I have been the indirect cause of all of this. Had I not so abruptly quitted my home, the deadly feeling of revenge against Rosetta and her parents might not have been aroused within his breast, and the poor girl might still have been happy in her native home. It would have been better, far better, had I and Rosetta never met; for then what misery might it have saved us both. But surely I was not to blame in loving one of nature's most perfect works, with a passion as pure and fervent as ever found place in human breast. Rosetta, could I have won your heart, what bliss would have been mine? But that hope is gone for ever. And that villain, Raymond Middleton; how terrible is the punishment he merits for the atrocious crimes he has committed. May the just retribution of Heaven overtake him."

He continued to ruminate in this manner for some time, while his feelings partook of mingled pleasure and anguish. To behold Rosetta again, to be near her, to have the indulgence of her sweet society, was indeed most transporting; but to know that he must never venture to breathe a word of love in her ear, was misery almost insupportable.

He could not at last resist the temptation to look into the tent to see that Rosetta was no worse, for he could not but apprehend the most fatal results from the effects of the trials she had undergone, and her immersion in the water; indeed he marvelled how she had found strength to support such severe sufferings as even the stoutest constitution might be expected to sink under.

He gently drew the canvas aside and looked in. Rosetta was reclining on the rude pallet, and seemed to be wrapped in a tranquil slumber. Her countenance was pale, yet Frank imagined that it had never looked half so lovely or so interesting. He gazed at her a few moments with pity and admiration; and then, fearful that she might awake, he withdrew, and again walked some short distance from the tent, pondering in his mind the remarkable events of the last few hours. Frank had erected his tent in that part of the island which commanded the widest view of the ocean, so that he might have the earliest opportunity of observing any vessel that might chance to appear in sight. He cast an anxious look across the wide expanse, and he sighed deeply as the apparently hopeless situation of himself and Rosetta presented itself with vivid truth to his mind.

"But a few weeks only," he said, "and my provision will be exhausted; and should no help, no succour reach us, we must perish of hunger. Oh, merciful Heaven, avert so horrible a fate!"

The bare idea was too much for him, and he beat his breast with agony. All signs of the late storm had now vanished, and the weather was particularly fine. The ocean was calm and beautiful, but it imparted little or no consolation to the breast of Frank Trevors.

Rosetta slept soundly, for she was completely worn out, but painful dreams haunted her imagination, and in fancy she experienced a repetition of all those horrors from which she had so recently escaped. At length she awoke and gazed around her, in the confusion of the moment not recollecting where she was or what had happened; but the whole truth at last recurred to her memory, and she arose upon her feet, and, walking to the entrance of the tent, looked out. She saw Frank standing with folded arms, and his eyes fixed earnestly upon the tent, at a short distance off, and immediately on beholding her he hastened towards her. He greeted her with respectful solicitude, which Rosetta returned with equal confidence, and he entered the rude tent, and, taking a seat by her side, he gazed at her with looks of the most unbounded admiration.

"Oh, Rosetta," he exclaimed, "so extraordinary are the events of the last few hours, that I can scarcely persuade myself of their reality. Never had I expected to behold you again; but, to meet with you under such circumstances, is indeed surprising and melancholy."

"Mr. Trevors," said our heroine, "I am convinced that you pity me; think of what my sufferings must have been, torn from my home, my beloved parents; persecuted by Raymond Middleton, and surrounded by wretches who exulted in brutality, and were only too ready to perpetrate any dreadful crime. Then the fearful scene of carnage I witnessed on the night of the mutiny of the pirates; subsequently the horrors of the storm, the shipwreck, and now to find myself on this desolate place, without hope, with nothing but the prospect of a miserable death; oh, God! my trials have surely been too severe."

"They have, indeed, Rosetta," said Frank, in accents which plainly shewed the feelings of pity he entertained towards her; "but do not despair, Providence will not abandon you, my poor girl; some assistance will yet arrive, and you will be rescued from your present situation, and restored to your native land, and to those dear relatives from whom you have been so cruelly separated."

"Alas! alas!" sighed Rosetta, wringing her hands piteously, "that can never be; my poor parents can never have survived my loss. It would be madness to suppose they could. What, oh, what have I to hope for? Why should I wish to live with all this weight of misery upon my mind?"

"But you will yet be happy, Rosetta," said Frank, "I am sure you will, notwithstanding your present gloomy prospects. Oh, my poor girl, can you wonder at the torture of my breast, when I think of my guilty father? I feel ashamed and disgusted to acknowledge myself his son, when I reflect that but for him you might even now have been happy in your native home."

"I forgive him, Frank," said the damsel; "and only hope that he may be brought to repentance."

"Amiable girl!" ejaculated Frank Trevors; "you act with more forbearance than he deserves. But for my conduct in so abruptly quitting my home, he would never have acted in the manner he did. Oh, I feel myself all to blame, and you must view me with disgust and abhorrence."

"Do not reproach yourself, Mr. Trevors, I beg," said Rosetta, in gentle accents, and sincerely commiserating in the anguish of mind he was evidently suffering; "I do not, I cannot blame you; Heaven forbid that I should."

"Generous girl!" exclaimed Frank; "this is more than I deserve; but if Heaven permit me, I will indeed endeavour to prove myself deserving of your friendship, your most implicit confidence; to merit and obtain that shall be my future study, my only hope of happiness."

Rosetta, by her looks, convinced him that she placed the utmost reliance in his assurances, and she extended her hand to him in token of her confidence, which he raised respectfully to his lips, and at that moment he felt happier than he had done for many, many months before.

It was fortunate for Rosetta that she felt no more of the ill effects of the extraordinary sufferings to which she had been exposed, and having been persuaded by Frank to partake again of some refreshment, she was greatly revived, and was enabled to make him acquainted with those melancholy particulars of her adventures since they had before met, which he was so anxious to learn. With what deep interest and emotion did he listen to her narrative, and he frequently interrupted her to give expression to the mingled feelings of pity, astonishment, and indignation, that laboured in his breast.

"Good God!" he exclaimed, when she had concluded, "how could you ever find strength to survive these accumulated horrors, poor Rosetta? Oh, what a villain must my father have been to suffer his unreasonable feelings of revenge to carry him to such a length! What had you done that he should seek your destruction?"

"Misguided man," said Rosetta, "I sincerely pity him, although the misery he has caused I fear is irremediable. Oh, Frank, think what must be my insupportable anguish when I reflect upon it, and anticipate the untimely fate which in all probability has befallen my unfortunate and beloved parents."

"Heaven knows how sincerely I pity you, my friend, my sister, for such I will hope to be permitted to call you," said Frank; "but still endeavour to encourage hope. The Almighty will watch over those so dear to you, and give them strength to bear up against their afflictions, dreadful though they be. You will be restored to them, and will yet be happy, though that can never more be my lot."

Rosetta shook her head and sighed deeply, for, alas! it appeared to her that it would be little better than madness to encourage such an idea; and when she reflected upon her present situation, the weight of anguish it inflicted upon her mind was almost too much for human endurance. She sincerely felt for Frank Trevors, whom she could not help viewing with the greatest esteem, which she was convinced he so amply merited; and the respect with which he behaved towards her increased the good opinion she entertained towards him. Frank read her thoughts, and most grateful did he feel for her kindness, and stifled the more powerful emotions that would, in spite of all his efforts, rise in his bosom. Had she but sanctioned his vows, all the troubles that had befallen them might have been avoided; and they would, in all probability, now have been happy; but he knew it was quite useless to encourage any hope of altering the sentiments of Rosetta, and he therefore tried to banish all such thoughts from his mind. From the observations that she had made, he was certain that the maniac youth, Julio, had made the most powerful impression upon her heart, and most bitterly did he regret that they had ever been introduced to each other, for then he might have hoped to have ultimately gained her affections. But it was no use to think of this; fate had decided against him, and he must endeavour to resign himself to it. But to be near her, and to gaze upon those charms which from the earliest youth had so enslaved his heart, was bliss which he had never dared hope to experience, and that he had been the humble instrument of saving her from an untimely death filled his bosom with the most powerful emotions of gratitude and satisfaction.

He now related to Rosetta the adventures he had met with since the time when he had quitted his home, and the damsel listened to him with attention, and expressed her sympathy in the misfortunes it had been his lot to encounter. It was now night, and Rosetta needed rest.

"The night is fine, Rosetta," said Frank, "and I will take up my lodging beneath the umbrageous foliage of the trees; good night, and may all good angels guard you. You have nothing to fear, for no danger can beset you, and Frank Trevors will protect you with a brother's watchful care."

Rosetta by her looks expressed her thanks, and having bade him good night, Frank retired from the tent.

How conflicting and tumultuous were the thoughts which crowded upon the brain of our heroine when she was left to herself, and it was some time before they suffered her to go to sleep. The deep kindness of Frank's behaviour imparted every confidence to her, and filled her bosom with gratitude, and she felt as safe where she was, under his protection, as if she had been beneath the roof of her own once happy native dwelling. At length she sank into a tranquil repose, and for awhile gained a respite from the cares that beset her mind.

Frank, for a time, traversed the island, buried in deep rumination upon the remarkable and almost incredible events which had taken place, and mentally invoking the interposition of Omnipotence to rescue them from the fate which must otherwise in a week or two befall them. The night was beautifully calm, and the moon shone brilliantly upon every object around. At length, tired with every thought, and the fatigue he had undergone, Frank stretched himself upon the earth beneath the shade of the trees, and soon fell asleep.

*   *   *   *   *   *   *

We should become tedious were we to particularise all the thoughts and conversations of our heroine and Frank during the time they remaned on the island. He was unremitting in the respectful attention he paid to her, and she gradually became more tranquil and resigned than could have been reasonably anticipated, considering all the melancholy circumstances of her situation, and the sorrows that had befallen her.

A week vanished, and still without any prospects of their deliverance presenting themselves, and, therefore, the most gloomy ideas haunted their imaginations, especially as their provisions were now getting very short, and a frightful death of starvation stared them in the face. Constantly were their prayers offered up to Heaven for mercy, and Rosetta became almost deaf to that consolation which her companion in misfortune attempted to impart to her; in fact, so completely hopeless was their situation, that he was at a loss for argument, and could only leave their future destiny in the hands of Providence, who he could not bring his mind to believe would altogether abandon them.

Rosetta would frequently accompany him in his rambles about the island; and for hours together they would strain their eyes across the vast ocean in the hope of seeing some vessel; but for some days they were doomed to experience nothing but disappointment, and they returned to their tent with minds oppressed with despair.

The eighth day had arrived since Rosetta had been rescued from a watery grave, and still nothing occurred to raise their spirits, but on the contrary, hope seemed, if possible, still farther removed from them. They had no more food left than would last them for a couple of days, and then they could no longer struggle against their cruel fate.

"Alas!" sighed Rosetta, "better would it have been for me had I perished in the storm than to die of hunger in this lonely place. Oh! how dreadful is the thought!"

"God help us!" ejaculated Frank; "but surely we shall not be abandoned to so horrible a destiny. For myself I care not, but to see you thus suffer, Rosetta, wrings my very heart."

"Father of mercy, if it be thy will, I must not murmur," cried our heroine, making a powerful effort at firmness and resignation.

The day was far advanced, and they were about to return to the tent, when Frank, once more casting a wishful glance across the ocean, suddenly gave utterance to an exclamation of mingled delight and astonishment, and Rosetta following the direction of his eyes, beheld the tall shadow of what appeared to be a vessel on the distant horizon, and which seemed to be sailing before the wind towards the island. Rosetta clasped her hands together, and involuntarily sank on her knees, while her bosom heaved with the most powerful feelings of emotion.

"The Almighty has heard our prayers, Rosetta," said Frank, in accents of joy; "and probably our deliverance is at hand. Should this ship approach the island we shall be saved."

"Alas!" sighed Rosetta, "the hopes raised in my bosom were but temporary, and now a dismal foreboding comes over me, which I find it impossible to subdue."

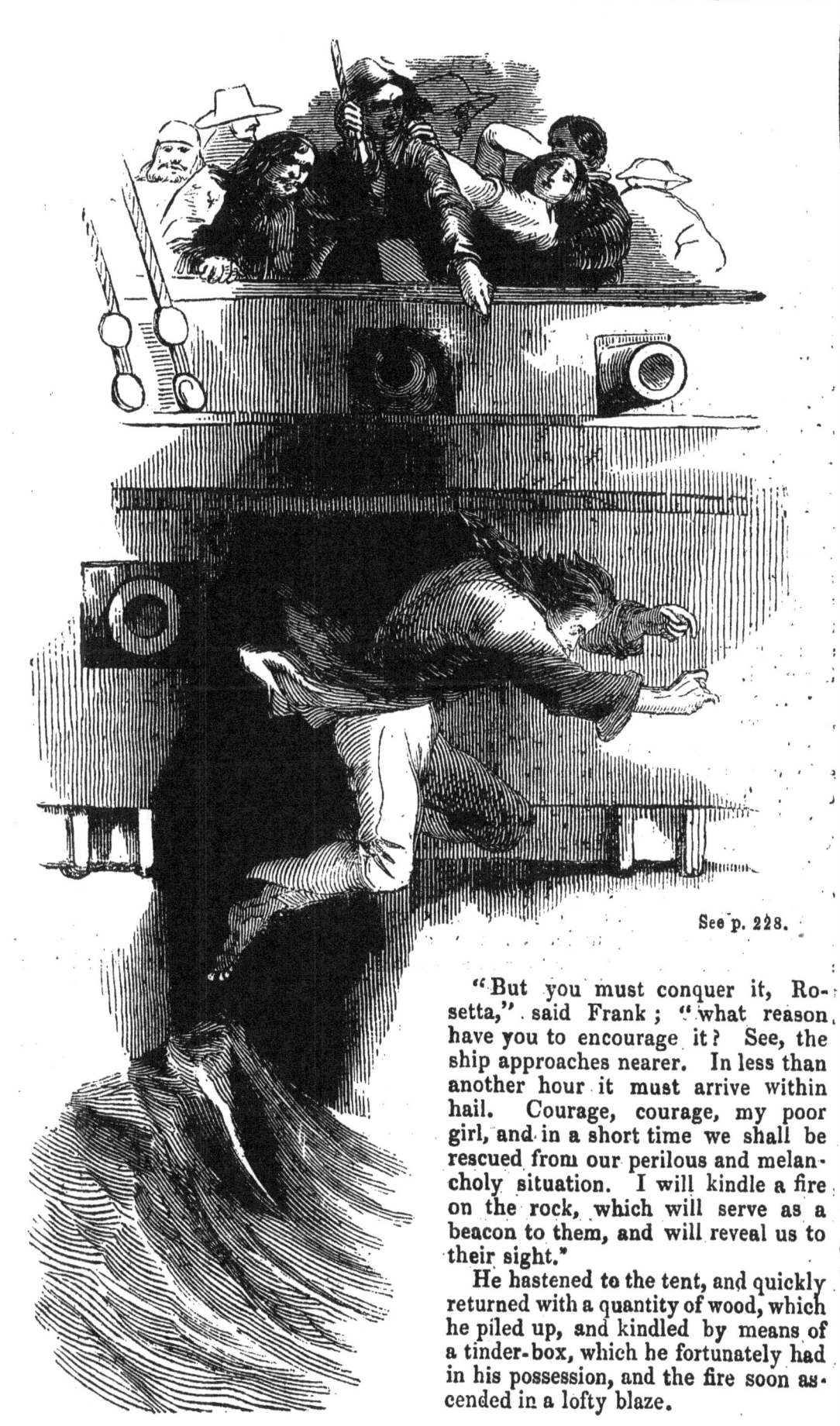

See p. 228.

"But you must conquer it, Rosetta," said Frank; "what reason have you to encourage it? See, the ship approaches nearer. In less than another hour it must arrive within hail. Courage, courage, my poor girl, and in a short time we shall be rescued from our perilous and melancholy situation. I will kindle a fire on the rock, which will serve as a beacon to them, and will reveal us to their sight."

He hastened to the tent, and quickly returned with a quantity of wood, which he piled up, and kindled by means of a tinder-box, which he fortunately had in his possession, and the fire soon ascended in a lofty blaze.

With streaming eyes they continued to watch the approaching ship, which gradually became more distinct. It seemed to be of very large size, was painted entirely white, and, as the declining rays of the sun reflected upon it, it had a truly strange and almost ghastly appearance.

Rosetta trembled, and the longer that her companion gazed at it, the less sanguine became his hopes, and an unaccountable feeling of dread came over him. But still he could not remove his eyes from the ship, and awaited its approach with the greatest anxiety.

"Surely I have seen that vessel, or one very much resembling it before," said Frank ; "Heaven send that those on board of it may be disposed to aid us."

"How its white sails glisten in the sunbeams," said Rosetta ; "it looks like some ghastly phantom of the deep rather than an honest vessel. See, with what lightning velocity it bounds across the billows, as though it bade defiance to their power. Oh, Frank, my heart misgives me."

"Nay, Rosetta," expostulated Frank, "surely there is no necessity for these apprehensions."

"Ah ! see, it approaches nearer and nearer, until we may perceive the shadows of men moving upon the deck !" exclaimed our heroine, clutching the arm of Frank. "And now behold, oh, God ! that flag, that terrible black flag, with those ghastly emblems upon it.   Horror ! horror ! this, this must be the Death Ship !"

Frank fixed an eager and terrified look upon the flag, which was hoisted at the mast head, and with a feeling of horror he was convinced that the surmises of Rosetta were correct. It would be impossible to describe his emotions, and for a moment or two he was unable to utter a syllable. Rosetta still clung to him, and trembled so violently, that had it not been for his support she must have sunk to the earth, for she saw plainly enough that his opinion coincided with her own, and all the horrors of the destiny that seemed to be in store for them, rushed vividly to her mind.

"Heaven preserve us !" said Frank, "for this assuredly is that terrible and mysterious vessel."

"Gracious God ! we are lost !" cried the distracted Rosetta ; "and see ! the fatal ship comes nearer and nearer. We may hear the shouts of the awful beings on board. They have observed us ; oh, whither can we fly? how escape them ?"

"Be firm, my poor girl," said Frank ; "they cannot, surely will not harm us. What motives can they have for doing so ?"

The Death Ship, for such it was, had now approached so near the island, that our heroine and Frank could plainly perceive a number of strange looking forms moving about its deck and rigging ; and they could hear the loud shouts they gave utterance to, which, under all the circumstances, sounded perfectly supernatural. The ship now hove to, and a boat being launched, several men got into it, and made towards the island. Rosetta uttered a cry of terror, and clung more frantically to Frank than before.

CHAPTER XX.

THE HORRORS OF THE DEATH SHIP.—THE FEARFUL DOOM OF FRANK TREVORS.

Scarcely knowing what he did, Frank took the hand of his trembling companion, and hurried her towards the tent, where he awaited the result of this adventure in a state of the greatest agitation. But a few moments, and they heard the voices of the men, as they ascended to the island.

"They come, they come, oh, God !" gasped Rosetta, with ghastly looks ; "we are lost ! death would not be half so terrible as this."

She had scarcely given utterance to these words when the canvass of the tent was pulled aside, and four of the most ferocious looking men that the imagination could conceive, and armed with swords and pistols, entered. Their features seemed scarcely human, and their general expression was enough to strike even the stoutest heart with terror.

" Ah! by all the infernal host," cried one of the villains, as he fixed his black and savage looking eyes upon the pale countenance of the terrified Rosetta, " a rare prize this for the captain of the Death Ship. Seize her, comrades, and on board with her ; I suppose, too, that we had better not leave this fellow behind ; we may, perhaps, find him of use to us, so away with him !"

" Use no violence, I beg of you," said Frank, interposing between them and Rosetta. " If you are indeed men, you will not harm two unfortunate beings, but suffer us to remain here until Providence may think proper to release us."

" Hold your tongue, you lubberly cur," said the pirate ; " the daring crew of the Death Ship are not accustomed to listen to such palaver as that. Chance has thrown you in our way, and those who once fall into our power, are never more suffered to escape from it. To the ship !"

" Oh, mercy! mercy !" shrieked Rosetta, as the ruffians seized her and Frank ; but, alas ! how useless were her supplications ; with rude and fiendish mockery they raised her in their arms, and, overpowered by the horror of her feelings, she became insensible.

She was aroused by a loud tumult, and, looking up, the novelty of the scene which presented itself to her eyes, filled her with the utmost astonishment, confusion, and terror. She was on the deck of the pirate-vessel, the so much dreaded and talked-of Death Ship, and surrounded by a number of the most singular-looking, and most ferocious beings, whose appearance was anything but human. The clothes they wore were of a sable hue, and each on his breast wore the same ghastly emblems of death as were inscribed upon the flag. In the centre of these, and immediately before her, stood the tall figure of a man, about forty years of age, and, as Rosetta fixed her eyes upon his countenance, she uttered a scream of astonishment and terror, when she recognised the exact resemblance of the portrait of Hugh Clifton, and remembered the strange emotion which poor Julio had evinced on beholding it. Frank Trevors, who was also upon the deck, immediately rushed towards her ; but he was fiercely thrust aside by the captain of the pirate-ship, and immediately afterwards seized by two of the other ruffians on board.

" Stand back, presumptuous dog !" cried the captain, " or you may suffer severely for your boldness. The girl is now mine, and the captain of the Death Ship welcomes his future mistress to his ocean palace."

" Merciful God ! protect me from these monsters !" cried Rosetta, as she fixed her eyes upon that terrific being, whose deeds seemed to be those of one who possessed supernatural power. " Horror !—horror !—horror ! for what fate am I reserved ? Oh, that I had perished in the storm, rather than have fallen into the power of these miscreant murderers. Oh, Julio ——"

" Julio !" interrupted the pirate-captain, with a look of amazement ; " that name. Did then the idiot boy escape, after he plunged into the deep? The vessel was destroyed by the flames, and, therefore, he could not escape that way. Speak, girl ; what Julio is it of whom you have spoken ?"

" Oh, spare her feelings, I implore you," said the deeply-agitated Frank Trevors ; " the boy of whom she speaks is a wretched maniac, who was saved from an untimely death by her father, about three years since, when your vessel made its fatal appearance on the coast of Cornwall."

" Ah! by the spirit of Hugh Clifton, the ocean doomed !" exclaimed the pirate-captain, " it is he !"

" Gracious Heaven !" exclaimed Rosetta, as the observations of the maniac youth, when he saw the portrait rushed to her memory ; " the guilty father of Julio."

" Girl, beware what you say," remarked the terrible captain of the Death Ship, with a threatening look ; " I am not the father of the boy, but he is the son of her who was my bride, by a man whom I detest, and whose blood I afterwards shed to gratify my revenge. In me you behold the son of Hugh Clifton by a second wife ; I am he whose very name has spread terror throughout the world. Who shall dare oppose the captain of the bark of death, over which the spirit of that man who formerly commanded it still hovers, and enables its daring crew to perform almost supernatural wonders ?"

"Murderer !" groaned Rosetta, turning away from the fearful man with a shudder ; but the secret concerning Julio was now partly revealed, and she felt her mind relieved from a weight of terror, notwithstanding her situation, to find that he was not, indeed, the father of that unfortunate youth.

" I thank my lucky stars that have placed so fair a prize in my power," said the pirate ; "henceforth you must view Redmond Clifton as your future lord and master, my beauteous damsel, and ———"

"Powers of mercy, release me by death from so hideous a fate !" interrupted Rosetta, her whole frame convulsed with terror.

" Away with her to one of the cabins below," said Redmond ; " to-morrow I shall commence my sweet courtship to my future bride."

" Oh ! spare her, spare her ! I beseech you, if you are indeed a man, which your atrocious deeds would almost temp. me to believe you are not," cried Frank ; " can you behold that gentle, helpless girl, without some feeling of pity ?"

" Bold dog !" fiercely exclaimed the pirate ; " who are you that thus presumes to talk to the captain of the Death Ship ? Take that, ye swab, and learn better manners for the future."

With these words Redmond struck him a violent blow with his clenched fist, which nearly felled him on the deck. The broad chest of Frank Trevors heaved with uncontrollable indignation, and he burst from the grasp of those who held him.

" Villain !" he cried, as he rushed on the captain ; " though I die a thousand deaths, I will resent this."

But before he could accomplish his intention, he was again seized by two or three of the ruffians, and several pistols were levelled at his head.

" Daring hound !" exclaimed Redmond ; " will you venture to show your teeth ? What should be the punishment of the rascal who would strike your captain ?"

" Death, death to the dog !" shouted the villains in a breath.

" Ay, string him up to the yard-arm !" commanded the captain ; and immediately the unfortunate young man was seized, and the pirates prepared to put the brutal order into execution.

" Oh ! mercy, mercy !" screamed our heroine, rushing forward, and sinking on her knees before Redmond ; " do not take his life ! you cannot be so monstrous as to put your threats into execution."

" Poor Rosetta," said Frank, in melancholy accents ; " do not appeal to these wretches, for it is all in vain. Farewell for ever, and may Heaven preserve you from the awful fate with which you are now threatened, when I am no more. But, monsters, surely you will not hang me like a dog in the presence of this poor girl ? My dying curse be upon ye all for this fiendish deed."

" Toss the lubber overboard," commanded Redmond ; " if he would prefer that death."

" Oh ! no, no, no !" screamed Rosetta, in the most frantic accents ; " spare him, this time spare him, and ———"

The murderers were deaf to her supplications, and before she could finish the sentence, they had raised poor Frank in their arms, and the next moment plunged him into the ocean. She uttered one piercing scream, as she heard the hollow splash of his body in the water ; her brain reeled, and she became unconscious of all around her. The pirate captain raised her in his arms, and gazed at her with looks of admiration.

" That headstrong boy was a lover of hers, I suppose," he observed ; " however, he has paid for his daring."

" He is still struggling with the waves yonder, captain," said one of the crew ; " he seems to be an expert swimmer, but it is not likely that he can save himself."

" Let the poor devil take his chance," said Redmond ; " for it is a very poor one. Ah ! he strikes out boldly, and should he be able to reach the rocks yonder, he may still prolong his life for a short time longer."

Frank Trevors was, indeed, struggling desperately against his fate, but in a few minutes the pirates lost sight of him, and the Death Ship proceeded on its way. Rosetta having been conveyed to a cabin by the captain, where he tried every means to restore her to her senses, but for some time without effect.

CHAPTER XXI.

THE GRIEF OF MR. AND MRS. BELFORD.—ATTEMPTED SUICIDE OF JULIO.—HIS SEIZURE BY MARTIN TREVORS.—HIS RESCUE FROM THE SECRET CAVERN.

WE must now return to the unhappy parents of Rosetta, whose sufferings at the severe bereavement they had experienced, were more intense than can readily be imagined. They were both for some weeks quite inconsolable, and it was quite evident they had received a shock which must speedily bring them to their graves, unless their daughter should be restored to them, of which at present, there seemed not to be the most remote chance.

In vain were all the endeavours of the officers of the law to discover Martin Trevors, and they could not form the least conjecture as to the place where he was concealed; although it was generally believed that he had quitted the country with his unfortunate victim, and it was feared that he would be able to set detection at defiance.

Michael and his wife had taken a small house near the residence of Mr. Hayward, who was almost a constant visitor to them, and did all he could to impart to them that consolation which they so much needed under their afflictions.

Weeks and months rolled away, and still without anything occurring that was at all calculated to banish their despair, and they now gave up their poor Rosetta as lost to them for ever, and formed the most dreadful conjectures as to the fate which had befallen her.

"Oh, what a monster must Martin Trevors have been," Michael would sigh, "thus at one fell blow to crush the happiness of two poor old people, who never wilfully injured him, but who, on the contrary, ever evinced towards him the most warm and disinterested friendship. A fearful retribution must and will, sooner or later, overtake him, for this inhuman deed; but, alas! he has blighted all our hopes for ever."

"He has, cruel, heartless man," said Mrs. Belford. "Oh, my poor child, little did I think that you would ever have been so cruelly snatched from us. It would be a mercy, my husband, if we were both now in our silent and peaceful graves."

Thus would the poor old people lament, until they were completely exhausted with the violence of their grief, and gained a short respite in temporary unconsciousness.

Poor Julio, too, how truly more wretched did he every day become, and how piteous were the wild and incoherent lamentations at the loss of "his pretty sister," he hourly gave utterance to. Frequently something like a gleam of reason would flash across his brain, and then his sufferings would become the more intense. Mr. Belford and his wife now looked upon the poor afflicted youth with a greater degree of melancholy interest than they had done before, for the sorrow he felt at the loss of Rosetta, and they lavished upon him the same affectionate attention as if he had been their own son; but, even amidst the sterner misfortunes of their fate, they often reflected with dismal forebodings upon what would become of the unhappy, bereaved youth, should anything happen to them, left alone as he might then be said to be in the world. He would sit for hours staring upon vacancy, and giving vent to the most impressive and pathetic exclamations; then he would suddenly start from his seat and leave the room, saying, that he would search the house for poor Rosetta, who he knew was only concealed from him in one of the apartments by her parents; and, when he had made his fruitless search he would return, and throwing himself on a seat, sit and weep as though his very heart would break.

Several more weeks elapsed, and still all the endeavours to discover the villain,

Martin Trevors, or to ascertain what had become of Rosetta, were fruitless, and it was with the greatest difficulty only that Michael and his wife were enabled to support themselves under such a weight of unparalleled afflictions. Julio remained in the same condition, and the sufferings of them all excited the deepest sympathy in the bosoms of every one who knew them. Sir Horace Middleton kept himself strictly confined to the old manor; and, had it not been for the information of Simon, who was seen occasionally, it would have been imagined that he had left the neighbourhood altogether; but the sordid old baronet had rendered himself so hateful that it was cared little what became of him. There were many who were anxious to fathom the mystery of his actions, fer it was generally believed that he had not accumulated all the immense wealth he was supposed to possess by fair means. One morning, about this period, Michael and his wife were surprised to find that Julio did not make his appearance to breakfast at the usual hour, and, after waiting a few minutes longer, Mr. Belford, fearing that something had happened to him, or that he was ill, went to his chamber, in order that he might ascertain the truth.

He found the room door standing wide open, and, entering it, saw that Julio was not there. He now became somewhat alarmed, and searched hurriedly the other parts of the house, and in the garden, but all to no purpose; it was evident that the maniac youth had left the place. He returned to the apartment in which he had left his wife, and found that Mr. Hayward had just arrived to pay them his customary morning visit. He informed them of the disappearance of Julio, and Hayward was as much astonished and alarmed as themselves.

"Alas!" ejaculated Mrs. Belford, "the poor lad has surely been driven, by despair, to commit some rash act, and we shall be entirely left alone. Oh, God! these trials are more, much more than human nature can support."

"Do not give way to unnecessary apprehension, Mrs. Belford," said Hayward; "probably the poor youth has only been tempted by the fineness of the morning to ramble forth into the green fields, or by the seaside."

"And is it not dangerous for him to be left alone, and to follow the dictates of his own wild will?" said Mrs. Belford.

"I confess that it is," answered Mr. Hayward; "but still I trust that no harm has befallen him on this occasion. Come, Michael, let us go in search of him, and I have no doubt that we shall soon discover him."

Mr. Belford endeavoured to impart some degree of comfort and hope to his wife, and then, taking his hat and stick, he accompanied Mr. Hayward from the house.

They made their way towards the cliffs, knowing that had ever been the favourite haunt of the maniac youth, and they had not proceeded far, when they beheld Gerald Wetherby and two or three other men approaching, and carrying what appeared to be the lifeless, or insensible form of a human being, in their arms.

A feeling of the greatest dread came over them both, and they hurried towards them, and their emotion was greatly increased when they perceived that it was Julio, pale and inanimate, and his clothes dripping with wet, as though he had recently been immersed in the water.

"Does he still live?" demanded Michael, in a voice of the deepest agitation, as he placed his hand upon the heart of the insensible youth, to ascertain whether or not it still throbbed.

"He does," answered Gerald; "but quick, let us immediately to your house, where I will explain everything. There is not a moment to be lost. I have sent for the doctor, and he will probably have reached your house by the time we arrive there."

Michael Belford cast one look of pity and anguish at the pale face of Julio, and then offered no further remark, but suffered them to hurry on their way to his dwelling with their insensible burden.

In a few minutes they arrived there, and the horror and alarm of Mrs. Belford, when she beheld the deplorable condition of the unfortunate youth, may be better imagined than described. They laid his insensible form upon a couch, and by that time the doctor had arrived at the house, and immediately proceeded to apply all the remedies to restore animation, that his skill suggested to him.

"Oh, how did this happen?" asked the old woman. "Who has made this awful attempt upon the poor boy's life?"

"No one but himself, Mrs. Belford," answered Gerald Wetherby. "I and my companions were out in our fishing-smacks, when we saw him wandering wildly upon the cliffs, and the moment afterwards he plunged into the sea; but we succeeded in rescuing him ere he had sunk for ever."

"Poor lad—poor lad!" said Michael; "alas! I fear that some melancholy fate will yet befall him."

After trying hard for nearly an hour, the doctor succeeded in restoring Julio partly to animation, and he then ordered him to be placed immediately in a warm bed, where every attention was paid to him, and, in the course of another hour, he was so far recovered as to be able to speak. He looked vacantly around upon Michael and his wife, who were in attendance upon him, and exclaimed,—

"Still alive—still alive! Oh, why was I not permitted to join my mother and poor Rosetta in the boundless deep? Let me hasten from hence, and seek repose in my ocean grave! Mother! Rosetta! I hear your voices calling upon me, and summoning me to ye. And shall I not obey? Oh, let me go—poor Julio has no business here."

We need not say how deeply Michael and his wife were affected by the words of Julio; but they did all they could to pacify him, and at length their efforts were crowned with some degree of success, and the medical man pronounced him out of danger, and for the present took his leave.

For several days, however, Julio continued in a very weak state, and was unable to leave his bed, and no change for the better had taken place in his reason; but of that ever being restored to him, Mr. and Mrs. Belford entertained little or no hopes. The only wonder was that, under such a weight of anxiety and affliction, they could themselves retain their senses. It was, however, the will of Providence, and events were on the eve of taking place, which they little anticipated.

In about a week after the attempted suicide of the maniac, he had so far recovered as to be able to quit his chamber; but Michael never suffered him to quit his sight, lest he should make another attempt upon his life, but did all he could to reconcile him to his situation, frequently taking him out, in order to afford him the benefit of the air, and change of scene.

One afternoon they had somewhat extended their walk, and it was twilight before they thought of returning home. By the time they had arrived to within half a mile of their dwelling, it was quite dark, and Michael, taking the arm of Julio, increased his speed, thinking that his wife would begin to feel uneasy at their protracted absence; but they had not advanced much further on their way, when, all at once, they were startled by a shrill whistle, not far from them, and the next instant they were surrounded by four or five men, armed and masked, and before Michael had the least opportunity to offer any resistence, he was felled to the earth by a heavy blow from the hilt of a sword, and became insensible. Julio was immediately seized by two of the ruffians, and uttering an exclamation of terror, he became insensible.

"Ah! the boy is now securely mine!" said one of the fellows. "Quick! quick! to the Manor-house. The coast is clear, and, if we delay not, we may reach there in safety. It was Martin Trevors who thus spoke; yes, it was he who was the author of this diabolical plot, and one of the most powerful of the miscreants whom he had hired to assist him, having raised the unconscious youth in his arms, they made their way from the spot with all the precipitation they could.

No one appeared to obstruct their progress, and they soon arrived at the Manor-house, and having proceeded round to the private entrance, Martin Trevors took the insensible form of Julio, and dismissed his companions, promising to meet them on the following night at a certain place. He then opened the door with a key, which he had secured, and, stealing up the staircase, entered the apartment in which the guilty Sir Horace Middleton was seated, and placing the youth upon a sofa, turned towards the wretched baronet with a look of triumph.

Had the ghastly phantoms of his unfortunate victims at that moment arisen from their graves to confront him, Sir Horace Middleton could not have evinced more horror than he did when he beheld Julio.

"Christ, save me!" he exclaimed; "take away that form from my sight. Trevors! Trevors! the fiends of hell could not inflict more tortures upon me than you do at present. Why, have you brought him hither? Oh! horror! horror!"

"Ha! ha! ha!" laughed the villain, scornfully; "you possess the most indomitable courage, Sir Horace Middleton, when you tremble at the sight of an idiot, and that idiot your own grandson."

"My grandson!"

"Yes; do you not recognise his features?" said Martin Trevors. "This is undoubtedly the son of Eveline Clifton, your daughter, who was murdered on board the Death Ship, with which you have been so many years connected."

"Hold! hold!" groaned the conscience-stricken Sir Horace, "or you will drive me to madness. What is your intention with that unfortunate boy?"

"To keep him here a prisoner while it answers my purpose, and to convince myself whether his insanity is real, or assumed.'

"And must I ever have him before my eyes? Oh! Martin Trevors, why do you delight to torture me?"

"Because, as I have often before told you, it is food for my revenge. However, I will convey this youth to another room, where your worthy servants must attend to his recovery; and then I will return to you, for, I feel inclined this night to explain to you more than I have hitherto done, in order that you may dread me the more, and see the utter folly and danger of attempting any opposition to my will."

"Fearful man," uttered the trembling Sir Horace, "I already know you too well, and would freely give half that I possess to release myself from your power."

"No doubt you would," returned Trevors, sarcastically; "but I am not going to agree to any such terms. Enough for the present; I will shortly return, when I shall have a tale to repeat to you which probably may not be altogether unfamiliar to your ears."

Sir Horace Middleton looked at him aghast, and trembled in every limb, and Trevors, raising the still insensible form of Julio, quitted the chamber.

"Madness! horror!" exclaimed the baronet, when he was gone; "the miscreant is bent on my destruction; I see it plain enough, and conscience tells me that the crisis of my fate is rapidly approaching."

He was interrupted by the return of Martin, who, taking a chair, gazed at him for a few moments in silence, and with looks of the most deadly malice. The wretched old man shrank appalled from his glances, but could not utter a word.

"Horace Middleton," said Trevors, at length, "I have, on a former occasion, reminded you of the events of five-and-thirty, or six-and-thirty years ago, when you were an *honest* clerk in the office of Mr. Luttrel, and Leonard Gresham was your fellow servant."

"Yes, yes; oh! torture!" groaned Sir Horace.

"Your *honesty* was well rewarded," continued Martin Trevors; "you became Mr. Luttrel's partner, and amassed wealth, but that was not enough for your soaring ambition, notwithstanding you had contrived to be promoted to a baronetcy. Your partner died rather suddenly, and you were for some time inconsolable for his loss."

"Are you a fiend in human shape, that you would thus rake up that which I would wish to be buried for ever in oblivion?" exclaimed Sir Horace, in a hoarse voice, and with blood-shot eyes."

"Nay, Horace Middleton, you surely cannot wish to bury in oblivion

the memory of your *dear friend;* of course you could not help the suddenness of his death. However, you consoled yourself for his loss, by making his daughter, his only child, your wife a few months after, and becoming the possessor of the whole of his fortune, in addition to that which you had yourself accumulated. Oh, she was a most lovely creature was Agnes Luttrel, at the time you married her; and beautiful, indeed, must she have looked in her bridal dress, that dress you have preserved with so much care in the cedar-chest, in the old vaults, eh?"

Sir Horace clutched his arm with a convulsive grasp, and glared in his countenance with an expression that was scarcely human. Big drops of agony started to his forehead; his chest heaved; his thin, withered lips quivered; but he could not give utterance to a syllable, and, sinking back in his seat, he groaned heavily.

Martin Trevors marked his emotion with unnatural satisfaction, and, after a brief pause, he resumed,—

"In due time, your beauteous wife presented you with a daughter, who was named Eveline."

Again Sir Horace groaned, and swayed his body to and fro in a state of distraction.

"Some years passed away," Martin Trevors went on to say; "and I suppose you was very happy with an amiable wife, a lovely child, an affluent fortune, and nothing to reproach your conscience with. Suddenly you became acquainted with a certain individual, called Richard Weldon, and with whom you soon entered into certain secret and extensive transactions, which bound you to him in a manner which you could not escape from. He had at that time a son by a second wife, about twelve years old. Have you any recollection of these facts, Sir Horace Middleton?"

"For mercy's sake, forbear, Trevors," gasped forth the baronet; "your words drive my very soul to madness!"

"Nevertheless, I must proceed with my story, and in which you are so deeply interested, in my own way," returned Martin, coolly. "Richard Weldon was supposed to be a fair trader, and a merchant of substance, and no one suspected that he was no other than the notorious Hugh Clifton, the captain of that pirate-vessel, which, from the daring and almost supernatural exploits of its inhuman crew, had gained the name of *The Death Ship*, and was at that time, as it is now, the terror of the sea. Your avarice, your love of gold, no matter how obtained, placed you in his power. You became his partner, his guest, his secret spy; yes, the wealthy Sir Horace Middleton became the instrument, the tool, the abettor of the pirate-captain, and it was through your means that he became possessed of that valuable information that threw so many rich prizes in his power. Deny this if you can, Sir Horace."

"Alas! I cannot," sighed the agonized old man; "oh, what a wretch have I been!"

"Hugh Clifton, as I have before said, had got you completely in his power, and had you dared to disobey his will, the gallows would soon have been your portion. So great was the power he held over you, that he bound you by a terrible oath, and on the pain of destruction, to unite your daughter to his son Redmond Clifton, when they should arrive at a proper age, and you yielded; they were betrothed, and, in order the better to secure you, he compelled you with your wife and child to leave England, and to join him in one of the islands of the West Indies. You did so in a merchant ship, taking with you the bulk of your fortune. Some months passed away, and your wife had no suspicion of your infamous connexion; neither did she suspect the real character of Hugh Clifton, who frequently visited you in disguise. I now come to the more tragic part of my narrative."

"Horror! horror! I shall choke with agony!" ejaculated Sir Horace.

"The beauty of your wife had inflamed the passions of Hugh Clifton, and he dared to make advances towards her, which she repulsed with horror and disgust. She made you acquainted with it, and 'tis true you reproached him; but he stoutly denied the truth of her assertions, and goaded on by feelings of revenge, he, in return, accused her of adultery, and you, blind infatuated fool as you was, believed him. Goaded on by his taunts and threats, you determined to have her life, ay, the life of her whose only fault was in loving a wretch like you too fondly; and you accomplished your bloodly and inhuman design."

"Cease! cease! hear you not that dismal groan?"

"Bah! but you shall hear me out. You shortly afterwards left home on a pretence of having some business to transact in a distant part of the island, which would detain you for a few days; but you only secreted yourself in the neighbourhood, and watched your opportunity to put your hellish design into execution. A few evenings afterwards, the unfortunate Agnes was found barbarously murdered in a wood not far from your dwelling. Whose hand was it that plunged the knife in her breast? It was yours, Horace Middleton, and you cannot, dare not deny, the hideous crime!"

Sir Horace started convulsively from his chair, and gazed at Martin Trevors with the livid aspect of a corpse; but his tongue clave to the pallet of his mouth, and he could not give utterance to the dreadful feelings that agitated his guilty breast. Martin Trevors exulted more than ever in his misery, and he again resumed.

"Two days after the horrid deed, you returned home, and pretended to be nearly distracted at the untimely fate of your wife. Hugh Clifton had now got you more than ever in his power, and he did not fail to take advantage of it. Some five years passed away in a manner you best know, and Hugh Clifton then insisted that you should complete the compact you had both formerly entered into, and bestow your daughter upon his son, Redmond. But Eveline had in the meantime placed her affections upon another, a young captain of a merchant vessel, and finding that she could not obtain your consent, she eloped with him, and became his wife. The fruits of that marriage was the boy Julio, and a girl who has been some years dead. But you did not behold your daughter for more than two years after, during which time Hugh Clifton died, making you in his dying moments sign a bond in your own blood, by which you promised to compel Eveline to become the bride of Redmond, at all hazards, if ever you should discover her, and to make him your heir, although at that time you had taken charge of your nephew, Raymond Middleton, who was then about seven years, and under the care of a confidential person in England. You dared not disobey, for the command of the Death Ship had now devolved upon Redmond Clifton, who was acquainted with all your secrets, and held you as much in his power as his father had done. On your daughter's return to you, she having lost her husband at sea, you received her with much apparent kindness and forgiveness, but after a few weeks you again presented Redmond Clifton to her, and urged her to become his wife. She yielded to your intreaties, not knowing the real character of Redmond, and became the pirate's bride, the bride of her husband's murderer; for I can prove that Captain Dashwood, your daughter's first husband, perished by his hand, in an engagement which the unfortunate vessel he commanded had with the pirates."

Once more the old man groaned, and beat his breast.

"I have not done yet," continued Trevors; "your daughter and her children were conveyed on board the Death Ship, you refusing to accompany her, but leaving her to the mercy of the wretch to whom her destiny was united. You were now permitted to return to England, on the condition that you should still continue your connexion with the Death Ship, and every five years contributing a large sum of money in proof of your good faith, and I was in secret deputed to follow in the same vessel, to ascertain where you went to, and to be the future spy upon your actions. I need not tell you how faithfully I have fulfilled my task; I need not mention to you how you have been compelled to keep your oath from the fear of being denounced, and the horror of your feelings whenever the Death Ship has made its appearance on this coast, for your fears ever conjured up on these occasions the grim spectre of Hugh Clifton, pointing to the bleeding body of your murdered wife, and your coward soul quailed beneath the power of its own disordered imagination."

"O, Trevors," gasped forth Sir Horace; "it was no imagination; I have ever seen them on those dreadful occasions, and then that awful cry which ever rings upon the air, and is heard by all around. Never, never, did I expect to hear this horrible story repeated to me."

"I have not quite done yet," said Martin.

"Oh, spare my feelings, Trevors," said the wretched old man; "already have you harrowed them up sufficiently by this dreadful recital."

"You acknowledge the truth of it then?"

"I do, I do; oh, l have, indeed, been a villain," replied Sir Horace, with a shudder, and scarcely daring to look up lest he should encounter the ghastly phantoms of his murdered victims.

"Hear me out, Sir Horace Middleton," said his tormentor; "you must know the full extent of the crime and misery caused by your guilt. What years of brutal suffering did your daughter, the unfortunate Eveline, endure, with that man to whom her fate was linked! She was the pirate's bride, and keenly did she feel the horrors and the degradation of her situation; but she bore it all with the gentle forbearance of her nature, and seldom even murmured at the cruelties that were inflicted upon her and her son; for Redmond Clifton, having gratified his sensual passions, treated his helpless victim with the most monstrous barbarity. At length, nature could support no more, she reproached him bitterly for his cowardly ruffianism, and he, wrought up to a pitch of fury, delivered her to the murderous hands of his crew; a dozen swords were immediately buried in her breast, in spite of the shrieks and supplications of her child, and then her bleeding and mangled body was thrown into the deep. From that dreadful moment the senses of Julio fled, and on the night of the destruction of the vessel off this coast by the Death Ship, he plunged into the ocean, but was rescued by Michael Belford. All this is the fruit of your avarice and villany, Sir Horace Middleton, and as a proof of it, whenever occasion may require, I have secured the boy. Now, old man, what think you of Martin Trevors?"

"Oh, torture, torture, most insupportable!" groaned the guilty baronet, and glaring upon Martin Trevors with blood-shot eyes.

"You feel it, do you?" said Trevors, with a malicious grin; "I triumph! This is rare food for my revenge."

"And who are you, that possess such knowledge of my guilty history?" said Sir Horace; "even after all the years we have unfortunately been connected together, I have been unable to penetrate your real character. Fearful man, you are not what you seem to be."

"I am not, indeed."

"Tell me, who are you, that I may know the full extent of the fear I have a right to entertain towards you?"

"Yes, you shall know me, Sir Horace Middleton, that you may see how much reason I have to hate you. Look well upon me; has time so changed my features that you still can have no recollection of them? They should strike terror into your guilty breast. I am he whose prospects in life you blighted for ever, and made me the guilty wretch l am. l am the victim of your base falsehood, unjustly punished on your evidence; look at me, I say, again, Horace Middleton, and tremble, for in me you behold him who was once known by the name of Leonard Gresham."

"Leonard Gresham!" repeated the old man, in a hoarse voice, and fixing his eyes wildly upon him. "Is it possible?"

"Ay, and it is true. Oh, you little thought how fearfully your villany would one day recoil upon yourself; that your very life would be at the mercy of him you had so basely injured."

"Oh, Leonard!" ejaculated Sir Horace, sinking on his knees at his feet; "I acknowledge the great injustice I did towards you, but many, many years have elapsed since then, and I have been most severely punished. Forgive me, l implore you; I have the means, and am ready to make you every atonement. Let us henceforth be friends, and ——"

"Friends!" fiercely interrupted Leonard Gresham, for such we must henceforth call him; "hated, despicable, old reptile, think you that my revenge can be so easily appeased? I hold you in my power; all that you possess I can make mine; and I will not rest until I have seen you swing at the gallows like a dog! But the time is not come yet. I have more torture in store for you, and will therefore spare your miserable life yet a little longer! Oh, this is glorious, to see the man, through whose guilty machinations I unjustly suffered, crouching at my feet for mercy like a slave!"

" Mercy! mercy! Leonard Gresham ; I am an old man."

" Mercy !" repeated Leonard, with a furious look ; " yes, such is the mercy I show you, dog !" and he struck the feeble old man a violent blow in the face with his clenched fist, which felled him insensible on the floor.

Leonard gazed at him for a few moments with the most deadly looks of malice and triumph. He then searched around the room, to see that there was nothing with which Sir Horace, in his frenzy and despair, could destroy himself, and quitted the chamber, locking the door after him.

Leonard hastened to the apartment to which he had conveyed the unfortunate Julio, who he found had recovered, and was giving vent to the most pitiable lamentations ; calling upon the name of Rosetta and her parents, and imploring to be restored to them. When he beheld Leonard, he uttered a cry of horror, and, grasping his arm vehemently, he exclaimed,—

" Ah, I know you. It was you who robbed me of poor Rosetta ; it was you who kindled those dreadful flames ! It was you who killed my more than father ; murderer ! murderer !"

" I did !" exclaimed Leonard ; " I have you now in my power, and you shall never behold those whom you call your parents, again."

The maniac youth stared at him vacantly for a few moments, as if he scarcely comprehended the meaning of his words ; and then, with a wild hysterical laugh, he threw himself on the floor, and once more became unconscious of all around him.

" See to his recovery," said Leonard, addressing himself to old Griselda, who was in the room ; " and harkye, in future, you must look upon me as your master. Sir Horace Middleton no longer holds any power in the mansion."

" Mercy on us !" exclaimed the old woman, with a look of astonishment, " what mean you, Mr. Trevors ? What have you done with my poor master ?"

" Mind your own business, woman," said Leonard, sternly, " and obey my orders. Sir Horace Middleton will henceforth be confined to his own room, until I may think proper to dispose of him in another manner."

Griselda looked terrified, and faltered out,—

" Oh, Mr. Trevors, you surely cannot mean to act so cruelly towards the good Sir Horace Middleton ?"

" The good Sir Horace Middleton !" repeated Leonard, with a sneer ; " canting old hypocrite ! you know him to be a villain ; after all the years you have been in his service, you are no stranger to his character ; and were you to see him, some day or another, mount the scaffold, it ought not to surprise you."

" Oh, good gracious !" exclaimed Griselda, raising her eyes and hands in amazement and consternation.

" There, that is enough of your foolery," said Leonard, impatiently ; " but mark you, you and that old clown, your companion, Simon Snipe, as he calls himself, must be subservient to all my commands, and, above all, keep my concealment here a secret, on pain of your very lives. Do you hear me, woman ?"

" Oh, ye—ye—yes, sir," stammered out the trembling old woman. " But what do you intend to do with this poor idiot boy, Mr. Trevors ?"

" Keep him a prisoner as long as it answers my purpose to do so. The secret vault will be a place of the greatest security."

" Oh, Mr. Trevors," said Griselda, " you surely will not confine the poor boy in that dismal place. What harm can he have done to you that you should thus act towards him ?"

" No questions, woman ; it is my will ; see to his recovery."

With these words, Leonard Gresham stalked from the apartment.

When the wretched Sir Horace Middleton recovered his senses after the blow he had received from his brutal enemy, and found himself alone, he staggered to his feet, and stared vacantly around him.

" Has this all been a frightful dream ?" he exclaimed ; " oh, no, the dreadful reality is impressed on my brain in characters of fire. Oh, horror ! what an appalling tale has been rung in my ears. The very recollection of it chills my blood to ice. Monster, miscreant that I have been; I do, indeed, deserve to suffer. From Leonard Gresham, goaded on as he is by hatred and revenge, what can I expect? He has threatened me with destruction; to bring me to the gallows, and he will not fail to keep his word. And must I, then, at last die the death of a dog, amid the execrations of the surrounding multitude? My own hand shall prevent that. Let me at once rid myself of this wretched existence, and thus, at any rate, frustrate the designs of my bitter enemy. It is but a blow, and all is over. Be firm, be firm, Horace Middleton, and you may yet escape a death of ignominy."

He now searched the room for some implement of destruction, but could not find one, and he again paused and reflected with feelings of the most unbounded horror.

"All is silent," he said; "can Leonard have quitted the house? No; it is not likely, after what he has said, that he would do so. He will never more leave me, but will continue to triumph in my misery. And that poor boy, too, must I again gaze upon his features, so like those of his murdered mother? Oh, I cannot. But why should I continue to drag on this wretched existence, and with no other prospect before me than an awful and violent death upon the public scaffold? Let me at once be determined, and I will yet cheat the hangman of his due."

The miserable man was worked up to a pitch of frenzy and desperation, and he tottered towards the door with scarce any defined purpose.

"The door fastened!" he exclaimed, as he tried it; "am I, then, a prisoner in my own mansion? Oh! the villain has indeed secured me, and I can no longer doubt his intentions. I cannot escape; I have not even the means of depriving myself of life, and must await the fate which my revengeful enemy has in store for me. Christ save me, or I am lost! Ah! dare I to call upon that holy name? I, the murderer, the monster! Dare a wretch like me expect mercy either from God or man? Oh, no; it is a terrible but just punishment for the hideous crimes I have perpetrated."

He sank on a seat, and beat his breast and tore his hair in the anguish of his thoughts. Then he gave utterance to loud exclamations of agony, and called upon Leonard Gresham to release him; but the echo of his own voice was all the answer he received.

His mind was now worked up to the greatest pitch of excitement and terror, and he heard the hollow sepulchral voices of his murdered victims on the midnight air, breathing curses upon his head. Then he feared to look around him lest he should encounter their ghastly and reproachful countenances. He suffered a thousand deaths in that dreadful hour; and madness almost seized upon his fevered brain. He approached the window with the desperate determination to precipitate himself from it, but he found it was so secured as to resist all his efforts to open it. Leonard had taken care to do that before he had quitted the room, and thus the wretched man was foiled on every side. He threw himself once more on his chair, and clasping his burning temples, swayed his body to and fro in a state of the most indescribable and uncontrollable agony.

"And this is the reward for all my years of care and anxiety?" he said. "Oh! avarice, you are the greatest curse that can attend wretched, erring mortals. Murder and every species of villany, follow in your train. Had I not knelt, the willing votary at your shrine, I might now have been happy, looked up to and reverenced in my old age, instead of being the poor, loathed and despised wretch I am now. And what good has my ill-gotten wealth done me? It has proved to me a curse instead of a blessing, as it would have done, had it been honestly obtained. And Leonard Gresham has it all in his power; he will rob me of it, and then consign me to the hands of the hangman. He has threatened to do so, and he will not fail to keep his word. Oh, I shall go mad, with all these terrific thoughts crowding upon my mind. Fool that I have been to remain here to meet with such a fate. Why did I not make my escape to some distant part of the country, while I had the opportunity, and where I might have lived unknown and unmolested? Surely I might have contrived to conceal myself from my terrible enemies, and by my future actions have endeavoured to make some atonement for the many dreadful crimes I have committed. But it is too late to repent now; I am completely in the meshes of the miscreant who gloats over my misery, and who will ultimately consign me to a shameful and ignominious death. My soul shrinks appalled at the thought. I see, in imagination, all the dreadful paraphernalia of my execution. I beheld the hangman gloating with hideous eagerness over his trembling, guilty victim. I hear the frightful shouts of the vast multitude assembled to witness my fatal and merited end. And then all the horrors of a dread eternity—an eternity of punishment arise upon my distracted fancy. Off! off! fiends of hell, ye shall not drag me to my endness doom! Flames of fire encircle me! I burn! Water! water! to quench this dreadful, this insupportable thirst! Oh, horror!"

The guilty, conscience-stricken old man, could no more, but with a wild, hysterical laugh, he sank senseless on the floor.

* * * * * * * * *

Several days elapsed, and Sir Horace Middleton was kept a close prisoner in his chamber, and was in a state of mind bordering upon frenzy. Leonard visited him two or three times a day, and exulted in his misery, and loaded him with the most brutal taunts and reproaches. Earnestly and piteously did the baronet implore him to take his life at once, but Leonard only replied to him with the most bitter scoffs and revilings, and again threatened him with the horrors of the gallows.

Leonard had now conveyed Julio to the secret vault, in which he intended to keep him confined for the present, until he had completely matured the diabolical plans he had in contemplation. It is needless to attempt to describe the sufferings of the poor maniac youth, who passed the dreary hours of his confinement, in the most melancholy ravings, and in calling upon the names of those who were ever present to his disordered imagination. He never beheld Leonard Gresham but with feelings of the greatest horror; but, nothing could move that stern and cruel man to relent; for he viewed the unconscious youth with abhorence, feeling convinced that he had gained the affections of Rosetta, and that it was for him she had rejected Frank.

He had taken entire possession of the mansion, and ransacked the coffers of Sir Horace Middleton, in order that he might secure his gold; and he now saw himself in a fair way to gratify the whole of his wishes, for he thought himself entirely safe from detection; but he little imagined how soon he was destined to be undeceived. In order the better to protect himself, he had taken several of his colleagues, on whom he could depend, into the house, and it was the scene of constant riot and revelry.

Simon Snipe and Griselda pretended to be subservient to all his commands, for they feared to excite his wrath, well knowing what the consequences would be if they did so; but they only awaited an opportunity to effect their escape; being resolved, if they could succeed in doing so, to betray Leonard Gresham to justice, let whatever might be the consequences to themselves. This opportunity soon presented itself to them. Julio had been confined in the secret vault about a week, when one evening, Leonard and his companions were engaged, as usual, in noisy revelry, and were drinking pretty freely, so that the two ancient domestics thought they could not have a better chance for putting their wishes into effect. They were in another part of the house, far away from the room in which Leonard and his companions were seated, and therefore they thought that they might easily quit the mansion without being overheard, and as it might be some time before their absence would be discovered, they would have a sufficient opportunity to escape altogether. They hastily packed up a few necessary articles belonging to themselves, and then descending a back flight of stairs, cautiously opened the door, and, to their no small satisfaction, found themselves in the open air. They for a moment hesitated what course to pursue, but at length they determined to make their way to the nearest magistrate, who resided about two miles from the Manor-house, and revealing to him all the particulars, throw themselves upon his protection. Fear added speed to their footsteps, and it was not long before they arrived at the house of the magistrate, who happened to be at home, and immediately granted them the interview they requested.

This gentleman listened to the account which Simon and his companion gave, and the hints they threw out respecting the real character of Sir Horace Middleton, with no little astonishment; but having felt satisfied that they spoke the truth, he instantly despatched a messenger to Michael Belford, to request his attendance.   In less than half an hour Mr. Belford arrived, and his astonishment on reading the account which Simon had given to the magistrate, may be readily conceived.

"Oh, my dear sir," he exclaimed, " I beg your prompt assistance to secure the apprehension of this bad, this cruel man, and to release the unfortunate Julio from his power.   There is not a moment to be lost; oh, Heaven, grant that I may be able to learn what the villain has done with my poor child."

"I fear, Mr. Belford," said Simon, "that you will be disappointed in that respect; Martin Trevors was foiled in his plans on the night he seized your daughter.   Some of his ruffianly colleagues, no doubt, had deceived him; they were attacked by several armed men, defeated, and Miss Belford was borne away by their assailants."

"Good God!" cried the distracted Mr. Belford, "this is more torturing and bewildering than all.   Oh! my poor Rosetta, what can have become of you? Never, never shall I behold you again.   Who can the villains be that hold her in their power?"

"They were masked," said Simon; "but Trevors feels convinced that the principal one, both from his voice and the observations he made use of, was Raymond Middleton, the nephew of my unfortunate but guilty master."

"Raymond Middleton!" exclaimed Michael; "is it possible? Oh! if that is indeed the case, the fate that has befallen my unhappy daughter, I must anticipate is of the worst kind.   He has turned pirate, and has doubtless torn her from her native land. Oh! Rosetta, would that you had died in childhood rather than such a terrible fate should have befallen you.   But what is best to be done, my dear sir? I solicit your advice and assistance."

"I will immediately despatch a sufficient number of men to the Manor-house, to apprehend the ruffians," said the magistrate; "they probably have not yet discovered the escape of these two persons, and will not have any suspicion of being surprised.   Know you of any part of the house where we may gain an entrance?"

"Oh! yes, sir," answered Simon; "I took good care to bring with me the key of the private door, and therefore you can gain an entrance without difficulty.   But no time should be lost, for should Martin Trevors discover our flight, he will be on his guard, and may be able to baffle your designs."

"I will see about his apprehension directly," said the magistrate; "and you say that he actually holds Sir Horace Middleton a prisoner in his own mansion?"

"He does, sir," replied Simon; "and I fear that unless he is secured, he will take the poor old gentleman's life."

"And know you any of the secrets of your master, and how it is that he has become connected with such a villain?"

"Oh! your worship," said Simon, "I would rather be excused from answering that question, but—but I fear that Sir Horace Middleton has been a bad man.   Nay, more, if I must speak the truth, I am afraid, nay, I am convinced that he did not obtain all the immense wealth he possesses by fair means."

"Ah!" remarked the magistrate, "this business must be examined carefully and minutely.   You must remain here, for your evidence will be required upon a future occasion."

"Oh! sir," said Michael, who was in a state of the greatest anxiety, "do not delay; the life of this poor boy, and the discovery of my poor and deeply injured daughter may depend upon our acting with promptitude."

The magistrate, who really felt a great interest in this event, immediately summoned a servant into his presence, and despatched him to order the instant attendance of such officers as he knew were at that time in the neighbourhood, and during the interval that elapsed, Michael remained in a state of the greatest sus-

pense and uneasiness. Rosetta, then, was in the power of Raymond Middleton. After what Simon had stated, he could not entertain any doubt of it ; and if such was the case, how dreadful must be the fate that had befallen her. He shuddered at the thought, and beat his breast in despair. The officers quickly arrived, and having received the instructions of the magistrate, instantly prepared to depart to the Manor-house.

"I will accompany them," said Michael ; "I shall be all impatience until I see the villain Martin Trevors secured, and behold the poor youth, whom I love as fondly as if he were mine own son, restored to liberty."

" I would advise you to remain here, Mr. Belford, or to return home," said the magistrate ; " you can do no good by accompanying them, and it may be attended with danger, for the villains will probably make a desperate resistance."

" Oh ! sir," returned Michael, " I do not fear, but I cannot wait here in suspense."

The magistrate did not offer any opposition, as he saw that Michael was determined, and they therefore departed, making their way with all the speed they could towards the Manor house.

Leonard Gresham, and his infamous companions continued to drink deeply, and to indulge in noisy revelry, little imagining the danger that was impending over them, or that Simon and his aged companion had escaped. They were suddenly aroused, however, by hearing a door slammed to, violently, as though it had been by the wind ; and then they thought they heard the sound of several footsteps cautiously ascending the stairs. Leonard started to his feet, and gazed eagerly towards the room door, as he exclaimed,—

" What sounds are those ? Some persons are ascending the stairs. Do you not hear them ?"

" Oh ! it is probably only old Simon, or the old woman," said one of his companions.

" There are no other persons in the house, except the old baronet, and he is secure enough in his own apartment."

" Ah ! by h—ll, we are betrayed," cried Leonard, as the sound of the footsteps became more distinct ; " stand firm !"

He had scarcely spoken the words, when the room-door was burst open, and Michael Belford and the officers rushed into the apartment, to the no small astonishment and confusion of Leonard Gresham and his infamous companions.

" Michael Belford," he exclaimed, while his eyes flashed with rage, " what rascal has done this ?"

" Martin Trevors," said Michael ; " cruel, guilty man ; destroyer of my home and all my happiness. The hour of retribution has arrived. Yield ; resistance is useless."

" Yield, old dolt !" cried Leonard ; " never with my life ; and thus take you my answer."

With these words, he felled Michael by a heavy blow, and the combat commenced with equal determination on both sides, Leonard and the other ruffians fighting their way towards the door, which they gained at length ; and, perceiving that they were likely to be defeated, they took to flight, Leonard leading the way towards the secret passage which led to the vault in which Julio was confined.

In the meantime, while all this was going on, events not less extraordinary and exciting were taking place in the vault. Gerald Wetherby, and several other fishermen, were on their usual avocation near the rocks. in one of which the cavern was excavated, when they thought they heard the sound of a human voice in deep and melancholy lamentation.

" It certainly is a human voice," said Gerald. " Hark ! There it is again. It seemed to come from the rocks yonder."

They now all plainly heard the voice ; and, satisfied that they were not mistaken, they made towards the rocks, and then they were enabled to distinguish some words that were uttered by Julio, and which convinced them that the rock must contain some secret cavern.

" There it is again," said Gerald ; " why, if that is not the voice of the poor maniac lad, I am a sinner."

" There must be some cavern here," said another of the men ; " we must penetrate this mystery."

" Ay," coincided Gerald, as he leaped from the boat on to a shelving portion of the rock, and was followed by two or three of his companions, the others remaining behind to take care of the boats. They now stood before that portion of the rock in which the opening to the vault or cavern was.

" Ah !" said Gerald, " we were right in our conjectures. Here is a cavern in the rock, sure enough, and probably it may have formed a smugglers' retreat. Could we but remove the rock which is placed beneath the aperture, we might effect an entrance and satisfy our curiosity. But it is quite certain that some person is confined here."

He now shouted aloud, and was quickly answered by Julio.

"It is the boy!" he said; "I cannot be mistaken in the voice. To work, my lads; let us apply all our strength, and we shall succeed in making the entrance clear."

They did so; and, after considerable exertions, they hurled the piece of rock from the mouth of the cave, and beheld at once that their suspicions were verified; but their astonishment may be imagined when Julio threw himself on his knees at their feet; and, with more of reason in his manner than he had ever before evinced, implored them to save him.

"Poor lad! poor lad!" said Gerald, "you shall, indeed, be rescued. But who has done this? Whither can this cavern lead? There appears to be a passage beyond this, which probably leads to some building, and yet there is none for some distance from this place, and the nearest is the mansion of Sir Horace Middleton. But, come, my lad, we will to the boats, and let this matter be investigated by the proper authorities."

"Julio will not have liberty without you restore me to sister Rosetta," said the youth; "and they snatched her from me, and bore her through the flames. Hark! Do you not hear her screams? Quick — quick! or they will murder her as they did my poor mother!"

"This way, this way, my lad," said Gerald, taking his hand, and leading him towards the mouth of the cavern.

Suddenly the chest, which Leonard had neglected to remove, notwithstanding its contents were so important, met their sight, and excited their curiosity. Gerald tried to open it, but found that it was locked, and, looking more closely, he beheld the initials of the baronet upon the lid.

"These are the initials of Sir Horace Middleton," he remarked; "and I begin to suspect that he has had something to do with the confinement of this unfortunate youth. I wonder what the chest contains. There can be no harm in gratifying our curiosity, especially since we have found it under such suspicious circumstances."

Gerald, now, after much difficulty, forced open the lid of the chest, and hastily examined the contents, Julio looking on at the same time with earnest attention. But what was the astonishment of every one at the curious contents of the old cedar chest—the damning evidences of the guilt of Sir Horace Middleton! They could scarcely believe their eyes, and looked at each other with mingled feelings of horror and incredulity. At length they came to the portrait, which has been mentioned in a former part of this narrative, and no sooner did Julio behold it, than he uttered a wild cry of emotion, and exclaiming,—"Mother! mother!" he sank insensible on the earth.

"There is some terrible mystery in all this," remarked Gerald; "depend upon it there has been some foul work perpetrated by the hands of Sir Horace Middleton. Ah! what noise is that?"

"It sounds like the clashing of swords," said one of the fishermen; "and seems to be approaching this way. Let us to our boats, or we may find the enemy too powerful for us."

Before any of them had time to make a reply, the door which led into the cavern was burst forcibly open, and Leonard Gresham, his companions, and their assailants, entered, fighting desperately. It would be impossible to describe the astonishment and confusion of the villain at the scene which presented itself to his observation; but no sooner did Michael behold the maniac youth, than he uttered an exclamation of mingled pleasure and amazement, and rushed towards him.

"D——n!" cried Leonard; "the boy discovered—hemmed in on all sides. The game is up. Oh, curses! but thus, at any rate, will I escape an ignominious death."

As he spoke, before any one could prevent him, he plunged a dagger into his side, and sank bleeding in the arms of the officers; his companions throwing down their arms, and suffering themselves to be taken prisoners.

"The deed is done!" gasped forth Leonard; "and although I have been foiled in my designs, at least I have escaped the hands of the executioner. But Horace Middleton shall swing—ay, swing on the gallows, and the certainty of that will be some consolation to me in my last moments. Take me to the apartment in which the old miser murderer, the wealthy Sir Horace Middleton is confined, that I may confront, and exult in his anguish when he hears me reveal his guilt. If you would see justice done, do not refuse."

"Oh, Martin Trevors—cruel man! what misery have you brought upon me, in order to gratify a revenge so unnaturally excited!" said Michael; "where, oh where is my daughter?"

"In the power of Raymond Middleton, the pirate," answered Leonard; "but I have not much longer to live; if you would hear all the explanation it is in my power to make, you will not delay to comply with my wishes."

"Do as the wretched man desires," said Michael; "and may his penitence be sincere. Gerald, to your care I commit poor Julio; convey him to my dwelling, whither I will quickly follow."

Gerald and his companions complied with this request, and lifting the insensible form of Julio in their arms, they carried him to the boat, and instantly made towards that part of the land that was nearest to the residence of Michael.

They staunched the wound which Leonard had inflicted on himself as well as they could, and then supporting him from the cavern, conveyed him to the room in which Sir Horace Middleton was confined.

CHAPTER XXII.

THE ACCUSATION.—THE FRENZY OF SIR HORACE MIDDLETON.—HIS DEATH.

It would be a fruitless task to describe the unutterable anguish and terror of Sir Horace Middleton, when he beheld the officers of justice, and beheld Leonard Gresham wounded and a prisoner. He saw at once that the crisis of his fate was at hand, and he trembled convulsively in every limb. Leonard eyed him with a look of fiendish malice.

"Mercy! mercy!" cried the old man, in piteous accents, and sinking on his knees. "I am not guilty; no, no, it is all false; Leonard Gresham, cruel as you are, you surely do not mean to accuse me?"

"Leonard Gresham!" repeated Michael, with a look of astonishment.

"Ay, that is my real name," said the wounded man; "that of Martin Trevors was merely assumed. Listen: in this trembling old miscreant you behold the murderer of his wife, and the father-in-law of Redmond Clifton, the captain of the pirate vessel, known by the name of the Death Ship. His daughter was the pirate's bride, and the mother of the boy Julio. She was murdered by her husband on the night when Michael Belford rescued the maniac from the deep. Redmond Clifton, however, was not the real father of Julio; he is the son of a good and honourable man, the first husband of the unfortunate Eveline."

"Great God! is it possible?" exclaimed Michael. "Guilty man, do you really speak the truth?"

"No, no," groaned Sir Horace, shaking with fearful agony, and his countenance becoming as ghastly pale as that of a corpse; "it is all false—false as hell; but you will not believe! Oh, spare me! spare me! I am a wretched, care-worn old man."

"I repeat," said Leonard, "that I have spoken the truth; and this guilty old miscreant knows it. Sir Horace Middleton, I told you that my revenge should be one day fully gratified. That moment has now arrived; I have escaped the halter, but you will die the death of a dog. Search the cedar chest in the cave, and there you will find sufficient proof of all that I have asserted."

"Off! off!" shrieked the miserable man, in accents of distraction; "you shall not, dare not charge me with those foul and hideous crimes. Am I not Sir Horace Middleton, and who dare accuse me of murder? Off, I say, or you shall dearly repent your boldness and injustice."

The blood gushed to the wretched man's brain, his countenance became perfectly awful, and he sank on the floor insensible.

Leonard Gresham was now exhausted with loss of blood and the excitement of the moment, and it was found necessary to carry him to a bed as speedily as possible, and to send for a surgeon. The magistrate was also made acquainted with the extraordinary particulars, and also with the statement of Leonard, and he lost no time in repairing to the manor, in order that he might commit the depositions of Leonard to paper before he expired, for the surgeon had given it as his opinion that he could not long survive.

Leonard was sinking very fast, but he yet found strength sufficient to make an ample confession of all those awful circumstances with which the reader has been made acquainted, and to which the persons present listened with the greatest astonishment and horror.

"But, tell me, Leonard Gresham," said Michael, "for you can have no motive for concealment now, and you surely will not carry your feelings of revenge to the grave? Do you not really know what has become of my unfortunate daughter?"

"I have told you all I know, Michael Belford," said Leonard; "but I firmly believe Rosetta is in the power of Raymond Middleton."

"Gracious Heaven!" groaned Michael; "what will become of her? I shall go mad."

"Compose yourself, Mr. Belford," said the magistrate; "she may yet be discovered, and restored to you. Guilty man, have you anything further to say?"

"Yes," said Leonard, in a faint voice; "I have a request to make, with which I trust you will comply."

"Name it."

"Should the young man, who has hitherto been known as Frank Trevors, ever return to this neighbourhood, I beg that he may not be reproached for my faults. He is good and honourable, and it would be unjust to cast any stigma upon him, especially as he is not my son."

"Not your son?"

"No; he is the son of Major Grenville, who, I believe, is still living in London."

"And how came he in your possession? and for what reason did you adopt him as your son?" demanded the magistrate.

"I seduced the affections of his wife from him," answered Leonard; "and she eloped with me, bringing with her her infant son. The major in vain tried to discover us, and I was fearful to make known to Frank the secret of his birth, when he arrived at years of maturity, lest I should be brought to punishment for the offences I had committed. This is the truth; and I wish Alfred Grenville to be made acquainted with it, should he ever return to his native country."

"Your request shall be complied with," said the magistrate. "Have you any other statement to make?"

Leonard shook his head, but was unable to speak. His sufferings now became more acute than ever, and it was quite evident that his end was rapidly approaching. His countenance was frightfully distorted, and he seemed to be suffering great mental anguish.

In less than an hour he breathed his last, giving utterance to one fearful groan of agony, and his guilty soul was ushered into the presence of its Almighty Judge. Thus perished the wretched Leonard Gresham, the victim of his own malignant passions.

Michael and the magistrate turned away from the corpse with a sickly feeling of horror, and they mentally invoked the mercy of the Supreme towards his crime-laden soul, notwithstanding he had been the cause of so much misery to his fellow-creatures, and those, too, who had never injured him.

The miserable Horace continued in a state of complete frenzy, and raved with all the fury of a madman. It was necessary to leave two of the officers with him, and it was arranged that he should remain at the Manor until he should be in a fit state to undergo an examination on the dreadful charges that would be preferred against him.

Michael now returned home, in a state of mind that may easily be conceived, and reflecting deeply upon all the events which had taken place within the last few hours, and on the dreadful uncertainty of the fate that had befallen Rosetta, whom he despaired of ever beholding again. The mystery of Julio's birth was now unravelled, and, on that point, he felt particularly satisfied, although he saw the absolute necessity there was of his using every precaution to conceal him from the power of Redmond Clifton, who would be certain to pursue him with his vengeance, especially when he should hear of the confession of Leonard Gresham.

Mrs. Belford had been awaiting his return with the greatest impatience, and some idea may be formed of the anguish of her feelings, when her husband related to her all the particulars of the confession and the death of Leonard Gresham. But her mind was almost distracted when she thought of the terrible fate that had befallen Rosetta, especially if she was in the power of Raymond Middleton.

Michael tried to console her, but it was with very little effect; for, in fact he was not in any better condition himself, and he saw that there was every reason to apprehend the worst.

Julio remained in much the same state during the night, but when he entered the parlour in the morning, Michael and his wife were astonished at the change which had taken place in his appearance and manners. There was no longer that wild expression about his eyes, the sure symptom of insanity; but, on the contrary, the light of returning reason seemed suddenly to have dawned upon his soul, and he seemed to have a recollection of all around him. He flew towards them eagerly, and, embracing them with every show of respect and attention, burst into tears. The old people were astonished, and so great, and so unexpected was the change, that, for a few moments, they could scarcely believe the evidence of their senses.

"Oh, I have been mad, or had a frightful dream," he ejaculated; "but recollection now returns. I know that to you I owe the preservation of my life. I know that you have been Julio's best friends when his mind wandered. Yes, yes, all is clear and lucid now. I am no longer mad; I am no longer mad!"

"Oh, thank Heaven!" exclaimed Michael and his wife, in a breath.

"Oh, yes," said the youth, passing his hand across his forehead; "my reason returns, and with it the recollection of all the horrible past. My murdered mother, murdered by her own husband, Redmond Clifton, the pirate-captain. Oh, God! let not the thought again drive me to madness. And last night I gazed upon her portrait in the dismal place where I was confined by that cruel man who snatched your daughter Rosetta from her home;—oh, what has become of her? Shall I never behold her again?'

Michael and his wife endeavoured to inspire him with hope, although, alas! they saw but little cause to encourage it, and they could not sufficiently express their delight at Julio's restoration to reason. They would fain have banished the recollection of the past from his mind, for they were fearful that if he dwelt upon it, it would again have the most dangerous effect on his reason; but Julio would persist in making them acquainted with all the melancholy particulars of his history, and which went fully to corroborate all that Leonard Gresham had stated. It was melancholy to hear the many afflictions, the horrible trials which that poor youth had undergone, and it was not at all wonderful that his senses should have fled beneath the shock of so many accumulated miseries; the only surprising thing was, that he should ever again recover his reason under such dreadful circumstances, and that in so sudden and unexpected a manner; but so it was, and the delight of Michael and his wife upon the occasion, may be better imagined than described.

"But did you never hear your mother mention the name of any relation you had living?" asked Michael.

"Oh, yes," answered Julio; "her own father. But she never mentioned him without a shudder of horror, for he was a bad man, who had abandoned her to misery and shame."

" And do you remember the name of your grandfather ?"

Julio passed his hand across his forehead, and seemed to be endeavouring to recall his scattered thoughts.

" Yes, yes," he said, " I should do so ; but my recollection has been wandering for some time. Ah ! it flashes across my memory now. Sir Horace Middleton, that was his name."

" Ah ! it is enough," said Michael ; " Leonard Gresham then was right."

" You know him, then ?" inquired Julio.

" Oh, yes, cruel, guilty man, as he undoubtedly is."

" And does he still live ?"

" Yes, my poor lad," replied Michael : " it was to his mansion you were taken by Leonard Gresham. He is charged with murder, the murder of his own wife, and is now in the custody of the officers at the Red Manor-house."

" Unfortunate, guilty old man," said Julio ; " may Heaven forgive him ! And must he then die an ignominious death ?"

" Such should be the punishment of his crimes. But for your sake, Julio, who are his only heir, I do hope that he will escape so violent and shameful a death."

" I cannot, dare not see him," observed Julio ; " my soul would shrink appalled in his presence."

" Well, I think it would be advisable to spare you the pain of such an interview, if possible," said Michael.

Julio returned no answer, but relapsed into deep thought. The image of Rosetta now rushed upon his recollection as vividly as if his reason had never wandered. Her kind solicitude and gentle virtues had made a most indelible impression even upon his then shattered mind ; and when he thought upon her loss, and the uncertainty of her fate, he could not control his anguish, and could not refrain from tears. In that feeling we need not say how bitterly Michael and his wife participated ; indeed, it was wonderful how they maintained their fortitude at all.

At length, Julio having become more tranquil, and Michael being anxious to know the condition of the wretched Sir Horace Middleton, departed to the Manor-house, on arriving at which, he found everything there in a state of the greatest confusion, for the guilty man had not many minutes before breathed his last, having ruptured a vessel in the violence of his paroxysms. The magistrate had been there all the morning, and from him Michael learned every particular of the baronet's end. It appeared that during an interval of reason, he admitted the truth of all that Leonard Gresham had stated, and made a full confession of the awful crimes of which he had been guilty ; and, therefore, it was satisfactory to know that there could no longer be any doubts upon the subject.

The magistrate was most agreeably surprised on being informed by Michael of the almost miraculous restoration of Julio to reason, and expressed his satisfaction to know that Sir Horace Middleton having escaped a shameful trial and condemnation, his wealth would not become forfeited to the crown ; but that Julio being clearly proved to be his heir, would, in future, be placed in circumstances of comfort and affluence.

These remarkable events caused the greatest sensation in the neighbourhood, and every one execrated the memory of Sir Horace, and shuddered when they reflected upon the hideous crimes he had perpetrated. In a few days the remains of him and Leonard Gresham were consigned to the earth without ceremony ; but it was long ere the awful events in which they had been the principal actors, could be forgotten.

CHAPTER XXIII.

THE RESTORATION OF ROSETTA AND FRANK TREVORS.—THE DESTRUCTION
OF THE PIRATE CREW.—CAPTURE OF THE DEATH SHIP.—CONCLUSION.

OUR eventful history is fast drawing to a close. Two months elapsed after the circumstances recorded in the previous chapter, and still nothing occurred to inspire Michael and his wife with any hopes of the restoration of their daughter, or of their ever being able to ascertain her fate, and we need not attempt to describe the poignant anguish they endured, and in which Julio so keenly participated.

It having been clearly established in a court of law, that Julio was the actual heir of the late Sir Horace Middleton, he came into possession of his wealth, which was found to be enormous. But as he could never make up his mind to reside in the Manor-house, it was sold, and Julio purchased another residence in the vicinity, to which he and his kind benefactors removed. It was a commodious but unostentatious dwelling, and they must now have experienced every happiness, had it not been for the loss of Rosetta, whom they could not flatter themselves with the least hope of ever beholding again.

Julio had a monument erected to the memory of his ill-fated mother, in the gardens of his residence, and there did he daily pour forth his devotions, and pray for her soul to repose in peace.

Several vessels had been sent out by the government in search of the Death Ship, and the vessel of which Raymond Middleton was supposed to be still the captain; but hitherto without success.

About this period, on the evening of a fine day, Michael his wife, and Julio, were seated in the garden of the mansion, when Mr. Hayward, who continued to visit them daily, suddenly made his appearance, and it was apparent from the excitement of his manner, that he had something of importance to communicate. Michael and his wife felt a strange and irresistible sensation at their hearts, as if something of a most interesting nature was about to happen to them, and they awaited with impatience for Hayward to speak.

"Good news, my friends," said the old man, at last. "Excellent news!"

"What mean you?" eagerly demanded Michael; "what has happened?"

"Most of the rascally pirates are destroyed," answered Mr. Hayward; "the Death Ship is captured, and has been brought in here about an hour since, by his Majesty's gallant vessels, the Vulture and the Tartar; and Redmond Clifton, and two or three others of his infamous crew, are brought home prisoners."

"Ah!" exclaimed Michael, "this is, indeed, good news."

"But not the best," remarked Hayward; "my good friends, there is happiness in store for you."

"Happiness!" repeated Michael and his wife, in a breath; "alas! I fear that can never again be our portion."

"But it will, though," said old Kit; "but I scarcely know how to break it to you."

"For mercy's sake, do not keep us in suspense."

"Well, then, the whole of it is, that the Vulture brings to their native land your daughter Rosetta, and Frank Trevors!"

Michael, his wife, and Julio, uttered simultaneous exclamations of mingled delight and incredulity, and starting from their seats, with throbbing hearts, they looked at Mr. Hayward as if they would penetrate his very soul.

"Mr. Hayward," said Michael, "I know you too well, or I might feel inclined to believe that you sought to trifle with my feelings. God of Heaven! hast thou, indeed, heard my prayer? But no, it cannot be; I dare not flatter myself with the blissful hope."

"I have spoken the truth, Michael," said Mr. Hayward; "Rosetta is saved, and ——"

"Oh, where—where is she?"

"Here! here! beloved parents!" cried a well-known voice, whose tones were even more sweet than heavenly music to their souls, and the next moment they clasped to their hearts their long-lost child.

*   *   *

Reader, picture to yourself the scene which follows, for we are inadequate to the task. Imagine how they embraced, and wept, and poured forth their gratitude to Heaven; while the transport of Julio was so great, that he could scarcely keep it within the bounds of reason. He knelt at her feet, pressed her hand to his lips, and bathed it with his tears, while Frank Trevors, or Alfred Grenville, as we must now call him, stood by and gazed upon them with mingled feelings of sorrow and joy. He looked at Julio; he saw the impassioned glances that he and Rosetta exchanged, and he felt more bitterly than ever that all his hopes were at an end.

Poor Frank, his was indeed a melancholy case, so fondly devoted was he to that one fair being who first won his heart; and now, after all the trials he had gone through, after all the various vicissitudes they had encountered, when he had entertained a slight shadow of a hope that he might win his reward, to find that *slight shadow of a hope* blighted, worked his brain almost to frenzy; but with the manly firmness of his character, he subdued his feelings, and endeavoured to conceal from Rosetta and her friends the thoughts that were passing in his mind.

Julio, too, with the light of reason now illuming his eyes, seemed at once to understand the thoughts that were passing in the mind of Frank, and to feel that he was the innocent cause of the misery he at that time was enduring. This conviction, in fact, he read in the eyes of the fair girl, whose unresisting form he now pressed with the most convulsive fondness to his bosom. He listened to the eloquent, but simple description which she gave of the various adventures they had together met with; and the respectful attention which he had paid to her when they were so miraculously cast on the same island together, called forth his most fervent expressions of gratitude. He seized his hand, and pressing it vehemently in his, exclaimed,—

" You have been the friend, the more than brother of Rosetta, her who in my dreaming, the wild vision of my wandering reason, I revered as a sister, but whom I now learn to view with a tenderer passion, and as my dearest friend I must ever esteem you.

Alfred Grenville, for such we ought to call him, returned the pressure of Julio's hand with a fervour that spoke much more than words could have done, but at the same time he averted his eyes from the glances of Rosetta, whose blushes, and whose heaving bosom, plainly evinced the emotions that were passing in her mind. With the fond transport that animated her bosom on the conviction that Julio's heart was devoted to her, and that his intellect was no longer overclouded by the sad feelings that had formerly benighted it, was mingled a sensation of melancholy regret, when she thought of the despair of Alfred, whose virtues she must ever admire, and about whose future happiness she was so sincerely and ardently solicitous. And Alfred well understood the feelings which were passing in her mind, and he endeavoured to think of her only as a dear friend, as a sister; for such their long intimacy, and the circumstances that had passed between them, authorized him to consider her.

He briefly narrated to Mr. Belford and the other persons present the extraordinary adventures he had encountered since they had last met, and the miraculous manner in which he had escaped the horrible fate to which the fearful miscreants of the Death Ship had consigned him; and they all expressed their admiration of the especial Providence that had protected him, and rendered him the indirect means of rescuing from destruction that one fair being who had endeared herself to all who knew her.

Alfred Grenville had struggled desperately with the waves, and at length succeeded in reaching the rocks, towards which the pirates had seen him making, and with difficulty clambering up them, he sunk down completely exhausted, and giving himself up for lost. But Providence watched over him; he had scarcely been in this alarming situation an hour, when the Vulture appeared in sight, and after considerable exertions, he succeeded in making himself observed and heard, and was shortly afterwards taken on board, where he was received with every kindness, and on his briefly relating his history, the captain determined to make sail in the course the Death Ship had taken. In the course of a couple of hours, they came in sight of that desperate vessel, and immediately bore down upon it. The combat that ensued was terrific; but the Tartar happening to come to the aid of the Vulture, it was soon decided. Most of the pirates were killed, the vessel captured, and the so long dreaded Redmond Clifton and those that survived of his crew were taken prisoners.

During the time that this terrific conflict was going on, the sufferings of our heroine were of the most intense and almost insupportable description. The groans of the wounded, the roaring of the cannon, the shouts of the victors, the execrations of the pirates, formed an amalgamation of horror it would be impossible for any language adequately to describe, and it was truly wonderful that Rosetta was enabled to support it with the fortitude she did. But when the defeat of the pirates became evident, and Alfred Grenville rushed into the cabin where Rosetta was confined, what a meeting was there. They embraced with all the unrestrained affection of brother and sister, and they wept tears of joy upon each other's shoulder.

"My sweet friend, my more than sister," ejaculated Alfred, "kind Providence, amidst all my calamities, has afforded me the opportunity of being the humble, but happy instrument of delivering you from a fate which I cannot even reflect upon without a feeling of the most unbounded horror, and I am more than repaid for any trouble I have encountered. You are now safe, and in a few weeks I shall have the happiness of restoring you to your amiable parents and all those whom you love."

He sighed instinctively as he made use of the latter observation, but he struggled with his emotions, and concealed from the penetration of Rosetta, as well as he could, the thoughts which were passing in his mind.

"Oh! Mr. Trevors," said the damsel, "Heaven knows the pleasure I feel at your preservation from the fate to which you were doomed by those merciless wretches, that have long been the terror of the seas. But, alas! although I am restored to liberty, I fear that I shall never behold my poor parents again. They could never, I am inclined to apprehend, have survived the terrible shock of my loss, and, if such is the fact, what is there left for me to render existence endurable?"

"Hope for the best, Rosetta," said Alfred; "I do trust that the same all-merciful Providence which has saved you from destruction, has watched over and preserved the lives of those who are so dear to you. You will once more be enfolded to their affectionate bosoms, believe me, Rosetta, and you will be happy; while I ——"

He checked himself, and turning away his head, sighed deeply. Rosetta perfectly understood his feelings, and fervently did she commiserate with him, but the image of Julio interposed, and she could not subdue the favourable prejudice which that unfortunate youth had gained over her mind.

During the remainder of the voyage our heroine and Alfred Grenville were almost constantly together, and they encouraged alternate hopes and fears; but, when the vessel came in sight of England, the feelings of Rosetta were far too powerful for utterance. Little did she anticipate the happiness that was in store for her, and far less that that being who had almost constantly occupied her thoughts during their cruel separation would be restored to reason. Certainly there was a special Providence watched over them all, and amply repaid them for the numerous troubles they had experienced, and which they had supported with much more fortitude than could have been at all expected.

On the vessel reaching the port, Mr. Hayward and several of his friends were on the cliffs, and the meeting between him and our heroine, when she received the assurance of the existence of her affectionate and beloved parents, was touching in the extreme. She sank on her knees, and, while tears of joy gushed from her eyes, she poured forth her gratitude to Heaven.

What were the feelings of all after they had entered into mutual explanations? They were almost too powerful for utterance, and it was some time ere they were restored to any degree of tranquillity. The astonishment of Alfred Grenville on hearing the extraordinary particulars that were related to him were unbounded; but it was a great relief to his mind when he found that he was not the son of that guilty man, who had been the cause of so much misery to those whom he so highly esteemed.

The restoration of Rosetta Belford was hailed with universal satisfaction by every one in the neighbourhood, and for some days they were fully occupied in receiving the ardent and honest congratulations of all who knew them.

The terrible captain of the Death Ship was conveyed to prison, and there, for the first time in his life, he felt some compunction for the numerous atrocious crimes he had perpetrated. He requested to see Julio and his friends, and in their presence he fully corroborated all that Martin Trevors, or Leonard Gresham, rather, had stated in his dying confession, and which removed a great weight of care from the mind of all parties interested, in proving that Julio was not the son of such an abominable miscreant.

Redmond Clifton and the other pirates paid the penalty of their numerous crimes upon the gallows; but it was many years before the horrors which had been perpetrated by the crew of the Death Ship were forgotten.

These remarkable events, having received full publicity in the newspapers, reached the knowledge of Major Grenville, who, though worn down with care and age, was still living. In a few days he had the felicity of embracing and acknowledging that son whom he had never expected to behold again.

Many years of bitter misery had the major endured, and fruitless had been all his endeavours to discover his faithless wife, or his offspring; but now that the latter was so unexpectedly restored to his arms, he returned his unbounded thanks to Omnipotence, and hoped to pass the evening of his days in peace. And most happy was he to find that son so worthy of his regard; and he could not help feeling something like gratitude to the seducer of his misguided wife, for the care in which he had brought him up, and for not having vitiated him by bad example.

Major Grenville was immensely rich, and he had, therefore, every opportunity of promoting the welfare of his son; but he was sorry to learn the unfortunate passion he had encouraged for Rosetta, and was fearful that it would be many years before he would be able to stifle it in his breast.

Weeks and months passed away, and all the principal actors in our tale were restored to tranquillity, and now did Julio and Rosetta venture to confess the mutual and ardent affection they entertained for each other, and received the consent of the aged Michael Belford and his wife to their union.

In a short time Julio led the lovely and blushing Rosetta to the altar, where they received the reward their virtues merited in the possession of every earthly happiness.

We have but little more to add; Alfred Grenville in time learned to conquer the unfortunate passion with which the charms and virtues of Rosetta had inspired him, and at length became the happy husband of a wealthy and amiable woman, and passed his future days in prosperity and peace.

Raymond Middleton was never more heard of; and there can be little doubt that he died a dreadful death of hunger on the desolate island on which he had been cast after the mutiny on board the lawless vessel he had commanded.

And now, reader, we have brought our narrative to a close; our object has been to show vice in its own hideous deformity, and to prove that it is only by a strict life of virtue and rectitude that ultimate happiness can be obtained. If we have so far succeeded, we are more than amply rewarded for our labours.

THE END.

www.ingramcontent.com/pod-product-compliance
Lightning Source LLC
Chambersburg PA
CBHW080733250626
47170CB00010B/2812